SONS OF
ROME

RISE OF EMPERORS

Also by Gordon Doherty

The Legionary Series

Legionary
Viper of the North
Land of the Sacred Fire
The Scourge of Thracia
Gods and Emperors
Empire of Shades
The Blood Road
Dark Eagle

The Strategos Trilogy

Born in the Borderlands
Rise of the Golden Heart
Island in the Storm

The Empires of Bronze Series

Son of Ishtar
Dawn of War
Thunder at Kadesh

Also by Simon Turney

The Damned Emperors Series

Caligula
Commodus

The Marius' Mules Series

The Invasion of Gaul
The Belgae
Gallia Invicta
Conspiracy of Eagles
Hades' Gate
Caesar's Vow
Prelude to War
The Great Revolt
Sons of Taranis
Pax Gallica
Fields of Mars
Tides of War
Sands of Egypt
Civil War

The Praetorian Series

The Great Game
The Price of Treason
Eagles of Dacia
Lions of Rome
The Cleansing Fire

Roman Adventures

Crocodile Legion
Pirate Legion

Collaborations

A Year of Ravens
A Song of War
Rubicon

SONS OF ROME

RISE OF EMPERORS: BOOK ONE

DOHERTY & TURNEY

HEAD
of ZEUS

An Aries Book

First published in the UK in 2020 by Head of Zeus Ltd
An Aries book

9 7 5 3 1 2 4 6 8

A catalogue record for this book is available from
the British Library.

ISBN (HB): 9781800242005
ISBN (XTPB): 9781800242012
ISBN (E): 9781800242098

Typeset by Divaddict Publishing Solutions Ltd

Printed and bound in Great Britain by
CPI Group (UK) Ltd, Croydon CR0 4YY

Head of Zeus Ltd
First Floor East
5–8 Hardwick Street
London EC1R 4RG

WWW.HEADOFZEUS.COM

SONS OF
ROME
RISE OF EMPERORS

THE ROMAN EMPIRE

RNUNTUM

R. DANUBIUS

ILLYRICUM

MATIA

NA

NAISSUS

THRACIA

PONTICA

ARMENIA

MOESIA

NICOMEDIA

TICUM

PROPONTINE
SEA

ASIANA

SYRIA

ANTIOCH

R. EUPHRATES

MESOPOTAMIA

CAESAREA
MARITIMA

ORIENS

AEGYPTUS

ROME
306AD

VIA FLAMINIA

VIA SALARIA

SEPTEM BALNEA

MILVIAN BRIDGE

R. TIBER

R. ANIO

ROME

PRAETORIAN FORTRESS

VIA LATA

NEW BATHS OF DIOCLETIAN

CAMPUS MARTIUS

QUIRINAL HILL & BATH HOUSE

THEATRE OF POMPEY

SUBURA

CAPITOLINE HILL

OPPIAN HILL

GARDENS OF TORQUATAS

FORUM

FLAVIAN AMPHITHEATRE

LUDUS MAGNUS

VIA CAELEMONTANA

DISUSED IMPERIAL PALACE

VIA PRAENESTINA

PALATINE

VIA LABICANA

VILLA OF MAXENTIUS

TIBER

CIRCUS MAXIMUS

CASTRA PEREGRINA

IMPERIAL HORSEGUARD BARRACKS

RIVER PORT

AVENTINE HILL

HORREA GALBAE

VIA APPIA

TO VILLA OF HERODES ATTICUS

Prologue

CONSTANTINE

THE ROAD TO ROME, 27TH OCTOBER 312 AD

*I*t was the eve of the battle that would come to define us: not
just my kin, nor my empire – that great and ancient empire
that sprung from the very city upon which I was poised to
march – but nigh-on every soul on this mortal realm. And
forever when they spoke of it they would whisper my name:
Constantine.

A clement breeze furrowed my greying locks as I looked
south along the Via Flaminia – the road that would take me
to my goal. Either side of the great highway, my loyal legions
were camped: a sea of goatskin tents, bright banners, honed
blades and polished helms glinting in the languid orange light
of the late afternoon sun. A soldier knows that the eve of
any battle is charged with emotions that take a man closer to
his god, but that day, something occurred which, some say,
instead brought the divine before me.

When it happened, the cornflower sky was unblemished
with cloud, so it was no surprise that all within my ranks
saw it: a bright, radiant halo that burst into life around the
sun; a crescendo of light that briefly illuminated the land as
if it were noonday once more. I shielded my eyes to the glare,

I

heard my legionaries gasp, the thud of their knees hitting the ground, the cantillating songs of fused faiths rising in awe. Within a few heartbeats it was gone.

Men still speak of what happened there. Some talk of that nimbate sun as a vision bestowed upon me to guide me in battle the next day. Others claim I conjured the story of the lights to mask my flinty and insatiable ambition. Every soul doubtless has a theory on this and my many other endeavours, and what is a man but the sum of his deeds?

Well let me be the one to tell you of my deeds, both light and dark. What happened that afternoon on the road to Rome was neither an omen from the divine, nor a shrewd yarn to disguise mortal ambition: it was a moment of great realisation, and the culmination of a journey.

Now every journey has a story, but this one is a truly dark and tangled tale – one that would end, the very next day, in battle against my oldest friend...

MAXENTIUS

By the Milvian Bridge across the Tiber, the next day

Off to the left a centurion screamed imprecations at his men, driving them on across the churned turf and into the press of battle, while the clash and clamour of Rome's armies at war filled the air around us.

I had to pause to adjust my rich wool hat, for it had become so sweat-sodden that it constantly threatened to slip down across my eyes, and it doesn't do for an emperor to be cursing and blind as he fights for his throne. In the searing heat of the sun's glaring fiery orb, my horse stank of sweat and my purple cloak clung damp to my back, sticking to the beast's rump behind me.

My sword had become heavy in my hand. I'd had only a brief chance to use it that morning, when I had managed to slip my overprotective bodyguard and join the cavalry in a brief push. But I had waved it around enthusiastically from time to time, giving orders to charge here and hold there. I knew my histories. Julius Caesar's men would have followed him into the jaws of Cerberus himself just because of that great general's presence on the field.

And I, Maxentius, emperor of Rome, had to be a new Julius Caesar this day, or I would be no one.

Briefly, across the sea of glinting helms and the forest of spear points, I caught sight of him. My enemy. The man who would wrest Rome from me. *Constantine.* My brother, my oldest friend, and yet my last and most bitter adversary. Like a hero of ancient myth, he rose in his saddle, sword rising and falling in a constant spray of blood.

The force I had in the field vastly outnumbered that of my old friend and there, at the centre, not far from my brother on his war horse, I could see Volusianus and his Praetorians, pressing home our attack, assuring our victory. Five thousand men clad in high-quality steel, their shields bearing the proud scorpion insignia of the Guard, heaved forward against Constantine's simple, chain-clad veterans, the enemies' shields invested with a bright new design as if it might ward off a Praetorian blade.

It was almost over. Half a day's fighting.

They had told me to stay in the city and prepare for a siege, but I could not. The time had come for confrontation. Even the Sibylline oracle had urged for this. Volusianus was close to Constantine now. Might my prefect even kill my old friend for me? Constantine lunged and withdrew – I could not make out his foe at this distance, but the way he lolled in the saddle suggested he had almost been skewered.

I had mixed feelings about that even now. Even here, at the end, when only he or I could leave this field as master of Rome, I could not have personally wielded the blade that took the life of my old friend. I was grateful to Volusianus for sparing me that pain.

How had it come to this? How had we ended our time together in this world here, each determined to witness the other's demise before the sun set? A friendship so close that its collapse tears at the soul must have deep, strong roots.

I barely flinched, impassive, as a lucky stray bolt from one of Constantine's artillery snatched a prefect from his saddle mere paces from me, hurling him back over his horse's rear with a shriek and into the dust.

So much death...

But once, long ago, things were different. My brother and I had been young and innocent.

Once, the *world* was innocent.

PART 1

Faber est suae quisque fortunae
(Every man makes his own fortune)
– Appius Claudius Caecus

1

CONSTANTINE

NAISSUS, MOESIA SUPERIOR, OCTOBER 277 AD

Thirty-five years earlier

My earliest memory is of a storm, a relentless tempest that battered my birth town of Naissus. It gathered at dusk as I lay in my bed. Through the cracks in the shutters I watched the black clouds clawing across the dusk sky as if to tear down the day. Night arrived and the winds grew fiercer, howling like a pack of lost wolves, the rain lashing like a torturer's whip. When the thunder came, I trembled like the timbers of our modest home.

I shivered under my blanket, watching as the shutters strained against the storm's wrath. Then with a furious gust, they were blown open. The icy gale searched through my room, tearing the blanket from me as the rain flayed the floorboards. I gawped at the open window, then glanced to the door leading downstairs and to safety. My parents often told me I was bold – too bold – and reckless. And so it was that night, for I found myself slipping from my bed, stepping towards the flapping shutters, shielding my eyes from the forked lightning that tore the dark asunder.

Chill rain soaked my nightshirt as I grasped the sill then stretched to stand on my toes. I felt the breath catch in my throat when I saw what the storm had done to the town: the swollen river had burst its banks and now murky water tumbled through the streets in dark torrents. The pained lowing of trapped cattle sounded from nearby, and the broken corpses of others bobbed and tumbled through the deluge. I saw crying families huddled atop wagons and market stalls. Across the narrow streets I saw faces gazing out from broken shutters, eyes wide with panic.

Every soul in this ancient market town cowered. Even the imperial garrison on the walls ran, hoisting their shields and taking shelter in the turrets. But I saw something that has stayed with me to the end: a lone, silhouetted figure standing tall and motionless on the battlements, as if bemused by the storm's wrath. A legionary. He wore a sodden crimson cloak and rested his weight on his spear. While his comrades sought shelter, he remained. The squall raged around him, the rain battering on his helm and lashing over his face and shoulders. The lightning came once again and I saw his youthful features, gazing from his post and off into the northern countryside, unblinking. Through each clap of thunder, every streak of lightning, he did not flinch. I noticed his spear hand, and how white his knuckles were. He reminded me of the tall statue of Mars by the northern gates. The God of War stood like that too, spear grasped firmly.

That was when I noticed that there was something else in the clenched fist of the legionary's other hand. I could not see what it was that he held, but when I saw him lift it, whisper to and kiss it, I knew it was his source of strength as much as the spear. The reckless streak in me took hold again and I strained to get a better look, leaning further and further from the window until the rain soaked my face and my flaxen hair was plastered to my forehead. The legionary uncoiled his fingers at last. The thing sparkled in his palm. A Christian Chi-Rho, I realised – an amulet just like the one my mother wore. My strained gaze flicked from the spear to the amulet and back again. One a symbol of Mars and the other of the Christ-God. It made me wonder: on a battlefield – like those my legionary father oft fought upon back in those days – which would be more powerful?

Just then, a cry sounded from the Temple of Jove, downhill from my home where the rushing waters were deepest. People waded from the temple in panic, splashing from the grand marble entrance, into the flood. A groan of timber and thick crack of masonry rang out, before a column crumbled into the endless rush of churning water. The screaming of one man was cut short as the capital of the column dashed him like ripe fruit, the crimson stain of his blood washing into the flood.

I stared at the spot, horrified but unable to look away. At that moment, the wind whipped up as if to tear the town from the land and it pulled me from my precarious perch on the sill too. I toppled forward, a boyish cry forming in my lungs.

But hands snatched me back from the window, bolting the shutters closed once more. *Mother.*

'Constantine!' she cried, going on to berate me for my foolishness. Soon though, her tone softened. As she held me to her rose-scented bosom, drying me with a rag, I traced a finger over the silver amulet dangling from her neck – just like the soldier's. It was more common for the women of Naissus to be seen worshipping the Christian God, which made the legionary's choice even more intriguing. The men, and particularly the garrison, tended to follow the old gods. Indeed, Father kept a small shrine to Mars in our home.

'You told me Christians do not make war,' I said. 'But outside, I saw a man on the walls, a soldier...'

She stopped drying me and held me at arm's length. Her eyes, azure like mine, affixed me. I thought I had spoken out of turn until she sighed and said: 'Men are men, be they Christians or otherwise, and men make war.'

I frowned. Father had often told me that I would grow to one day be a soldier like him. I had listened in awe to his prayers to Mars. Likewise, I had been spellbound by Mother's Christian tales. 'What brings a man to war?' I asked, then my frown deepened. 'What brings a man to choose his god?'

She smiled weakly and brushed a droplet of water from my cheek with her thumb. 'That is for each of us to find out, Constantine. Our choices in this life define us. That is the journey we each must make.'

She kissed me and laid me down. Soon, the storm faded and I drifted off to sleep. My dreams were riven with the image of the legionary on the walls and one echoing question: where might my journey take me?

THE ROAD TO TREVERORUM, MARCH 286 AD

Nine years later

It was a frosty morning on the kalends of March when my father told me the news that set in motion such a great chain of events. We were in the hearth room of our villa outside Salona. He knelt before me on the tessellated floor and clasped his hands around mine, his sallow and sunken eyes pinning me to my seat. The fire crackled nearby as if trying to disguise the echo of his words.

'Emperor Diocletian has called upon you?' I said, my heart sagging as I realised he would be gone for some time. That he had been summoned by the emperor himself was no great surprise to me, for my father was no longer a mere legionary as he was in those early days in Naissus. Now he was Constantius, Governor of the Province of Dalmatia. He was often on his travels, seeing to the province's tax affairs, listening to the gripes of the citizens and going even further afield on occasions like this to attend the imperial court.

'He has,' he said solemnly.

I tried to hide my sadness.

'But you will be coming with me,' he added.

The words were like a stirring song: *I was to stand in the presence of the emperor?* An ember of fear and excitement sparked into life in the pit of my belly. I was keenly aware of Father's eyes searching mine for a reaction, so I glanced through the open doors, over the courtyard outside and the frost-speckled gardens beyond, trying to appear indifferent.

'You are fourteen now, and no longer a boy,' Father added.

'Then we must arrange for the villa to be tended to in our absence,' I agreed, further feigning nonchalance – but the fire of angst and intrigue was roaring within me now. I must point out that I was no stranger to journeying through foreign climes: in the first few years following that storm in Naissus, Mother and I had been with Father on his travels as he forged a fine career in the legions, fighting in the dank wilds across the Danubius and in the arid wastes around Palmyra. But since he had gained his governorship, I had rarely ventured beyond Dalmatia's borders. I wondered how much the world beyond had changed in the intervening years. More, I wondered how Mother felt about undertaking such a voyage. But when I looked over to her, standing by the old oak table, I saw that there was something wrong.

'It will just be you and me, Constantine,' Father replied, glancing at Mother as well. 'We are to ride to Gaul. Diocletian has been in Augusta Treverorum for some months. It seems that in that time he has finally accepted that the empire can no longer be ruled by one man, and he seeks to end the wasteful wars of succession. Maximian is to become Emperor of the West in Augusta Treverorum, while Diocletian will rule the East from his palace in Nicomedia as the senior of the pair. Power will be shared between the two... and others.' He paused, again looking to Mother. I saw firelight dance in his eyes. And something else... *guilt?* He looked back to me. 'That is why we must be there. Now ready yourself, son. Our escort will be here before noon.'

As I made for my chamber to pick out my travelling garments, a fresh shiver of excitement marched across my skin. While selecting my doeskin riding boots, a woollen tunic and cloak and two linen tunics, I mouthed the name silently. *Augusta Treverorum.* A fortress city on the banks of the Mosella, so very far away. Then I thought of Father's guarded behaviour. For a moment, I tried to piece together his agenda. Why was I to accompany him while Mother remained here? He had told me often that I would one day be a soldier and then a leader like him. Maybe this was the first step beyond my daily swordplay and study of battlefield tactics and fortifications?

No, I realised, there was more to this journey. My mind was all but tied in knots with this guesswork, and so I laughed and let it all go. *Perhaps by the time we reach the West, I might have figured out his strategy.* Whatever it was, it was doubtless well thought out. Father had always been restless in his efforts to catch the eye of his superiors, to claw his way through the ranks and to secure his governorship. While some men bought favour or were born into nobility, Father had worn himself to the nub to earn all he had.

As I drew a leather belt around my light brown tunic, my thoughts grew sober. Despite Father's rise, he had never found contentment. And in recent months, rumours had been circling like vultures. The people of Dalmatia whispered that his role as governor was coveted by others, others with the leverage of noble blood. It had further darkened the rings around his eyes and added a clipped edge to his already terse moods. Indeed, one night last month, I had seen him at his worst. He was sitting by the table nursing wine, raking a white-knuckled hand through his thinning hair. Mother was weeping by his side. Neither knew I was watching, and Father certainly never intended me to hear his serrated words to her.

I have no choice, Helena. Graft will never change the colour of my blood.

The memory stilled me as I again wondered what matter had riven them so.

Just then, Mother's gentle sigh startled me. I looked up to see that she had entered my bedchamber silently. She walked over to stand by the window, the morning light betraying the first lines of age around her eyes and threads of grey in her otherwise dark, thick Cypriote curls. She watched me as I buckled my belt then fastened on my riding boots. 'So tall and such broad shoulders for such a young man.' She spoke in a hushed tone, her delicate face creasing in a doleful half-smile.

I caught sight of myself in the bronzed mirror opposite. My daily practice with the wooden sword, duelling with

13

Batius, Father's ox of a bodyguard, was draining, but the more I practised, the more I ate. The effects were clear to see; my limbs were lean yet muscular, my posture proud. My jaw had grown too, widening to match my flat-boned face and broad nose. She stepped over to stroke my flaxen curls from my forehead. She rose on her tiptoes and kissed me there, and I saw the tears quivering in her eyes.

'Father could not avoid this journey, Mother. You realise that, don't you? Emperor Diocletian has summoned him and thus he must go.' I said this to reassure her, but I knew it would not suffice.

'Remember me, Constantine,' was all she said in reply.

The words cut me to my heart. 'You are never far from my thoughts, Mother. It will always be so. Why would it be any other way?'

'Constantine,' Father cut me off abruptly. He stood in the opposite doorway of my chamber, beholding both of us suspiciously. His muscled bronze cuirass was designed to exaggerate his physique, but that was the first day I noticed that his once burly limbs seemed to have grown sinewy, his powerful frame ever so slightly wilting. I wondered whether I should dare ask after his health. Before I spoke, he stepped forward and proffered me his *spatha*, still tucked into its scuffed leather scabbard. 'You'll need it for the journey, Constantine.'

I stared for a few breathless moments, dumbfounded. The lengthy slashing sword of the legions had been by his side all throughout his time in the ranks. Now, it seemed, it was to be mine.

For the journey, I mouthed, taking it by the hilt.

His hand clasped my shoulder and I felt a frisson of excitement. The blade caught the morning light as I unsheathed and weighed it. Light and perfectly honed. The hilt was well worn and devoid of opulence. It was Father epitomised. 'Batius might feel he is at a disadvantage if he has to face me with the wooden training sword?' I grinned.

'Batius will gladly strike steel with you.' Father chuckled, his demeanour lightening a fraction.

Outside, a clopping of hooves signalled the arrival of our escort. I glanced from the open shutters and into the ivy-clad colonnaded courtyard below. A *turma* of *equites* – thirty riders in iron helms, mail shirts and crimson cloaks – cantered in through the gates and came to a halt. Their mounts snorted and scuffed in the small space. The shaven-headed Batius strode from the shadows to greet them, then mounted his mare beside them, holding the tethers of Father's black stallion and my white gelding. I turned to my parents.

Father beheld Mother. 'Helena,' he said through taut lips as he beckoned me to the stairs.

'Farewell, Constantius,' she replied, again refusing to meet his gaze.

We boarded an imperial *bireme* at Salona's city docks and set sail northwards, cutting through the sapphire waters of the *Mare Adriaticum* before coming to the port city of Aquileia on the morning of the seventh day. Then followed nearly a month of riding. First we journeyed through the green hills of Noricum, then we came under the shadow of the Alpes as we passed through snow-capped valleys and high passes where the air grew thin and fresh. Hot stew and dry, warm beds awaited us at each imperial way station dotting the roadside. After several more days of travel, we descended from the chill mountains, through Raetia before entering Germania

Superior and riding the military way along the banks of the River Rhenus. Spring had taken hold of the land by then, turning the air clement. At night, we camped in the open, roasting rabbit, cooking stew over the fire and slaking our thirsts from the cool shallows of the great river. Then the wine came out.

I had my first taste of unwatered Rhodian red that night. At first it burned like fire on my tongue. But after a few mouthfuls, the bitterness was tempered by a rising, warm contentment in my blood. I watched as Father talked ribald with the equites as if he was one of them. In many ways he still was – perhaps he might have been a happier man had he accepted his lot as a soldier or a low-ranking officer. I watched him, seeing the reflection of the campfire in his eyes, as if it had kindled his spirit once more. Batius joined in, recounting tales from his time with Father during the Palmyrene revolt: battles, epic treks through the desert and a somewhat dubious story about how he had won a suit of solid golden armour in a game of dice only to swiftly lose it again. He guzzled a mouthful of wine and grinned, his teeth stained red as he flashed a look at Father. 'Remember the hag?'

Father looked back blankly at his big, scarred bodyguard for a moment, then wagged a finger in recollection. 'How could I forget that?' The equites leaned in to hear the tale and so too did I. 'We were trekking through the desert towards the rebel city when a toothless crone shuffled onto the road before us. We stopped. A whole legion halted by a withered hag,' he said, his eyes widening. 'She glowered at us, her face like the edge of a blunted axe, her skin like a prune. That part of the world is stranger than most – every man seems to worship a different god, and some of those I wouldn't even call gods.' He shook his head and sucked air through his teeth. 'Anyway, we were waiting on some mystical prophecy, a curse, a warning against marching on to Palmyra.' He looked up, seeing the men hanging on his every word, seeing me with them, then he grinned. 'Then she pulled open her robe and showed us her tits!'

The men around the fire gawped, then erupted in fits of laughter.

'She stood there, screeching like a crow, demanding a bronze denarius for her "services". When we marched past, she shook her coinless fists at us...'

'Aye,' Batius cut in, wiping wine from his chin, 'and *then* the curses came, let me tell you!' The riders roared again. Batius' shoulders jostled and a tear of laughter spilled from one eye.

Father seemed more carefree by the moment. I noticed how the dark lines under his eyes seemed to have lightened momentarily, his posture righted just a fraction too, his shoulders almost filling the cuirass. Was it the travelling, or the comradeship, or this brief hiatus from the day-to-day duties of his governorship that lifted him? Or was it the absence of Mother?

Remember me, Constantine. Why had she said that? Why?

We set off again the following morning, nursing foul heads as we turned west, away from the Rhenus. More than a moon after we had set out, we were in the lands of Gaul and the Province of Belgica, a land of green meadows dappled with a mist of purple irises. Our trek was almost over.

'Look, Constantine, what do you see?' Father asked one mid-morning.

I gazed ahead. The lush green grass and low woods were interrupted by the valley, edged with steep bluffs of pale sandstone. A river meandered through it, sparkling like liquid sapphire. The Mosella, I realised. We followed the river until a sturdy walled city rolled into view. It dominated the eastern banks of the Mosella. More, a stocky stone bridge linked the city to a robust-looking *castellum* on the western side, affording total control over the waterway and its banks. Inside the walls, a jumble of marble and brick and a medley of fluttering banners jostled for supremacy.

Again, I trilled the words: 'Augusta Treverorum.'

Father smiled. 'They say it was first founded by an Assyrian prince. The Gauls held on to it in some of the bloodiest wars this land has seen. Then it saw Caligula draw his first breath. Today, within those walls, the empire's future will be decided.'

I noticed Father's eyes narrowing. 'Decided? I thought the elevation of Maximian was but a formality?'

This seemed to break Father's thoughts. 'It is, but there is more to this gathering. Diocletian aims to set out the rules of succession for generations to come. For centuries. Forever.'

I saw a hunger in his eyes at that moment. I recognised it. Just like the night when I saw him nursing wine, Mother in tears by his side. I bit my lip to stifle the question I had held prisoner behind my lips all the way here, but this time I could not hold back. 'Why did Mother not come with us?'

Father seemed nervous then. He blinked and squinted into the horizon, as if trying to discern the glinting shapes of the sentries on the city walls. A time passed and I was unsure if my question had gone unheard. 'Not long after Palmyra, Emperor Aurelian bestowed me with the title of *Protectores Augusti Nostri*,' he said at last. 'I was by the emperor's side like his shield. He treated me like a brother, spreading my name, championing my deeds.' His jaw stiffened and his lips drew taut. 'Yet look at me now. Aurelian is gone and I have nothing but the running of Dalmatia to show for the blood I shed in that desert war. And there are plenty who look to take even that from me.'

That was all he said. We reached the valley floor and rode for the twin arches of the city's eastern gate, joining the stream of wagons and traders heading inside. The walls, smoke-blackened from the watchmen's braziers, loomed up over us, the sentries glaring down from the top of the gatehouse until we passed under the archway. Inside, the city was thronged with activity. The streets were packed with faces and the air was thick with the stench of manure and sweat. Bells clanged and traders yammered; dogs yapped and whips cracked over the backs of sumpter mules. I noticed that between the finer marble buildings, there were vast wards that were run-down, with cracked flagstones on the streets and row upon row of crumbling brick *insulae* where most of the many souls of this city lived. The crowds were thickest here – shuffling around bread stalls and bargaining with hawkers and pedlars.

We were almost at a standstill in these parts until – with a burst of whinnying and clopping – a clutch of imperial riders barged through the throng and came before us. There were twelve of them, each wearing polished scale vests, pale blue cloaks, plumed helms and carrying pale blue shields adorned with a perched eagle. They beheld us with grim faces. 'You are the last party to arrive,' the lead rider hailed Father icily, then wheeled round, motioning for us to follow. Like this, we negotiated our way towards the domed basilica in the centre of the city where the emperor waited.

'Who are they?' I whispered, captivated by the gloriously garbed riders.

'The Joviani,' Father whispered by my side as we trotted behind them. The populace seemed in no mood to anger or delay these riders, some even dropping that which they carried to leap clear of their path. 'Wherever Diocletian treads, these men will be nearby. Likewise, the Herculiani will seldom be far from Maximian's side.' He pointed through the bustle of the forum, past the *thermae* and on to the steps of the basilica. There, two parties of eight black-cloaked legionaries in baked leather armour lined either side of the steps. Their shields bore the image of a soaring black eagle on a background of pure, blood red – the same colour as the plumes on their helms.

I remembered my early years once more, when people spoke of how the emperors had been protected by the Praetorians. I had only heard the rumours of their decline; once they had stood by the emperor's side, now they had been reduced to a mere garrison in faraway Rome. It seemed that Diocletian had chosen these two faithful legions to replace them.

Just then, a triumphal chorus blared out as three musicians atop the basilica blew into their *buccina* horns. The populace broke out in a keen babble, all heads turning toward this, the centrepiece of the city.

'It is time,' Father said, eyeing the building with a strange look.

We reached the basilica forecourt, where the eager citizens were kept at bay by a wall of spear-wielding garrison legionaries. Their leader recognised our Joviani escort and waved Father, Batius and I through into the clear space before the entrance. We dismounted, giving our steeds to stable hands and surrendering our weapons to the sentries. The escort gone, Father led the way now, striding across the flagstones, shoulders back, head held high. Walking by his side, I felt the eyes of the crowds upon me. Maybe it was saddle-weariness, but every breath felt stolen and every footstep somewhat clumsy. I felt suddenly conscious of my simple, dust-stained linen tunic and travel-worn doeskin boots – dress more like that worn by the peasants of this city than the son of a nobleman.

We climbed the steps past flanking lines of Herculiani, then passed through the entrance portico and into a miasma of incense smoke and sweet wax scent. I looked up and around. On later reflection, I realised the domed basilica was modest in size, but at the time, I felt dwarfed by it. A central nave ran from the doorway to the far end of the hall, with rows of well-dressed spectators – nobles, governors and senators – standing in two blocks, backs turned to us. Every rustling or coughing of those gathered there was amplified tenfold. In the apse at the far end of the hall to which all eyes were turned, two odd figures stood atop a petal-strewn plinth, facing this gathering. At first I thought they were statues, for they each wore paint on their faces – one gold and the other silver. I studied this pair as we took our place near the front of one block of spectators. Around the two, the sweet smoke coiled from bronze burners on the altar behind them. The pair wore immaculately polished bronze armour, fine purple silk cloaks and glittering laurel wreaths.

'The two emperors?' I whispered to Batius.

'Aye – and I bet they painted each other's arses too,' Batius whispered just as a hush began to descend on the hall, then disguised his words with an embarrassed cough when he heard his own echo bouncing around crisp and clear. Father glared at him and he dropped his gaze to the floor, admonished. A moment later and there was barely a sound to be heard bar the occasional crackling from the wood in the burners.

I studied the two on the stage. The older of the two men was a foot shorter than the other. His gold-flecked face was pinched and his gaze cold, his dark hair and tightly curled beard neatly trimmed – just like the many coins bearing his name. Emperor Diocletian, I realised with a frisson of excitement. The master of the Roman world. In all my time I had never been in the presence of such an individual. Suddenly, a chorus of *cornua* blared from the back of the plinth, the horns filling the hall with a majestic tune. When they fell silent, Diocletian stepped forth.

He looked out over the silent crowd like a crow, then raised his arms to either side, his silk sleeves gathering at his elbows as he turned his palms towards the ceiling as if about to proclaim some great, lost truth. 'The empire will flourish once more,' he said in a pinched, nasal tone. 'Like brothers, we will guide the East and the West. Twin eagles, overseeing imperial fortune. I, Gaius Aurelius Valerius Diocletianus Augustus, will serve the lands of the East, bestowed with the power of Jove, God of Sky and Thunder.'

At once, this conjured the image of that storm in Naissus. Then, I had witnessed a man empowered by a god. Here, this man seemed to be claiming to *be* a god. Jove, no other. The image on the coin had always held me in awe. This pompous display was somewhat dismantling those feelings.

The other then stepped forward. He was maybe in his mid-thirties – Father's age. His silver-painted face was broad and his hooded green eyes gave him a lackadaisical look. He carried the thick flesh of a man well used to palace life and his bushy beard seemed tailored to hide a bulging chin. *Maximian?* I wondered. I saw him glancing down at us and froze as he nodded, almost imperceptibly. Then I realised the gesture was aimed at Father. I shot a sideways look at Father to see him nodding back.

Maximian then held out his arms as if to embrace all before him. 'And I, Marcus Aurelius Valerius Maximianus Augustus, will pursue glory and fortune for the West, like Hercules, the great hero and son of Jove.'

Jove and Hercules. I stifled a snort of derision. I watched and I listened as the two professed their closeness to the divine pair. Their pompous and well-rehearsed address lasted a long time. Long enough for Batius to begin shuffling and scratching at his nether regions. My eyes wandered around the hall. Glancing left and right, I saw many more faces either feigning reverence or fending off boredom. Then there was one that snagged my gaze. Dark eyes shaded under a heavy brow, a large, shapeless nose and mirthless lips all framed by a square face. He was tall and well built, with close-cropped fair hair, wearing an eastern-style military robe and slippers. I reckoned he was in his late twenties.

'That is Galerius, the Herdsman,' Father whispered.

'A shepherd?' I replied.

Father smiled faintly. 'Once, long ago. Now he is anything but. He is a man of the legions, and a fine tactician. He is here only because power is being meted out...' He fell silent, as if stung by his own words.

I glanced once more at this Galerius and the younger boy standing with him. Well, he was younger than me – maybe ten or eleven years old – but like his father he was tall, with a stocky build and ham-like hands. He wore a lavish, gem-studded silver necklace.

'And that is his son, Candidianus,' Father whispered.

It was then that the boy noticed me looking. I averted my gaze instantly. I let a few moments pass then risked another furtive glance; now the boy was whispering to Galerius, who said something in reply that caused the lad to grin coldly and stare back at me. I bristled at this, sure they could know nothing of me. Perhaps they were mocking my simple clothes?

He quickly grew bored of whatever had amused him, and of the ceremony as a whole. I watched with a cold eye as the young one left Galerius' side and slipped from the crowd with six boys of his age, heading to the side of the nave and disappearing from sight.

I was stirred from my thoughts when, finally, Diocletian brought the ceremony to an end with a valedictory salute to the gods. His last words echoed around the room, then the doors along the sides of the hall swung open, and painted slave girls carried in amphorae of wine and platters of roasted pheasant, rabbit, pork and cheese, stacks of polished apples and grapes and baskets of freshly baked breads. At once, the gathered crowd broke out in a relieved prattle, the ordered rows breaking up into clusters as they ate, drank and chattered.

From the moment Father told me of our journey here, I had longed to see the city, to witness the acclamation of the two emperors. Yet after the affectation I had just witnessed, I felt nothing but hollowness. The masks of gods were farcical.

Just then, Father stepped away from me, saluting the silver-skinned Maximian as the new Emperor of the West waded through the crowd, flanked by a pair of Herculiani legionaries. Maximian stopped and spoke with Father, the pair sharing hushed words. Up close, I could see the ruddiness of the skin around his neck where the silver paint stopped, and the kink in his nose where it had been broken in the past. His heavy-lidded green eyes gave the impression that his mind was elsewhere but then his gaze flicked up to lock onto mine, and I knew nothing could be further from the truth. I saw a bead of sweat trickling down Father's neck as he continued to speak to this silver emperor, and he jabbed out his tongue frequently to dampen his lips. Curiosity piqued as to Father's words, I stepped a little closer to see if I could overhear, when Batius slapped a hand on my shoulder.

'I'm no senator and I care little for politics. You know me well enough, lad: give me a spatha, a bastard Goth to gut and a temple to share my honour with Mars afterwards and I'm a happy man. But I'd advise you to stay out of their dealings.'

I glowered up at the big bodyguard, momentarily angered that he had drowned out whatever Father was saying. But his sardonic grin quelled me. I acquiesced, turning from Father and Maximian. I thought of Mother, of Father's tension in these last months – it all seemed to be leading up to this moment. 'Aye, but I get the feeling it will soon entangle me,' I mused plaintively.

'Then enjoy yourself while times are still simple.' He winked, casting a bulging eye at a pair of round-hipped slave girls gliding past nearby.

With a grin, I left him, but not to chase slave girls. I picked my way through the chattering crowds and over to the side of the hall. A door lay ajar there. Silence and space to think.

2

MAXENTIUS

'Maxentius!'

I jumped at the edge in Mother's voice. Her legacy of a Syrian accent lent her Latin a strange harshness that made her sound as though she were angry even at the best of times, and Father had shouted my name in a heated tone often enough that I had developed something of a nervous disposition at that tender age of eight summers.

I looked up sharply, my startled hands knocking over the figures and blocks that I had so painstakingly organised. My mother – Eutropia, wife of the newly raised co-emperor Maximian – stood in one of the room's three doorways, her finery carefully selected to bring out the swarthiness of her skin and to offset the lustrous dark sheen of her intricately plaited hair.

'Mother?' I replied, a little shakily.

'Where is your stepsister? She disappeared from the celebrations just as your father was about to introduce her to someone important.'

I blinked. I remember being somewhat surprised that anyone would expect me to know anything at all. I was generally ignored until I was required to perform some dull duty or display my knowledge of the empire's great history for the edification of Father's guests when they'd all had too much wine to discuss deep matters themselves.

'I have no idea, Mother. I've not seen Theodora since this morning.'

Mother huffed and tutted for a moment, clearly trying to decide what to do next, and then turned to leave, pausing with an afterthought.

'Make sure you clear all this rubbish away, Maxentius. This room could be required at any time – there are so many guests present.'

As she left, shutting the door behind her just a little too hard, I stared after her and twitched a little. Mother was kind – always had been – and to see her so flustered that she passed her irritations on to me was a worry. Father must have been rough on her once again. I watched that door for a long moment, and then turned to regard the other, more important entrance that led from the basilica hall proper via a small ambulatory. The general hubbub of the gathering of nobility was audible, if dulled a little by distance and doorways, and I knew that Father would be there, in his element, enjoying his newfound celebrity.

No one would come in here, regardless of what Mother had said. It was one of the reasons that Father had suggested I come here to keep myself occupied in the first place. Of all the rooms and spaces in the basilica complex, only those with décor befitting the presence of the imperial court would be used for today's gathering. This rather drab room with its stained window and sparse furniture was perfect for the glorious, silver-tinted Maximian to leave his bookish, quiet son.

I returned to my toys.

There were many blocks, carved by an expert to resemble towers, walls, gatehouses, temples, rotunda and many other civic and military structures. It had been a birthday gift from my parents three years earlier and remained my most treasured possession, brought with us from Mediolanum along with my sister's possessions and my seemingly endless piles of court clothes – Mother despaired of my habit of lounging on floors and wearing threadbare my expensive silks and linens.

I placed the blocks carefully. I was always excessively careful with my toys and my mother marvelled at my need to tidy away all my games when they were done, placing each piece in its assigned position and making sure it was secure and in perfect condition. But for now the floor was their home, as they grew into a great ligneous city.

The temple was central, of course, raised upon a podium formed by a wide, low rectangle, itself carved with a delicate staircase. This, I decided, would be the temple of Jove in pride of place, at the centre of my great urban design. I cannot remember the details of my other structures, though I know it would resemble a grand forum and *Capitolium*, with a great basilica off to one side, and that I would use the military tower and wall blocks in a somewhat pacific fashion as the boundary walls for grand villas and as aqueduct sections. It annoyed Father to see me do so, I know, but I was not building a fortress; I was building a city... I was building *the* city.

'Maxentius?'

I turned and smiled. The same door had opened once more, but this time the figure standing in the opening was that of my elder stepsister Flavia Theodora. I had known as much before I looked up, for she was the only person in this grand complex who would call me by name without an inflection of irritation or harshness. Theodora's voice lilted with a slight upturn so that everything resembled a question, whether intended as such or not.

I loved Theodora more than anyone else in the family, I think. Even Mother. She had comforted me when Father railed at me during his worst moods, or when he slapped me, chiding me for what he considered to be my 'womanish habits'. He never did understand that strength comes in many forms and not all of them involve the flexing of muscles. Theodora salved my conscience and my soul when needed, and despite everything even Father seemed to love her – insofar as he could truly love anyone.

'Sister?'

'It seems I am to be paraded in the manner of a prized sacrificial bull before the drooling, leering megalomaniacs of the court. I feel sometimes that Father cannot wait to foist me off on some rich noble to further advance his position.'

I remember giving her a sad smile. The thought of her being torn from my life and sold into marriage was a blow to my soul, though I knew it would happen soon enough – she had already been of legal marriageable age for several years.

'Father will be kind in arranging your marriage, Theodora. He loves you, and now he is made co-emperor with Diocletian. How can he hope to advance beyond such grand status? I think you are safe. Go and be paraded, dear sister. You are beautiful and I will hear a dozen hearts breaking even from here.'

Theodora smiled then and the glory of it lit the room for me. I was still grinning a little inanely myself after she left and closed the door. I sat for some time staring at the patterns in the marble by my feet and contemplating the very idea that a man sharing the most powerful position in the empire could consider striving for more. How foolish to wonder such a thing. Age has taught me that the ambitious never stop striving, even at the top, and more importantly that even the throne is far from a secure place to rest.

Finally, I turned back to my wooden city and noticed with consternation a shadow cast across it. A whispered voice from the room's periphery hissed 'Candidianus,' in a nervous tone. My eyes rose across the marble floor and I felt impatience rise within – the result of an irritability I had inherited from my father. With these constant interruptions and visitors I would never finish adjusting my wooden Rome. Why were these people even coming here? They should all be bustling around Father and the great Diocletian.

This new arrival in the room, though, was not someone I knew. No hassled lady seeking her wayward children, or recalcitrant daughter attempting to evade her destiny...

The figure whose shadow stretched across the room and threw my glorious civic centre into an oppressive gloom was a stocky, well-built young man, perhaps half as old again as I was, with bear-shoulders and close-cut fair hair. He was dressed in relative finery – not as rich as mine, I would say, but costly enough to make most families wince and touch their purses for reassurance. And yet something about its cut, colour and make-up spoke more of the battlefield than the throne room. He wore a thick leather belt with a place for a sword and dagger, though neither was currently in evidence. Even before he stepped forward and the light from the leaded window threw his face into sharp relief I had seen enough to form an instant dislike of him.

His face took things so much further.

It brought a fear that chilled me from the roots of my hair

to the soles of my feet. The boy's mouth was twisted into an expression of casual cruelty and his eyes were flinty hard and devoid of compassion or joy.

His shadow was the most pleasant part of him. The warmest. And it showed no sign of moving away.

As if his brooding appearance was not enough, there was a small gaggle of boys loitering behind him at the door that led back to the main hall. Each and every one had that look of a bully. Piggy eyes and leering faces, made no less brutal by the fine court clothes they wore. Even at perhaps eleven or twelve summers they would have looked more at home nailing a peasant to a cross and stripping him of his flesh than attending the court of the most powerful men in the empire.

A cold shudder ran through me at the sight, and at the realisation that I was at their mercy. I glanced at the other two doors in the room but they were both closed, and even as my eyes shot back and forth between them, the wicked-looking thug's cronies entered the room at his silent cold-eyed instruction, moving around the perimeter and effectively sealing me in.

The main door – through which they had entered – was closed with a quiet, gentle click that might as well have been the resounding leaden boom of a mausoleum door slamming shut.

I tried to find my voice, but it seemed to have become lost somewhere beneath a layer of fear, and all that issued from between my dry lips was a faint croak.

'What is *this*?' asked the leader of this small pack of brutes, the distaste clear in his voice, as though he had come across a mangy dog eating its own waste.

It took me a moment to realise that he was actually

referring to my city rather than to my person, and I knew then what would happen. I had met this boy's sort before in my few short years, and had learned a few hard lessons. Such boys – and men, when they grow into them – exist only for the pleasure of causing distress and pain. There is no arguing with them or reasoning with them. They will not stop unless forced to do so.

My immediate future was bleak, and I was astute enough to recognise that.

Strangely, a calm settled over me at the thought that the thug had fixated upon my glorious wooden invention rather than upon my person. I was not a martial boy by nature. I shunned the sickening sights and sounds of inflicted wounds that the arena produced and had little interest in lessons from the swordsman Father had retained to 'toughen me up', my forays into the military largely restricted to reading from ancient masters such as the great Julius Caesar.

No. Not a warrior. Not yet.

I accepted that then, but despite my quiet, pacific demeanour, one thing had come down to me from my father's personality, other than a tendency to anger easily: a bloody-minded unwillingness to bend. There was a steel in me, as yet untempered but beginning to show even as a child. Despite the fact that I knew this boy was here for violence, I found a disinclination to accept my fate, and my jaw hardened just a little.

The thug must have seen the change in me and recognised it for what it was, for one eyebrow twitched upwards just a little, and he goaded me beyond words by taking a step forward and deliberately knocking aside one of my carefully planned commercial centres with his foot.

'I said what is *this*?'

The blocks tumbled away, distorting the immaculate lines of my city, and anger rose in the pit of my stomach. But I was no fighter – the anger had no outlet through fist or blade. My rage instead hardened to a diamond within me, amplifying my resolution to weather the storm.

'*That*,' I replied with the same inflection that he had used, 'was a careful, thoughtful and artful construction of Rome as it should be. As I see it. That is what it *was*. What it *is*, is a mess of ruins and fallen buildings, knocked carelessly aside by an uncultured and mindless barbarian.'

I watched the fire ignite in his eyes. Had I not already hardened myself to my fate, I would have panicked then, for this boy was more than a mere ordinary bully, and I had just pushed him as far as he had likely ever been pushed. Given his build, his garb and the ease with which a weapon belt sat on his hips, likely no one had ever answered him back in his life.

There was a strange, pregnant pause as the boy fought to restrain his anger and keep hold of himself.

'Watch those doors...' he said to his gaggle of brutes and ruffians without taking his eyes from my own. Then, to me: 'Piss on Rome. Shit on Rome. It'll only improve it. Rome is a ruin already. A shell. The dank, stinking hole that gave birth to our empire, as the Dikteon cave gave us Zeus.'

At the time I saw only a dreadful and destructive lust in the boy's eyes, sure that he was intent on destroying both my wooden city and my whole self. I saw my doom in his dreadful gaze. Looking back, I realise that my grown self would have recognised so much more in those fiery eyes: an easterner – given his referring to Jove by his Greek appellation; one of the new breed of soldier-born nobles without the intelligence to recognise the value of our heritage, which was rapidly slipping through our fingers. A bitter and twisted young man, taking out his own failings on the world around him.

I had read sufficient tales to know that the only thing a bully respects is strength, and I had little enough of that in my scrawny arms and thin torso. But the strength that I lacked in my frame I made up for in my heart. That steel within hardened me.

'Rome is the hearth of the world where the eternal flame burns. Only a clot-brained moron would fail to see its importance.'

I saw the attack coming, but that pig-headed, unyielding part of myself was very much in control now, and the sight of his soft leather boot smashing aside my temple of Jove and crushing one of the precious wooden figures as he lunged did little to assuage the anger I felt at this mean and wicked intrusion.

I may not have been strong or brave, but I *was* nimble, I think. The first swing he made for me swept through the empty air a foot above my head as I ducked away to the side. I danced off, staying out of his reach as his swinging fist came round again, leaping back as he made a concerted effort to connect.

I was doomed, of course. There were half a dozen of them and, although only the leader was attacking me at this point, I knew that the others would likely leap into the fray if their master demanded it of them, given that they would hardly find me a difficult target. But for the moment it looked as though I would be able to keep him at bay for a while, and a delay might be my saviour. At any time, someone could enter from the hall, or Mother or Theodora could come for me, and then this would end relatively harmlessly.

My undoing was, indirectly, my own fault.

As I ducked out of the way of yet another punch thrown from those ham-like fists, my foot came down on the wooden military gatehouse that I had found no civil use for, and it skidded. My leg disappeared from under me and I collapsed painfully to the floor.

The youth allowed me no time to recover.

His kick caught me below the ribs and drew every tiny fragment of breath from me. The first blow that landed had sealed my fate – with such a strike there was little chance of me making any comeback and we both knew it.

I withdrew into myself, hoping to gain some distance from the pain as I curled into a ball around my bruised midriff and what I felt sure must be a broken rib or two. If I could hold off the pain I might pass out soon and enter a blissful dark world.

'Candidianus, that's enough!' called one of the lackeys, his voice audible even over the flurry of blows being landed upon my form by this titanic adolescent monster and even above the racing torrent of my pulse that beat out the 'ramming speed' in my ears.

The boy who shouted may have believed it was enough, but clearly Candidianus did not. A kick to the knee sent shockwaves of pain up and down my leg that had not cleared even when the next two punches landed in my kidney.

'Candidianus! That's Maximian's son! Are you mad?'

And I realised then where I had heard the name. Candidianus, the son of Galerius. A veteran officer of the legions and a war hero. My father had expounded on the merits of Galerius more than once, especially when trying to push me into physical training. Candidianus, they said, already showed promise and would likely soon follow his father's path.

'Be silent!' Candidianus snarled at his companions, pausing in his beating to stand and glare at the speaker. 'You think I am afraid of a runt because his father paints his face and calls himself a god? Hardly! Fat, painted, self-made gods have fallen before.'

The pause in the attack continued as the thug looked me over, deciding what to do with me next and, as I saw the gleam of hatred in his eyes, I realised with dismay that Candidianus truly felt no fear of reprisal, believing his father powerful enough to make him untouchable. Or possibly under the impression that I was just too weak and cowardly to press for retribution.

As he stood, deliberating on my future, I felt that nebulous anger reforming once more. Strangely, perhaps, it was not anger directed at my fate or even at this monster for what he was busy doing to me. It was anger at his blind denial of Rome. At his wanton destruction of my glorious wooden city. At his lack of nobility.

It is almost laughable to charge him with a lack of nobility and then to recount what I did next, but it was the one shining moment for me in that unpleasant encounter, and I can make some account of myself when the occasion demands. I uncoiled like a snake, feeling the pain in my cracked ribs as I did so, but ignoring it long enough to lunge out and sink my teeth into his ankle.

I caught him on the tendon rope between ankle and heel and snapped my jaws tight until my teeth all but met.

Candidianus' howl echoed around the chamber like some primal monster of legend and it amazes me that it was not heard in the crowded basilica hall, though by then the chatter would be cacophonous and the musicians would be playing.

I tasted the tin-salt tang of blood flowing into my mouth

and felt my teeth ache as he wrenched his ruined heel from my mouth, almost taking teeth with it.

I do not rightly remember, but I feel sure that I giggled like a madman then as I curled into my defensive ball once more and waited for the assault to begin afresh. I knew that I had sealed my own fate, of course. Now he would not stop until my soul had crossed the river.

The punches came again, thick and fast and heavy, but no more kicks, and now he fought from his knees, his heel unable to take his weight.

I felt the blows land and I felt my body react to them the only way it could: I began to distance myself from the pain; to withdraw and disappear into my own dark subconscious as my death approached. I waited for the Ferryman to come for me, no longer coherent enough to consider what would happen when he found me bearing no coin for the journey.

I do not know how long it was or how many blows I had taken, but I knew I was out of endurance and beyond pain. I had already lapsed into unconsciousness twice, brought back by the next sharp agony only to fade again, and I felt sure that this third time would be the last.

And suddenly the blows stopped.

Miraculously, thank Jove and the gods of Rome, the blows ended.

I wondered why, but my mind was past conscious thought and my sight was fading, one eye crusted shut from the punches. I managed to flicker my other eye open just for a moment and saw something that I could not quite understand.

The door from the ambulatory and the main hall seemed to be open once more, admitting a white-gold glow and, haloed in that brilliance, was a tall, bear-shouldered figure, seeming to me like Hercules himself.

I said something, I think, but it was lost in the noise that now erupted. I was blissfully unaware of everything that followed, my body succumbing to the agony and locking my mind away in my slumbering form.

But I felt certain that I had been saved.

3

CONSTANTINE

Raucous chatter and speedy flute medleys echoed around the basilica behind me as I strode from it and into the narrow corridor. The door swung shut behind me, mercifully dulling the discordant echoes. I had longed for a moment like this for the last month. Time alone. Time to address that which lay unresolved in my thoughts. Mother and Father – what was going on between them? I paused in that short hallway for a moment, resting my hands on the dusty marble sill of a window.

Looking back now, I wish I had not been so hard on myself. At fourteen, I was old enough to wear the *toga virilis*, yet the garment that symbolised adulthood unfortunately did not bestow upon me any great gift to see inside my parents' minds. But I was a tenacious soul, even then, and I refused to let it go. Something just wasn't right. I tried to piece it all together: Father had been acting strangely for a long time. In these last months he had been ever more guarded; Mother seemed to be almost grieving for him. My head throbbed as I tried to imagine what had gone on between them. Then a bout of shrieking laughter tumbled from the main hall, scattering my thoughts. I scowled at the doorway, my temper flaring, then swung to the one opposite that led further from the gathering.

I butted the door open with my palms, hoping to find some other forgotten, quiet and empty chamber. Instead, to my astonishment, I beheld a poorly lit, drab room, wholly unremarkable were it not for the pack of baying youths at the far corner. They were huddled around something on the floor – no... some*one*. The largest boy in the group was raining punches and kicks onto this figure. Toy wooden blocks lay scattered nearby.

I froze, my eyes locked on the cowering victim: a dark-haired boy, wiry and lean, some years younger than his attackers. His narrow, tanned face was spattered in blood and his eyes were swollen almost shut, but his bloated gaze met mine. When his lips moved, I did not hear his words, but I understood.

Help me.

Suddenly, one of the young thugs looked up, his eyes widening upon seeing me in the doorway. 'Candidianus, stop!' he yelped in warning to the big one.

At once, the ring of youths broke away from the bloodied lad. The ringleader snarled, dragging his foul glare around to fix upon me, eyes shaded under his heavy brow as he struggled to discern my identity in the gloom. But I recognised him immediately – it was Galerius' son. His nostrils were flaring like a bull's. The gemmed necklace was spattered in the beaten boy's blood... and I noticed a bite-wound on one of his ankles too, the blood trickling from that and staining his boot.

'One man?' Candidianus snarled at the six with him while jabbing a finger at me. 'You crumble in fear at the sight of one man? You will never serve as my bodyguards – never!'

I noticed the six looking around sheepishly. At first, I had assumed they were Candidianus' friends. Now it was clear they were merely acolytes.

Just then, the bloodied boy groaned and tried to prise himself from the floor.

'You stay put!' Candidianus roared, turning painfully back to the boy, lifting his fist and readying to swing it down.

I cared little for either of the two strangers before me, but the scene was sickening: a burly boy readying to strike at the face of a younger lad who was already beaten and near-unconscious.

I lurched across the chamber and caught the bully's wrist before he could strike. His eyes bulged and he bared his teeth, his clenched fist shaking in my grasp. He tried to wrench free of my grip but I twisted his arm up his back and he winced like a whipped dog as I held him, back turned to me, using him like a shield against his cronies. At this, he cried to the nearest of his acolytes – a stocky, snub-nosed boy: 'Get him off me!' This one stepped forward, fists clenched. I turned a gimlet stare upon him that broke his stride, halted him and turned his scowl into a pallid, fearful look. I flashed the same look at the rest, and issued a silent thank you to Batius who had taught me the power of a confident glower. The truth is my gut was churning, but I had those six beaten with no weapon other than my demeanour.

Candidianus struggled in my grasp until it became clear he could not wriggle free. I growled in his ear. 'Now I'm going to let go, and I want you and your group to leave. Do not make a fool of yourself by trying anything.' He nodded, yet I could sense he was keen to become a fool. But what else was I to do? I relaxed my grip on him and he stumbled away, panting.

He did not head for the door, as I had urged him. Neither did he fly at me. Instead, he turned to face me, standing tall, a few feet away. Despite the few years I had on him, his shoulders matched mine and our eyes were level. 'You dare to lay a hand on the son of a nobleman?' he growled.

I snorted at this. 'Something of a contradiction, is it not?' I gestured to the young lad on the floor. 'Going by this one's fine robes I'm certain he is no slave or peasant. Perhaps you should discuss this with his father—'

'It's you! Constantine, the son of Governor Constantius!' Candidianus cut me off, one finger wagging, his eyes sparkling in recognition, grinning like a cat that had just spotted an injured mouse. 'I saw you in the main hall.'

'Aye, son of the Governor of Dalmatia,' I snapped. 'So perhaps *you* should avoid the habit of picking fights with men of noble blood and be gone, as I urged you.'

'You?' Candidianus continued with a burgeoning grin. 'Noble blood?' Then he threw his head back with a lungful of painfully forced laughter, clearly learned from another – doubtless his father. 'He doesn't know,' he roared in delight, meeting the gaze of each of the six with him. One by one, the six laughed too. Sycophantic yet mocking laughter. 'Your father brought you all the way here and didn't think to tell you why?'

I saw a look of gleeful triumph in his eyes. My thoughts jumbled and my skin burning, I felt the urge to blacken this cur's eye. 'You know nothing of me or my father!' I spat, cringing at the angry tremor in my words – in just those few heartbeats this sneering bully and his group had snatched away my air of gravitas. But what he said next was like a blow to my gut.

'Your mother, she does not travel with you, does she?'

My eyes darted over his confident rictus now. 'She remains at home. What of it?'

Candidianus almost squeaked with delight. 'She knows. She knows that while today she can call herself the wife of a governor, by tomorrow, she will be a forgotten concubine. And you—' he stabbed a finger at me, barely containing his delight '—will be little more than her bastard. A stain on your father's past.'

I felt only numbness. What wicked lie was this? I didn't realise it, but I must have risen up then, gestured as if I was coming for them, for they turned and hurried to the door leading back to the basilica hall. Candidianus was the last to leave, casting one final malevolent grin at me as he limped away. It was then that feeling returned to me. My chest was heaving, sweat snaking down my skin. I wanted for all the world to rush after them, grab the thug by the neck and choke the life from him. Then I thought of Mother, alone and so far away. Pity quelled my rage and my shoulders slumped.

'You humiliated him in front of his cronies,' a weak voice spoke from the floor beside me. 'Take no heed of his words, they were all he had left to hurt you with.'

I turned to see the beaten lad. His face was a patchwork of flowering bruises and he was spattered in his own blood, yet his first thought had been to soothe my anger. I instantly liked him for that. I knew that by stepping in to save him, I had chosen wisely. I only wish I could have disregarded Candidianus' parting words as the boy suggested. But they nagged at me, tangling with the troubles that had taken me away from the gathering in the hall. Blinking and shaking my head, I crouched by the boy. He seemed uncertain, shy. 'What's your name?' I asked.

43

'Maxentius,' he croaked weakly, wincing and clutching his ribs.

'Maxentius,' I repeated, then glanced again at his fine robes. My memories of the journey from Dalmatia spun through my head. I had heard that name before. My eyes widened. 'Hold on... the son of Maximian? *Emperor* Maximian?'

'Aye,' Maxentius replied meekly.

I glanced to the door through which Candidianus had left and uttered a gasp of disbelief. 'Then that brute is a bigger fool than I first thought.'

'His father, Galerius, is a war hero, and many will expect Candidianus to match or outdo his achievements. Perhaps such weight of expectation on his shoulders has twisted his mind and turned him into a thug; his father must watch his every move and compare it to his own high standards. Indeed, I know the feeling.'

He managed to grin weakly as he said this and I found it infectious. I chuckled and sat beside the lad. Despite his wounds, he seemed keener to gather and organise the collection of wooden blocks on the floor than anything else.

'What are you building?' I asked.

He looked up at me. I saw a glint in his swollen eyes at the question. 'You'll see.' He grinned wider this time.

At that moment, the dull babble from the main hall seemed to fall away, as if all there were pausing to witness another piece of ceremony. I looked up. I knew Father would be angry if I was not there. I placed a hand on Maxentius' shoulder. 'Those thugs will not be back to bother you, but get your wounds seen to – you might well have a cracked rib or two, and that eye will close up unless you put a cooling salve on it.'

His head bobbed in agreement, although his attentions

were now fully on his blocks. As I reached the door, he said just one last thing.

'Thank you for helping me, Constantine. I won't forget it. One day I will be grown, and if I can fend off Father's plans to have me leading legions, I should find myself a position where I can help the empire grow and prosper. Perhaps then I will be able to return the favour?'

I twisted round, smiled at him then left the room to return through the corridor to the basilica and the ceremony. When I came to the basilica door, I opened it gingerly, slipped through and eased it back into place so as not to make a noise, for the hall was deathly silent. All were formed up again in two vast squares, either side of the central nave. I glanced over the many heads, unable to see what was going on at the apse of the hall where they all looked. In any case, all I cared about was getting back to stand alongside Father before he grew too annoyed. I kept my head down and picked my way along the sides.

Finally, I saw big Batius' shaved scalp, so I pushed into that row. When I reached him, I saw that Father wasn't there, just a space where he should have been. It was then I noticed Batius' face: the big man rarely showed much emotion, but at that moment he looked at me as if he had the most terrible news to impart.

'Batius?' I whispered.

He opened his mouth to reply, then shook his head, the words choking in his throat. Just then, booming words spoken from the apse filled the hall.

'And one of my first acts as Emperor of the West is to form strong bonds with all parts of the empire,' Maximian said. I looked up to see the silver-flecked emperor striding to and fro. But there were another two figures with him.

It made no sense. Father… and some young woman, side by side. Maximian's next words answered all my questions, brought all of my fears and doubts together like two swords clashing. To this day, I have never felt shock like it, despite all that has come to be. 'Thus, I give the hand of my daughter, Theodora, to Marcus Flavius Valerius Constantius, Governor of Dalmatia. Let the marriage bring with it the favour of the gods.'

I tore my eyes from Father and the woman. Maximian's words rang around the hall, then the watching crowd cried out in joy, clapping fervently, cheering. At once, the neat squares of observers dissolved again into revelry, the flutes whistling and the maidens bringing out more wine and food. Shoulders barged past me. Laughter seemed to echo all around me. Then I heard the shrill words of some unseen loudmouth. 'There he is, a mere low-born – no longer part of the family he followed here like a lost dog!' Loudmouth and his audience erupted in hilarity at this and my skin felt like it was aflame.

I felt big Batius rest a hand on my shoulder.

'Why did he bring me here?' I croaked.

'Because he couldn't bring himself to tell you. I'm sorry, lad, I urged him to speak to you about it before today. I didn't want you to find out like this…'

His words faded. I glanced up to the apse once more. Father and Theodora were stepping down from the decorated plinth, offering smiles and accepting the congratulations of the many around them. But I saw through the mask that Father wore. I recognised the glassiness in his sallow eyes. For just a heartbeat, he met my gaze across the crowd. He had given up the woman he loved to take another. Another who brought with her power and a step up into the new imperial order. So Father's name was now indelibly linked to a noble lineage – just as he had sought for so long. Father had made his choice.

Worse, just a sliver of me understood – even accepted – what he had done, and I hated myself for it.

4

MAXENTIUS

'You are the son of the Emperor Maximian, not a common brawler!' Mother chided me as she fussed at my clean tunic, eyeing with distaste the blood-spattered garments in which I had previously been clad. I declined to respond, knowing that any protestations over my innocence would fall upon deaf ears. She simply would not countenance that Galerius' boy had done such a thing, and believed the whole thing to be some sort of dreadful mistake.

After initially viewing my condition with panicked horror, Mother had called for the palace *medicus* and begun cleaning off the worst of the blood. I had limped into the room, bent almost double and clutching fractured ribs, largely feeling my way, with one eye crusted shut and the other blinded by a steady warm crimson trickle.

I had yelped and hissed as the healer worked on me, all the time my mother fretting around us, demanding to know my precise condition. The upshot was delivered in studious, flat tones by the medicus as though I were not even there: my ribs would be fine in a month or so, my eye would at least open a fraction despite its state, and the pupil was responsive. Most of it was apparently *superficial* and of *no real danger*

48

to me. Despite the waves of pain that smashed at me, I was somewhat taken aback when the man told Mother that my condition was only of concern because I was so fragile and that, had I been more robust, the injuries would not have seemed quite so grave.

The medicus finished applying his foul-smelling pastes to my various abrasions and then sprayed me with a perfume of oiled rose petals that I knew would do little to provide the rugged masculinity that other boys at court found so readily but which continued to escape my academic nature. Seemingly my fragility was to be highlighted over my non-existent robustness. Still, better to smell of roses than whatever he had smeared into my wounds – a pungent stench that brought a tear to my eye and a tingle to my nostrils and may have been made from some sort of terminally sick rodent. It smelled a lot like Belgica to me, in fact.

Satisfied, the medicus pronounced me healthy and *on the mend.*

I felt less than healthy. In fact, I felt as though I had been dragged into Hades and back by wild horses – along a cobbled road. However, according to the medicus, either my attacker had sought not to do me any permanent damage, or he had simply not been informed enough to aim his blows for true wounding. Remembering the look in Candidianus' eyes, I suspected the latter.

Thinking back on the thug who had attacked me for no reason brought a whirl of images, finishing with my unlikely saviour. It seemed a work of the Goddess Fortuna herself that the son of the Dalmatian governor had happened across the scene just in time to save me from the worst of the beating. Another dozen heartbeats alone with Candidianus and cracked ribs would have been the least of my worries.

'Constantine,' the thug had called him, 'son of Constantius'. I knew a little of his father – my own had spoken of him, mostly when he wasn't aware that I was listening. It seemed he held the governor in some esteem, which was a touch perturbing, since my father only truly respected ruthless strength. But I had seen more than merely that in the broad-shouldered Olympian who had driven off my attackers. I had seen more than strength, ruthless or not. I had seen compassion, a nobility in this low-born saviour that Candidianus lacked.

My reverie was cut short by Mother as she dampened a linen wipe in the pink-tinged water bowl and dabbed at the slow trickle of blood from my nostril, a dribble that refused to clot.

'Your father is in conference, but he will want to know of this incident.' Mother sounded uneasy – she knew as well as I how Father would likely react. 'Go to his office – the room of the golden snakes – and speak to him, but be circumspect.'

I heard the raised voices before I even reached the door.

The room was sealed from the majority of the court. The hallway leading to it was guarded by two black-cloaked legionaries in tunics of blood red, spears crossed to bar the way: the Herculiani who seemed omnipresent in those days. Recognising me, the men saluted, displaying mild surprise at the state of my face with its swollen eye and trickle of blood from nose to lip. Probably at the mixed aroma of rose petals and swamp-like poultice too. I informed them shakily that my mother had sent me with words for my father, and the pair deliberated for a long moment as to the proper course of action before uncrossing their spears and permitting me access. They had no intention of being the ones to interrupt the new 'Emperor of the West' but neither would they bar his son. I walked on towards the door a couple of dozen paces beyond them and paused there, listening to the slightly muffled voices issuing from within.

'The borders are sparsely defended at best.' A thick, pompous voice that was dark and – for an indefinable reason – sent a shiver up my spine. 'Barely trained border forces patrol the forests of the Alpes Mountains under orders to keep out the barbarians. And who are these forces, but those self-same Germanics conscripted into uncivilised and barbaric cohorts? Since the loss of the mountain wall two decades ago the area between the Rhenus and the Danubius has been a prize fruit waiting to be picked by the first tribe with the balls big enough to try it.'

There was a pause and finally a sibilant, pinched and nasal voice replied quietly: 'Your tone is dangerously insubordinate, Galerius. Remember to whom you speak.' *Diocletian!* I knew his voice, of course, from the many occasions upon which he and Father had spoken. My heart thumped in my throat. It was bad enough having to interrupt Father's meeting and announce my humiliation in front of his court, but in front of the senior emperor as well? My mouth was drier than a Persian's sandal.

'Apologies, *Domine*, but if I am to command the armies of the Upper Rhenus, I have to consider the unprotected mountain terrain between my province and the Tenth Legion's base at Vindobona.'

'You will have three legions in addition to your border cohorts, Galerius. *Generations* of men have held the Upper Rhenus and the mountains with that number – or with less. Maximian pushed the Alemanni and the Burgundiones back across the Rhenus and put down the Bagaudae here over the past year, and without any need for additional troops. You inherit a command that he found in chaos and left in order.'

Father had been away for much of the previous year on some campaign or other, though until now it had never occurred to me how immediate or important that war might have been. For me it had been a distant rumour as I sat at home with Mother and played and read. Now, I could almost feel the tension in the room from beyond the door as the most powerful man in the empire continued: 'I am done with the affair, Galerius, and if you seek an increase in your forces, you will need to petition my colleague, who now commands in the West.'

There was another tense silence and I could almost picture Galerius glowering at the junior of the two emperors. Finally, it was Father who broke the spell.

'The treasury is not a bottomless pit, Galerius. We cannot simply raise new legions to shore up your weaknesses. The money for such decisions has to come from somewhere. And given the fact that little more than a hundred miles from where I now sit – and little more than a decade ago – legion fought legion to drag the rebellious *Gallic Empire* back to the fold, I am unwilling to reassign any of the other western legions. I will not risk losing the imperial grip on the oft-seditious north. Reassign the men you have as best you can.'

A murmur arose in the chamber as the various noblemen and officers within made known their approval of my father's words or grumbled irritably at them. With a deep breath, I took advantage of the general hubbub to quietly open the door and slip inside.

The room of the golden snakes was a large meeting chamber decorated in an archaic style with red and gold plastered gaudily across each wall and a monochrome mosaic floor depicting the twelve counsellor gods. I remember, despite the importance of the occasion, my attention being captured and held by the writhing golden sea serpents surrounding the room in their blood-red water. When my focus finally returned to the scene before me and the door behind me closed with a quiet click, I scanned the two dozen or so occupants.

I had entered at the rear of the chamber in shadowed obscurity. At the far end, upon a dais, rested two thrones, occupied by my father and the great Diocletian, both of whom had removed their glittering face paint, but still fair dripped with jewels and ostentation. Around the room stood men in the currently fashionable Persian-style robes or the more traditional toga that was still favoured for state occasions by some westerners. Clearly many were military men, while others were courtiers of one form or another.

Attention was largely focused upon the two emperors and the three men who stood closest to them, almost on display before the rest of the court. I had no idea who the three were, of course. Though I had been present at many court occasions – as befitted the son of such a high official – I was young and had previously found no reason to pay close attention to the goings-on of the elders around me. Now, hidden at the rear of the room, behind the crowd of courtiers and peering between two swarthy men in Persian dress, I waited for the hubbub to subside, squinting at the three men. One of them must be the father of my new nemesis. I waited for the conversation to begin again so that I could pick him out.

'Respectfully, Domine...' Galerius began again in his unpleasant, strangely glutinous and booming tone, cutting across the general murmur with a gesture to my father, and loading the honorific with as little respect as he could summon, 'those men who held the Upper Rhenus have done so with full legions and in times of relative security. Despite your laudable successes last year, Domine, the Germanic tribes remain active, the peasants are still unhappy with their lot, the region still seethes with discontent after the collapse of the rebel empire, and according to my records these legions and cohorts have seen excess action with insufficient recruitment, their numbers falling well below official strength on the books.'

With the benefit of hindsight, I see that last statement as little more than a complaint to my father for leaving the legions of the Rhenus undermanned. It may have been a legitimate concern, of course, and looking back on it, it almost certainly was, since for all Galerius' faults, lack of military skill was never among them. But still, my dislike of his son had already painted Galerius as a pig and an enemy to me.

Tall, and with a rustic appearance, bull shoulders and a flat, fleshy, un-expressive face, Galerius was imposing in only the most unpleasant way. Perhaps, again, that is my later opinion informing my remembered image of him, but he repulsed me in an indefinable way. His voice was equally spine-chilling, sounding like pitch slopping from a vase. I hated him. For the son, of whom he was a nightmarish magnification, for his voice, for his wide, blocky face and his lank hair and coal-dark eyes, for his Persian robe and slippers, for his apparent disdain for my father. For everything, I chose to hate him in that single moment, and that hate never lessened throughout all the time I knew him.

'If I may?' interjected another of the three – a soft-spoken man of equal height, though slighter and with a more delicate form, a shapely face, and an expression that seemed somehow sad – even haunted. The fact that he wore a plain toga rather than the silky eastern dress that many favoured endeared him to me.

'Constantius?' my father acknowledged. I smiled painfully to myself, happy that my early opinions seemed to have fallen so perfectly in line with my expectations. This was the Governor of Dalmatia – the father of my unexpected saviour. How could I do anything other than like him?

'With all respect to my colleague, Galerius, there is currently a surfeit of able fighting men in Latium. Since the glorious emperor's thinning of the Praetorians, there are close to two thousand veterans pensioned out early, many of whom would probably willingly take a transfer to the Rhenus legions. Old soldiers often fail at peace and yearn for war. Add to these the early-settled veterans in your own province, Galerius, and you could quite feasibly return your army to a good strength without the need to transfer any unit in the West.'

It was well said and, though I had no experience of – or interest in – military matters, I could see that the rest of the gathering saw sense in the words. Even Galerius was forced to agree.

And then the third man spoke. A well-built and lantern-jawed fellow of average height, he wore a plain but expensive cloak over a military-style tunic and trousers, eschewing the glamour of the court. His voice cracked and rasped as though he suffered some illness of the chest, yet he was clearly hale and strong, and his words held a power that his voice itself lacked.

'There is *one* unit that could be spared, Domine?' The man's address had been directed at my father, who leaned forward in his seat with a deep frown.

'Go on, Severus?'

'The Second Parthica, Domine.'

I blinked my good eye in surprise.

I knew little of the army, or the disposition of legions, for I was still a child, playing with toys rather than lives, but two units of the empire's military I knew:

The Praetorian Guard, who the great Diocletian had reduced from an imperial bodyguard to a simple city garrison of diminished strength, and the Second Parthica – the only legion based on the sacred soil of Latium, some dozen miles south of Rome at Castra Albana. The legion tasked with the defence of the capital, should it ever find itself in danger.

Unseen behind the crowd I shook my head, waiting for my father to laugh at such a proposition. However much these new soldier-born nobles lauded their hometowns in the East and would see them raised in glory, Rome was still the capital – still the heart of the empire. The very idea of stripping out its only defence was ludicrous.

'I must decline,' Father replied with a wave of his hand that swept aside Severus' suggestion. For a moment I felt a pride in my father that was rare enough to be remarkable on those few occasions when it arose. 'You cannot take the Second Parthica,' he added boldly.

Good!

'For the Second will be coming with me to Germania Inferior,' he went on. 'The Saxon pirates are still untamed, despite Carausius and the Britannic fleet's best efforts, and the Heruli and the Franks are causing trouble at the Rhenus' mouth. I have settled Germania Superior for you, Galerius, and now I must do the same for the river's lower reaches.'

My pride in my father shattered and crumbled to dust in the face of that decision. Even Father – now the master of the West – could not see enough value in Rome to afford it the same protection that such great men had before him.

I listened on to the argument and counter-argument between Constantius, Galerius and Severus – the former seemed determined to aggravate the latter pair, often by gainsaying them in agreement with Father – and shuffled my feet uncomfortably. I was acutely aware that I was not supposed to be witness to these monumental events. After all, neither Constantine nor Candidianus were present, and both were older and more martial in their manner than I. The very fact that I was here could fetch me a switching from my father, but still I stood silent, wondering how long I could dither before I was discovered and accused of eavesdropping.

My question was answered, heart-stoppingly, a moment later as the two men who limited my view of events decided to cross to another courtier and whisper something to him.

Upon the dais, Diocletian was preparing himself to interject before the argument became rabid. His pinched features folded into an irritated scowl and then changed again in an instant, and he leaned forward, gesturing with a bony finger.

'You, boy!'

I felt a thrill of panic course through me. The richly dressed courtiers randomly moved aside and left me in full view of the dais, and now Diocletian himself was singling me out. I stepped forward into the circle of the powerful and bowed respectfully, almost collapsing as I whimpered with the pain the move brought to my cracked ribs. I rose slower than I had bent, tears of pain in the corner of my open eye, a drip of crimson splatting onto the mosaic visage of Minerva from the end of my still-bloody nose.

'Domine,' I stammered.

'Come here,' ordered the most powerful man in the empire.

As I took a few hesitant steps towards the dais, I saw Father realise that this misshapen and bloodied mess in an expensive tunic was his son, and spotted a dozen emotions flitting across his gaze before puzzlement won out.

'The son of Maximian!' the intrigued Diocletian announced in sibilant surprise. 'It appears, colleague, as though your offspring has been engaged in his own border dispute with the barbarian. Mayhap he has already quelled the Heruli for you?'

The courtiers dutifully laughed at the senior emperor's joke. So much for remaining unnoticed until the end of the meeting.

'What happened to you, boy?' Father demanded, with a quick, apologetic glance at Diocletian to hide his irritation.

I hesitated once again. My throat had dried to a husk and I could feel my bladder pulsating at the thought of having to describe the incident in front of the most powerful men in the empire, including many celebrated military veterans. Including Galerius, who was watching me with almost tangible disdain.

For a moment, I considered hedging around the story – a lie to ease the difficulties that would surely arise from the truth. A simple story of clumsiness that my father would very easily buy into, coming from my split lips. But the very fact that I had apparently deemed the matter important enough to insinuate myself into the council of Rome's rulers uninvited made such a lie unrealistic. Nothing short of the truth would do.

I took a deep breath and then began to recount the fight in the barest terms possible. I will not describe in minutiae the sparse detail into which I went, but know that it was scant enough that both my father, and Diocletian himself, asked of me more detail than I cared to impart over the ensuing uncomfortable moments. For some indefinable reason, I omitted the bite I had given the brute's ankle – perhaps through fear of reprisal, or perhaps through embarrassment at my desperate, low response to his attack. I tried not to name my tormentor, but Candidianus' identity was drawn from me at my father's insistence. I was careful not to look at Galerius as I brazenly indicted his son, and he remained silent, but I could almost feel his wrath radiating across the room at me. Constantine's name was also drawn from me, though with considerably greater ease.

Barely had I finished than my father summarily dismissed me with his usual manner of casual negligence, sending me back to my mother. I was truly grateful to leave that room and scurried off painfully, my departure announced with the fanfare of Galerius' raised voice back in the chamber. Though I could not hear his exact words, I was grateful that distance muffled his angry tone more with every footstep that I took.

I sincerely hoped that I would not be called back to answer yet more questions in the presence of the brute Galerius. Intent instead on returning to my own quiet pursuits, I sought the solitude of the chamber with my wooden city, hoping against hope that Candidianus would not deign to return to the scene of his crime.

Looking back on it I realise that, while I slowly and painstakingly rebuilt my imagined Rome, Candidianus had concerns of his own in the hour that followed.

5

CONSTANTINE

Sometime later that day, I sat alone on a marble bench in the almost-deserted basilica. Occasionally, slaves would scuttle past, or a clutch of noblemen would swagger by, braying and congratulating one another. Outside, the shrieking, hooting and laughing revellers in the forum and streets sounded like the mad cries of gulls. My thoughts swirled like a gale. Everything I had known lay in disarray, spinning crazily. That pig of a boy, Candidianus, had been right: Mother was now little more than an inconvenience to Father's ambitions. And what was I? Constantine, the bastard son of an ambitious man and his concubine? Mother did not deserve this. I did not deserve this. There had to be a way to make this right. There had to be a way to gain control once more. I curled both fists tight, my breathing slowing at last as I grasped on to this notion. *There has to be a way.*

'On your feet, boy,' a voice snapped in my direction, mean and clipped. 'The two emperors summon you.'

The words were like a slap in the face. I blinked, reality returning. I looked this way and that, then spotted the black-cloaked legionary nearby, glowering at me. One of the Herculiani – Emperor Maximian's guardsmen. He was unshaven, with a dagger of a nose. He rested his hands on his spatha pommel and flexed his fingers on the grip of his blood-red shield. 'I said, *on your feet!*' he snapped, then wrenched me from my seat by my collar.

It was like a flint hook striking light to a torch. With a savage surge of anger, I ripped myself free of his grasp then thrust out the heel of one hand. It slammed into his nose. He staggered back, eyes going in every direction for a moment, gasping. Stunned, he raised his fingers to the droplets of blood that trickled from his nostrils. His face turned feral and he strode for me, making to draw his sword.

I braced, maddened, ready to fight this seasoned, armoured and armed legionary with my bare fists. Then a huge shadow stepped between him and me.

'Are you sure you want to do that?' Batius said, facing the legionary.

The bloodied soldier hesitated for a moment.

Batius sniffed nonchalantly. 'You were sent to bring Constantine to the emperors, aye? So I would say that running him through isn't the best idea, hmm?'

Finally, Dagger-nose slid his sword, albeit reluctantly, back in its sheath with a low growl. 'Follow me,' he snapped, swinging away from us with a swish of his cloak.

'Come, lad,' Batius beckoned, following.

Dagger-nose's boots click-clacked through a long, echoing corridor.

'What's all this about?' I asked Batius quietly as we headed into the basilica's depths.

'It seems you were involved in some trouble earlier?' he whispered as we passed through one corridor after another, then veered towards an office at the rear of the basilica.

'No, well, yes, but—' My words were cut off as Dagger-nose

swept open the door leading into the chamber. It was a striking room – the blood-red walls veined with gilt asps. Before me stood a row of nobles, eyeing me like a line of starved crows might behold a single scrap of bread. Dagger-nose gleefully motioned for me to step forward so I did, albeit gingerly, gesturing for Batius to remain at the door. As I approached the nobles, I noticed that most were adorned with fine silks, trousers, slippers and jewellery, only a few dressed in military attire or simple robes. If the mood in that room had not been so grave and had all eyes not been upon me I might have laughed aloud at their frivolous ostentation.

When I was only paces from them, the line parted like doors, revealing a dais at the end of the room. The co-emperors, Maximian and Diocletian, were enthroned there. Maximian wore a deep frown, his eyes masked in shade, while Diocletian sported an irascible scowl, as if this affair had interrupted some far greater matter.

Only two men in that room offered anything other than black looks; two men perched either side of the co-emperors. Father stood by Maximian's side, dressed in his simple toga and offering me a poignant, almost apologetic gaze. And – surprisingly – Galerius, standing alongside Diocletian's throne, regarding me with something of an impassive look. With a chill I noticed Candidianus standing in the shadows behind his father. Then the Herdsman's gaze swept past me for a moment to fix upon the bloody-faced Herculiani who had been sent to fetch me, and I'm sure his lips played with a smile, as if impressed by my handiwork.

When I halted before the dais, everything was perfectly still, eerily so. Both emperors stared at me mutely, the only sound in the room the guttering of an oil lamp in the corner.

Then Emperor Maximian broke the silence, leaning

forward to behold me, the half-light from a narrow window high on the walls illuminating his hooded eyes. 'My son, Maxentius, was brought before me today, bloodied and bruised. And the son of *Tribunus* Galerius was injured too.' Maximian clicked his fingers. At this, Galerius turned to the shadows behind him and bundled Candidianus forward to the edge of the dais. The burly lad was now limping badly from the wound on his ankle and stood with his head bowed, clutching his wrist – bruised where I had wrested him back from the boy Maxentius. I noticed with interest that Galerius cast a look of demonic contempt upon his son before turning back to me with that curious expression of near-affability. Which of the Herdsman's two Janus faces was the real one, I wondered. I can only laugh dryly when I recall such naïveté – for in the years to come the man would answer that question time and again with his deeds. In fact, only moments later, I would see his true colours.

'I am told that you, Constantine, son of Constantius, had a part in this incident?' Maximian spoke shrilly. '*You*, standing before us now with not a bruise or mark on your person. Some might wonder if you were the aggressor, harming the other two?'

I glanced to Father. I don't know why, for he had only hours ago disinherited me and Mother. I should have realised then that I could no longer rely on anyone but myself. In any case, Father failed to meet my gaze.

'I did play a part, Domine,' I answered Maximian. Then I looked askance at Candidianus, who repaid me with equally sour eyes before returning to studying his feet. 'This one was polishing his boots on your boy Maxentius' face. I stopped him.' I heard a chorus of surprised muttering around the hall. A few of the words were a little too loud.

'Saves the emperor's son – after his share of imperial favour, just like his father,' I heard one whisper to another behind me. I felt my temper flare again at this. It took all of my will to resist swinging round to confront the gossiping pair. Instead, I directed my words to those who mattered. 'I helped your son, Domine, *before* I realised who he was.' Then I looked to Galerius. 'And I subjected your son to no more force than was necessary to end the brawl, Tribunus.'

At this, Galerius smirked and his eyes narrowed. One of his many masks, I realised. I was sure then that this one they called the Herdsman saw me as one of two things: a prospect or a threat. Or perhaps both? Galerius stepped forward and cupped a hand under Candidianus' chin, raising his son's head so their eyes met.

'So the boy Maxentius' tale was accurate, then. *You* were the aggressor?'

Candidianus slid his chin from his father's hand, his head slumping again in a tacit confession.

Galerius' nose wrinkled. Ire flared in his eyes as he glowered at his son. This was the real Galerius, I began to suspect. A brute of a man. Truly angered at his son's indiscretions, or simply at the bearing they would have on his own career? I was sure I knew the answer.

Candidianus' pluck from earlier was utterly gone. All he could manage was to stammer: 'Father, I, I...'

'You dis-*gust* me,' Galerius finished for him in a thick accent. 'And you will never be fit to ride in my retinue.' The Herdsman grappled the gemmed silver necklace the boy wore and tore it free. Precious stones spilled from his grasp, bouncing and scattering across the dais and mosaic floor in every direction. 'I lavish you with finery and you reward me with shame. *Shame!*' Galerius swept an arm back then brought his knuckles raking across Candidianus' face, sending the boy spiralling across the dais before collapsing to his knees in a sobbing heap. Despite everything, I felt a twinge of pity for the crumpled boy. No man is born a bully, and it was now clear to see where Candidianus had learned the art.

Candidianus rose and then shambled past me, limping heavily, head bowed to disguise his sobs as he fled the room. Emperor Maximian sighed, massaging his temples, his eyes screwed shut. 'I shall leave it to you, Tribunus, to mete out what further punishment you feel is appropriate.'

'It will be so, Domine,' Galerius said, his top lip twitching like an angered dog's. Then the man caught my gaze and at once that mask of serenity settled on his face again.

'Governor Constantius, you will see to it that your boy is disciplined too?' Maximian continued, looking to Father. I did not flinch at this, for I knew that, even though my part in the incident had been well intentioned, there had to be some form of nominal redress for bruising the son of a nobleman. Then I realised something: *I'm not the son of a nobleman, I'm a bastard! He deserted me and Mother!*

'I was minded to bring my son into my entourage,' Father said, 'to be trained and put into some station in the Western provinces.'

I stared at him, and could not help but recall Mother's strange words: *Remember me, Constantine.* It all clicked into place now: she thought I was never coming back. Father had already shared this plan of his with her – to divorce her and take me with him. I almost shook with disbelief.

'But indeed, he must suffer some form of penalty for his part in the affair,' Father continued. 'Perhaps a few years serving as a messenger on the northern shores of Gaul might serve to straighten him out.'

I stared at him still. Suddenly he seemed like a stranger. All around the hall had fallen silent, and it was a lasting silence.

Galerius' tactical cough broke the tension. 'I think this lad is ill-deserving of such punishment,' he said. 'Perhaps instead he could aid me? My legions are depleted from the wars on the Danubius, and I see potential in him. He could learn much by my side in the Eastern armies, Domine.'

The moisture drained from my mouth and I swear my heart stilled for a moment or more. *What had he just said?*

Galerius twisted to Diocletian and continued: 'And in times of peace, when I am at your court in Nicomedia, he could learn from your finest teachers?' he said this and gestured into the watching crowd towards a slight, weary-looking fellow with black eyebrows, greying hair and a long, grey beard. Despite the bags under his eyes and the bloodshot whites, he had a friendly face – a rare commodity in that room – and I noticed he wore a Chi-Rho amulet on his neck chain. 'Lactantius always welcomes new pupils.'

Diocletian had seemed utterly disinterested in the matter until now. But there was something in Galerius' words, perhaps his tone, or maybe even in some unseen look, that snagged the senior emperor's curiosity, for the man's eyes narrowed to slits and he leaned forward on his throne. 'Aye, perhaps this would be the most satisfactory outcome.'

Maximian beheld Diocletian and Galerius, eyebrows arched as he contemplated this, then turned back to Father. 'Well, Constantius? He's your son – do you agree to this?'

I saw Father's eyes widen momentarily, a sadness in there, looking at me. 'Let Constantine decide. It is his future.'

All eyes fell upon me once more. The Herdsman, the two

emperors, the noblemen. The tutor, Lactantius. Father, gaunt, sorrowful, yet with true power in his grasp at last. At that moment I felt my earlier panic return. My chest tightened, the blood-red walls drew closer and the gilt serpents seemed to writhe, as if coming for my throat. Standing there in that snake pit, I wondered just how much rested on my next words. All I knew then was that two very different roads lay before me.

I could take my punishment and place by Father's side. And leave Mother, alone and disinherited in Salona. *Remember me, Constantine...*

Or, I could accept the Herdsman's offer and step right up and into his armies. There, I would be close to Mother, and I would be paid a good purse, enough to provide for her.

The truth is that even if my father had offered me all the silver in the empire at that moment, I would have thrown it back in his face. But Galerius, this brute of a man... why would any sane person want to serve him?

I raked over my thoughts, searching for an answer, trying to blot out the many expectant eyes upon me. It was an unexpected memory that came to the fore: the lone legionary from the night of the storm, standing on the walls, grasping his spear, empowered by his god and facing the storm. I glanced to the twin emperors, still bearing flecks of paint from their imitation of Jove and Hercules. Gods and power remained entwined after all these years, it seemed. Then I realised I had my answer.

Alongside Galerius I might achieve fame in the wars. Fame and power. Power was the only thing that could make things truly right again. With it, nobody could question my station in life. With it, perhaps I could not only provide for Mother, but also restore her and me to some form of nobility. With it, I would no longer be at the mercy of other men. With it, I could forge my own destiny.

I genuflected towards Galerius then returned his half-smile with one of my own.

Power it was then.

6

MAXENTIUS

I reached across the wooden city that had sprawled to seven imagined hills within the quiet room, a forum of glorious structures the centrepiece to a city of a million fictional souls, to place the last block, sucking air through my teeth at the pain in my ribs as I did so. My hand knocked an insula to the city's south in the process and I had to quickly nudge it back into position.

Slowly, I stood and examined my city. It was complete, though it still lacked something... grandiose. Something worthy of the glittering centre of the world. I moved about it, slowly and painfully, trying to ignore the fact that I really should have been dismantling it as I went, instead adjusting the position of various structures, realigning streets and tweaking stacks of bricks. Though this room was rarely visited, occasional visitors had crossed through it and the breeze of their passage shifted my city fractionally each time.

I nudged the aqueduct back into line and perused the streets, my mind furnishing them with a million imaginary figures going about their daily business. I have always been blessed – or possibly cursed – with the vivid imagination that often goes hand in hand with an impractical nature, and I saw myself walking through that wooden world.

Fishmongers called out their wares from the *tabernae* at the street sides, beggars cried out for alms, equites and patricians with their hired escorts strode down the wide pavements, city folk shoved roughly aside by the paid mercenaries. Off-duty soldiers drank and ate in *thermopolia*, their unshaven features dark from the sun's rays over a score of years serving in distant lands. Slaves scurried this way and that, desperate to complete their chores and avoid a beating. A microcosm of the world in carved pine.

My good eye strayed to the forum again and for a fleeting moment, I imagined Father there, addressing the people of the great city as I stood in awe nearby. I tried to open my other eye for a better view, though it seemed unwilling to comply with my will, and eventually I gave up, surrendering to the dull ache I had intensified with my attempt.

'So this is Rome?'

I turned in surprise. I'd not heard anyone approach, and the voice was close behind.

'Constantine?'

The young governor's son – soon to be my nephew I realised with a start – stood with his fists balled on his hips and a strange, haunted, sad smile. Something gnawed at him, I thought: something deep-rooted and soul-tarnishing. My memory furnished me with an image of the young man's face during the scuffle in this very room, when Candidianus had revealed the truth of Constantine's mother and her anticipated fate. My heart went out to the boy who had saved me from such a beating. He was losing the mother he loved to the maelstrom of power in much the same way I would be losing Theodora, though my sister's fate could be assumed to be considerably brighter than that of Constantine's poor mother.

'Your city is magnificent.' The governor's son strode around the periphery of my ensemble, perusing it and weighing it up. 'Such attention to detail. Is it an accurate depiction of Rome?'

I smiled weakly. 'I'm not sure. I've never actually been there, though I've been told much about it. It is how Rome looks in the eye of my mind.'

'It is how Rome *should* look.' Constantine smiled. 'Perhaps one day we will both visit the centre of the empire and compare it with your design?'

A strange silence fell – that silence old men who consult the auspices suggest is indicative of gods paying close attention. Perhaps they were. Gods like a joke, after all, and that last might just be the greatest and most wicked joke of all time.

Uncomfortable and unable to define exactly why, I found myself speaking somewhat out of turn. 'Things will be good for you, Constantine, I am sure. I know being separated from your mother will be difficult... and from your father,' I added, the discomfort only growing as I fumbled to sound supportive, remembering too late that the decision he had made might still not sit well with him. 'Serving with Galerius will give you the chance to become a hero, and then perhaps he will take you to Rome.'

I spun to gesture at my wooden facsimile of that city and, hissing with the pain turning brought to my side, I moved to lean against the wall, blinking my good eye. Constantine gave me that sad smile again, but this time I saw something new in it. A resolve that had not been present before.

'Thank you. My path, it seems, shifts like the surface of the sea. My galley set out north for friendly ports and has been blown off-course into deep and troubling waters. But I will learn to pilot this ship and command the seas, and I heartily advise that you do the same, young Maxentius. Your father is a power in the empire, and such men attract trouble like a corpse attracts flies.'

I shuddered at the image. 'Still, our families are united now, through my sister. Perhaps the future holds great things for us?'

Constantine made no reply, turning his attention once more to the wooden city spread across the marble floor.

'I see you have been very careful with your planning. The forum is magnificent, and the radiating districts are well organised. A good series of potential firebreaks, interspersed with meadow and baths. All good, but your city is missing something.'

I chewed a lip as I scoured the city with my gaze. I remember being puzzled as to what that certain missing something was.

'I was thinking the same,' I replied, licking the fresh blood from my reopened lip. 'It needs something majestic; something glorious that even gods would envy. A showpiece worthy of the world's centre.'

'No.' Constantine rolled his shoulders and crouched by the southern edge of my city. Without warning, he reached out and smashed his flattened palm against a series of insulae, scattering the blocks into one another, knocking a whole district aside. I leapt forward, aghast at this sudden destruction from a boy who I'd already come to trust. Had my instincts been so far adrift? Only as I failed to reach him and fell to my knees, battered by fresh waves of agony in my ribs did I realise how limited I still was, two days on.

'Why?' I moaned in pain, slowly pulling myself back up.

'Sometimes the best lessons are learned the hard way,'

Constantine murmured. 'Forget your palaces and grand edifices. What you are missing is defences.'

I blinked.

'If you hold the greatest city in the world – a glittering jewel coveted by all others – the first thing to set your mind to is its protection,' Constantine declared, bending to collect up some of the blocks he had knocked aside, his expression slightly apologetic. 'Your city lacks walls. High ones. Strong ones. Walls that might have stopped my hand. Commission your carpenter to make you new blocks, with turrets and buttresses, gates and watchtowers.'

I sighed, watching my city in dismay. It was time to pack the blocks away anyway, I told myself, though my friend's destruction still rankled, for all he now crouched, placing blocks back into place. 'Rome already has walls.'

'Yours didn't.' The young man straightened and handed me back the top of a temple. 'Anyway, I came to say farewell. I came here with Father, but I am to leave with Galerius' court, and he is twitching to be off. Candidianus will travel with us, so you'll be safe from further attacks, though I gather your father is also preparing to leave. It seems the world is moving on rapidly following his accession.'

I rose painfully to my feet, still eyeing the fallen blocks with the growing urge to rebuild. I had for some reason not registered that awful name among Constantine's words and simply smiled in discomfort. 'Perhaps, since we are to be kin, we will meet again in more personable circumstances? I think I should like that.'

Constantine ruffled my hair. 'It would be good, but unlikely, I fear. Father will travel towards the cold northern sea, to serve with your father in senior command, but Galerius takes Candidianus and I south and east where he seeks to fortify the border against the Marcomanni. The Herdsman's company is to be endured rather than enjoyed, or so I have heard, but while I love my father... I simply cannot remain at his side, for it would suggest I agree with his choices.' He fell silent for a while, and then looked up, a spark of realisation in his eyes. 'I mean no offence to your sister, of course.'

And there it was. This time, I caught the name. I stared. 'Galerius, I can understand, for he is an emperor, but to travel with *Candidianus*...' I left my disgust hanging.

'I know that we both feel the same about that unpleasant creature... but what Father took from me today, the Herdsman offers: a chance to make a name for myself, a chance to walk my path in my *own* boots, even if it is beside his son.' He gestured at the tumbled blocks as though I should learn a lesson from Galerius. 'Remember what I said about defence.'

'I will.' Strangely, despite the fact that we'd shared only the briefest of moments, Constantine's departure felt like something of a wrench deep inside. I would be moving off to play whatever role Father saw fit in his new life as Western Augustus until the day I was of an age to take my place in the succession. Constantine was to accompany Galerius. I wondered, as I watched his troubled eyes, whether he would be a good influence on that unpleasant officer, or whether – gods forbid – the opposite.

Constantine smiled sadly one last time and strode from the room with no farewell spoken. I mouthed my own at his back, though my throat was dry and only a scratchy sound issued.

I turned the ruin of my face to the ruin of my southern district.

In my mind's eye an invading army rampaged through the wooden streets, gutting citizens and leaving their carcasses mouldering in the gutter, the insulae ringing to the panicked cries of the victims of rape and looting.

Father could wait a little longer. He would have plenty of other folk to shout at.

With a grim, determined expression and Constantine's words rattling around my skull, I set about demolishing the scattered insulae and using their blocks to wall in my city.

7

CONSTANTINE

SIRMIUM, JULY 294 AD

Eight years later...

It was a dog-hot day and the streets of Sirmium sweltered like the air above a cauldron. The meaty behind of Galerius' stallion swayed before us as we marched down the city's main way, the hooves kicking up dust from the flagstones into our faces.

A sudden splattering sound erupted, and a horrific stench hit us.

'Mars' arse!' Batius gagged. 'That stallion needs pulling through with a spruce tree. That smells worse than the tent that night after we ate that "spiced" boar.'

Breath held, trying not to chuckle at the memory, I let my eyes drift up to the rider, murmuring sideways to Batius. 'Are you so sure it was the horse?'

Batius rumbled with dark laughter and so too did a few of our fellow Fifth Macedonica legionaries marching immediately abreast and behind us. Galerius, unsurprisingly, was too caught up in his own fame to notice. He sat proud as a peacock, waving and saluting to the cheering, adoring crowds. What a reputation he was building for himself.

In contrast, my first four summers in his service had been surprisingly quiet, spent in the city of Nicomedia, capital of the green, sun-baked Province of Bithynia. Galerius wanted me to be educated, you see, so that I would be fit to serve with him. He assumed, wrongly, that I had not been given any sort of education given my 'humble' bloodline. I was happy to capitalise on his ignorance. Thus, at Nicomedia I had studied under the tutor, Lactantius. They were pleasant years when the old goat taught me the histories of Rome, of the Greeks, of the Trojans. Poetry, architecture, rhetoric, philosophy of the mind and of nature, music and languages of the East and West.

The old teacher had swollen my mind with so much information and wisdom. He had also helped me to disobey Galerius, and I loved him for that alone. You see, Galerius had stipulated that I was not to leave Nicomedia for any reason. Yet every few months when the Herdsman was away on campaign or on official duties, old Lactantius gladly arranged boats and horses to take me to Salona to visit Mother. Batius, with me as ever, always came along too. We would sit on her villa balcony, drinking the estate wine with the workers, sharing fond old memories.

Nobody mentioned my father in front of Mother. Quite right, for he had never spoken to her since that day when he left to wed another. Equally, his path and mine had not crossed but for once, when he visited Nicomedia. I had passed him and his bodyguards in the street, not even recognising him at first. There was just a moment when our eyes had met and both of us realised who the other was. I stared back at him as blankly as he did at me. Then I found the first lane, shambled to its dead end and wept until I was hoarse. That was the one dark stain on those wondrous few years of happiness, growth and love.

In the fifth year, Galerius decided that I was old enough and had enough tuition behind me, and so he called me to the legionary fortress of the Fifth Macedonica. It felt like a cold shower of rain, a reminder that those few years of learning and peace were not why the Herdsman had brought me to the East. Batius joined the legion proper, whereas I was installed as a glorified stable hand at first, marching alongside the Herdsman when he led the Macedonica and two other legions across the River Danubius and into the Gothic forests.

During the days, we had marched through the woods, hearing bird calls and strange whistles that were surely from the lips of watching Goths. 'They're tracking us,' Batius had whispered. 'Stay close to the soldiers, lad. If arrows start flying, get behind the shields.'

In the shadowy, cold nights, I had lain awake, sure that every crunch of twigs or shuddering fern outside the marching camp was a tribal warrior. You see, although big Batius had taught me how to handle myself in a fight, and Lactantius had taught me how to use my mind... The old goat had also told me of the great Teutoburg massacre, when a train of legions had been betrayed, set upon and obliterated in that wild German forest.

But character, as they say, is forged in the fires of adversity. So when the Goths ambushed us in one wooded vale, I was stricken with fear, aye, but it did not last; I found myself reacting in a way that belied my dread. I threw down the reins of the horse I was leading, took up a sword and squeezed into the soldier line alongside Batius. The big man guided me through it all. But the battle line had broken down into single combat. A giant of a Goth came for me, strong as a bull, his longsword relentless. Sparks flew as he hacked at my sword and I parried as best I could. His topknot juddered and his pale animal face grew red with fury while my sword arm turned numb and shaky, my mouth dry and my guts in knots.

I knew to defend and wait for him to tire, just as Batius had trained me to. And the Goth did tire. I felt the first spray of another man's blood on my face that day, suffered the horrid streaks of guilt and confusion afterwards. I've never forgotten that first kill. Yet most others since are but a numb, crimson blur.

The next day, word reached me in my filthy tent that Galerius was pleased with my efforts. I was now to serve as an *optio* to Batius – a true soldier. Many more battles followed before the Goths were beaten back from the imperial borders. The struggle had been long and hard, and I found that the longer I was out there, the more I came to understand them, to understand the horrid, insatiable, violent game of war. Yet all the time, I knew that we were there for one reason alone: to spill enough Gothic blood and sacrifice enough of our own lives in order to propel Galerius up the ladders of power. And rise he did.

I gazed at him again, catching glimpses of the smug expression on his blocky face as he led us through Sirmium. Now he was almost at the very top. Diocletian's system of co-emperors had evolved in the past years. Now there were no longer two emperors, but four. A Tetrarchy, they called it. A senior emperor in the East and in the West, each known as Augustus, and each aided by a Caesar – junior emperors who were guaranteed to succeed their Augusti. This tetrarchic system had been designed to put an end to the wars of succession, but it also allowed ambitious men plenty of room to manoeuvre. True to form, my father secured the post of Western Caesar, answering only to Maximian. At the same time, Galerius had manoeuvred his way right into Diocletian's pocket like an eel. Now he was Diocletian's Caesar, heir apparent to the Eastern Empire. More, he had even wed his superior's daughter to strengthen his position to the extreme.

And it was another wedding that brought these huge crowds to Sirmium. Galerius had been buoyant with pride that this city – perched near the border between the Western and Eastern Empires – had been chosen as the venue. For it was officially the capital of his quarter of the tetrarchic realm. It made sense for other reasons too, mainly that it was his daughter, Valeria, who was to be wed. Thus, guests had travelled from far and wide, some from distant Hispania and Africa, even. The Herdsman could have come in a carriage with a small bodyguard, but of course he insisted on parading like this with a full century in tow. Some said it was because he had not been awarded a *triumphus* following his victory over the Goths... although they only ever said it very quietly.

We were nearing Sirmium's forum, I realised. Lyre players skipped and danced alongside us, slaves up on street-side balconies tossed down petals from baskets and trumpets keened across the red-tiled rooftops. The sea of singing, drunken faces filled the forum and every single avenue and alley leading to it.

'Halt!' the legion tribunus blared as we came to the rostrum. Here, Galerius dismounted, grinning like a shark, basking in the adulation.

'Anyone would think it was him getting bloody married,' Batius murmured as we fell into a drill formation of tight blocks.

'If it was, he'd be marrying himself,' another whispered

behind us. 'I can just imagine him, tarted up in a tall wig and wearing a pretty stola, the daintiest of brides.' A burst of sniggering escaped from the legionaries close by.

We watched as two corridors opened up through the crowds – helped as ever by the steel of the urban guards – one coming from the west end of the city, the other from the east. The groom approached from one side, sparkling in old-fashioned white armour, flanked by a troop of Praetorians – that old ceremonial unit from Rome. From the other direction, two slaves wearing rich silks walked, one carrying a bowl of water and the other a crackling torch – fire and water from the bride's hearth in her Sirmium residence. Four more slaves carried Valeria in a litter. Her face was veiled in red gossamer, her robes saffron and shining in the sunlight, clinging to her curves and lending her a swan-like beauty. I gazed at her, probably for a little too long.

'It could have been you,' Batius said. 'Regrets?'

'Ha, none!' I replied a little too quickly, almost as quickly as I had risen from the ranks of optio, to junior centurion, and then to centurion of the first century, first cohort – one of the most prestigious ranks in the legion. Galerius had paved my rise as much as I had earned it, to be truthful. He clearly thought that I could become very useful. So much so that, earlier in the year, he had dangled before me the possibility of taking Valeria's hand. This would have set me up to become Galerius' direct subordinate, a huge advance in power. *Power,* I mused once more, flexing the fingers of one hand. All I had to do was reach out and grasp his offer. But the proposition was made in the way a master might throw a scrap of meat before his dog. I realised that as long as I climbed the imperial ladder hanging on to the hem of the Herdsman's cloak, the power would never be truly mine. At any time he might disown or disinherit me as Father had done. That was not true power, nor control over my own destiny. And so I had declined.

'You *decline*?' he had seethed through clenched teeth. Galerius had never been friendly in any way with me. At best, I think he saw me as a prospect and a threat – a cast die yet to settle and yield a result. But ever since I spurned that offer, it seemed the die had come to a rest and he had been less than impressed with the result. It poisoned our already fragile relationship. All talk of further advancement was shelved for now. 'You'll have to work like a dog to earn the plumed helm of a tribunus,' he had drawled, swishing away from me. 'And you will look back on this moment as the biggest mistake of your life,' he cast over his shoulder like an eastern horse archer.

Shaking my head and bringing my thoughts to the present, I looked sideways at Batius. Back in Treverorum on that fateful childhood visit, after I had agreed to go with Galerius, the big man had asked to be released from my father's retinue so that he might accompany me. 'What about you? Do you never wonder what life might have been like had you stayed in my father's service?'

The big man issued a nonchalant chuckle. 'Way back when you were a boy, your father tasked me with making you useful and protecting you.' He shrugged, unable to meet my eye. 'So that's what I'm doing.'

'I never did thank you,' I said.

'Eh? What for?'

'For everything. You gave up everything for me.'

'What are you mumbling about?' he said, shuffling and scratching, pretending he didn't know. He never was the best with his emotions. 'Anyway, eyes front.'

We watched as Galerius stepped up onto the marriage

plinth, where a gaggle of priests and a hooded *haruspex* waited with two bleating lambs and a sickle. These were for the bride and groom to sacrifice before the gods, but the eager Herdsman looked almost as though he wanted to do the job himself.

The groom's party neared the plinth, and I saw him then. The boy with the wooden blocks. The man who had said yes where I had said no. Maxentius. Eight years had changed him so much. He was only sixteen summers old, but none would mistake him for a boy now. He walked with perfect statesmanlike poise and measured strides, head held high – not like the peacock, Galerius, but with an air of confidence and an earnest half-smile. His eyes and mine met for the first time since the halls of Treverorum. I wondered if he would remember me. I had never forgotten him or his sincere yet boyish way back then, when I was so lost in those moments after my father had torn our family apart.

His lips moved. *Constantine?*

His eyes seemed to brighten as he said this, and the half-smile became a full one. I felt a wonderful sense of gratitude at that. Apart from my comrades in the Fifth Macedonica and the villa workers at Mother's villa, the world was a place of hard-faced strangers or enemies who wanted to slit you from groin to neck. I had grown used to behaving like them.

'He's laughing at you,' a voice hissed from beside me.

I did not need to turn to see who had spoken. 'You were never good at reading people, Candidianus,' I sighed, feigning disinterest. He had shuffled his way along the line of our century just to goad me like this.

'You were never good at making decisions... *bastard*,' Galerius' son sneered.

I had no right to insult him back, for he was *primus pilus*, second in command only to our legion's tribunus. In the years since that first unfortunate meeting with him in the side-room of Treverorum's basilica, he had become a twisted ball of angst and anger. His father's bullying and scapegoating of him had been commonplace throughout the Gothic campaign. In truth, I pitied him. Empathised, even: for his father and mine were shit-sacks, and so too was Maxentius' sire. There were times when I even considered approaching Candidianus to offer him advice or the chance to talk, but then every so often he would do something that tore away any empathy: like the time in the northern woods when he stole extra rations and blamed a member of his *contubernium*, then watched that tent mate lose the skin from his back to a barbed flog. It was only later that Batius and I had discovered the truth about the whole affair, finding the missing, legion-stamped grain sack in Candidianus' tent.

I sensed his malevolent, sideways glances at me. Despite losing Galerius' favour, some said I was destined to rise above his boy. Candidianus, my legionary comrades said, was more a *primus cunnus* then a primus pilus.

Bleating startled me from my thoughts. I glanced up at the wedding plinth to see the second lamb, stained red and jerking, being laid on its side by my friend. The priests began their incantations. The ceremony was nearly complete. As Maxentius descended from the stage first, leading the way to the wedding quarters, I wished him all the luck in the world, and hoped the gods saw fit to afford us a chance to speak before Galerius marched us off on his next campaign.

'Escort, ready!' our tribunus bellowed.

Batius elbowed me. 'That's our cue.'

I jolted, realising I had been brought here to do more than merely gaze around and reminisce. Valeria was descending from the plinth now, the slaves with the fire and water leading her across the forum. Me, Batius, Candidianus and the first century fell into line, forming screening files to either side of the new bride.

Bells clanged and cups clacked as the citizens – pickled and stuffed with free wine and bread – crowded and celebrated along the wayside. Soon, though, we came to the quieter ward of Sirmium – a palatial quarter on a low rise overlooking the green River Savus. Here the applause and cheering grew quieter and more refined, coming from the thinner crowds of rich men and nobles, watching on and raising cups from their marble balconies. The shady streets also provided welcome relief from the sun, petals drifting lazily along in the air with us.

'Perhaps I should speak first, then,' she said.

I blinked, sure I was hearing voices. So engrossed with the drifting petals and the opulent villas was I that I had almost forgotten about the veiled bride bobbing in her litter just beside me. She was smiling, at least.

'Considering what went on between you and my father in the spring,' she added.

'Forgive me, *Domina*. I... I did not think it was my place to speak on this of all days.'

She snorted with disdain in a rather unladylike fashion. 'And so plays out the life of Valeria, daughter of Galerius.'

Batius, marching adjacent to me on the other screening file, pretended that he couldn't hear, all the while his ears were twitching. The big man was a salacious gossip.

'You will live well as Maxentius' husband, My Lady.'

'I live in a cage of guards, slaves, servants. I don't see it being any different now,' she said bitterly.

I could not think what to say. My mouth turned dry, similar

to that way it often did in the moments before battle. 'I... I must tell you that I did not turn down your hand for any reason other than personal ones. You are a beautiful woman, learned and wise, from what I hear.'

She seemed to ignore my comment, gazing off over my head. 'I have been told since I was a girl that I was born to be married off. When my father said I was to be your bride, I told him instead to take me to the nearest cattle market and let men bid for me there.'

I smiled, barely suppressing a laugh. She was colder than a northern winter, but I liked her. I liked anyone who stood up to Galerius. 'Maxentius is a good young man. I dare say you will find greater freedoms in his house than you have known so far.'

She cocked a doubtful eyebrow, her mouth a thin, unsmiling line.

I glanced ahead, seeing Candidianus marching at the front along with our tribunus. Every so often, he would glance back at me. 'You do realise that your brother and your new husband hate one another?'

'I heard some story about a boyhood fight in Treverorum,' she said.

'I was there too. I saved him.'

'How brave,' she said with a haughty look.

When I looked ahead again, I noticed that Candidianus had peeled away from the column head. To where, I did not know. Soon, we came to a marvellous palace gleaming with silver architraves, blue-flecked marble columns and a lush garden sparkling with fountains and summer blooms.

The litter was set down in these gardens and Valeria alighted. Maxentius waited in the atrium to their bridal manor, his face bright with enthusiasm. The two slaves entered first, one touching the torch to a hearth inside, the other decanting the bowl of water into an empty urn on an otherwise stacked feasting table. It was an age-old practice: fire and water taken from the bride's residence to the groom's. A further symbol of joining. The last thing was the bridal dowry. A slave rummaged in the chest at the back of the litter, but seemed to be taking an age.

'Be quick,' Maxentius said, 'before the gods grow old!'

Everyone nearby laughed. Our tribunus was given some signal to have us fall out. When we did, a manor slave brought cups of wine to us legionaries. Batius gulped his down like a desert hound and demanded another. I took a draught of mine and sighed, enjoying the fiery goodness of it, the near-instant softness it brought to my blood.

'We should enjoy this,' Batius mused, gazing around the gardens fondly. 'It'll soon be a distant memory, eh?'

'Persia,' I rumbled, the moment of carefree cheer fading. The Goths were beaten, for now at least. But out in the blazing east, something was going on. Narses had been crowned *Shahanshah*, the King of Kings, master of the mighty Persian Empire. He had sent the usual gifts of accession to Diocletian to mark the ongoing peace with the Roman Empire. But the four tetrarchs had been hearing things from their spies in the Persian realm. Narses was not minded to stay peaceful for long. Rumours were that, should trouble arise, Galerius and his legions might be posted to those desert borders.

Batius pointed at our Macedonica tribunus. 'If we go there, you won't be marching for him. You'll be leading a legion of your own.'

I laughed. 'My career has stalled. The Herdsman detests me.'

Batius grinned. 'Hate you or not, you're one of his best

men. He *needs* you.' He patted my shoulder roughly. 'Just like you need me, eh?' With a rough laugh at his own joke, he wheeled away and called out to a slave for a third cup of wine, barking with more laughter – incredulous this time – when the slave offered to water it for him.

I drifted past the flower beds, now pleasantly merry. Batius was right. I should enjoy this day, for who knew when we would next be in some infernal struggle, consigned to tent life for months on end. I was just about to intercept the slave and ask for more wine myself, when another voice cut across the gardens.

'I can't find it,' the litter attendant moaned, his voice heavy with anguish. 'Domine, Domina,' he pleaded, looking into the atrium where Maxentius and Valeria still waited, 'the dowry... I, I put it here, I know I did.'

Many faces around the gardens paled. The bridal wedding dowry was often an item of great value. For the daughter of a tetrarch, it was surely a gift *beyond* value.

'You idiot!' Candidianus snarled, shoving the slave aside. He rummaged in the chest himself only to look up, sweating, lost for words. 'Sister, the slave is right. It is gone.'

The slave started shaking madly. 'Forgive me... forgive me!'

'Search him,' Candidianus barked. Two legionaries pinned the slave to the ground and others ripped the clothes from him. In a moment he was naked and cowering, but clearly not in possession of any treasure. The other slaves were searched like this. Nothing. Candidianus' eyes swept around the garden. He whispered to our tribunus, who looked ashen-faced as he nodded in agreement. Candidianus stepped up on the edge of a fountain. 'Legionaries, fall in,' he barked.

Batius, on his sixth cup of wine, looked at him with

red-veined eyes and a line of drool hanging from his bottom lip. 'You fall in. You're the one standing on the edge of a fountain,' he slurred, before roaring at his latest joke.

I hooked an arm around his and led him back to the space around the litter, the rest of the first century doing likewise despite varying degrees of intoxication.

'Turn out your kit bags,' Candidianus demanded.

'Who... who you do are you think?' Batius slurred in a jumbled babble.

'Just do as he says,' I urged the big man. As I took my own kit bag and began to untie it, I had the most terrible creeping feeling of prescience. My things – the simple goods of a soldier – tumbled out onto the grass: hardtack, string, a flint hook, a copper measuring cup. Then something else, the sight of which sent a lance of ice through me.

No, I mouthed, seeing the gleaming edge of the thing. It tumbled out on top of the other things, incongruous in such basic company. A solid golden sceptre, encrusted with carnelian and ruby stones. I felt my guts twist and pulse downwards. *How, how could it be?*

'You thieving dog. You dirty Pannonian *bastard!*' Candidianus roared, striding towards me. 'You'll have the skin taken from your back for this,' he screamed, pointing down at me, foam spraying from his twisted lips. 'My father will have you thrown into the copper mines when he hears about this. Arrest him.'

He stepped back. Two fellow legionaries, somewhat dumbfounded, stumbled forwards to seize me by the arms, lifting me to my feet.

Batius roared in complaint, but I couldn't hear or even think at that moment. I saw Candidianus lift the sceptre and sink to one knee before the bride and groom, his lips moving in some sincere apology. I heard all sorts of gasps and whispers around me. I thought of the mines – a common punishment for theft. Or death, just as likely. For Candidianus was right, despite it all. I was nothing but a disinherited bastard who owed everything to his father, Galerius. The Herdsman had given me all I had so far... and now he would see it all taken away.

'Release him,' a voice said quietly.

The storm of thoughts quietened to a gentle wind, then a whisper, and then it was gone. Maxentius stepped before me, looking me over. 'I said release him.'

The two legionaries did so, quite gratefully – for they were friends of mine in any case.

'Domine,' Candidianus protested, 'he must be punished.'

Maxentius slid his head around to affix Candidianus with a gimlet stare. 'Shut your lying mouth, dog.'

Gasps all round again. Nobody noticed a wagon drawing up into the gardens.

'I watched the procession from the high balcony, you idiot. I saw you take the sceptre and plant it in Constantine's bag. When first we met in boyhood and you planted your boots in my face, I thought you were a fool. Today, you proved it.'

Candidianus sneered, growing tall. 'I am the son of a tetrarch, just like you. Your word is not enough to prove what you claim.'

'No, but mine is,' Galerius hissed from the wagon window. 'I was riding behind the procession. I saw what you did.' He alighted from the wagon as he spoke, striding over to his son, towering over him, the veins in his neck pulsing.

I would like to say I felt pity once more for Candidianus for what was about to happen to him, but I did not. He had drained that well dry. We watched as Galerius led his son to the wagon. The door closed gently with a click, and the vehicle pulled away.

'By all the gods, there is nothing more terrifying than the sight of the Herdsman leading his prey away quietly,' Maxentius said.

I turned to him. 'Thank you. If you had not spoken up for me...' I stopped, seeing his growing smile.

'If you had not come to that tired little room in the Treverorum basilica all those years ago...'

Now I smiled to match his.

'Come, walk with me.' He gestured to a path that led around the gardens. So confident and assured, I thought once again, yet gentle and softly spoken at the same time.

'Your new wife will not be cross if you leave her alone?'

Maxentius chortled, nodding over to the corner of the gardens where she was roaring with appreciation as two acrobats performed a fire dance for her. 'She will be well for now.'

'She can be somewhat... icy,' I remarked, 'but there is a warmth in there. I told her she had married a good man.'

Maxentius took two fresh cups of wine from the tray of a passing slave, gave me one and clacked his to mine. We drank to that.

'Life has been something of a journey for me since that day back in Augusta Treverorum,' I said. 'And from what I have heard, life has swept you up also, and carried you far from your days of building cities from wooden blocks.'

He laughed once, a short barking sound. 'I still have those blocks, you know. I find it soothing to look upon them from time to time. Perhaps one day if I have a child they might play with them as I once did.'

'High walls though, eh?' I smiled.

'High walls.' Maxentius laughed again.

'What comes next for you, Constantine? I hear rumours of unrest on the desert borders.'

'Aye. They say the legions will be shipped to Antioch before long. Probably for several years. But before I set foot on any ship, I will do what I promised I would when I first pledged myself to Galerius. I finally have enough silver to pay off Mother's debts. I will buy a good home in Antioch and arrange for her to move there. Whatever this Persian War throws at Rome... it will not come between me and my mother. My father cast our family aside that day at Treverorum. Now, I will bring what is left of it back together.' We drank again. 'What about you, my friend?'

'Ah,' he sighed jauntily. 'Back to my father's court, I expect, once he is done with the trouble on the Rhenus. Debate, tangled finances and building projects.' He paused and winked. 'More than just wooden blocks, this time.' Then he looked back at his new wife. 'In between, I hope to get a chance to know Valeria. It would make me whole, Constantine, if we were to have a child. I know... I just *know* I could be a better father than my own.'

I gulped at this, sadly and in agreement. 'You and I both, my friend. You and I both.'

The wedding celebrations carried on long into the night, and in the following days my legion was given leave. Maxentius and I met to talk about all we had learned about this vast and perplexing world into which we had been thrust. He was incredibly bright of mind, and I found it enriching to discuss with him all I had learned under Lactantius. We played dice, enjoyed food together. Batius and I even joined him and Valeria on an afternoon at the odeum to watch Plautus' Adaptation of Menander's *Dis Exapaton*. All too soon, however, Galerius mustered us and led us from Sirmium, back to our legionary fortress where we were to prepare for this potential new excursion out to the Persian borders.

We left the city early the next morning, once more with the back end of Galerius' steed for a view. A black-eyed and silent Candidianus walked with his head down beside his father, and a horrendously hungover Batius marched beside me. What a visit this had been. When I cast a last look back at Sirmium, I saw Maxentius up on the sun-bleached walls – high walls – watching us depart. He cast a hand up to wish me farewell, and I did the same.

With that, I faced forwards again, looking to the horizon. *To the distant east,* I thought, with a frisson of excitement.

8

MAXENTIUS

Antioch was alive with excitable citizenry, whether they be hungry for the glory and glamour of an imperial visit or filled with morbid fascination over the disaster whose details were still the stuff of rabid rumour in this ancient metropolis.

As befitted the scion of an emperor, I had accompanied the imperial court of the great and remarkably unpleasant Diocletian from Nicomedia, and had brought my wife and baby boy Romulus, even packing my wooden blocks, ever hopeful despite him being far too young to take an interest in them yet. The fact that we were here to see the equally unpleasant Galerius had been the only real reason Valeria had agreed to come, leaving the comforts of home.

'Perhaps new surroundings will change things for us,' I had mused as we travelled, attempting to get her to open up to me somehow. Two years of marriage had done little as yet to uncover any bond of affection from my cold wife.

'My life's threads are woven for me, without my design,' Valeria had replied with more than a touch of bitterness. 'Sirmium or Nicomedia, it matters not, for both are cages no matter how gilded. Had Father sold me as chattel to your friend Constantine instead, I would still be in golden chains and still at this place, and likely still with a mewling infant bothering me.'

I had lapsed into silence then, having tried and failed yet again, as she left me and crossed to the stern of the ship to spend time with her mother. I truly had no idea what Valeria wanted from life. Clearly it was something she was never likely to find, for her circumstances were as much of her making as of mine. I never placed bars about her, and I would have loved nothing more than to share a bond with her.

It was clearly not to be.

At least my hog of a father was not present, for he and his Caesar, Constantius, were off in Gaul, dealing with northern barbarians. This would not be a joyous affair either, though, as had been made clear by the emperor's expression throughout our journey to Antioch.

Persia was playing her games once more.

The new Persian ruler, Narses, had invaded Roman lands and those of her allies, razing, enslaving and looting with wild abandon. Persia has, of course, been the great enemy of all civilised men in the East since the days of the Athenian empire, and upon receipt of the tidings, the senior emperor had unleashed his war dog of a Caesar, Galerius, to teach the Persian a lesson.

Galerius had ridden east with a powerful army, full of hubris and plans to humiliate the new king of kings. Their armies had met at Carrhae, site of one of Rome's most ignominious defeats centuries earlier, and the result had been utter catastrophe. The overconfident Galerius had marched his vast army into Narses' trap and had paid the price, limping away with a newfound sense of humility. He'd barely had a chance to breathe and recover his wits before the Persian forces leapt upon the retreating Romans and dealt them repeated hammerings as they ran.

The Roman forces had moved back into reputedly safe territory and lurked there, licking their wounds as Narses and his men once again moved around the East freely, ravaging and thieving. When it became clear that Narses was content to lord himself over the border regions and was not planning to actually invade Rome, Galerius pronounced his disaster a success, that the Persians had been contained, and began to return to the heart of the empire with little more than half his original number.

Unfortunately for the Herdsman, word of the defeat had already reached the palace in Nicomedia, and Diocletian had immediately gathered his court in a fury and raced towards his junior with thoughts of castigation and even removal from office. Whether the emperor had calmed somewhat on his journey, or perhaps some other influence had been at work, I know not. When we'd set out from Nicomedia, everyone shied away from the great man who seemed ready to lynch Galerius on the spot for his failures, but now, while we waited in Antioch, the man had settled for chastisement and simply embarrassing his junior.

Scouts had placed Galerius and his entourage only a few miles from the city this morning, his army far behind, slowly approaching and still keeping Persian strikes at bay. Diocletian made his plans accordingly and I had decided to observe it all, not really for the sake of Galerius, who I cared for about as much as the diseased carcass of a stray dog, but for the two junior officers who would return with him. The loathsome Candidianus, who had somehow achieved minor command under his father despite his constant failings, and my friend Constantine, now a tribunus and watched over with interest by the Herdsman. I was fascinated to see what had become of the pair in their first outing to war, especially in the disastrous crucible of Persia.

Diocletian and his cronies, accompanied by appropriate guards, had left the city to clamorous applause earlier, planning to meet Galerius on his approach some distance from the city. Word of this had leaked out, by design of course, and the whole of Antioch filled the streets, watching, waiting for the spectacle of two emperors riding into the city in glory. The reason for Diocletian's temporary departure became clear to me as the horns announced his return.

The imperial procession back into Antioch was a joke, and a cruel one at that, befitting the wicked mind of the senior emperor whose design it was. As the gates stood wide, the first figure to enter the city was Galerius. Instead of his battle panoply, he was dressed in his imperial silks and finery with gold-braided slippers, more reminiscent of the Persian he had fought than of a traditional Roman. As soon as I saw him I made the decision that the day I came to power it would be wearing a toga like the great men of Rome before me, not like this sickening easterner. But even though I loathed him, I could still find a touch of sympathy. He may be dressed like a sumptuous king, but he was covered in dust and blood, his hair awry, and even from the street-side with my guard I could smell the body odour and the aroma of dung that clung to him. Diocletian was making a very clear statement about his junior.

Behind Galerius came his officer corps, the very men whose duty it had been to avoid the disaster that had befallen them. Prefect and tribunus, *praepositus* and general, they trudged past, dirty and unkempt, still covered in the blood of their latest failure, for it appeared that Narses had given them one last beating even recently before letting them retreat to the safety of Antioch, which even the King of Kings would not easily approach.

My eyes searched out the two men I knew and found them with ease. Candidianus, now my brother-in-law, shuffled disconsolately, dirty but seemingly untested, his face bearing an expression of impotent thunder. The damage from my childhood bite on his ankle was still in evidence in the form of a noticeable limp. Constantine came behind him, bearing scratches and scars, attesting to his hard fight and, though this entire parade was intended to humiliate, my friend's head was held high as though he'd accounted himself well.

I watched them pass and for just a moment, Constantine's eyes caught mine. His face lightened for the blink of an eye, and then he was past. It was odd. Antioch had gathered to cheer its emperors, yet instead the population watched in silence as the beaten Galerius and his men trudged past. The sight was so unexpected that even when Diocletian appeared astride a white horse in glittering glory and with his attendants and guard about him, still the people watched in silence.

Two hours after that awful parade of ruination I was back in my apartments, alone. Valeria had gone to see her mother once again, keeping safely out of my way. Euna, the nursemaid, had taken our baby boy somewhere more pleasant. I had been alone for an hour and was already bored, and so a knock on my door was both unexpected and welcome.

Outside, a slave hovered, looking nervous.

'Domine, the tribunus Constantine wondered if you were free and might spare him an hour in his apartments?'

I found myself grinning and reached out, gripping the

slave's shoulders with both hands as though I were about to kiss him. He recoiled in panic despite the grin. 'Good man,' I said, 'lead on.'

Locking my rooms on the assumption that neither Euna nor Valeria would be back before me, I followed the slave through the palace to a rather inauspicious door in a dilapidated wing that did not exactly scream *imperial glory*. I waited as the slave introduced me and then stepped deferentially aside. I dropped into the man's hand a coin that I'd been fiddling with – small change for me, a lifetime's dream for a slave. He made astonished noises and was gone before I could take it back.

I entered the room to find Constantine standing at the window, leaning on the sill. Three large jugs of wine stood on a table nearby with only one jug of water and half a dozen glasses. Constantine turned to me, his face split with a weary and uncertain smile.

'Have you been entertaining a crowd?' I asked, pointing at the jugs. 'Or has Persia enhanced your love of the grape?'

Constantine frowned in incomprehension, then looked to the side and noticed the three jugs, smiling easily. 'I asked for wine, and someone seems to have overdone themselves. Still, I shall not go short.'

I laughed. 'Batius, I suspect, if my memory of him serves. Perhaps I might help relieve your supply.'

Constantine chuckled and poured us each a good-sized wine, peering into the water jug. 'I fear we may need either more water, or otherwise stretchers in due course.'

'I see you are quartered in a salubrious part of the palace,' I said, my voice heavy with sarcasm. 'Galerius' favour still eludes you?'

'I have already arranged a villa nearby but for tonight the

Herdsman wants me close. I fear he does not like me out of sight where he cannot keep an eye on me. Until he spots a shapely slave, of course, whereupon he promptly forgets that I exist.'

I took the wine and looked about. He'd dropped a rough, soldier's kit bag on the bed. I grinned. 'Is there a golden sceptre in there perchance?'

Constantine snorted. 'I doubt it. Candidianus has his own problems these days.'

I laughed. 'It is good to see you, my friend.'

'So I am still your friend, even though I fight in the East and you navigate the treacherous currents of the court?' Constantine said. It sounded like easy jest but there was something of the real question in there too.

I gave him a shrug. 'I have a wife who resents me; a son too young to do anything but burble; a father who is overbearing, bombastic and unpleasant, though fortunately also absent; and a full court of unpleasant and ambitious politicians. How many friends do you think I have?'

He laughed then. 'I have found little more in the East, truth be told, serving a gilded turd of a master alongside his bronzed turd of a son.'

'Tell me about Persia.'

Constantine sagged back against the windowsill and took a swig of wine. 'You don't want to hear the details. It was a nightmare from beginning to end. Galerius is strong, and tactically shrewd, but his ego oft-times overrides his sense, and his brood of sycophants would rather die in Persian sand than speak out against him. Even I fought against doing so until it was almost too late, but at least when I did stand up to him my advice saved our hide as we pulled out. He is grateful... for now. It will take some time for any of us lesser officers to shake off the stigma of this, though Galerius already plots with his master how to take the fight back to the Persian.'

I nodded. 'I suspect you will escape much of the blame. Surely most will land with the Herdsman?'

Constantine snorted. 'He is as adept at shifting blame as he is incompetent at planning a war. Already Galerius sloughs his snakeskin of failure, labelling Candidianus as the one who walked us into the trap. There is an echo of the truth in there, but only an echo. Still, if there is one thing we will come out of this disaster appreciating, it will be the failure of Candidianus. His father has told him pointedly not to expect to be included in the succession, or even to anticipate high office. It seems our old adversary is finally sliding out of the light. He may yet try to win back his father's favour, but I would be exceedingly surprised to see him achieve it.'

'Sometimes I wonder if there is a father in the world a son can rely upon,' I mused, then grinned. 'Still, such troubles could not happen to a more deserving whelp.' With that, I downed my wine in a toast to the failure of Candidianus and poured another, completely ignoring the water jug like some old sot. 'In the meantime I have had a son, Constantine. A *son!*'

His face brightened. 'Just as you always wanted.' Then he grinned mischievously. 'Did he thaw upon leaving your wife?'

'You are talking about the woman I love, old friend.' I snorted. 'Well, the woman I *like*.' I laughed aloud. 'All right, tolerate...'

Now Constantine laughed. 'Very well, young Maxentius, father and husband, courtier and politician, we shall forget my tales of bravado and we shall drink wine as you do, unwatered and in anticipation of brutal headaches. I may have tempered steel, but it appears that you have tempered flesh, and learned to use an entirely *different* lance.'

I gave my old friend a shocked glare before we both exploded into fits of breathless laughter. Finally, I sighed. 'I have to admit to being a little jealous of you. I know you have had a bad time of it so far, but I am also sure that you will win glorious victories in due course, and all that time I shall be playing with counting blocks with my son and on occasion listening to my father bluster and argue and call me names while he creates divides between himself and the other rightful rulers of this empire.'

For a moment, I thought I had ruined the easy mood, and my old friend fixed me with a very serious glare. 'Are you telling me the miserable old hood-eyed toad can stay sober long enough to play politics?'

I chuckled, the buoyant mood returning in an instant. 'Gods, Constantine, but let us never allow such rifts to push us apart as they do these dogs we serve.'

Constantine laughed and poured neat wine for us both with a humorously arched eyebrow. We sat in his poor apartments at the arse end of the palace and drank wine until I could hardly remember how my legs worked and until every sentence had us howling with laughter. I had never been as happy and I hoped that such glee could last forever.

PART 2

Salus populi suprema lex esto
(The good of the people should be the highest law)
– *Cicero*

9

CONSTANTINE

ARMENIA, JULY 298 AD

In battle, the stench of death is never stronger than on the cusp of victory, and now, after twelve years with Galerius, I had become well accustomed to both death and victory. And this day was bloodier than any yet. As the sun dipped behind us in the heart of this rugged land, I could sense my mentor's glee as he swung his spatha to tear out the throat of another Persian.

'Finish this!' the Herdsman roared, his face and muscled cuirass spattered in gore. He grabbed a legionary standard and swept it towards the nearest hillside, his cry trailing off into a low, almost Bacchanalian growl through clenched, grinning teeth. His inky-black eyes glinted in anticipation as he beheld the Persian *Derafsh Kaviani* standard fluttering up there on the peak, part-masked by smoke and swirling, red-brown dust clouds.

I echoed his command, waving my legion – the Third Gallica – towards the slope. Batius had been right, you see, and my career had progressed; this war had pushed me into the boots of the previous tribunus, who had fallen last summer. We surged across the valley floor, littered with countless Persian and Roman dead. White bone and red mire churned underfoot. All around us, screaming, wounded men and whinnying beasts thrashed and shuddered. For their deaths and grievous wounds to have any meaning, there could be no hesitation, the Persian royal standard had to be seized.

We charged up the scree-strewn hillside, our ranks closing on the crest like an iron noose. I gripped my spatha, stained red since dawn, the blood pounding in my ears. The legions following in my wake rapped their spears on their shields and roared like lions.

I glanced at the hilltop with every few steps. Persian guardsmen stood in a thick circle protecting the lip of the plateau there. Nigh-on one thousand of them, I reckoned. *Pushtigban* – Shahanshah Narses' royal guard – resplendent in iron scale and plate armour and crested with pointed, plumed helms and iron masks. Hubris, terror, fury – nothing showed through the expressionless eye and mouth slots. Fearsome warriors, I knew. But my will was strong, my dander piqued; after four years of bitter conflict across Mesopotamia and Syria, this war would end. Here. Now.

The Pushtigban presented a nest of spear tips to our ascent, their masks hiding any emotion. My chest rose and fell rapidly, my thighs numb, quivering with fatigue at the steep climb. Over the din of roaring, panting men, boots and rustling armour I heard it again – a thrumming sound from somewhere atop the plateau. *Archers!*

'Shields!' I cried out, my throat parched, seeing the dark volley of arrows sailing out from behind the Pushtigban line, dipping like hawks then plunging down towards us.

The cry seemed to reach only those nearby the impending danger. Precious few shields were raised overhead and only moments later a whooshing sounded and then the punching of iron tips into flesh rang out in a sickening rhythm. Legionaries all along the front sank to their knees. Persian arrows quivered in their legs, arms, throats, eye sockets, some in their open and still-screaming mouths. A hand slapped on my shoulder and I spun to see a young lad built like a sapling. An arrow had pierced his cheekbone and dark blood pumped from the wound in gouts.

'Sir, I...' he stammered, his eyes darting in panic.

'Be still!' I hissed, halting, lowering my shield then steadying him with one hand and grappling the arrow shaft with the other. No sooner had I snapped off the exposed section of shaft than another volley arced over the Pushtigban line on the plateau and rained down on us. The young lad was punched back from me, two arrows embedded in his throat. I stared at his corpse for a moment, numb more than anything else. It was then that I realised he was one of Candidianus' century. When I looked up, I located Galerius' foul son, a good hundred paces downhill behind his own men, his face pale with fear. His century was being torn to pieces and the craven-hearted cur had hung back to save himself from the worst of the fighting – exaggerating the effects of his limp from Maxentius' ankle bite so long ago.

That had been the way of it with him: ever since his father had shifted the blame for our earlier defeats onto him, he had sunk into lower ranks, lost all of his pluck and confidence. Ruined by his own sire. *Not me,* I thought, briefly recalling the horror of that moment in Treverorum when Father had chosen to abandon us. I squared my shoulders as if chasing away the memory. *Not me.*

'Onwards!' big Batius cried, snapping me from my momentary trance, shoving my shield back into my hand.

He forged on ahead, leading his century like a titan, his face spattered red, his helm dented and his mail shirt torn. Inspired by him as always, I burst uphill to join the ascending front once more.

The arrow hail slowed and the defiant roars from both sides grew intense as we closed on the hilltop. Within a few more strides, the lines clashed. The roaring swiftly died, replaced by the clattering of shields, discordant clanging of iron, crunching of bone, tearing of meat and the feral shrieks and grunts of dying men. Spears jabbed at me and my shield shuddered again and again as if under assault from Hercules' club. A stink of freshly spilled blood and ripped bowels wafted across the struggle. Men by my side who faltered and let their guard drop, exhausted, were run through by Pushtigban spears. But I held on, I waited, knowing the Persian resistance had to ebb.

'Stand together, stay close, keep your shields up!' I croaked, exhausted.

Just when black spots began to grow at the edges of my eyes, I felt the relentless strikes slow. The Persians were tiring too. The next blow came and I swept my shield forward and up, the boss barging away the spearpoint aimed at me. In the same motion, I lunged forward, driving my spatha-tip into the guts of the Pushtigban before me. The impact of my blade was dull, his scale armour blunting most of the blow, but the tip had slid up between the scales and pierced the leather underneath and his flesh.

He staggered back, glancing in disbelief at the gouts of dark lifeblood that followed. In a heartbeat, he was on his knees. The smallest of gaps in the Pushtigban line lay before me.

'Forward!' I cried.

'You heard your tribunus! Into the breach!' I heard Batius bellow in support of my order.

The Pushtigban either side of the gap were too slow to close the fissure. I shouldered into one of them, knocking him back from the line, then ducked the spear jab of the other, before bringing my spatha up to swipe across the gap between the bottom of his mask and the collar of his scale vest. With his throat opened, blood pumped from the wound and from the mouth-slit on his mask, and his strength vanished.

I stumbled beyond the ruptured Pushtigban line and onto the flat ground of the hilltop plateau – a small stronghold of tents and wagons. The brigade of archers who had moments ago rained death upon us as we climbed now gawped at me as if I had emerged from another realm. Their surprise lasted only a trice though, as they threw down their bows and drew their *shamshir* swords, then rushed towards me.

Panic had me, for there was only me and the big man and two other Romans on the hilltop at that moment. But the gods must have been watching, for that was the instant when the ring of Pushtigban crumpled. At all different sections of the plateau edge, scores more legionaries pierced through as we had, and the order of battle had dissolved. One group sideswiped into the archers coming for me, the two forces tumbling into a frenzy of hand-to-hand fighting. Within a breath, the plateau was awash with fighting men.

I parried and blocked madly, then the severed head of one of the Persian archers bounced past me.

'Archers trying to join in the real fighting?' Batius cried over the din of battle beside me. 'That means it'll be over soon!'

'Perhaps, but until then, keep your sword high and your

shield close,' I panted in reply. 'Someone told me that once.'
I grinned.

The fighting was brutal and swift. The Persian warriors
fought manfully but could not match the legionary spirit.
There was just a tinge of daylight left on the horizon when
the clatter of swords and spears being thrown to the ground
rang out and the Persians cried for mercy.

The tumult of battle faded, replaced by the moaning of
the injured and the panting of exhausted Roman and Persian
alike. *It's over,* I mouthed, letting my spatha drop, the tip
stabbing into the red earth, quivering.

I heard the men cry out, many to Mars, God of the Legions.
I had worshipped at his altar keenly in my years in the ranks,
and felt his power like an inferno when I marched with
legionaries. But today there were cries from the Christians
too. Their voices were less ferocious – poignant almost – as
they called out to their deity. The centuries-old cult seemed to
be capturing the hearts of many.

Yet all I could see before me were ghosts of the recent
battle, and my ears still rang with the screams of those who
had died. On and on it went. I closed my eyes and pressed
my thumb and forefinger together – something old Lactantius
had taught me to do as a means to rid my mind of horrors.
My thoughts began to drift towards other memories. Sweet
ones that would spirit me away from the carnage all around.
It conjured sweet thoughts of Mother, her mantras. And all
my efforts had been for her. Now, thanks to my military
purse, she was set up in a comfortable villa in Antioch – my
billet house for this campaign. When I fought, I fought for
Rome, but I also fought to live, just to have the honour of
returning to her. And not only her... for out here in these
eastern borderlands, I had found love.

I thought again of her smile, her dark cheeks dimpled, her eyes mesmerising. *Minervina*. Daughter of a Syrian wine merchant, she was as obstinate as she was beautiful. Her father need not worry for her well-being with me, for she was quite capable of looking after herself. She allowed me to spend time with her in a medical house in Antioch's lesser palace, where she oversaw a school of healers. On occasion she agreed to join me on the riverside taverns to eat fish and drink wine. But always, she complained that I was like a clam, closed up, too stiff with my feelings. Her reserve had only made me mad with the desire to win her over fully. Now, perhaps, I could return to Antioch and do just that.

Conjured by these thoughts of pleasant things, a smile began to appear on my weary face. Only for terrible cries of angst to ring out nearby, tearing my thoughts away. All heads looked up and around. The disarmed Persian prisoners glanced anxiously to each other, sure, no doubt, that despite their surrender these cries signalled the start of an ignoble butchery. My eyes snapped onto the Persian royal tent at the far end of the plateau. The noise seemed to be emanating from there. A woman in pain.

'Rope the prisoners together,' I called to Batius hurriedly, my eyes never leaving the tent. 'See to it that they are watered and fed with what scraps are left after our ranks have eaten.'

'Aye, sir,' Batius replied.

But I was already off and jogging towards the tent. Now I heard the woman scream again. I saw a pair of legionaries from one of Galerius' favoured legions standing either side of the tent entrance, pinning two Persian guards to the ground with their spears. The pair saw me and made to say something, but then both simply looked away, ashen-faced.

I swept the tent flap back and ducked into the gloomy

interior just as an animal roar of pleasure rang out and the woman's whimpering died away. The scene before me was nightmarish. Galerius, still in his cuirass and helm, plastered with blood and with strips of skin and hair dangling from the rim, stood, back arched, face contorted in ecstasy. His tunic was hitched up as he issued a final few pelvic thrusts into a dusky-skinned young woman lying broken on the table before him.

'This is just the start,' Galerius purred in that thick, pitch-like accent, backing away from the woman, tucking himself away and pulling the hem of his tunic back down. 'I have filled your wife with my seed. Now I will proceed to take every last morsel of your empire. My armies will dine in the halls of Ctesiphon by the end of the summer.'

I followed Galerius' gaze, across the gory trail of four Pushtigban in gilded armour lying dead on the floor – one impaled on the staff of the Derafsh Kaviani standard – to the corner of the tent. There, in a bubble of orange lamplight, two more legionaries held a kneeling, dark-skinned, long-haired and full-bearded man at bay with their spathas. The kneeling man wore a gold-threaded purple robe and a fine, gemmed gold necklace. Shahanshah Narses, I realised. King of Kings. Ruler of all Persia. The one my men and I had talked of as the enemy for so many years, and here he was on his knees before the Herdsman. At that moment I felt only pity for him. This was not a fitting end for a noble adversary.

'Take her away, have fun with her if you will, then put her in chains,' Galerius snapped his fingers, prompting one of the two legionaries guarding Narses to scoop up the weeping woman and carry her from the tent. 'We'll keep her in Antioch as a reminder of Roman power,' he called after the legionary with a grim chuckle.

'Be wary of pushing your advantage too far, Roman,' Narses cut in, barely controlling the tremble of rage in his voice.

Galerius swung to the man with a look of incredulity on his face. 'Pushing my advantage? Just as your forefathers did when they had Emperor Valerian skinned alive?' He chuckled darkly and swept up a goblet of wine from a table, draining it in one gulp then hurling the vessel down with all his strength so it clattered across the floor. 'I'll seize all that lies before me. However, you won't be here to see it.' Galerius made eye contact with the legionary guarding Narses, who read the signal and raised his spatha, ready to drive it down into the King of King's collarbone.

Throughout my years in the legions I had learned so much: the disciplines of strategy, tactics, formations; the arts of diplomacy and leadership; the fine balance of mercy... and ruthlessness. *This is not right, I know. But if one more death brings the war to an end... is it truly wrong?*

Yet before I could choose to remain mute or speak out, shouting echoed from outside. I heard panicked cries outside and the thundering of hooves drawing closer.

Suddenly, the tent pole wobbled and toppled then the tent came crashing down. The goatskin fell upon me like a shroud and I was blinded and deafened momentarily. As I fought to pull myself from the tangle, I heard Galerius cry out in terror, his hubris of moments ago utterly gone. There was a brief clash-clash of swords, then the hooves thundered off into the distance again to a chorus of hurled Roman curses. I struggled from under the collapsed tent and righted myself. All eyes on the plateau were looking to the east. There, galloping down the eastern face of the hill and off through the owl-light was a cluster of mounted Persian horsemen, and Narses was clinging to the saddle behind one of them.

'*Cataphractii* riders,' Batius said, sidling up next to me. 'They broke onto the plateau to save their king. Probably for the best.'

I saw Galerius struggle from the other end of the tent, rise to his feet and seethe at his escaping prize. A handful of equites and a clutch of legionaries had set off in pursuit, but the Persian riders were clearly fresher and swiftly sped off into the darkness.

'For the best?' I said, thinking of my musings from moments ago.

'We broke the Shahanshah's armies today,' Batius reasoned. 'Now we will surely be able to press for terms and Narses will be obedient. Had we slain him, the Persian people would have been outraged. A martyr can be more powerful than an army ten thousand strong.'

I cast the big man a grave look. 'You did not witness what just happened in that tent, Batius. Never is a wolf more dangerous than with a thorn in its paw.'

I looked once more to Galerius and felt only utter revulsion. I offered him only a terse nod, disguising my true emotion. This was a skill I had refined in my time with the Herdsman.

Campfires blazed all across the plateau and on the valley floor below. I sat by one fire holding a skewer of goat meat over the flames. The meat was charred and crunchy on the outside, succulent and fatty inside, and it invigorated my weary limbs. I washed each mouthful down with a long pull on my skin of watered wine. I looked across the sea of smoke-blackened, scarred and gaunt faces, then latched on to one. Narses' wife sat, hugging a woollen blanket around her shoulders, her eyes glazed, haunted. I had found the legionary who had taken her not long after dusk. Just in time too. Now she was safe, with warmth, food and water.

Memories of Galerius defiling her scudded across my mind, uninvited. *One of the four most powerful men in the Roman Empire, nothing but a black-eyed beast,* I thought. Perhaps it had been the scale of Diocletian's public shaming of him that had driven him to that new low? Yes, Candidianus had shouldered much of that blame, but not all. Had the Herdsman taken some purgative pleasure today in defiling Narses' wife? *An explanation, but not an excuse,* I affirmed sourly.

Despite all his flaws, Galerius had proven himself again today as an astute strategist. He had understood that the Persians excelled at warfare on flat, open terrain where they could utilise their ironclad, centaur-like cavalry to great effect. Luring them to these dust- and rubble-strewn Armenian highlands had been a shrewd and ultimately telling move. I had learned much from the man – a cunning military mind – but that aside, he was the antithesis of all a man should strive to be.

It was then that the Herdsman interrupted my thoughts, appearing beside me unnoticed. He stood there, swigging wine, armed men flanking him. He looked down on me with his inky-black eyes and an almost pitying grin. He had a way about him where – despite his loathsome boorishness – he seemed able to perceive the thoughts of others.

'Do you ever wonder what might have been?' he offered flatly, stepping forward then crouching beside me. In the background I was aware of his two bodyguards chewing on bread, watching us like gulls waiting on their share of fish scraps. 'You could have joined me, followed in my trail of glory... and entered the line of accession. Just like me, like your father. Instead, you are a tribunus. Merely a hardy soldier whose name will quickly fade with the mists of time.'

I looked to him, hiding my disdain behind a gentle smile. 'What is done is done, Domine. My choices are what they are, and they will define me,' I replied, thinking of Mother's words to me on the night of the storm. 'They will guide me on my journey.'

Galerius stood tall again and swigged greedily on his wine, before leaving at last. As much as he disgusted me, I had little option but to show him obedience. As a Caesar, the Herdsman was poised, ready to one day rise to the apex of the tetrarchic system as Augustus of the East, and the thought chilled me to my marrow.

Now you might wonder why I had remained with Galerius' retinue for so long given such bleak thoughts. Well, it was my own mule-headedness for one thing. That and one of the maxims I had learned from the old tutor, Lactantius:

The best way to outwit your enemy, is to convince him that you are his friend.

ANTIOCH, SEPTEMBER 302 AD

Four years later...

Some say the Persian War ended on that bloodstained plateau in Armenia, but like a stubborn ember, the remnant of the Shahanshah's armies fought on – years of insurgency and bitter retaliation followed as the great empire of the desert tried to strike back against Rome. It was only after four summers of such wretched skirmishing that a truce was declared. At long last the army was stood down and I was free to retire to my billet chambers in the great eastern city of Antioch, straddling the River Orontes, perched on the edge of the arid wilderness. I had come here fleetingly during the Persian War, sometimes just for days, sometimes to winter between campaigns. Now, in my thirtieth year and with the war settled, I was here to see out the year. Rumour was the legions would be shipped back to Nicomedia after that.

I rested my palms on the villa balcony and inhaled deeply, realising how much I would miss Antioch, vowing to appreciate these few months of indolence. A clement autumnal breeze brought with it a taste of the desert dust, rippling my overgrown hair and faded blue military tunic. The sun was dipping into the horizon behind the city's imperial palace, throwing a languid orange light over the crush of marbled halls and red-tiled roofs of the city wards and the sweeping, burnt-gold and shrub-studded slopes of Mount Silpius. I eyed the great slopes from which the city's eastern walls jutted, seeing the shadows of the coming dusk gradually obscure each rugged feature.

The sunset framed my thoughts perfectly: the war here was over. Likewise, it seemed that troubles elsewhere in the empire were ebbing: a rebellion in Aegyptus had been quelled and the barbarian incursions over the Rhenus had been beaten back too. More, Father, far away in the damp and often frozen north, was taming the revolutionaries in distant Britannia. I did not need him anymore, and I hadn't for some time. As much as I hated him for what he did to Mother and I, I could not help but fear for him now. For I had gotten wind of rumours about his health. Constantius 'Chlorus', they had taken to calling him – 'the pale one'. I wished him no ill-health, but I wondered if he was truly happy with his lot. He had gotten what he wanted. As Caesar of the West, power and respect were his. He had spurned Mother and me to grasp these 'precious' things.

Such a fool, I thought, for in this burning land, during my odyssey of war and campaigning, I had spurned nothing. I had built a fine reputation on the battlefield, I had brought Mother here and had given her the life she deserved. And the love I had found in these lands had blossomed, for Minervina and I were now married.

My eyes slid down to the temple gardens near the villa. Amongst the date palms and lemon trees, fountains babbled and exotic birds chirruped – two sand-martins play-fighting as they flitted from branch to branch. Then I spotted her. *Minervina,* I mouthed fondly. She knelt on the grass in the shade of a tall, bronze statue of Mars. I watched, mesmerised as always, as she tucked her dark and sleek locks behind her ears and coaxed a bright emerald butterfly along the length of her finger, towards her wrist and the Christian Chi-Rho bracelet that hung there.

I knew we would be wed not long after that dark day, four years ago, when Narses' armies were routed. The legions headed back to make camp outside Antioch, and I delivered the Shahanshah's captured wife to her new residence in the lesser palace to be cared for by Minervina and her healers. The poor woman was trembling, certain that every Roman eye cast upon her was wicked. I assured her that although she was a hostage, she would come to no harm and would live the life of a noblewoman.

It was then that Minervina had finally seen through my stubborn, iron shell. She heard my words to the frightened Persian woman. She said my deeds revealed God's place in my heart. I like to think there were other good things she might have seen in me, shining through the black pall that war drapes across a man. But then we all deceive ourselves at times, do we not?

We were wed in a ceremony similar to – if less expensive than – that of my friend Maxentius. Minervina wore a flame-red veil and pure-white robes, me in – for once – opulent crimson silk garments with an overly ornate muscled cuirass and greaves. One slave even offered to paint my skin silver. I declined. Minervina's father had insisted on bringing his fattest swine to the ritual slaughter and chartered a trade cog to bring in sixty amphorae of Chian Red for the feasting and festivities that followed.

The nights Minervina and I shared after that were fraught with passion. Heady times, the memory of which, even now, brings me exquisite joy. However, in the few years since our joining, we had been together only fleetingly, in between my forays with the legions. Yet this only ensured that returning to her was golden, simply golden. And the last time I had come back from the march, she had greeted me with the greatest news of all. Entranced, I watched her, dusky eyes fixed on the butterfly, full lips bent in a smile... and her other hand resting on her pregnant belly. Aye, after so long theorising about the scruples of my father, now I was to be one myself.

The notion drew me into some haze of introspection. Did I have it in me to be a father? I was the flesh and blood of a man who had failed utterly at that role, after all. I brought sad memories back, of Mother weeping, and of the hot shame I had felt for years afterwards.

I realised I was staring at an empty space by the statue now, the figure of Mars casting shade where Minervina had been. Where had she gone? Then I felt a delicate set of arms wrap around my waist from behind. I tasted her floral scent in the air. I grinned as she caressed me, muttering something in her lilting accent. I turned away from the balcony edge to embrace her, holding her head to my chest. I stroked her delicate neck, the nape richly scented. She looked up, her dark locks falling away as she tilted her head back to meet my gaze. Her eyes were sleepy, accentuating the rounded beauty of her face. 'Our boy will be a handsome fellow if he inherits your looks,' I said, stroking her cheek.

She saw my grin and failed to fight off its advances, her lips stretching into a smile too. 'Who said it will be a boy?' she gasped, moving a hand to her belly.

'I need some reinforcements,' I said, arching an eyebrow and adopting an overly serious expression, 'otherwise you'll have me completely at your beck and call.'

She issued an indignant snort. Before she could reply I stooped and hove her from her feet, cradling her and bringing her eyes level with mine. We gazed at one another then shared a passionate kiss that seemed to bring with it the twilight, for when our lips parted, the sun had left the sky. It was another voice that spoke next.

'Come, Minervina, the congregation of Babylas is gathering and evening prayer will take place soon.' I looked up to see Mother, standing in the archway that led out onto the balcony, black-robed and beholding us in adoration. I returned her smile with one of my own. For how could I be anything but joyous that Mother was safe now, living here with me in the villa? She was treated with respect and wanted for nothing, for everyone knew I was her son. Constantine the Tribunus. Constantine the war hero. Distant memories of her shameful estrangement from Father had faded, and those of her lonely years in the villa at Salona were ebbing too.

When she had first come here to Antioch years ago she was frail, ravaged by time and having been denied the company of her oft-campaigning son. But as the Persian wars had gradually ebbed I made sure to be with her as often as possible. The company of Minervina and me seemed to have revitalised her. Yes, her hair was now near-white and her once radiant skin was hidden behind a network of lines. Yes, she seemed to have shrivelled; her shoulders were frail and rounded. But her azure eyes were sharp and lively once again, her spirit strengthened simply by being close to me once more – and being near the land of the Christian Prophet and the Apostles. She had used her time to help grow the strong Christian community in Antioch. Every summer too, she had journeyed south to the city of Jerusalem, taking Minervina with her.

My smile faltered as a dark thought cut across my mind. The faith had flourished in these last years, but so much so that followers of the Roman gods had become suspicious, jealous even. In some parts of the city there had been reports of beatings of these Christ-worshippers. Worse, I had heard whisperings in the court, ever since Emperor Diocletian had arrived here from his campaigns in Aegyptus in the late summer. He and Galerius had grown increasingly disparaging about the Christians, claiming it was some affront to their place as demi-gods. Any man with a keen eye could see they were in fact afraid of the cult – a religion that cared little for falling into line with imperial doctrine and emperor worship.

Some emperors of the past had highlighted their disdain for the irksome faith by inciting bloodthirsty persecutions. If Diocletian and Galerius – dangerous creatures when calm – felt truly threatened by the Christians... I pressed my thumb and forefinger together and closed my eyes, sweeping this dark possibility from my thoughts with a confident smile. *I am Constantine the war hero,* I assured myself. *None can harm my beloved few.*

'Until tonight,' Minervina whispered in my ear, bringing me back to the present. She tucked a scented, silver silk scarf into the belt of my tunic, slipping away from me. She seemed to glide across the marbled balcony, her rich red robes accentuating her rounded hips. Then she was gone, Mother with her.

I watched the space where they had been standing and wondered. My loved ones were safe and well. Nobody could harm them. Had I found what I once sought all those years ago in Augusta Treverorum – the power to protect and keep safe those I loved, to steer my own fate?

I was torn from sleep by a raucous jeering. I fell from my bed, fearing some Persian horde had bested the wall garrison overnight. Rushing to the balcony, I blinked the sleep from my eyes. It was mid-morning and the sun blazed over the city, the reflections from the pools and sun-bleached structures below blinding me. It seemed I had slept longer than intended. But not even a drunken boar could have slumbered through this racket. My eyes slowly acclimatised to the light; thousands, it seemed, had gathered in the forum across the river, beside the dome-roofed thermae. Bathers had even emerged from the bathhouse semi-dressed, their skin still slick with oil, to join the jeering rabble.

'Constantine, what's happening?' Minervina croaked, sitting up in our bed, gathering the blanket around her naked form.

'Stay here,' was all I said. I dressed quickly in soft leather boots and my trusty legion tunic then rushed from my chamber, stopping at the font only to sweep a handful of water over my face and through my hair. I hurried down through the villa, ignoring the cold glares of Diocletian's Joviani legionaries stationed outside. I darted over a humped stone bridge to join the crowd.

A chariot cut through the throng, round and round as if led by a runaway mount. A lone man stood upon it, behind the driver. *A triumph?* I thought and then instantly scoffed at the notion. Indeed, such a conclusion was swept away when I saw that the fellow was bound to the carriage, fixed upright by ropes around his chest and wrists to some wooden pole jutting from the floor. He was maybe only a few years my senior, but was so drawn and pallid he could have passed as someone much older. He wore a tattered brown robe. His bald head seemed to be badly sunburnt and the dark locks around the back and sides were flailing in the breeze. Suddenly, the jeering intensified and the crowd began hurling things at him: rotting cabbages, stale bread, even stones. What had this poor fellow done?

His head snapped back when one well-aimed pebble smacked into his forehead, sending a swift trail of blood snaking from the wound, forking across the bridge of his nose. The shower of missiles thickened, and the vitriol grew ever more heinous. Throughout it all, however, his eyes remained bright, strong – and there was something about that defiant gaze that reminded me of Mother. More, he was muttering some mantra as if to give himself strength.

Forgive them... he seemed to be repeating over and over.

A foul-smelling and squat man in front of me hefted his arm to hurl a blackened and unidentifiable root vegetable at the chariot. I grasped his wrist. The cur shot a glare over his shoulder at me, his black and yellow bottom teeth – his only teeth in fact – jutting out over his top lip. His ire subsided instantly when he recognised me. 'Who is that?' I demanded, gesturing towards the chariot.

'That is the man who laughs at the glory of Jove! Yet another *milites Christi*,' he insisted with a wind of foul breath. 'Romanus, Deacon of Caesarea!'

At that moment I saw the silver Chi-Rho the poor soul on the chariot wore around his neck, just like Mother's. 'Who gave permission for this?' I seethed.

'Emperor Diocletian,' he said, his chest puffing out and a hint of confidence returning to his tone.

I followed the dog's gaze and saw the pair of them then. Diocletian and Galerius, seated on thrones atop a sun-bathed plinth at one edge of the square. The steps leading up to this platform were lined with Joviani legionaries. I could have laughed aloud had the bloody form of the poor deacon not been hovering in the corner of my eye; for the Herdsman's flesh was painted silver and he was wrapped in opulent purple silken robes – a transparent attempt at emulating Maximian that day back in Augusta Treverorum – surely now purporting to be the Eastern Hercules to Diocletian's Jove. He glittered in the morning sunlight like a hideous, oversized carp.

The chariot came to rest at the foot of the dais and the driver hopped from the vehicle. He ascended the marble steps and then – in the most un-Roman fashion – fell to his knees and prostrated himself before the emperor and the Caesar of the East. Most nauseatingly, this man – probably of noble birth, going by his attire – had to then crawl forward like an insect and kiss the hems of the pair's purple robes.

Diocletian – his dark hair now flecked with grey and his face somewhat age-lined – glowered down his nose at the driver as if eyeing a mangy dog. A wave of the emperor's hand brought the driver gingerly to his feet once more.

'Domine, I bring to you the preacher of the false god.' He bowed, gesturing to the beleaguered deacon. 'The one who has been causing so much unrest in the southern city of Caesarea.'

Diocletian ignored the driver, simply glaring down the steps of the dais at the deacon. 'Let all who look on know this, and spread this word to all who walk the lands of our empire. The gods have chosen.' He gestured to himself and Galerius, then raised a cupped palm, fingers tensed as if crushing some invisible fruit. 'Their power, their judgement and their wrath will fall upon any who do not heed and worship them.'

He stood, Galerius rising with him. I saw the Herdsman's lips flicker into a sadistic smile and felt great dread for the deacon.

Diocletian raised his arms up and out wide, as if addressing the azure morning sky. 'The false prophet of Nazareth and his fanciful delusion of a god are cancers in the imperial flesh, gnawing at the foundations of empire in these lands. The false faith must be purged. It must be reduced to ash.'

At this, a raucous cheer went up from the crowd. It was then that I noticed a handful of men stacking timber and kindling to one side of the dais. A thick timber pole jutted from the centre of this pile. A Joviani legionary stood beside it, his eyes and his blued-steel armour and shield illuminated by the flames dancing from the torch he clutched in place of a spear. So the deacon was to burn, it seemed. I saw the man's eyes dart to the torch. For a moment, his resolve foundered, a low, tremulous wail spilling from his lips. But moments later it returned: he shuffled behind his bindings to stand tall, his eyes glancing skywards and his lips moving as he spoke with his god again. Diocletian looked to this then turned to the soldiers nearest the chariot. 'Untie him!' he said.

The two Joviani nearest the chariot cut the deacon's bonds and then bundled the man over to the stack of timber. They hoisted him up to the centre pole and bound him there. As they fumbled to tie the ropes, I thought of the many souls of the empire who followed the word of the Christian prophet. *Mother, Minervina,* I thought numbly. Panic rose in my breast.

'And let word spread across the sands. Worshippers of Christ will *burn!*'

Another raucous cheer, this time so spirited that the flagstones I stood on seemed to tremble. The blood in my veins turned to ice at that moment. Then, just as the torch-wielder made to touch the flame to the firewood, I saw that Galerius was whispering something in Diocletian's ear. The emperor seemed to approve. 'Wait!' he called out, halting the torch-wielder.

For a precious moment, I wondered if he had seen the folly of all this – that burning and martyring these people would only strengthen their faith and forge a hardier devotion.

'Bring him up here,' Diocletian purred.

The two soldiers acted without question, untying the man, grappling him by a shoulder each, leading him from the firewood pile and bringing him up the stairs of the plinth. The chariot driver frowned, confused. Galerius grinned rapaciously.

'Come!' Galerius beckoned with flicked fingers to the archway at the back of the dais. There stood Candidianus, shoulders slumped as if trying to blend into the shadows. 'Bring the tongs.'

Candidianus emerged from the shaded archway and into the glare of the sun. Physically, he was every bit his father's son, but while Galerius carried himself like Hercules, Candidianus walked under a cloud of self-doubt, his steps erratic due to the old ankle wound. The loathsome young man's mind had truly been poisoned and confused beyond repair by his father.

If I had known what was to happen next, I would have leapt onto the dais and plunged a merciful dagger into the poor deacon's heart. Instead, I have lived with the memory – and many more even darker – ever since.

Candidianus looked to the Herdsman for reassurance, then lifted a leather wallet from his belt. He opened it to reveal a set of glinting iron torture implements. The crowd fell silent in a foul mix of horror and intrigue as Candidianus lifted a set of iron tongs from the selection. Then he plucked the dagger from his belt and moved towards the deacon. The Joviani grappled the deacon's shoulders, Candidianus raised the tongs to the man's mouth, then hesitated, his eyes widening in panic.

'Do it, whelp. You said you had the stomach for it... so *do* it!' Galerius snarled, clutching the deacon's jaw and prizing his jaws open. Candidianus probed the tongs inside the deacon's mouth, his hand badly shaking, then pulled them back out, stretching the man's tongue with it. The deacon's stance faltered, his legs buckling and his eyes bulging, dry retching as his tongue was dragged out until the flesh lost its colour.

'Cut it!' Galerius hissed.

I saw Candidianus' chest rise and fall and was sure I could read the panic on his face as he lifted the blade. But it hovered there, the Herdsman's son struck with horror at the act he had seemingly agreed to carry out in order to regain some scrap of his father's favour. The moment seemed to last forever.

'Useless boy,' Galerius growled in disgust, and snatched the blade from his son. With a flash of the dagger, the tongue was severed. He and his shaking, pallid boy were sprayed with dark blood from the stump. It came in gouts as the deacon slumped to his knees. His skin grew pale white and then slowly greyed as his jaw and robes were sodden with blood. The crowds gasped as Galerius took the tongs from his son's hands and raised them, the bloody tongue hanging limp in their grasp. The Herdsman pumped the bloody trophy aloft and stuck out his own tongue as if mimicking the poor deacon, except his mouth was wide in a roar, eyes aflame.

This ignited the crowd into a matching chorus of frenzied cheering. Candidianus, shaking madly, backed into the shadows. I knew then that was where he – once the promising scion of a tetrarch – was destined to remain.

I turned away when I saw Galerius run his fingers over the other torture implements to select another one. As I strode back to my villa, I saw a few in the crowd turn mean eyes upon sober-faced individuals, accusing them of being Christ-worshippers. One confrontation even came to blows, the accused being thrown to the ground in a storm of fists and feet. Moments later, many such incidents had broken out.

Seeking strength to understand what was happening, I thought of Mars, sought some kind of strength from the War God. I thought of my childhood and the Christian legionary on the walls of Naissus, how he had been grasping spear in one hand and Chi-Rho in the other. *Hide your Christian symbols,* I thought, wondering where life had taken him, *and keep your spear close.*

I thought again of Mother and Minervina. A cold hand swirled my guts. In this fiery land, sun-maddened minds were often quick to ignite, and the emperors' words were sure to stoke a conflagration. The deacon's fate would be shared by many others of his faith – all across the desert cities of the East. In zealous fervour, men would surely strike out at all things Christian, heedless of nobility.

I stumbled across the Orontes bridge, across the gardens towards the villa. I came to the bronze statue of Mars – where Minervina had been sitting just the previous day. I knelt before it, the spiked shade of the god's solar crown cast across my skin. I sought some words of tribute, searched for some pledge I could make if only he would see my loved ones spared from these persecutions.

I gazed up into the lifeless bronze eyes and realised it was futile. It was the very followers of this god, packed into the square, who cheered every twist of the torture going on there. It was the pair who claimed to represent Mars' sibling deities, Jove and Hercules, who cajoled them. Then, behind the statue I saw two forms, leaning from their balconies, faces wrinkled in angst and confusion as they peered into the heart of the city.

Mother, Minervina.

I realised then just how fragile my power and my fine reputation really were. If this persecution took hold I could not save them. I was to remain stationed here for another three months at least. *Three months?* I thought, smelling the first wafts of burning wood and flesh drifting from the forum, heard the piercing, animal screams of the deacon. In just one morning the city had swung from haven to Hades.

My mind exploded in a storm of thoughts as to how I could spirit them from this land at haste. My spinning head slowed at last as I thought of the cool, pleasant halls in the city of Nicomedia, my place of tutelage before the Persian War, hundreds upon hundreds of miles away to the north and west. My old teacher, Lactantius, could take them in. There, I tried to assure myself, they might be safe from this desert storm.

10

MAXENTIUS

'Euna? Get in here and take the boy somewhere!' Valeria snapped, pointing at her son – our son – as though he offended her merely by his presence.

'But, Mother, I...'

'Quiet, child. Go and busy yourself somewhere. Euna will find you some food.'

'But I'm not hungry, Mother, I...'

'Silence. Do as you are bid before I take the back of my hand to you!'

I watched in dismay as my son, Valerius Romulus – the light of my life and the core of my heart – turned away, his lip trembling and his eyes lost and saddened. Euna, the Syrian slave woman who all but played the part of Romulus' mother these days, scurried in from the next room with the boy's freshly laundered clothes under one arm, bowing to my wife as much to avoid her draconian gaze as out of deference. She grasped Valerius' forlorn hand, shot me a sympathetic look and then scuttled from the room.

'To what do we owe the pleasure of this morning's buoyant mood, light of my life?' I murmured with heavy irony, scrubbing my hands through my short hair and rubbing vigorously at the short, neat beard I had taken to wearing, largely because it annoyed Valeria.

As my wife spun and the full contempt of her gaze pierced me, I looked her up and down in the heartbeat before she reacted. She was beautiful in a cold, hard, ice-sculpted way. I would say on reflection that despite the fact that I loved her, she was far more beautiful on the outside, her soul and personality tainted with some permanent anger.

Since our wedding, I had learned that Valeria had railed against the match and had threatened to join the cult of Vesta as a virgin rather than follow her father's wishes and join with me. At the time I took this as youthful reluctance and rebellion. With the benefit of hindsight, it was a warning. In any event, no one defied Galerius the Herdsman – least of all his own daughter – and our wedding had gone ahead as planned.

The years since had done little to bring us closer together. In fact, apart from the duties a wife owes her husband, it had soon become a rare event that we even exchanged words.

I tried. The gods will remain my witness that I *tried* to make it work. Every long, cold, endless month of those years – and beyond – I tried to make it work. I did my best to love that cold marble woman who was less yielding than the statue of Minerva that stood outside our bedroom's window. But she appeared to have nothing but revulsion for me, as had quickly become apparent.

I am reasonably certain that if it weren't for the commands of her father and her own hubris she would have left me or fallen on a sword like a defeated general.

But despite the coldness and distance that ever existed between us, we had managed to sire Romulus, who was born healthy and strong but cursed with my looks – possibly a contributing factor to her indifference towards him. For while Romulus was to become the very light at the centre of my being and my hope for the future, he was to Valeria little more than a reminder that she was shackled to me in cold matrimony.

She had showed him little love, if any, and foisted him off on a series of wet nurses and then maternal slaves. I did my best to play the role of a true father, for I loved him deeply, and the bond between my son and I grew and strengthened. It made me smile to find him playing with my old wooden building blocks and soldiers, and further pleased me to see him so carefully aligning the streets in a mirrored reflection of myself those long years ago in the north.

Our relationship would never be enough to make my life truly companionable and warm, but it took away some of the bitterness I might feel towards his cold mother. Valeria might hate me, but she had given me Romulus and whatever she might do in life, I would always owe her for that.

This morning, though, she was close to unbearable – simply cold and angry and heedless of her family. And despite my almost playful needling, I knew why.

Messengers from the coastal watchtowers had reached the gates of Nicomedia this morning with news that the imperial fleet had been sighted out in the Propontis. Today, the great Diocletian was returning to the city, along with Valeria's father, Galerius...

...and his protégé, my first – very possibly my *only* – true friend: Constantine.

Valeria was in a state of agitation, desperate to see her father, who had been absent fighting in Persia and attempting to recover his reputation after the disaster at Carrhae, leaving her to wallow in the cesspit of her loveless marriage. Some might think she was simply excited to see her father; I had spent eight long years with her and knew her better. She saw only an opportunity to persuade her father to grant her a divorce, which we all knew he would not do, for bonds between ruling families are things to be tightly maintained.

I might have been downhearted at the thought, since there was still a part of me that clung to her, despite everything, and I could not imagine the horrible effect her departure would have on the boy. I might have been dejected, but for the thought that finally the long years of ennui at an empty imperial court might now be over. My father – who periodically stayed here, apparently solely to make clear his disappointment in me – would have his peers to bother with and might leave me alone.

And I was, I have to admit, interested to see what another half decade of warfare had done to my friend. While I had been languishing, he had been making something of a name for himself by all accounts. Word of his heroic exploits had reached Nicomedia regularly and I am forced to admit that despite my lack of interest in things military, I still envied him the excitement and exoticness of his time in the East while I played husband to an unresponsive wife and wandered a court bereft of excitement and activity.

My mother had eschewed the stresses of the court, choosing to raise my eight-year-old sister Fausta – who I had yet to meet beyond correspondence – in her home city of Apamea, far south in Syria. I missed her, particularly in the cold silences instilled by my wife.

Aside from the growing bond with my son, the only figures with whom I had found a personal connection had appeared a few months previously and taken up residence in the palace. Minervina – the young wife of Constantine – had arrived with her entourage, with child yet in the early days of the process, accompanied by the war hero's mother, for whom he had somehow managed to secure a residence at court, despite her estrangement. I had paid them a courtesy visit in their first days there and had found them to be pleasant and engaging ladies. I spent much time over the next few months entertaining them, and watching Romulus make them smile – my stony wife, of course, had nothing but bile and invective for the women and disapproved of my befriending them, but her antagonism towards them merely threw me ever more into their company.

And through the ladies, I also came to know Lactantius, who had been at court for some time, but who had been less than prominent until this pair arrived. I had apparently met the old man those many years ago in Augusta Treverorum, though at the time I had been young and he just a face in a sea of courtiers. Since then, he had been Constantine's tutor and therefore a friend of his mother, and with Lactantius I found the opportunity to expound on a number of engaging subjects over the cold autumn nights when Zephyrus blew the wind east across the Propontine Sea. He was a member of the Christian faith, though I found him to be pleasant and intelligent and in no way as arrogant and hostile as that strange sect are said to be.

Indeed, from his carefully couched words I harboured the suspicion that Constantine's mother followed that same sect, which somewhat explained his moving out of the shadows on her arrival. I simply enjoyed the exchange of intellectual debate and the opportunity to speak to an adult who did not treat me as an inconvenience. He argued the value of his faith admirably and, though I could hardly see it as a replacement for the *true* gods, such debate gave me a healthy opportunity to practise my rhetorical skills. I even contemplated asking him to take on my son as a student.

But on that morning, when activity boomed and life flooded back into the palace, my association with Constantine's former tutor was to come to an end. For as Valeria glared coldly at me and opened her mouth to bury me under fresh invective, the door slammed back against the frame and my father strode in, a purposeful gait about him.

'Where's the boy?'

In his wake, body slaves and other minions flustered about him, fastening his rich cloak with an obscenely expensive gilt brooch, buffing his Persian-style footwear and sliding rings onto fingers, straightening his tunic and generally preparing him to be seen by the public.

'Outside,' I managed, surprised at the interruption. 'Valeria sent him...'

'Never mind!' Father cut me off with a dismissive wave of his hand, which he then turned on the body slaves. 'Diocletian is closing on the city with Galerius and the commanders of the army.'

'So I hear, Father. There will be celebration tonight, I presume.' This would not be like the last time at Antioch, when the pair entered the city in a parade of humiliation. Now, the war had gone well at last, and this would be a more exiting, uplifting affair.

'Doubtless,' Father said gruffly. His eyes narrowed as he regarded my calm, open face, my mouth tilted to humour with the uplifting thought of the coming liveliness. 'Have you been listening to the reports of Antioch and Diocletian's pronouncements?'

'I hear little, Father, apart from my myriad failings as a son or as a husband.'

The comment was lost, seemingly unnoticed by either of the room's other noble occupants as Valeria ignored me and adjusted her gold hair net in the bronze mirror, preparing for her father's arrival, and my own sire traditionally disregarded whatever I said unless it impacted directly on his current thought process.

'Those Judean cultists have been causing trouble again. Diocletian has had to deal with one of their leaders in Antioch and there is talk of wider repercussions – a new swathe of Neronian burnings.'

My expression remained unchanged. I had little or no connection with Judeans, barring my visits to Constantine's family and my late-night discussions with the ageing Lactantius. The Christians were ever a troublesome bunch to the imperial pride, in their staunch unwillingness to bow to the emperor's clear divinity, but I had never seen any of their actions as more than a flea on a dog's back. What were such troubles to me?

'You will have to stop visiting those people.'

'Who?'

'The family of Constantine and their old fool. They are... they are *Christians*, boy!' he hissed in a disapproving, almost conspiratorial voice.

'His father is an emperor,' I responded in disbelief. 'They carry powerful blood. They will not be treated like common criminals, even if that is true.'

'You are still young and naïve, Maxentius. You are weak and spend too much time with your nose buried in your books and too little listening to your betters and improving in the practice fields. But Diocletian is a man of action – a man who wrested the empire by force from that lunatic Carinus. And Galerius, who moves with him, is a lover beyond reason of blood and torture. If they are turning their gaze upon these Christians it matters not whether their followers are commoners or half-divine; they will experience his wrath as deeply as anyone.'

He grumbled as though he were trying to explain Vitruvian principles to a hog.

'You are a grown man now, Maxentius, and destined for the purple when I am gone, despite your failings, and so I will not *tell* you what to do, but I will urge you one time only: break off your friendship with those women and that doddering old fool. They are destined for Tartarus in the empire's cleansing flames.'

My father was ever immune to reason, and so I simply nodded. It was noncommittal, of course, but Father seemed to accept it as an agreement to his request, and I left it at that – life would become unutterably dull were I to eschew my only intelligent sources of discourse. With the flurry of events that would be set in motion by the arrival of the full imperial court, such quiet social engagements would seem unlikely to continue anyway.

I thought with a smile of my boy, busy in the gardens playing the part of Horatius saving the Sublician bridge from the army of Clusium, their part taken by a variety of shrubs. The boy had a love of playing such games and reminded me more in truth of Constantine and his ever-eager sword arm than of me and my own more passive tendencies.

But Romulus and I were still two parts of a heart regardless of any differences. Fatherhood had changed me; saved me, to some extent. Fatherhood changed most men, not that it was always for the better, as our own sires had demonstrated.

11

CONSTANTINE

Thirteen days after leaving Antioch and taking to sea, we were almost within sight of Nicomedia. I stood at the prow of the quinquereme as it sliced through the placid, turquoise waters of the Propontis under the power of three hundred oarsmen. The fleet – some forty vessels strong – followed in our wake. The crisp and still January morning air was spiced by the salt spray and my eyes darted to the flash of leaping silvery fish shoals that broke the surface as we cut past one verdant island after another.

Yet despite such a pleasant vista, my guts churned. The events that had taken place back in Antioch in the last few months dangled at the forefront of my mind. The flayed Christian corpses, the savage beatings, the burnings. I glanced over my shoulder to the imperial flagship at the heart of the fleet. Diocletian and Galerius were but two purple-robed blotches on the deck.

I faced forward again and gazed to the northern horizon. There lay a faint outline of land – the two outstretching fingers of rock where Europa and Asia Minor almost touched. It was a sight I oft marvelled at. Little did I know then just what significance that place would hold in years to come. But that day, I thought little of anything other than my immediate future in Nicomedia. Mother and Minervina, alone. I had sent them to this city thinking that here they might be far from the tide of religious violence in the desert cities. Yet the words of the Eastern Augustus and his Caesar in Antioch had spread like fire. The Edict of Persecution, as it was now known, was being pursued with a fervour in cities all over the desert provinces. Some gossiped that it would soon spread further afield.

As far as Nicomedia? I fretted. I longed to know that my loved ones had not come to harm in the fervour of the anti-Christians. I drew the silver silk scarf my wife had given me when last we had embraced. I pressed it to my lips and inhaled her sweet scent. I felt the urge to pray at that moment, then scoffed at the notion. 'To the old gods, who seek to burn my loved ones? Or to the Christian God who stands back and watches as his people are slain like lambs?'

'Nicomedia is in sight!' a cry came from a member of the crew straddling the mast.

I grasped the rail of the vessel, realising we had turned east, to sail into the Gulf of Astacus. Then I saw it for the first time in nearly five years; the beetling, sun-bleached walls of Nicomedia, perched at the end of the gulf. This was Emperor Diocletian's grand seat of power. The thriving port city had served as my place of tutelage and then as my winter quarters during the years of campaigning with Galerius in the Gothic lands.

When we docked at the walled harbour, it seemed the entire city had come out to greet us. Coloured ribbons flitted in the gentle afternoon breeze, hands waved, beaming and often ruddy faces cheered, filling the wharf side and the square adjacent. Children climbed on the recently hewn columns and statues, eager for a better view.

The cohorts spilled from the decks first, and I was quick to follow. We waded through the throng, a line of mail-clad urban guards making a path for us. Prostitutes pressed against them, their breasts bulging and jiggling as they sought to catch the eye of the men at the front of the column – the men with the biggest purses. Likewise, traders cried out in a polyglot babble, waving trinkets, wineskins and some rather abrasive-looking sexual implements.

As eager as I was to push on to the palace, Galerius and Diocletian, seated on litters, seemed intent on milking the applause, savouring every moment of what was tantamount to a triumph. When Galerius barked at the Urban Cohort to slow the advance, I felt my blood boil. I looked ahead, over the sea of faces, past the towering *horrea* grain silos, the vast marble cistern, the great colonnaded halls and temples, on along the main way to the palace complex at the heart of the city. *That* was where Mother and Minervina waited. *That* was where I wanted to be.

I spotted Batius just ahead of me, weighing up a two-pronged device one trader had handed him.

'Two denarii, and I make nothing from it!' the trader insisted.

'Hmm.' Batius curled his bottom lip, moving the contraption back and forth, his tongue poking out and one eye closed as if imagining the possibilities.

'She will scream like a harpy... and then beg for more, guaranteed!' the trader added.

'I'll take two.' Batius shrugged, tossing the man some bronze coins.

Two? I gawped, then shook the somewhat unsavoury

image that followed from my head and grabbed the big man by the shoulder. 'Batius, come on, let's forge ahead.'

'Hmm?' Batius said, confused. His mind had clearly wandered to salacious ground.

'The palace. Mother, Minervina!'

The big man's face lit up in realisation and he nodded hurriedly, then ploughed ahead, breaking past the urban guard and on ahead of the triumphal procession. I followed close behind, evading the well-wishers and profiteers until at last we were clear of the crowd.

We hurried through the streets and I thought that nothing could slow us, but slow we did. An acrid stench of burning flesh wafted across our path. A shiver crept across my skin as I located the source: a dozen stakes with crumpled, blackened and smouldering corpses tied to them.

I spotted the charred form of a Chi-Rho pendant dangling from one corpse's neck, and all my fears rose a cold blade through my insides. News of the Edict of Persecution had indeed reached this city – just as I had feared. A grinning, cold-eyed garrison legionary stood by the smouldering corpses, watching us, seeing our horror, knowing he had the weight of the emperor's word behind him.

'What's wrong, soldier?' the legionary sneered at Batius and I, seeing our basic military tunics and mistaking us for off-duty rank and file. 'Are your sympathies with these dogs who deny the true gods?' He levelled his spear as he said this, clearly eager to agitate. Another pair of legionaries appeared at this point, flanking the aggressive one and adding their own growling expressions.

Batius approached them as if they were unarmed, walking until the tip of the cold-eyed one's spear pressed against the breast of his tunic. 'You, runt, will address me as centurion, and my companion as tribunus!' he growled like an angered mastiff. The cold-eyed one retracted his spear at this, the colour draining from his face.

'I'm sorry, sir,' he stammered.

Likewise, the other two backed away a step, dropping their gazes to their feet.

I stepped forward next. 'I have spent nigh on fifteen years fighting far from my home, always but an inch from the blade edge of some wild-eyed Goth, Aegyptian rebel or Persian giant. Every night I have bowed my head before Mars, begged for his wisdom to guide me, prayed that he would be with me on the battlefield.' I cast a grim look beyond him to the burnt cadavers. 'Never once in those years did I seek to shame him by slaying defenceless citizens in his name.'

'But... but the emperor has decreed it!' the legionary stammered.

And if I draped a purple cloak around the shoulders of a rabid wolf, would you obey its demented howls? my thoughts snarled as I cast him a blistering look.

The man sensed my ire and sensed it well, his gaze dropping to his boots.

'Tell me, how many have died like this?'

The legionary gulped and poked out his tongue to dampen his lips, droplets of sweat darting across his face. 'Hundreds,' he croaked. 'There have been burnings every day.'

Madness consumed me at that moment. I lunged forward and grappled the man's collar. 'If you have so much as troubled my family—'

Batius' hand pressed on my shoulder. 'Sir. We should hurry, to the palace.'

I closed my eyes, pushed the dog back and sent him staggering.

We hurried onwards, then passed through the palace gates and gardens in a blur of salutes, soon arriving at the main portico and entering the great hall. The noise of the city fell away almost instantly and, as usual, I felt dwarfed in this vast, domed chamber. Torches crackled along the walls, but the air was cool and the green-veined marble floor and porphyry columns lent a polished sheen to everything, uplighting the gilded busts and fine frescoes. Silence. Sanctuary?

Suddenly, the chaotic sound of paws and claws scraping on the smooth floor arose. An Agassian hound came skidding round one corner, ears and tongue streaming like banners in the wind. Batius fell to one knee: 'Ferox!' he cried in delight, extending his arms to catch the hound and embrace it like a beloved child. The creature had been little more than a pup when we had last been here.

'It's been some time, eh, sir?' Batius cooed as Ferox licked his face in a frenzy.

'Nearly five years,' I agreed, glancing round the vast hall. In my years alongside Galerius, I had been either at war or here, in this great palace complex, studying. I thought again of my tutor, old Lactantius, at that moment. We had spent many days and evenings discussing the sciences of nature, the stars, the empire's origins, religion – all that was non-martial. The old man – a staunch Christian – was forever eager to bring me to the religion, I recalled with a smile. And sometimes he would focus on the power of the mind.

Press your thumb to your forefinger, think of the good times. Do this often and one will conjure the other.

I found myself doing just this yet again.

'Ah, yes, the mind is both devilishly complex and divinely simple, is it not?' a familiar, frail voice echoed through the chamber. Ferox' ears perked up and his head tilted to one side. Batius and I swung to see the old tutor hobbling through towards us with the aid of a cane, his white hair and beard more unruly than ever. I was both elated to set eyes upon him and saddened to see the toll these last five years had taken upon him. He pointed to my finger and thumb. 'The last time I saw you, Constantine, you dismissed that technique as a pile of horsesh—'

'You are well?' I grasped him by the shoulders, cutting him off.

'I wouldn't put it like that. My bones ache in the colder months and—'

'I mean these persecutions,' I hissed in a hushed tone, cutting him short again. My eyes fell to the spot where he usually wore a Chi-Rho necklace. It was absent.

'Ah!' Lactantius said, smiling wryly, then he pulled me close, embracing me as he whispered: 'The burnings began last month. My faith is as strong as ever – stronger even. But I am not one for martyrdom – alas I am not brave enough. Thus, I chose to stow my amulet and bite my tongue whenever those animals came looking for more people to throw on the flames.' He pushed back from me just a little. 'Sooner than they think, they will be judged for their sins, and me too, perhaps, for my cowardice.'

'Nonsense, tutor. You are alive and that means more than another blackened corpse. You can use your silver tongue to conjure sense into the pair who brought this about.'

'Diocletian and the Herdsman.' His face fell. 'So the rumours from the desert cities are true – they have returned? Then I fear the brutality will only escalate.'

This brought my thoughts spinning back to my two loved ones. 'Tell me, old tutor. Please, tell me they are safe also – Mother, Minervina?'

Lactantius' face remained grave and for a heartbeat I felt my blood run cold. Then, like a dawn ray, a smile split his features, furrowing every age line. 'They are well, Constantine. I encouraged them to worship discreetly as I do. Go to them – they are in your old chambers.'

I spent the next days shut away in the southern wing of the palace, in the high-vaulted chambers that were my home in this city. I nuzzled into Minervina's neck and whispered in her ear. I stroked her pregnant belly and we chattered lovingly about our unborn child, just a few months away from coming into the world. Mother sat with us through those days, her eyes sparkling, alive with the promise of her first grandchild. Slaves brought delicate fare to the chambers – grapes, fine wine, cheeses, fresh bread, dates, baked mackerel, garum and pheasant. Lactantius and Batius visited us every other day. The only other person to come to us was a red-cheeked older woman – an *obstetrix* who had been helping with Minervina's morning sickness. In there, away from the throng and the goings-on in the city, we were well, bellies full and hearts hale.

But we were living under a shield. Whenever we opened the shutters to walk out onto the balcony and stand in the crisp winter air, or late at night when the bustle of the streets had died away... we heard it: screaming, crying, baying. Soon afterwards, a faint and acrid tang of charred meat would spoil the air.

We tried to ignore it and remain in isolation, but I knew I would have to face up to the duties my post demanded. The first of which would be attending a ceremony to divine the future, to justify the persecutions. That evening – the kalends of February – there was a rap on the door. I looked up.

Minervina and Mother looked up too. Our smiles dissolved like morning mist. 'I won't be away for long,' I said, throwing on my woollen cloak.

I slipped outside into the corridor to find Batius and Lactantius awaiting me. Old Lactantius looked as enthusiastic about the coming ceremony as I did, but Batius wore something of a satisfied grin – no doubt refreshed from trying out his two-pronged devices with the local prostitutes.

'So what can we expect from this?' I asked the pair of them – conscious of how long I had been locked away from reality.

'A bull will die, a man will rake through its innards, then he will throw together some tale to pander to the silver- and gold-painted fools,' Lactantius said flatly, his wooden cane tapping as he walked.

Batius snorted, shaken from his filthy reverie. 'Nah, this haruspex they've brought in to read the animal's entrails – apparently he's well thought of. Tagis of Etruria. He'll divine only what he sees.' He scratched at his freshly shorn scalp. 'No arse-licking for the painted pair.'

'Then this could be… interesting,' I said, my guts tightening.

We came to the great hall of the palace. As always, Diocletian and Galerius had taken centre stage. They stood in the middle of the marble floor by a red porphyry water font. Courtiers and acolytes stood in a thick circle, with Joviani legionaries ring-fencing the Eastern Augustus and his Caesar. We walked to join this ring of spectators. When our footsteps died, only the crackling of the torches around the chamber walls served to stave off total silence.

The spell was broken by an absurdly incongruous animal groaning along with a scraping and stamping of hooves on the polished floor. All heads turned to see a group of Joviani sentries leading in a bulky old bull. The creature had been fed some vicious concoction to sap its strength, I was sure – its eyes were bulging and wild, its step erratic and weak, hooves sliding this way and that. I caught the creature's eye for just a moment and sensed the fear in its heart. Two non-military men walked with the bull. I recognised one of them as Tagis, the haruspex from Italia, from the long-sleeved silver robe and the pointed white hat he wore. The other was the *Rex Sacrorum*, the master of sacrifice – unmistakable in his hooded dark robes that covered all but his pale lips and withered jaw. A ceremonial axe hung from his belt.

The circle parted to let the dazed bull through to the centre.

Diocletian watched with narrowed eyes. Galerius looked on with a chill grin set on his face, like a crow readying to feast. As the Rex Sacrorum and Tagis the haruspex set to work, circling the beast, chanting in booming tones that filled the hall, I wondered at the outcome of this show. The lives of many thousands of Roman citizens would hang on Tagis' divinations.

'Tagis is a good man,' a voice whispered next to me, 'but his words will be twisted to suit the imperial agenda.'

I turned to see a young, lean man who had sidled up next to me. I eyed him for a moment. Behind the neatly trimmed hair and beard, I recognised that fine-boned face, the tanned skin and the dark eyes.

He offered me a nervous smile. 'I have never forgotten you, Constantine,' he whispered, extending an arm gingerly.

For a moment I forgot all that was going on in the centre of the circle before me. I grasped his hand with mine and pulled him closer to embrace him. 'Nor I you, Maxentius,' I said in reply. A few eyes turned from the circle and glowered upon us in disapproval, so we returned to standing tall and facing the proceedings. As soon as the disapproving eyes were averted, I leaned in to whisper in Maxentius' ear: 'How long has it been, friend?' I eyed his muscled bronze cuirass, hanging awkwardly on his lithe frame. 'Seven years? How goes it with Valeria?' I smiled at him, naïvely assuming he and his wife must enjoy the same kind of love shared by Minervina and me. But he did not return the smile. Indeed, he struggled to maintain eye contact, reluctantly watching the fate of the bull instead.

'Valeria is… she has her ways,' was all he said.

I pitied him then, remembering the strong, sometimes glacial woman I had met on their wedding day. I had figured then that it would take a man with an iron fortitude to keep up with her. Something else struck me then, and I felt like a fool for forgetting. 'Your boy!'

'Romulus,' he said, grinning as if I had just handed him the keys to the Palatine villas in Rome. 'He is golden, friend, he is everything. You should come with us one morning to the circus stables. Romulus has a love of horses and chariots. He could learn a lot from you, I am certain.' I noticed his eyes taking in the nicks and scars on my hands and face. 'We've been living here for some years. In that time we've heard many tales of your exploits in Aegyptus and on the Persian borders.' Then he leaned closer to be sure that only I would hear, flicking a finger at Galerius. 'But the agents of that foul bastard have been sure to champion his part in it all, as if he alone won the Persian War.'

'And you think this haruspex will have his words altered to warrant these persecutions?' I said, watching Tagis.

'I am certain of it. Remember, I have spent many years in the court of my "great" father, the Emperor of the West. I have seen the truest of words tied in knots.'

I looked up to follow Maxentius' gaze across to the far

side of the circle. There stood Maximian, here in the eastern provinces for the first time in many years. The years seemed to have doubled the man's size. Portly and ruddy-faced, his beard spiralled down the breastplate of his oversized cuirass and his eyes were hooded and bloodshot.

'You have been back to the West?' I asked. 'Tell me, what do the people there say about my father?'

Maxentius offered me a grin. 'Relax. He may be Galerius' western equivalent, but that is where the similarities end. Constantius has proved to be a fine ruler. He is still locked in war with the rebels of Britannia, and we hear nothing but praise for his exploits – much like your own. To achieve such glory despite his illness is...' His words trailed off when he saw my troubled expression.

'He is growing weaker?' I asked. 'I have heard how the men now call him the pale one.'

'He takes it all in good heart. Constantius Chlorus – Hammer of the North! He is still strong enough to rise from his bed every day and lead the legions to battle. So do not trouble yourself with his state of health,' he tried to assure me. He looked awkwardly around the room for something else to say, then clicked his fingers. 'We should meet and talk more. As I say, come to the stables. A new stock has arrived recently. Romulus has been training and grooming one stallion, a dappled grey named Celeritas who is almost ready to serve as a war horse. Perhaps he would be ideal for you?'

What a fine gesture, I thought. I returned the smile and tilted my head to one side in agreement.

We both hushed when Tagis and the Rex Sacrorum stopped chanting. Silence dominated the hall once more. Tagis stood back while the Rex Sacrorum pulled a hammer and a set of shears from a bag. The bull looked up, terrified, its glazed eyes searching the shade under the pontiff's hood for some sign of mercy. The Rex Sacrorum snipped a lock of hair from the bull's brow, causing the beast to dip its head in fright.

'See how the creature assents?' the pontiff asked the audience in a rasping tone, his arms extended and his palms upturned.

'Proceed,' Diocletian said.

With ferocious swipe of the hammer onto the bull's skull and a crack of bone, the beast groaned, stunned. Then, with an equally nimble swish of an unseen dagger, the creature's throat was opened. Blood sheeted out onto the marbled floor. In moments, the bull's legs wobbled and collapsed under it.

Tagis crouched by the creature, then set to work eviscerating it. The tearing of flesh echoed through the hall and the stench of innards permeated the air. I looked on with glazed eyes, seeing the bull's liver and entrails laid out on the pool of blood while Tagis studied them. I noticed then a bead of sweat darting down the haruspex's forehead, and the pulsing of the veins in his neck.

'Well?' Diocletian asked.

'Come on, man, *come on!*' Galerius snarled unnecessarily.

Tagis looked up, shaking his head. 'The signs are not good. They say the persecutions are wr—'

'Silence!' Galerius strode forward to loom over Tagis. His towering presence was enough to still the haruspex. 'Now, Haruspex...' Galerius' gaze was intense '...are you *sure?*' He said this with a wicked grin. In the background, a pair of Joviani legionaries moved a little closer to the circle, their hands on their spatha hilts.

Maxentius sighed. 'As I suspected,' he whispered in my ear.

Tagis' wide eyes darted to the Joviani legionaries and then fell slowly to the bull's innards once more. 'Perhaps there is a bad presence in the air – skewing the divination?' he mumbled.

'Aye, there is,' Galerius roared. 'Christians!'

Diocletian stopped his Caesar then called him over. The pair remained deep in discussion for a short while, then swung round to address the circle of spectators. 'If this bull has died in vain,' Diocletian shrieked, 'because the Christian presence in the city has marred the abilities of our haruspex, then perhaps we should cleanse the air?'

I saw Tagis' face pale. His words had not just been twisted. They had been pulped and mangled beyond recognition.

Galerius continued. 'Tomorrow, we will begin the sacrifice tests. Every citizen will be forced to come forward and prove they are faithful only to the true gods. No Christian will offer sacrifice, and so they will be rooted out. Then they will burn more brightly than ever before – enough to light up Nicomedia's streets on the darkest of nights. All efforts will be channelled into ridding this city of them by the month's end. No one will be spared. Beggars, whores, palace guards... noble families.'

His words cut into me like a cold dagger. And I am sure that he swept his gaze over me as he said that. I looked to the haruspex. Tagis' face was awash with sweat now. His lips quivered.

'Domine, Caesar,' he said at last. 'I was mistaken.' Tagis bowed his head, his eyes screwed shut tight in disgust with himself. 'The signs are good. The Edict of Persecution is favoured by the gods.'

I felt a dull nausea in my gut, rising to my throat. The earnest Tagis had been forced to falsify the reading of the bull's entrails and to validate the persecutions – merely to stave off an accelerated cull of the Christians of Nicomedia.

'Excellent!' Diocletian stepped forward and threw his hands up, his face bent in a joyous smile. 'Now, let us celebrate with a feast!'

The bull's corpse was taken away to be butchered. Barely an hour after its death, it was served up to a lengthy dining table, hemmed by the ruddy-faced pigs who had watched the creature die. They set about gorging on the cooked flesh, laughing like jackals and spilling wine down their robes. Across from me, I saw how uncomfortable Maxentius was, flanked by his fat boar of a father and some pallid and equally corpulent bald senator. But I would have given my last denarius to be in his place and away from the pair who flanked me. Galerius on my left and his loathsome son, Candidianus, on my right.

Galerius supped great mouthfuls of wine then stood to speak across the table to all who would listen. 'A triumph – that's what this was. Just as the Oracle of Didyma gave her support to our edict... eventually... now this most famous haruspex has lauded our decision.' He grinned at the sweating, pale-faced Tagis, who seemed to have lost his appetite.

The acolytes amongst the diners applauded his words, then the Herdsman sat down once again. 'You see, men do not act on the word of gods, Tribunus,' Galerius enthused to me as he gorged on a cut of rare meat. The blood, fat and juices ran down his chin, and strings dangled from his teeth as he spoke. 'For gods cannot speak. Power lies in the hands of those appointed to speak *for* the gods.'

My patience was just about holding out, when Candidianus rocked back in laughter from the conversation he was having with some other courtier. His laughter was shrill and piercing like a gull's. Worse, his elbow barged into mine, knocking a splash of wine from my cup and over my tunic.

'Those who speak *for* the gods,' Galerius repeated, his foul breath offending me.

'The weakest dogs tend to howl the loudest,' I snapped.

Instantly, I regretted it. The inebriated sheen drained from the Herdsman's eyes in a heartbeat, his pupils shrinking, his lips pursing, twitching with ire.

'Be careful, Tribunus. You are fortunate to even have my ear. You have not grown to become what I hoped you might in our years together. I once thought you would succeed me, become my Caesar when I eventually ascend to become Augustus of the East,' he said, waving a dismissive hand. Then, so sure he had crushed my spirit with his clumsy rhetoric, he once again fixed me with his gaze. 'But despite your failings over the years, you are not a wasted labour... yet.'

'What do you want from me, Caesar?' I asked, trying to stave off the emotion that trembled in my chest.

He leaned in close at that moment, his lips an inch from my ear. 'I want your *heart!*' he hissed like an asp. 'No more recalcitrant behaviour. No more whispers of your poisoned words about me. From now on, you will exist only to obey me.'

I backed away, seeing from his inky-black eyes and the contorted grimace on his face that he was serious. 'You demand fealty?'

His grimace faded and a cold smile played on his lips. '*Now* you understand. The way you act around me, the way you look at me... makes me think you are not entirely loyal. And that is not good for you... not good at all.' He tutted, then picked up an apple and turned it over in his hand. He drew a knife and rested it on the apple's flesh. With a jerk of his wrist, he sliced the apple in two. 'Nor is it good for those you care for – especially if they are Christian.'

The threat struck me dumb. I dropped my gaze to my untouched food and struggled to resist the urge to vomit.

12

MAXENTIUS

'It appals me, Maxentius. It is simply abhorrent; not just un-Roman, but inhuman. Most of all, it is short-sighted.' I looked at Constantine out of the corner of my eye as we leaned on the marble balustrade of the balcony, which offered us a grand view of the great city of Nicomedia, the eastern hub of Roman power, with all its nobility and culture. This shining jewel of civilisation was illuminated by a glow that would have been simply breath-taking, had one not been able to divine the source of the radiance.

Two *horrea* – the grain stores that held supplies for the city – blazed in the early morning light, still burning after hours of attempting to halt the inferno. The city's *vigiles* were stretched too thin to be truly effective, further units still active with other blazes over by the city gates, near the docks, in the warehouse district and across the slums. A quick glance to my left, tearing my gaze from the granaries, and I was treated once again to the sight of the palace's northern wing, standing like the charred and blackened bones of some great monster.

The riots had been sporadic and extremely hard to control as the instigators melted away each time before the authorities could even reach the troubles, leaving only angry citizens, burning buildings, seething sedition and a number of execution spots empty and awaiting their next victims. I wasn't so sure about the persecutions being 'inhuman', but they were certainly short-sighted and badly handled by our imperial masters.

Following the initial flash of the persecutions, Diocletian had ordered the new, glorious – and I have to admit as a life-long lover of great architecture, it was *truly* glorious – temple of the Christian God in Nicomedia razed. All the belongings of that strange, insular cult were confiscated and their books burned. The emperor's edict had then been published officially, his pronouncement of the criminal status of Christians set in inflexible words, and those words had been sent like storm crows to every corner of the empire, heralding charred and blood-soaked torments wherever they were read aloud.

The burning of the palace had been the first great act of defiance in the wake of the edict, and had the emperors perhaps taken a little more care in how they had dealt with the matter, the situation could have been defused and the city returned to normal. Instead, a bloody hunt and extraction of confessions had begun, tearing through the population of the Christians – and in some cases simply those who were unpopular enough to land them the label 'Christian'.

Four men of Diocletian's own household had been deemed responsible for the palace blaze, and their fates had been horrifying even to those who spat upon that sect. A palace chamberlain, a government official and an officer in the palace guard had all met their end protesting their innocence, each tortured to the limits of human endurance and then their broken corpses burned as an example to the people.

Yet these three had been but accomplices of the emperor's

own valet, Peter the *Cubicularius*, who had denied nothing as they hung him by the wrists before the palace walls and scourged him expertly, never enough in so short a time to drive from him his wits. And when his bones were broken and his skin torn, they saved him from the agonies of his ravaged flesh by peeling it from him in strips, leaving him raw and shrieking. I had watched that afternoon as they had taken down the thing that had been Peter – a man whom I had known in no small measure – and poured salt and vinegar over his glistening pink form before lowering him onto red hot irons and roasting him slowly before the jeering crowd.

Peter Cubicularius departed the world of men suffering a fate the likes of which no Roman had witnessed since the wicked days of Nero. Like his 'accomplices', his execution was meant as a message to the people of Nicomedia.

It worked.

Not as Diocletian and Galerius had intended, though. As Peter left the world, so did sense and security. For days on end riots raged unchecked and unresolved, random insurgents spitted and roasted in place of the real culprits, who remained unknown. Spring came to the land, bringing a spray of colour to every flowerbed, greenery to the trees and energy to the wildlife. Yet the relief of spring was subdued by the endless executions, burnings and troubles.

And this morning as I stood on the balcony with my friend was no different. Six more men were scheduled to die in another hour or two, including the head pontiff of the Christian sect in Nicomedia – Anthimius. Good firewood was becoming scarce in the city and so Anthimius and his companions would be sent to meet their curious God under a blade. My father had required my attendance, and I was already hardened to the fact. I had used every fragment of my energy in refusing his demand that my son also come to watch, and had little reserve left to argue on my own behalf.

Constantine would not be attending.

During the announcement of the edict and that farcical bull sacrifice, my friend had found himself at odds with Galerius. I had watched as the two men faced off against one another at the meal and had worried for Constantine's future, given his tendency to speak his mind heedless of the consequences. But he had managed to contain himself somehow and in the days that followed, he had stayed out of the way of his 'mentor', claiming the need to be close to his wife, who was largely restricted to her suite during the later stages of her pregnancy.

Consequently, he and I had the opportunity to spend time together, he distancing himself from Galerius and the horrors of the edict, and I keeping myself away from Valeria and the coldness of her gaze and sharpness of her tongue. Young Romulus, always a figure to lighten my days, came with me on my visits, and Constantine was good to him, like a favoured uncle – the pair spending many mornings training and grooming my horse Celeritas at the stables, while Batius and his hound would play by the paddock. Looking back, I suspect that apart from myself, my old friend was the only real family Romulus ever experienced.

I turned from the balcony and poured two glasses of wine, watering them appropriately, and then shuffled back, handing one to my friend. Back inside, through the thick drapes, I could hear Romulus entertaining Constantine's ladies with his rendition of a song his tutor had been teaching him. At only eight years of age, he was blissfully immune to the terrors going on around him, and I ever strived to keep it that way.

Taking a sip of my wine, I watched the roiling smoke darkening the sky above the granaries.

'It is not inhuman, Constantine. In fact, it is *all too human*. You have been away fighting wars, witnessing the nobility of the honoured enemy and revelling in the glory of the hard-earned victory. And in that time I have sat and watched the discoloured underbelly of this empire with all its sickening ugliness.'

Constantine turned to me then, and I almost stepped back from his expression. He pinned me with that cold, unyielding stare and his voice issued almost in a hiss.

'You know *nothing* of war, Maxentius. You have no idea the things I have witnessed, the things I have done. You are innocent, my young friend. Pray to whomever you wish that you never have to stand in the blood and filth of friend and enemy alike while you watch acts of evil perpetrated in the name of the empire.'

I fell silent, then. I could see in his eyes that pushing him further would gain me nothing. In the silence that followed, I could hear Romulus and Minervina reciting the names of the consuls from the time of Augustus, a seemingly endless list his tutor had been drilling into him for days now. A change of tack was required, perhaps?

'I know you worry for them, Constantine. And yet they remain safe.'

'So far.'

'They have followed Lactantius' example and kept their beliefs to themselves. Whatever Galerius might threaten, the consequences of him accusing your family would be extremely troublesome for him, and unless you push him he will do nothing.'

'They should not *have* to hide their beliefs, Maxentius.'

I frowned as I took another pull of my wine. 'Don't tell me you *share* their creed?' I asked in whispered incredulity.

Somehow it seemed reasonable that the old man and the ladies might be influenced by this strange cult, but the idea that a hero of Rome and man of the sword like Constantine might do so struck me as absurd.

'No,' he replied, 'but nor do I feel threatened by them. Their God is used as an excuse to confiscate whatever the emperors desire and murder those whom they fear. Whether I be one of them or not, they should have no cause to fear simply on account of their beliefs.'

I pursed my lips. It was a subject with which I had some difficulty. After all this time, I was still undecided in my opinions on these Christians who defied the law and burned cities and yet claimed a moral high ground I could not quite see for myself. In truth and in retrospect, I would have found *no* redeeming features in the whole cult had it not been for the examples of Constantine's family.

'No one wants to stop them worshipping their God, Constantine, but to deny the divinity of the emperor is simple treason. There can be no refuting it. The Christians' blind refusal to acknowledge Diocletian's Godhood—' it never occurred to me for a moment to apply the same term to my father for some reason '—is what brings this upon them. And while I would not have heaped harm upon them in the manner of this vicious edict, neither would I rush to argue their case. I, for one, worry for the future of the empire if a sizeable portion of its people will not honour their ancestral gods.'

'And what future is there for an empire that does not recognise its people's changing beliefs?'

'Now you sound like Lactantius,' I said with a slight smile, hoping to lighten the subject, though my friend met my words with an inscrutable silence. 'What will you do?'

'Stay with Minervina and Mother until the child is born. Until the painted Titans who occupy the thrones summon me. Until Nicomedia is nothing but ash.'

His tone had darkened with his mood and as I opened my mouth to try and placate him with some soothing words of support for his increasing isolation, he threw down the rest of his glass and turned a dark look on me.

'You had best attend your father before he has to come looking for you,' he said. 'If you wish, you can leave Romulus with us while you go to warm your hands over the embers of the bishop of Nicomedia. The boy will be safe here.'

I sighed unhappily but agreed. When I turned to leave and strode from the balcony, he still had not looked up, and I worried for my friend. For all his glorious exploits, he was languishing here in a dark place under the dread gaze of his master, with only the women to brighten his days. Sadly, given my father, my wife and my child, it was a situation I shared in some small measure.

I stood on the raised dais shivering despite the heat. My father and Diocletian sat upon their thrones as befitted the two men who shared god-like control of the empire. Yet the pedant in me could not help but baulk at the sight of Galerius on the senior emperor's far side. Constantine's father, second in command to my own, was still busy in Britannia fighting back endless waves of blue-painted barbarians. But here was Galerius – his peer – seated in power, displayed to the public almost as my own father's equal. The favour the Herdsman enjoyed from Diocletian gnawed at me. Though I felt no great paternal ties to my father, he should not be so blatantly outshone by such a black-hearted swine.

My chewing over such matters was soon brought to an end as the murmur of the crowd faded away to reveal the rumble and clack of cart wheels and the drumming of hooves on the stones of the street.

Two carts appeared between the long line of Herculiani with their black eagle on red banners and their opposites – the Joviani with their pale blue. They came slowly, as befitted a funeral, the cart wheels bouncing and jolting on the uneven flags, the figures inside thrown around like a child's ragged dolls, held in only by the fact that they were tied with restraining ropes to upright poles, which kept them visible.

Pieces of rotten fruit and browned vegetable matter bounced off the figures – three in each cart. All had clearly suffered torture prior to their arrival in this place of execution by the city walls. The carts rumbled slowly to a halt; the population jeering at the condemned Christians. I had no idea whether I was the only one who noticed, or whether others did but no one cared, but here and there in the crowd of onlookers were wails of anguish for the prisoners. Indeed, as the second cart slowed behind the first, one citizen managed somehow to wriggle through the barrier of soldiers and over to the cart, where he began to intone some prayer, reaching up to the doomed men only to have his skull split by the butt of a Joviani spear and be dragged back and thrown, dazed and bleeding, into the crowd.

While I had no great love for – or hatred of – these Christians, I found it hard not to admire the poise and nobility with which they seemed to be facing their fate. It was then it first struck me that the deaths of such men was an unnecessary waste. Whatever they believed, such steel of spirit was sadly lacking in a lot of the more 'noble' Romans with whom I was acquainted. I thought back on my earlier words to Constantine: *while I would not have heaped harm upon them in the manner of this vicious edict, neither would I rush to argue their case.*

There had to be a way to *use* them rather than *abusing* them...

The first man to step from the cart, like the other five, was dressed only in a dirty, ragged sack, covered and stained with dirt and blood. But his bearing was military. He stood proud, with his chin high and I knew, just looking at him, that he was a soldier. What had brought him so low, I couldn't imagine. Surely such a man would have the sense to tell his accuser whatever they wanted to hear and maintain his grip on life?

But as he walked defiant, limping from some unknown wound, towards the open space before the emperors, I knew that this was a man who would bend his principles for no one. Again, something to be harnessed, not destroyed. The crimson lines across his arms and back and the stains on his garb spoke of some horrible, bladed torture, and yet he stood proud.

The men who followed, each in turn untied from the cart and led down for the walk to their place of execution, were more miscellaneous. Simply citizens who had the temerity to refuse the true gods. Yet for all their commonness, they each displayed that same defiance and nobility as they moved to stand in front of the emperors. The man who came last was the infamous Anthimius, high priest of the Christians of the city. A single glance at his white-bearded face, serene with self-belief, was enough to confirm that.

I tried to look as though I was paying close attention, eager even, as the six men were nudged into a neat line by the spears of their guards. I feigned shock as their 'crimes' were listed, along with their names and former positions, though no feigning was required at the discovery that the soldier, one Georgios, was a prefect in Diocletian's own elite Joviani!

I waited tensely in the silence of the equally pensive crowd as the six men were all given one last chance to renounce their God, kiss the robes of the emperors and sacrifice to Jove – an example of Diocletian's 'munificence'. I had never expected any of them to do so, of course, though I found myself urging at least the soldier to.

But no. I stood impassively as the six men were officially condemned and the executioner came forth, drawing his outsized sword from its black sheath. No sharpened point down into the neck for a swift, clean merciful kill here.

The first man was made to kneel, though he seemed disinclined to struggle anyway. I grimaced as the executioner lifted his massively heavy blade and brought it down on the man's extended neck. Surely with such positioning the sword would clatter onto the stones after it sliced through the neck, and damage the blade?

Then I realised, as the sword bit into the man and cracked his spine. This blade was deliberately blunted, chipped and dull, so as to cause the maximum agony and all but negate the possibility of a single-stroke kill. Indeed, as I watched, the poor creature received four blows, hacking away at his neck before the sword made it through and the head rolled away. And even by the fourth strike the man's mouth was working in an attempt to scream. There was no doubt in my mind that he felt every nuance of that death. I hoped that his God was more forgiving in his next world than in this, wherever that might be.

And so it went on, the soldier's head mercifully bouncing free after only two cuts. Whether by accident or careful design, this 'bishop' Anthimius took six blows to sever. I suspect the latter, given the gleeful, hungry looks on the faces of the three seated figures.

Looking at the lust plastered across Galerius' face I was grateful that Constantine was busy with his pregnant wife and not here to see this. I was ever a diplomat and able to suppress my true feelings for the sake of expediency. Constantine was not that kind of man, and I fear that, had he been present, he would have done something that saw him take a seventh place under that dulled, crimson blade.

In the end, Constantine's immediate burden was lifted soon after. A few days after the bishop's demise, Galerius had called together a meeting of the court and made his opinion plain: Nicomedia was unsafe, undermined by Christian treachery and ready to topple and burn. For every conspirator they caught and executed, three more names came to light. With little aplomb he announced his intention to leave the festering city to burn and sail for Rome.

Galerius' entourage were packing their things for travel that same day, and when I called in to see Constantine, saddened at the prospect of another parting, I found him in equal parts relieved and enraged. He and his patron had clearly argued and, though he would not reveal the nature of the dispute, it had been serious enough that Galerius had ordered my friend to remain in Nicomedia and not travel west with him.

The atmosphere in the more peripheral areas of the court brightened noticeably at the discovery that the Herdsman and his unpleasant son would soon be gone, though I envied them the fact that they were bound for the city that still held a fascination deep in the chambers of my heart.

Among the official entourage that attended his departure,

we watched Galerius and his pig of an offspring standing between the steering oars at the rail of the ship, as the small fleet took him away from us and to darken the lives of the inhabitants of the eternal city. I actually smiled, placing my hand on Constantine's shoulder. The city might still stink of charred wood and burned flesh, but one of its worst monsters had departed.

'Do not smile too broadly,' my friend remarked as we turned from the rapidly retreating ships. I threw a sidelong look at him as we began to walk back towards the waiting horses, along with the others, surrounded by Joviani and Herculiani guards. He gestured to a small group of glittering, lavishly draped figures, at the front of which stood my father, deep in conspiratorial discussion with Diocletian. 'The word is that those two will follow in due course. Diocletian does not wish to appear to be abandoning Nicomedia to its fate, but both of them mutter about leaving, and they will be gone before the weather begins to turn and drives the already agitated masses to lunacy.'

'How do you hear these things, secluded in your family's apartments?'

'Lactantius hears many things, my friend. Diocletian had already planned upon travelling to Rome by winter, to celebrate his *vicennalia*.'

'He will take my father with him. They must celebrate such an event together.'

'And that means he will take you.' Constantine smiled sadly.

'Perhaps, perhaps not. No one knows my father as I do, and he will likely consider me far too insignificant to attend such a celebration. In fact he is for the most part embarrassed by my presence, and to have me at court alongside Candidianus would cause difficulties. The memory of our trouble may be old to you, but my father never forgets an embarrassment. After all, you hear nothing of him sending for his wife or the sister I have not yet met, both of whom wallow in peace at Apamea. If he does take me with him it will be as excess baggage and probably under duress. More likely I will be left here with my ice-hearted wife.'

I smiled a tired smile and slapped my friend on the back. 'Anyway, if by some miracle Father decides to take me with him, that will not be until the summer is past, and my boy would be heartbroken if he were not here to welcome your own child into the world. Don't forget that they'll be cousins. After all, for all your advantage in years, since Theodora married your father, I am your uncle!'

We grinned at one another in silence and for just a moment the world was a better place.

13

CONSTANTINE

JUNE 303 AD

It was the blackest day I had yet endured.

Absurdly, it began as one of the finest. I awoke to a soft dawn chorus and an unblemished blue sky. The city was blessedly quiet for the first time in months, and the black plumes of smoke mercifully absent. Had the storm of persecutions abated? With more than fifteen thousand dead from the burnings and the rioting, I certainly hoped so. Indeed, in the months since the vile Galerius had been gone from this city, the ferocity of the persecutions had eased. Even better, the two Augusti, Diocletian and Maximian, were this very day due to leave Nicomedia and join Galerius in Rome in preparation for the vicennalia at the end of the year.

I spent that fine morning sitting with Minervina and Mother on the balcony of our chambers, blissfully unaware of what was to come. We ate bread and honey and sipped well-watered wine, with Mother regaling us with stories of my childhood – particularly the time I tried to saddle an angry old goat to be my war horse. Minervina listened intently, giggling, her face radiant as she stroked her pregnant belly, no doubt imagining the larks that our child would enjoy. She was but days from giving birth, according to the red-cheeked obstetrix who called in every day to check her condition. And it was when the somewhat formidable lady arrived that morning that things changed.

She brought with her a vial of tincture that she reckoned would bring about labour. Minervina thanked her and swallowed the contents of the vial. We talked while the obstetrix fussed and organised her things. Barely an hour later, Minervina stopped, halfway through a sentence. Her mouth widened as if in shock, and she clutched her belly.

'Constantine?' She looked up at me, her face contorted in fear, the waist of her robes suddenly soaked through and water pouring down her legs.

I fell to my knees by her side, clutching her hand, looking to the wet nurse, terrified. 'What's happening?'

The ruddy-cheeked woman was entirely unmoved. 'Excellent,' she said. 'The potion worked.'

'Your contractions have begun,' Mother added, her eyes as bright as her smile.

Minervina and I gazed at one another in shock, then erupted in nervous laughter, embracing. It was happening, at last. Another contraction and she winced, pulling away from me.

'Come on, let us bring her to the birthing stool,' Mother fussed, waving us to the bow-shaped timber seat that had been set out for months in preparation for this moment.

We carried her there and the obstetrix set to work, bringing in basins of olive oil and water, sea sponges, towels, lemons, some sharp-smelling crystals and a pair of rather vicious-looking iron callipers. Minervina clasped my hand tightly as we helped lower her into the chair. The obstetrix crouched before her, lifted her robes and checked her condition. My knees ached from kneeling beside her, but I was not for moving, not for anything. I often wonder that, had I stayed true to those intentions, then perhaps things might have been different. But a knock on the door changed everything.

Rap-rap.

At first I ignored it.

Rap-rap-rap, the noise came again – this time more urgently. I cast a sour look at the door, willing whoever it was away.

'Constantine?' a muffled voice called from beyond. The tone was insistent.

Minervina, sweating heavily now, pulled her hand from mine. 'Go, see to it!' she demanded like a scolding mother.

With a gruff sigh, I rose and stomped over to open the door.

'Maxentius?' I said, seeing the young man's weary expression. 'I thought you had left on the ferry for Rome this morning?' And I was sure this was the case. We had said our goodbyes the previous day – for he and his family were all set to travel west to the eternal city with the two Augusti.

'We were ready to depart,' he explained, 'but Diocletian wanted to make one last statement before he left. So he has delayed the voyage. The ferry will leave this evening instead.'

'Diocletian wants to make a… *statement?*' I frowned, sensing Maxentius' unease.

'We have been summoned,' he said flatly.

'I have a wife on the cusp of giving birth—'

I stopped, seeing Maxentius' face light up, his eyes trained on the goings-on behind me. 'It is her time at last?'

'Aye, by this evening, I will be a father!' I exclaimed, my heart thundering with a frisson of excitement at this truth.

'For months Romulus has talked of how he and your new child will be friends,' Maxentius said with a glint of love in his eyes, 'how he might show the youngster the art of grooming and feeding Celeritas – and that they might walk Batius' hound together!' But his face fell again.

'It is a great pity that your lad will not be here to greet our newborn...' I said, noticing that he was alone. 'They are not with you?'

'He and Valeria are at the forum near the docks, waiting to board the ferry,' he said with a half-smile, 'and I am to meet them there later, after Diocletian's gathering. Come, we should be swift, attend this spectacle so you can be back here in good time for the birth.'

'Spectacle?' I said, feeling a sense of unease rise in my belly. This sounded less innocent than a mere *statement*. 'Another execution?' I lowered my voice so Minervina and Mother would not hear.

'I was with Father this morning at the emperor's breakfasting table. Someone is to burn at noon. He did not say who, but he said it would leave no doubt as to the place of the Christians under his rule. And,' Maxentius added, his brow furrowing, 'he said it with a tear in his eye.'

'I care little for the man's tears and I have no wish to watch another poor beggar die horribly at his command, especially when my first child is about to be born. I will not attend. You go.' I planted a hand on his shoulder and squeezed gently. 'My thoughts will be with you and your family for a safe voyage to Rome. I hope it will not be long before we meet agai—'

Minervina screamed in pain. I swung away from the door towards her, but Maxentius grabbed my forearm. Confused and surprised by the strength of his hold, I stared back at him.

'You *must* come, Constantine.' He lowered his voice and I saw panic in his eyes. 'Diocletian has demanded that you and I attend. Any who do not will be arrested and sent to the burning pyres.'

I recoiled in disgust. 'Has the old fool lost his mind entirely?'

Maxentius looked this way and that down the corridor, as if fearing that my words would be heard.

I looked back to Minervina. She was panting and her face was creased with discomfort. A sharp cry of pain escaped her lips. I made to approach her but when I stumbled over a pan of water the ruddy-cheeked obstetrix scowled and waved me back. 'Stay back, clumsy man!' she scolded me.

Mother was by Minervina's side, I noticed, clasping her hand, talking her through her pain. She was in good hands. Mother met my gaze. *Go!* the look said.

'I will be back soon, to be with you when our child comes into the world,' I said to Minervina. Through a veil of sweat and pain, she nodded as best as she could. Reluctantly, I turned back to the door, swept on a cloak and left with Maxentius.

The arena stank of sweat and garlic. All eyes in the dense crowds looked askance at the pile of firewood and vertical pole in the centre of the arena, and many mouths whispered and murmured variations of the same question. *Who was it for?* All others seemed as confused about this event as I was. I could not help but tap both feet in torment. Every passing moment was torturous: my wife was locked in labour and I was here. *Why?* I screamed inside, scowling at the still-empty imperial box. *Show yourself,* I mouthed to the absent Diocletian, *subject us to this 'spectacle' and let me be back by Minervina's side!*

As if my lamentations had been heard, two figures at last emerged from the rear of the box to take their seats.

Diocletian and Maximian settled into place, shaded under a purple silk awning. Then, with a blare of trumpets, the arena fell silent. A pair of Joviani – armour glittering like jewels – marched into the arena, dragging behind them a woman. They pulled her over to the dark smudge of piled firewood, hauling her up there and binding her to the central stake. In the heat haze I could not identify her. Maxentius, seated by my side, squinted too. Then we both gasped along with the rest of the crowd as the identity of the woman dawned on us all.

'No!' Maxentius gasped. 'This must be some mistake?'

'Alexandra?' I mouthed, recognising the grey-flecked locks and worn features of Diocletian's wife. I looked up to the imperial box. Maximian gazed around the crowd with hooded eyes as if relishing the reaction. Diocletian looked down at the pyre in a cold, expressionless silence. His eyes were locked on his wife of many years. I had heard whispered rumours that she had been so appalled by the executions that she had turned to the Christian God as a measure of defiance; perhaps in hope of showing her husband the folly of his ways? This, it seemed, was to be her reward.

Another Joviani legionary stomped out of the tunnel and onto the arena floor, carrying a crackling torch. The crowd fell utterly silent as the soldier held the torch near the firewood then looked up to Diocletian. Maxentius and I looked on, the breath held captive in our lungs. We, like the rest of the crowd, were sure that the emperor would intervene, give his wife a reprieve. This was statement enough, surely?

At that moment, I noticed how Diocletian jolted in his seat, lurching forward as if shaken by some great moment of understanding. His fingers clasped the arms of his seat and his eyes grew wide. His lips opened as if to speak.

Free her, I mouthed, willing him to speak those words. I noticed Maxentius' lips move likewise by my side.

Silence... then the emperor nodded to the torch-bearer and slumped back in his seat.

The torch touched the kindling, and the flames took hold of the pyre. Alexandra gazed up at the box, her face contorted not in pain or fear, but in great sadness... pity, even. My gut churned at this nightmarish spectacle. For a fleeting and tortuous moment I saw instead Mother or Minervina down there, tied and doomed to burn. I glanced back to the imperial box; Diocletian seemed trapped by his wife's haunting gaze.

When the flames licked at her robes and seared her flesh, she screamed. Within moments she was ablaze, the breath stolen from her lungs, her blackening form thrashing for an eternity, great blisters of skin swelling up and then popping, seared tendons snapping. The stench of garlic and sweat was stolen away by the all too familiar reek of burning hair and skin. Her back arched as if in one last effort to break free of her bonds, then the charred corpse fell mercifully still.

Without offering as much as a word to those gathered, Diocletian stood and left abruptly, shambling away into the shadows at the rear of the *kathisma*. His point had been made. The recent lull in the persecutions had been meaningless – nought but the passing eye of the storm.

We wandered from the arena in a daze, unspeaking amidst the other fearfully babbling spectators. Those who had not been there to witness the burning erupted in confused shouts, hearing that their emperor had just burnt his wife alive but not believing it. The snatched words and cries were like the first gusts of a storm. Moments later, the babble had turned into angry jeers. The crowd swelled and began pushing and shoving, the shouting deafening and incessant. Fights broke out all around us, stalls were kicked over and objects were thrown.

Like wolves and lions, Christian sympathisers fought those fastidiously loyal to the Roman gods. Gnashing teeth, venomous curses, swinging fists and pained cries. We stumbled through the bedlam that ensued. Soon, rocks were being tossed, doors broken down, sculptures toppled. Chaos reigned in the streets all around us. I had so far only heard the riots from the safety of my chambers. Now, it seemed, I was at the heart of the latest and most ferocious one.

I ducked a thrown chair and staggered clear of a drunkard's flailing fists.

'Come, Constantine.' Maxentius beckoned me, shouting over the tumult, sensing the atmosphere turning utterly black. 'Valeria and Romulus are awaiting me at the forum – we should hurry there.'

I could see the fear in his eyes. Not concern for himself, but for his family. Or for his boy, at least. We barged through the throng, dodging more punches, ducking under hurled plates and urns. I was thankful then for my choice of simple dress – for I saw the crowds pounce upon some palace dignitary in gold brocade. They thought him the embodiment of Diocletian's edict. The old fellow was beaten to the ground, then one citizen set about clubbing the man with a timber cudgel. My instinct was to intervene, but all around me there were too many similar scenes.

A lone Joviani legionary backed away from a circle of citizens. He levelled his spear, switching it this way and that to keep them at bay. Then he skewered one before the others leapt for him, pummelling him with a storm of fists before smashing a rock down upon his head, crushing his helmet and skull, spraying brain and blood across the street. Up above, I saw members of the mob spill onto the rooftops of the temple of Jove dragging the pontiff with them. They rushed to the roof's edge to throw the pontiff to his death on the street below. In a grim reflection, another lot burst onto the rooftop of what had been outed as a Christian shrine, throwing a black-robed man they had found within from the roof's edge, his body plummeting like a rock until the thick rope they had tied around his neck snapped taut and stole the life from him. A supply wagon headed for the palace was stopped, the mob swelling around it, pulling the drivers from their berth to bludgeon them, then toppling the cart over. Bread, baskets of fruit, vases of honey and fine meats spilled across the main way. Finally, one rioter put a torch to the wagon. 'You seek fire?' the man screamed towards the palace gates – where a thick pack of the rioters clamoured – as if Diocletian could hear. 'Have your fire!'

We forged on and, mercifully, the trouble thinned. Indeed, the ward near the docks was all but deserted. Breathless, we hurried through the archways leading onto the forum. As if oblivious to the chaos only streets away, Valeria sat there, by a fountain, tracing her finger across the water's surface. Maxentius rushed to her, then stopped suddenly, halted by the pinch-faced scowl she shot him.

'Where have you been? You said you would be here immediately after noon.' She jabbed a finger at the sundial in the centre of the forum, which showed it was nearly an hour past midday.

I gawped at this. *An hour past midday?* I thought. *Minervina!*

'There is no time to talk,' Maxentius said, grabbing Valeria's wrist. 'The heart of the city is gripped by rioting. Come, before it spreads this way.'

She shook off his hand with a snort and a cold laugh that echoed around the square. 'And you think I need *you* to protect me?' She stood and stepped back from him.

Maxentius ignored her rebuke. I could see he was well used to her ways. And he seemed agitated about something else, his eyes darting around the forum, deserted bar a few shopkeepers hastily closing their doors and bolting their shutters at the sound of the nearby riots. 'Where is Romulus?'

Valeria frowned. 'You mean he didn't find you?'

Maxentius' tanned skin seemed to drain of blood at this. 'What?'

'He has been like a caged cat since the ferry voyage was delayed this morning. He wanted to go and find you and Constantine and take Celeritas to the racing grounds one last time. So I let him.' She gestured in the vague direction of the arena.

'You let him go... alone?' Maxentius stammered.

'You cosset him too much – filling his head with nonsense, encouraging him to play with wooden blocks and indulge in his Horatian games. He needs to learn to be a man—' she looked him up and down, her nose wrinkling '—as does his father.'

I stepped forward, between Maxentius and her, and pointed a finger back in the direction from which we had come. 'Do you know what is going on back there?'

She flinched at the naked ire in my tone. Clearly she was unused to being spoken to so. 'Ah, Constantine. You are still here? I thought you might have tired of city life by now. Does the dog of war not hanker to return to the battlefields, to chase the carrion crows?'

'Which way did he go?' Maxentius cut in, the anger in his own voice now matching mine.

She swept her robe around her shoulders and flicked her head towards one of the archways leading from the forum.

Maxentius looked that way then hissed to his wife: 'Go to the docks, board the ferry for Rome and wait there. Our legionary escort are on board and will see that you are safe.' Valeria scoffed at his good-hearted words, then stood and swept away towards the wharf as if hugely inconvenienced. Maxentius grimaced at his departing wife for but a moment. Then he turned to me, beckoning.

We set off in search of Romulus. Following in his footsteps, I glanced all around at the turmoil. The streets near the forum were now thick with rioters. Even the Joviani legionaries and the garrison troops deployed to quell them had proved ineffective. These soldiers swiped their spathas at the fighting citizens like farmers cutting down wheat, mindless, ruthless, but this only fuelled the outrage. Further up the street, I could see that the swell at the palace gates had grown, demanding the emperor come forth. But those iron-studded timber gates were well bolted and a line of legionaries stood on the walkway atop those walls, some hurling spears and weighted darts down upon the aggressors. The palace was safe. Diocletian would not come to any harm from the storm he had conjured. Neither would Mother or Minervina, I realised with a surge of relief.

That relief lasted but moments until my thoughts returned to my wife. Had our child had been delivered yet? Memories of Minervina's pained cries that morning came to me and my thoughts swam, building into a panicked flurry. It was the chillingly similar, piercing shriek of some woman in the crowd that shook me from my thoughts.

'By the gods, no!' Maxentius cried, seeing what she had seen. I turned and saw it too. Before us, the giant grain silo was ablaze. The great timbers roaring like a titan's pyre. And the vigiles were nowhere to be seen. The piercing scream sounded again. A woman fell to her knees, reaching out with one trembling hand to the timber huts around the base of the silo.

'Caius!' she screamed again and again.

I followed her tear-streaked gaze. Inside one of the huts, a pair of children huddled in the far corner, surrounded by a wall of flames. Trapped.

I heard Maxentius gasp. My friend stepped forward, his lips trembling. 'Romulus?'

I saw beyond the curtain of flame at that moment. The face of his boy. Trapped with the one named Caius, both soot-blackened and wide-eyed.

'Father!' Romulus cried back over the thunder of the inferno.

A shuddering crack sounded from the towering silo as the fire devoured the timber. Then it groaned, slumping just a fraction to one side. 'It's going to collapse!' a man cried, dragging the screaming woman from her knees and hauling her back.

Maxentius clasped my shoulders with shaking hands. 'Please, *help me!*'

'We... we must find water!' I stammered, looking this way and that.

'The cistern is too far away,' Maxentius panted. 'But the stables!' He jabbed a finger to a lean-to timber shack on the opposite side of the street. We bundled inside, seeing the deep water trough there. We snatched up a bucket each, clumsily filling them with water. I swept off my cloak and soaked it too. We hurried back across the street once more, hurling our water at the flames trapping the children. With a hiss, the water was gone, but the flames burned no less brightly – perhaps they even grew fiercer. I swept my sodden cloak around my body and made to push through the blaze, but the heat threw me back. Just then, another titanic groan erupted as the blazing silo leaning overhead creaked, listing further askew, like a fiery axe waiting to chop down.

'It's useless!' Maxentius said, falling back from his own attempt to broach the fire, tears running down his face.

Thick black smoke billowed around us, staining us, snatching away our hopes.

At that moment, bodies rushed around us. More rioters? No – men and women hauling water, just as we had. A clutch of them, spilling into and from the stables, ferrying water in whatever they could find – buckets, vases, amphorae. They lashed the precious water onto the flames over and over. The fire roared in defiance. Maxentius and I joined them in bringing more water. More and more citizens joined us. Finally, the orangey veil lessened. While the rest of the timber shacks and the near-to-collapse silo itself still blazed ferociously, we had tamed this tiny part of it. Another splash and the flames almost parted. Maxentius and I shared a knowing glance. 'Now!' we cried in unison.

We leapt through the gap. The heat inside stole the breath from our lungs. The black smoke stung our eyes and blinded us. But we grasped up those tiny, frightened bodies, bringing them back out to safety on the far side of the street, Caius fell into his weeping mother's arms, coughing, retching. Maxentius and Romulus embraced and wept also.

When the silo groaned angrily I knew the structure was doomed. 'Back!' I roared to the water-bearers. The snarl of the silo and my hoarse cry somehow pierced the throng of those rioting nearby, for even they seemed to stop. Hundreds of faces gawped up, stumbling to the far side of the street as the tall silo roared, crumpling to the ground with a whoosh of dust, embers and splinters that swept through the streets. The din seemed to still the riots and the collapse blessedly smothered the worst of the inferno too, but many more smaller fires raged nearby.

I felt a hand squeeze my shoulder. Maxentius offered me a tear-streaked smile. 'Thank you... brother,' he said, panting until he regained control of his lungs. 'Without your help...' he started, but could not finish. A tear-flooded look at his boy said it well enough. He took a moment to compose himself. 'It hurts me that I cannot repay you, for I must hasten to the ferry. But know that I will not forget what you did for me today.'

'I would do the same for any true friend.'

Maxentius grinned at this. 'Now, I should go to the docks, board the ferry for Rome and wait for it to set sail. Gods, it will be safer on that vessel than on these streets!' Then his eyes darted and he added with a weak smile: 'On the other hand, if Valeria's mood has soured further...'

I chuckled and clasped my hand to his. 'Go, and be swift! All will be well, my friend.'

'And you, you should hurry to Minervina's side. My thoughts will be with you both. Until we meet again, Constantine.' He smiled. We beheld each other, both knowing we would not meet again for some time.

Maxentius backed away before at last the crowds came between us and we could see each other no more. 'Until we meet again,' I whispered after him.

I turned, intent on heeding his advice and hurrying to be with Minervina. But the crowds on the street seemed lost at that moment. Men glanced at each other, some with fire in their eyes, some with fear, many still bearing clubs and rocks. Those who had helped rescue the children – Christian sympathisers and Roman Pantheists – seemed frozen by the profundity of their instinctive cooperation. That hiatus, that delicate balance, might have leant either way. But in the end, it was the blunt aggression of the garrison legionaries that tipped the streets back towards violence. A century of them spilled into the end of the street and fanned out in a line.

'Lock shields! Draw your blades! And... *advance!*' their centurion bellowed.

At once, the crowd erupted in a babble of panic and anger once more. The wall of legionaries stepped forward, spathas raised, ready to chop through the agitators. The chaos seemed set to swirl into a new, steeper crescendo, when a single word burst from my lungs.

'Stop!'

It was a throaty and visceral cry. I did not think for a moment that I would be heard, let alone heeded.

But many looked to me, faces agape. The line of legionaries halted, even their centurion gawping at me. Some of his men recognised me now. *Constantine the Goth-slayer!* one legionary gasped. Then I heard whispers from the crowd of stilled rioters: *Constantine, the killer of Persians.* I winced at the epithets. But their tones were reverent, as if these were noble soubriquets. And so all was still on the streets once more apart from the scudding smoke across all those staring faces. All staring at me.

What did they want from me? A million things came to my mind. What I should say? What I should be careful not to say? But all this mental chatter fell away. Because sometimes a man is compelled to speak from his heart, and when this happens, he can surprise even himself.

'This is not the answer!' I cried out, waving a hand at the crackling remains of the silo and the myriad other plumes of smoke all around the city skyline, glowering at the bludgeoned corpses of soldiers and citizens alike staining the streets. The rioters offered no denial of my words. Even the line of legionaries put forward no challenge to this. 'The emperor's edict stokes pride in the hearts of some and indignation in the hearts of others. I stand here not to justify or deny the persecutions. I stand here as a man who is weary of seeing his people tear each other apart. Let this black day end. Now!'

I felt my heart thunder on my ribs and the blood pound in my ears. I can only liken what happened next to that moment at the end of battle, when the chaos melts away, when snarling foes are once again merely men. I heard myself bark orders to the legionaries, having them perform the duties of the vigiles in taming the fires. The crowds obeyed me too, moving back from the heart of the riot, parents taking up children, young men helping elderly from the ruined streets. Some stayed and formed groups to aid the legionaries. It was some time after, when my muscles were weary from aiding and directing these groups that I realised the riot had ended. Not just here by the silo, but in the surrounding streets too. The storm was over.

Or so I thought.

As soon as the chaos was under control, one name screamed in my mind.

Minervina!

How long had I been away? I turned for the palace gates, sped through the crowd then hurried inside. Suddenly, two pairs of hands seized me, halting me.

'Emperor Diocletian has summoned you,' a gruff voice said with little thought for my troubles.

★ ★ ★

The throne room was cool and free of the tang of smoke that seemed to fill every other corner of the city. Diocletian, enthroned before me, was a perplexing sight. His skin was pale – almost white – and streaked with sweat. He drummed his fingers on the arms of his throne as if in extreme agitation, the thick gold rings on each finger clanking. His eyes were distant, wild, even. Most tellingly, his dark, greying hair now sported a stark, white flash like a streak of Jove's lightning, from his hairline to his crown – a feature that had appeared in the hours since Alexandra's burning, seemingly.

I shuffled where I stood. I seldom felt discomfort under the gaze of my so-called superiors, but Diocletian's haunted demeanour had me very much on edge. And I was still not sure why I had been brought here – to be commended, or to be committed to the pyre? The pair of Joviani legionaries flanking him gazed straight ahead, giving nothing away. I certainly had never previously been subject to a private audience with the emperor like this. And I had never imagined I would do so in a smoke-blackened tunic, my face plastered with sweat, dust and soot. More, this maelstrom of thought was but an annoyance compared to the weightier issues on my mind.

Minervina! a voice in my head screamed again.

I risked glancing past the emperor's shoulder, to the huge, coloured-glass window behind him. The sunlight was distorted through this murky yellow pane, but I reckoned it was late afternoon. I had intended to be back by her side no later than an hour past noon.

'It seems Galerius was wrong about you,' Diocletian said absently, startling me from my thoughts. I braced at the ambiguity of his words. And the cur left me dangling for some time before he clarified: 'He thought you a troublesome whoreson, brave in battle but eager to defy your superiors.'

Despite the somewhat exotic reply I yearned to give, I thought it best to remain silent.

'You managed to break up the worst of the riots, I hear. None of my men in this city have managed such a feat. Not even those who have been by my side for some time – those who profess to be indispensable,' the emperor said. Shrewd words but spoken as if from a great distance, somewhere behind that lost gaze of his. 'A man who can compel the people to accept my edict is a man I would rather have alongside me in future. And there is always a seat by my side.' He held up a trembling finger, wagging it at me once. '*That* is the beauty of the Tetrarchy, is it not?' he said, suddenly gazing around the empty throne room with a weak smile as if expecting a crowd to be there.

I disguised my confusion well. It seemed Diocletian had heard that I had broken up the riots by talking down the Christians. Words between men are oft misunderstood, and I learned that day that it is sometimes best to leave them so. I nodded graciously.

'Perhaps I will involve you more in my daily court, to begin with,' Diocletian surmised.

My heart sank at the prospect of a daily meeting with this dark soul and his pig-faced, squealing courtiers. 'I would be honoured,' I replied with an earnest half-bow.

'But, as you know, I am to leave on the ferry for Rome this evening. So your mentor will be overseeing the court in my absence. Galerius is to return from his sojourn within the next few days—'

My heart plummeted.

'—to oversee affairs here. I feel he should have a spell in charge of this crucible of a city, to see through the... challenge... of enforcing the edict.'

'Then I look forward to working with him once more,' I lied.

Diocletian beheld me for a while. Was he judging my sincerity? Then I noticed a sharp twitch in his cheek, and realised he was looking not at me, but through me. It took little guesswork to imagine what he might be seeing in his mind's eye.

Finally, he flicked a finger towards the tall, arched doorway behind me. 'That is all.'

I swept along the corridors of the palace, each one seemingly longer than the last. At last I came to the southern wing and saw the chamber door up ahead. Batius and Lactantius stood outside. It brought a wave of relief to see that they had gone unharmed in the chaos of the riots. I rushed to the door, but something was wrong. They both wore the most sullen of expressions.

'Constantine!' Batius said, blocking my way.

'What is it, Batius? Let me past!'

Lactantius' withered hand rested on my chest. The thumb and forefinger of his other hand were pressed together and he gestured for me to do the same. His age-lined face was sullen. 'I wish there was something I could say to make this easier, Constantine...'

I could have struck the pair of them, so angry and confused was I. Then, like a droplet of cool, calming water in a boiling pool, I heard a noise that changed everything.

A baby crying.

Batius made to say something, but the words dissolved into a resigned sigh. He stepped aside. The breath stilled in my lungs. I pushed open the chamber door. There stood Mother. A baby in her arms. A healthy baby boy. There have been few moments of such joy in my life, and none so short-lived. For when I saw Mother's face, drawn and tear-streaked, I felt a wretched apprehension creep over me and claw away the joy.

When I looked beyond her shoulder, past the empty birthing stool and over to the still, blue-lipped and staring form of Minervina on the bed, I realised what had happened. Fiery talons reached deep inside me and tore my spirit away. I fell to my knees and heard a distant, low moan topple from my lungs.

14

MAXENTIUS

ROME, APRIL 304 AD

My body slave fussed around me, adjusting the positioning of my toga as though a fraction of a finger-width difference in its hang might constitute a matter of life and death while on public display. I could hear Valeria in her own chamber three rooms away, snapping waspishly at her slaves and occasionally backhanding them sharply as they attempted to conceal her condition. Perhaps I should have found it saddening that my wife and I had fallen into such frosty distance that we only met at formal occasions or by unhappy accident, each staying within our part of the villa and trying not to cross into one another's.

I cursed silently at myself, for whenever I started feeling sorry for myself over the state of my marriage, it brought a slow wave of gnawing guilt that Constantine had missed the last chance in this world to speak with his own wife while busily saving my son. I pushed down the guilt to join its fellows in that seething green sea of similar culpability that lurked at the edge of my consciousness. Time enough to make amends to my friend. For now, I had my own problems.

Valeria and I had never had the best relationship, of

course, but the past four months had seen a descent of almost Orphean dimensions. One night in the depths of winter, I'd had an argument with my father – the latest of many since we had reached Rome – and had turned to unwatered wine to soften the aftermath. My indulging coincided with Valeria returning to our villa outside the city on the Via Labicana in a similar state and, well nature had taken its course. It had been the first time we had shared a room – let alone a bed – in well over a year, and it was to be the last.

When she had missed her next cycle and realised that she was carrying our second child it had almost pushed her over the edge, and she had thrown things at me, cursing until I retreated from her presence. My spirits had plummeted for when I had learned that Romulus would have a sibling, I had vainly hoped that it might bring us closer together. I'd been wrong.

One night I'd had a little too much wine and found myself questioning Euna over her mistress, hoping that she might have more insight for me. She had, though it had taken some drawing from her and it improved things in no way. It seemed that my darling wife had once more asked her father to agree to a divorce from me, but Galerius had been adamant, noting that a second heir should secure our bond all the more. How odd it was that the Herdsman and I should be of accord in something.

After that Valeria stopped speaking to me altogether. Had it not been for the need to appear side by side in public on such an important day as today, I am certain that she would have refused to accompany me anywhere ever again. But in the circumstances, she was determined to hide the increase in her waistline and appear as cold, statuesque and imperial as ever, as befitted a daughter of Galerius.

She sounded less than imperial that morning as she called her *cosmeta* names that would make a whore blush.

Romulus, standing proud at eight summers now, waited in the corner with a calm and patience beyond his years, trying not to listen to his mother's invective.

I was only grateful that we had this sprawling ancient pile to ourselves to hide our family's rift. Father had taken up residence in the old imperial complex on the Palatine after the departure of his fellow emperor, Diocletian.

And *that* had been something of an eye-opener.

I had come to Rome to revel in its ancient glory – a city I had longed to visit my whole life – and had not been disappointed. It was everything I had hoped. Or rather it had the *potential* to be so, once the faded paint was replaced and the fallen walls rebuilt, but I could see it in my mind's eye exactly as it should be. Young Romulus was equally eager and enthusiastic. Father, of course, treated the place as a political stage, exactly as I would have expected, and Valeria was clearly unhappy to be here.

But Diocletian...

The senior Augustus and master of the world had arrived in Rome to celebrate his vicennalia festival the previous autumn with the pomp and power of the entire imperial court. The people of Rome from the highest patrician blood to the lowest homeless beggar had turned out to greet the great man who, in his twentieth year of rule, was setting foot in the ancient capital for the first time. There had been cascades of flowers and petals and extravagant gifts and gestures. The crowd had loved the spectacle and cheered when their emperor waved his hand paternally – if half-heartedly – at them as he passed.

But I, from my position close to his side, could see what the crowd could not: I could see the boredom, the emptiness and even the hint of revulsion in Diocletian's expression. He would rather have been almost anywhere else. He had been like this every time I had seen him during that interminable trip from Nicomedia – withdrawn, distant and empty, as though what he had done to his own wife that dreadful day had snapped a crucial thread inside his mind. Indeed, once, on the sea voyage, the most powerful man in the world had been found at the bow of the ship staring down into the waves, and had seemingly forgotten how he had made his way there.

The man had aged critically in a short time and seemed constantly on the edge of something monstrous – either a complete mental collapse or a fearsome eruption. Even those who gloried in their position among his close council had begun to distance themselves. And arriving in the world's greatest city, he had displayed little to no interest as he was shown the new arch that had been raised in his honour on the Via Lata, the numerous columns with vicennalia inscriptions and carvings, the almost-complete bath complex, which would be the largest the city had ever accommodated. Had he even seen them?

Yet while his true condition remained unnoticed by all but the central court, still the lesser value Diocletian placed on Rome and its populace quickly became common knowledge. The emperor lodged himself on the Palatine and rarely showed his face over the next few months. On one occasion in the great Theatre of Pompey, on a day when he seemed to be close to his former strength and chose to attend a performance of Seneca's *Phaedra*, he made such disparaging comments about the city in comparison to his own Nicomedia that he drew boos and murmurs of discontent from the crowd, order being restored only at the sword points of the Joviani. Few had seen the tears in his eyes as he had left the theatre.

The increase in agitation among the populace merely pushed Diocletian into ever deeper seclusion and had his vicennalia not been prepared for December, he would certainly have abandoned the city before then. As it played out, he appeared in public briefly to go through the motions of the anniversary, his gaze distant and lost, and then shut himself up on the Palatine once more, deigning thereafter only to show himself to the city's elite and even then rarely.

Rumours began to spread among the senate following a feast at the palace that had been held as part of the festivities. It had been announced as the greatest banquet the Palatine had ever seen. The very best garum had been brought in from Hispania and slathered upon mullet from Cosa. Assorted *brassica* from Belgica filled heaped platters. Ibis from Aegyptus steamed in a cherry sauce, oysters from the southern coasts of Italia, the leanest of rare beef from southern Gaul... the list went on. Delicacies that few Romans would ever have the chance to taste.

Diocletian had taken the lightest of nibbles from the most expensive foods in the world and declared them tasteless and worthless, settling for a simple plate of cabbage, which he dipped liberally in vinegar, labelling even these sour and unpleasant before finally casting them to the floor in disgust.

My father stepped in as often and as carefully as he could, diverting attention away from his colleague's erratic behaviour, but there could have been little doubt among those nobles who left early, before the feast's end, that the master of the world had changed – that he was no longer the man he had once been.

A mere six days following the festival's anti-climax,

Diocletian and the bulk of his court set off for Ravenna for the winter, from where it was rumoured that he planned to take command of the Danubian armies for the next season. No one dared voice a question as to how a man in such a bewildered state hoped to wage a war.

The only ray of light that shone in the grand vicennalia of the master of the world had been that, being so far from the unhealthy influence of Nicomedia, in a place far removed from such religious turmoil, he had relented and granted an amnesty to the Christians as part of the proceedings. How long that peace would last no one would care to guess, for the great emperor was becoming noticeably more changeable and unpredictable just as his physical ageing seemed to accelerate.

To my disgust, my father had argued against the amnesty, declaring that many enemies of the empire still clung to their Chi-Rho, but without the unhealthy influence of Galerius, calmer hearts managed to wheedle the decree from Diocletian anyway, and I noted with interest how a weight seemed to have been lifted from the ravaged emperor's shoulders with that one act. It is entirely possible that the magnanimous gesture contributed to better spirits city-wide and prevented riots breaking out that had previously seemed inevitable. One ray of light...

Father had been left holding the unhappy city and, to his credit, had set upon a campaign to bring the people back onto his side. Following the failings of the 'great' vicennalia, Father looked ahead to the *dies natalis urbis Romae* – the festival honouring the founding of the city. It was normally one of the lesser festivities, but this year would be a grand affair to promote the value of the city after Diocletian's diminishing of it. Of course, Father was ever a political animal, and he could not care less about the city's self-esteem in truth, but he did care for the ongoing support of the people. Too many emperors have found themselves with a blade in their heart because they heeded not the wishes of the people. But regardless of his selfish reasons, I was pleased to see the plans unfold.

I sat in the carriage, feeling the heavy weight of the sweat-sodden toga dragging me down in the unseasonal heat. Romulus peeked out of the window from behind the curtain with unconcealed excitement, clearly displeasing his mother who sat opposite us in stony silence, rarely lowering herself to look upon her family. Oddly, when I did catch her looking at me, it was not with the icy disdain with which I was most familiar, but with a worrying hint of calculation. What to make of that I had no idea and, while I would ponder it in due course, confronting Valeria about it could have no helpful outcome, I was certain.

The curtains of the carriage were drawn across for privacy and I could hear the crowd cheering as we passed. I knew it was at the sight of my father's Herculiani guard, a small unit of which had been assigned to protect us at our suburban villa, but it was heart-warming to hear nonetheless.

The wheels settled into the ruts worn in the road over the centuries and only occasionally bucked and bounced and, with time to spare, I smiled at Romulus and took my cue from him, drawing the curtain back a hand-width or so to peer out.

I was just in time to see the city walls go past, here surrounding a disused palace constructed over a century earlier by one of the empire's more infamous rulers, complete with its own circus and amphitheatre. I had heard that Father had constructed a small private arena in the gardens on the Palatine for his own private amusement and wondered at the sort of man who found the shedding of a small lake of blood relaxing. When the day came to build my own villa, I would not bother with such entertainments. Chariot racing, yes, but Rome was host to enough bloodletting without my adding to the torrent with private fights.

I watched the great gate pass by overhead and noted with dismay the poor condition of the battlements and the towers, a huge crack running down one of them. A good hit from a siege weapon and that tower would be little more than rubble. I had a sudden happy flash of memory to that day so long ago on the floor of the basilica anteroom in Treverorum, covered in wooden blocks. 'Your city lacks walls,' Constantine had declared. 'High ones. Strong ones. Walls that might have stopped my hand.'

I made a mental addition to the list of necessary city improvements I had been noting since my arrival. Walls. High, strong walls. Assuming Father and I would be staying in Rome for some time, someone had to look to the needs of the city. Father was only concerned with the support of the people, but I would produce for him a list of matters that needed attention in due course.

As we passed the defences, I gazed back along their line and was further disheartened to see the shocking condition of the walls. Staircases had collapsed, bricks were missing, whole sections without solid mortar holding them together. Astonishingly, it seemed the Urban Cohorts had allowed citizens to construct their dwellings butting right up against the defences with no thought for military efficiency and the need to manoeuvre along its length. Appalling. A single legion would overwhelm the city in an hour had it a mind to do so.

My mind strayed momentarily back to my old friend, the memory of the wooden block walls bringing him to the fore again. He and I had gone our separate ways once more in that square in Nicomedia, he to the birth of a son and I to the heart of empire, yet I felt oddly as though something of him had remained with me. The man who had saved me all those years ago in Treverorum had now done the same for my beloved son in Nicomedia even at the expense of his last moments with Minervina. The debt for my own life was a powerful one, but his selfless aid in saving Romulus had bound us to him forever. If I lived a dozen lifetimes I would still owe him for that.

Inside the defences the carriage turned left, clonked, rumbled and bounced on down the Via Caelemontana alongside the great aqueduct into the heart of the city, the blanket of silence inside broken by a series of exchanges between Romulus and myself.

'What are those, Father?'

'Those, my boy, are the grand gardens of Torquatus. Note the way they are so sculpted to the landscape that the surrounding press of buildings seems to be diminished and somehow made calm by them.'

'And that?'

'That used to be the barracks for the imperial horse guard. I actually don't know what they're used for these days, now that the *singulares* are based near the walls. Clearly they're in use by somebody, mind.'

Another place I would have to look at. Another mental note.

Soon we turned again, and again, and our destination loomed above the buildings around us.

'What's that place, Father?'

'Mmm?' I blinked as I focused on the long, squat heavy block, with barred windows and guards on the door, the walls scrawled upon with obscene graffiti. 'Oh, it's the sailors' barracks.'

'Sailors, Father? Here?'

'Wait and see.' I smiled.

And then the carriage was past the *ludus magnus* and into the square that surrounded the greatest amphitheatre in the world. Built by Flavius Vespasianus more than two centuries ago it remained one of the great symbols of imperial power and *Romanitas*. Three tiers of graceful arches – each containing a statue of a *loricate* or *togate* Roman – with a great white wall above, topped with the poles that supported a great sunshade. It was a stunning building. Having seen it a dozen times now, it still never failed to draw the breath from me.

This was the first time I had seen it on a day of games, though. Once, it had been busy almost continuously. These days only occasional festivals filled the great arena, and Father had spared little expense to make the dies natalis a huge affair, so the crowds massed around the square, trying to secure a place. Those outside stood no chance now, and many were climbing to the top of nearby rickety wooden insulae in the hope of getting even a poor view of the action. Now, with events already in motion, whoever was not already seated in the amphitheatre would be staying outside, disappointed.

Apart from those in the imperial family, of course.

Valeria threw me an arch look. She still would not exchange words with me, but her meaning was clear.

'We will be there for the main event, beloved. I weighed up the programme and decided on balance that we would arrive an hour late for the sake of our son.' Her look failed to return to normal, so I explained. 'We have missed the parade of exotic animals, which I would have liked Romulus to see, but my father has chosen to do away with a few troublesome outspoken Christians despite the amnesty granted by Diocletian, and I have no heart to make the boy sit through such things.'

Romulus' brow wrinkled. 'Will that not turn Rome into another Nicomedia, Father?'

I often underestimated the boy, thinking of him as an infant and forgetting that he was more than capable of reasoning through my words. 'I think not. Rome is not so much a hotbed of that cult as the eastern cities. Here, the rule of the Olympians still holds strong. Jupiter, Juno and Minerva still stand proud on the Capitol.'

Valeria fixed me with a look. 'You shield the boy from too much. You transfer your own weakness onto him. A little horror is good for the soul.'

Once again, she wore that strangely calculating look until she swept her gaze away, and I wondered whether it had something to do with being in Rome itself, or perhaps with the fact that dressed now in a toga I would look different, somehow akin to the statues of emperors and generals of old that we passed. In the end I decided it was probably wishful thinking and that she was truly as detached and unhappy as always. They do say that bearing children does unpredictable things to a woman's emotions, after all.

'I don't want to watch executions anyway,' Romulus said, for which I was immensely grateful.

'Weak,' said Valeria again.

I was saved from further discussion and thought on the matter as the carriage rolled to a halt and the Herculiani made way for us, their glares filled with the threat of drawn iron. I stepped out first, followed by Romulus, and then held out a hand to help my wife down. She flinched at my touch, but smiled coldly for the sake of appearances.

Within moments we were being admitted to the great amphitheatre and escorted up the staircases to the imperial *pulvinar*, where my father sat with a few ageing senators and notables, half a dozen Herculiani on guard, resplendent in black and red and glittering steel.

My father turned at the interruption, his now ample frame still large and powerful, his bushy, unfashionably long beard sending trickles of sweat down his neck, a flash of irritation passing across his face.

'About time. I was wondering if my overly sensitive offspring would deign to grace us with his presence!'

A few of the senators dutifully mumbled their agreement, and I bowed from the waist, politely, but not deep.

'Father. We had matters to attend to. Or perhaps I need remind you that your second grandchild grows within even as we speak?'

For the first time in months, Valeria opened her mouth and aimed words directly at me. 'Do not presume to use me as your excuse for weakness. Better that you make true account of your deeds and be found lacking than hide behind others.' Without another word she sank to the seat left clear for her and began to pick at the tray of foods awaiting her.

Father gave me a meaningful look, but I was saved further questioning as Romulus scurried over to him and grasped him in a hug. My father shrank back a little, dismayed at such a display of emotion in public.

'Enough, boy,' he admonished, though not unkindly. 'Come. Have a seat beside me and I shall give you some of my own wine.' He flashed a glance at me. 'Your father's tardiness means you have already missed two of the best sights of the day – the parade and the execution of four Christian priests. See: the slaves rake the blood into the sand even now.'

I rolled my eyes and then smiled as I heard a low rumbling and scraping sound. I looked up to confirm the noise was what I thought and then stepped across and tapped Romulus on the upper arm, pointing up to where the huge sunshade was being slowly extended across the arena.

'Sailors.' I smiled, pointing at the blue-tunic'd figures moving about the winches and ropes, where their nautical skill with sails and rigging made them indispensable. Romulus grinned at the discovery and watched until the shade was in place, covering the seating. His attention was drawn once more by my father, who turned him round and gestured to the sand of the arena.

I followed his pointing finger. To the slightly discordant melody of the water organ and the cornu horn, two slightly larger than man-sized crates were being wheeled out from each end of the arena by teams of workers. Perhaps nine feet tall and five in each other dimension, they could only contain a human.

'Gladiators?' I frowned. Father nodded and I scratched my head. 'But the fights should be scheduled for the afternoon. The morning's for the beast hunts.'

'Sometimes things need stirring up. I want to feast the people on blood today. Only with oceans of the stuff can we truly satisfy the populace and repair the damage done by my colleague's actions.'

I held my tongue. I knew my father well enough to know when not to bother arguing. Instead, I turned to the arena. I had to admit to a little curiosity over the display. While I had no desire to expose Romulus to the pointless and excessive murder of priests and no interest in private bloodlettings, I had no argument with him watching the public games. I had come to appreciate and even enjoy the games since the days of my youth. Indeed there is a level of skill and style involved that cannot be seen elsewhere, and Romulus was already becoming acquainted with the abilities of the different classes of gladiator he watched.

I took my seat and poured myself a glass of wine as the workers lowered the boxes to the sand, facing one another at opposite ends of the arena, and then removed their wheeled contraptions and returned to their shelter, closing and barring the doors behind them.

The music built to a climax and the referee, who had hitherto been standing in the shade at the sand's edge, stepped into the centre and threw out his arms.

'On behalf of the Ludus of Galicatus, I welcome you to the first fight of the day – a contest to the drawing of blood.' He bowed to the imperial box. 'Domine, I give you the greatest warriors beneath the gods. Titans of the arena. Slayers of a hundred men. Brothers in blood...' His voice reached up an octave and burst into the air as the fronts of the two crates fell open to the ground. 'Hercules and Jove themselves!'

I watched, dumbfounded, as the two gladiators stepped out of the boxes onto the sand. Before the Gate of Life stood a *dimachaerus* – a warrior with two swords – only lightly armoured, painted head to foot in silver and almost painful to the eye in the bright sunshine. Opposite him, in front of the Gate of Death, was a *murmillo* with the familiar heavy, crested helmet, arm guard and greave, wielding a sword and shield of old-fashioned legionary type. Unbelievably, his skin was painted head to toe with gold.

Was this supposed to be flattering? A homage? Maximian and Diocletian represented as warriors in the arena? I hardly dared look at my father. Clearly it appealed to the crowd in Rome, as the people roared their approval at the two gleaming, glinting warriors. Finally, taking a deep breath, I turned to my father.

He was looking at one of the notables sitting sweating in a toga. Titus Galicatus, I realised, the owner of the gladiators on show today. The man had a curious expression formed of mixed hope and dread. I knew which I would favour, especially having caught a glance at my father's eyes.

'Explain,' said Maximian, emperor of Rome, in a quiet, dangerous voice.

'Well, Domine, we thought that with your esteemed colleague's departure, it would please the crowd to...' His voice trailed off as he realised how large an error in judgement he had made. His eyes began to flicker and dart. 'Rest assured, Domine, that the fight has been carefully planned such that your august self will win. See how he stands before the Gate of Life in preparation.'

'You feel it is appropriate to insult your emperor simply because peasants are peeved? And you think that victory on my behalf will balance that?'

'Well, no, Domine. It was not intended...' The man was running with sweat now. My father turned back to the arena. The crowd were baying and howling with bloodlust. It could hardly be stopped now, so all Father could do was grind his teeth and make the best of it. With a grunt, he waved irritably at the referee to begin the bout.

Even as down in the arena the silver-painted Hercules swung his paired swords at his golden adversary, in the imperial box Father made an offhand gesture to one of the

Herculiani, at which the man stepped forward from the back of the pulvinar, blade drawn.

As the crowd's passion for violence surged all across the stands, their eyes locked on the battling Titans in the arena, the trainer of gladiators up in the imperial box jerked and bucked forwards, looking down in horror at the gleaming crimson blade emerging from his chest. I stared at the man's silent shock as my father hissed: 'Get rid of him before the crowd notices,' and two soldiers dragged the spasming, kicking *lanista* into the shadowy archway at the rear, a hand clamped over his mouth.

I kept my gaze on the gurgling, gasping shadows for a moment, unable to make out the figures within, and then turned my sickened gaze back to the arena as the grisly job was finished. Whatever the blood I was born to, I could never condone acts of pointless cruelty. Honour was something that should be synonymous with Rome, and I had tried to show Romanitas and honour in everything I did since I had come to this ancient city.

Neither was visible on the arena's sand that day, either.

In fascinated shock I watched as the figures representing the two emperors retreated from their first strike and whirled into another, the silver warrior smashing down a heavy blow that forced his opponent to raise his shield, while the second blade flicked low and almost took a piece out of his leg. The golden murmillo managed to drop his own sword in the way to block just in time.

Three more exchanges and I was beginning to wonder how the fight had been planned. It certainly looked as though they were doing their level best to murder one another. Pirouetting and leaping, ducking and spinning, sliding and leaning, the two men struck and parried like dancers, the ring of steel on steel and the clonk of metal on wood echoing out even above the hungry roar of the crowd.

And then the blow came. I had seen enough fixed fights in my time, often at the insistence of my father, that I could frequently spot the deliberate mistake, and this was a familiar one. As golden Jove swung wide, he brought his shield round too far, exposing his open shoulder to the silver man's second blade.

A sharp, red line across the shoulder, which started to run with blood as the golden man hissed with the pain. The two stepped apart and the referee moved in to check and confirm the blow. With a deep breath, he held out his arm and announced the victory.

'Now will we see beast hunts?' Romulus grinned. He had always liked the bears and wolves most of all in the arena. I smiled back. 'I imagine so.'

But my father had risen to his feet. 'I find this somehow lacking,' he announced, the crowd falling into a subdued hush at his words. 'A poor showing from this ludus. I feel the people of Rome have been short-changed. Continue the bout to the end.'

'The end, Domine?' asked the referee, incredulous.

'The death,' confirmed my father. 'And nick Hercules' shoulder to make the match even.'

The referee looked past my father, trying to search out his master.

'Don't concern yourself with your lanista. Galicatus will not be worrying about the loss of a valuable man today.'

Shaken, the referee nodded his understanding, licked dry lips and had a brief conversation with the two gladiators. The silver dimachaerus drew up his sword and sliced a matching line across his own shoulder. Having reached some kind of agreement with them, the referee stepped back and held out his hands.

'Begin.'

I watched as the two men resumed their fight. There was a subtle difference now as the two men were no longer choreographed, instead fighting to the bitter end. I glanced around at my family for a moment. Romulus was rapt. My father's face was dark. Valeria had finally perked up. It was the most alert and interested I had seen her in months.

'That poor idiot,' I said, looking down on the fight.

'Who?' asked Romulus.

'The poor idiot controlling the bout. He'd just better hope Hercules wins. If golden boy walks away from this arena, your grandfather will have issues to take up with the referee.'

Romulus simply shrugged off that worry. Children are so resilient.

I watched the bout again, but it was clear early on that the referee had little to fear in that matter. The twin-bladed warrior was dancing rings around the murmillo and even as I watched he managed three quick cuts, two to the already-wounded shoulder and one to the unarmoured leg. I saw the murmillo begin his long, slow descent into death then, oddly mirroring the great Diocletian's recent decline, in my eyes. His leg gave way once, twice, three times, and he found it hard to turn quickly. His thrice-wounded shoulder lost strength as it lost blood, and finally the large square shield fell to the ground.

It was almost painful watching the golden Jove trying to counter each blow and failing almost every time. Hercules was dancing around him, a lithe silvery figure, drawing line after line in the man's flesh, such that soon there was more gleaming red than gold.

Finally, almost anti-climactically, the murmillo sank to his knees, shuddering, and cast his sword across the sand, struggling to unbuckle his helm with his remaining good hand and sending it after the sword. Hercules stood over him and lowered the tip of his sword into position above the meeting point of the man's gleaming collarbones, looking up and awaiting the order. The crowd surged with cries to kill him or spare him – so few of the latter – and my father gave his gesture with thumb turned across throat.

I watched the death blow impassively and then shuddered as the figure dressed as Charon stepped out from the Gate of Death, wielding his huge, heavy mallet. The gladiator was clearly dead. We'd all seen it happen. Surely they would not heap insult on Diocletian by having his avatar's body brutalised? And yet my father did nothing to prevent it.

I stared in sick horror as Charon approached the prone corpse of the golden murmillo, raised the mallet and then brought it down on the man's head, bursting it like a blister.

'Now we can see some beast hunts,' my father said, patting Romulus on the head and leaning back to eat a morsel from his plate. My own appetite had vanished.

As the din diminished while the mess was cleared away and fresh sand scattered on the blood, I turned to my father. I don't know what made me bring up the matter then, but I put it down to a need to change the subject and raise something positive over the wreckage of this awful scene.

'Father, I have been thinking…'

'Something you do too much of.'

'There are parts of the city that need work, Father, just as much as the people's esteem. If we are to stay here and revive it as a capital of note, there are things that need attention.' He remained silent and unmoved, so I continued. 'The walls need repairing and heightening. There are unused barracks and abandoned palaces that could be reassigned or sold off. There is much waste and a lot of rundown structures. There is no camp for the Herculiani, even.'

Father waved aside my comments with a hand as though meaningless. 'I will likely be moving on to Mediolanum soon with an eye to the next campaigning season. I have almost had my fill of this place. I begin to appreciate what my colleague saw.'

What he saw? Sour cabbages and the shade of his burning wife, perhaps?

'But, Father, there are things that need...'

Again he cut me off with a hand. 'When I am in Elysium, you will be Constantius' Caesar in the West, and one day you will supplant him. You will rule, and then you can deal with your run-down ruin of a city. Do not pester me with the matter now, lest I lose my temper with you!'

Silence fell between us for a moment, and eventually Father rolled his eyes in irritation and gestured across the imperial box. 'See the man with the close-cropped beard over there? That's Anullinus, the Praetorian Prefect. He's sent me a list of engineering works he thinks we need to look at. Go talk to him. As long as you can find the money for it without touching my treasury, help yourself. I'm sure the two of you will have plenty to discuss.'

I glanced across at the Praetorian. There was something about the man's face that I instantly warmed to. He was not the greedy, fat senator that most of this gaggle appeared to be. He exuded purpose and strength. As I stood and turned to cross and introduce myself, I realised what it was: he reminded me of my friend back east.

'I will build your high, strong walls, Constantine.' I smiled as I strode towards the man.

15

CONSTANTINE

The marble hall was still and silent as I swept my gaze over the courtiers. Each of them glowered back at me, so reminiscent of the vultures that day in Augusta Treverorum. But there was one huge difference: this time, I felt no fear. Indeed, in this past year, I had felt little of anything at all.

'The Goths are restless.' I swiped a hand to the north, thinking of the beleaguered legions posted on that edge of the empire to face those savage tribesmen. 'The central section of the River Danubius needs a stronger garrison.' My words echoed around the hall; all eyes remaining fixed on me. 'We need to levy fresh cohorts – a new legion, even – to reinforce them.' I then cast my hand towards the east, imagining the sun-baked farmlands just beyond Nicomedia's walls, where countless souls toiled with their herds, wheat fields and vineyards. 'So I urge you to look no further than the Bithynian valleys. The people of these lands need to believe in their empire once more.' I didn't mention the source of their disenchantment. I hardly needed to. The city and surrounding countryside still bore the scars of the riots and the faces of the people were still weary and fearful, memories of the Edict of

Persecution remaining tender like an open wound. It had been some six months since Diocletian's amnesty, but it would take far longer for people to trust the emperor once more.

'We can train them with our best men,' I said, thinking of big Batius and his ilk. 'We can mould a new legion. We can give the people back their pride and belief.' I said these words with such conviction I almost believed them, my head held high, my gaze distant and austere and my shoulders square – just as old Lactantius had taught me. *Say it with hubris and you could sell horse shit to a king!* The applause that followed filled the hall, yet I heard nothing but an echoing voice in my head.

Constantine? You said you would come back to me?

Her voice wavered with fear, as if she was lost in some dark place, alone, calling for me. I closed my eyes as if lapping up the applause, only just managing to stifle the stinging tears as I did so. *I'm so sorry,* I offered to the memory. Then I thought of baby Crispus, our boy. So neglected by me in the year since Minervina's death. *I'm so, so sorry.* I pressed my thumb and forefinger together in a vain attempt to stave off the sorrow. In vain, because it simply brought back the images of the flames and the burning silo that had diverted me from her side, cost me the chance to spend those last few moments with her. That *damned* silo. Right at that moment I would have burned a city of silos to the ground just to have another instant with her.

When I opened my eyes, I saw not the clapping, cheering courtiers, but the only two in the hall who abstained. Diocletian and Galerius; the pair had been reunited in this crucible of a city for a few months now. Diocletian watched me with a curious look. Intrigued, encouraged, even. Was there some affinity there, under the layers of bitterness? He had lost his wife just as I had mine. The vile manner in which he had been widowed surely plagued him more, and he still wore that haunted, lost look. All I knew was that he saw me as a prospect for his beloved Tetrarchy. Did he really mean to raise me one day to Caesar? Perhaps he meant only to tempt me with the possibility to see how I might react or to keep me hanging on?

No, I realised, there was definitely something afoot. Many of the courtiers had been acting strangely recently and even down on the streets, there had been rumours and whispers of some impending shift of power. Some said that the Tetrarchy was on the verge of change. Had my head not been in such a mess I might have foreseen what was to come in the near future.

'And so it shall be; the levy will begin in earnest within the month,' Diocletian said lazily, as if dismissive of the fact that the order would affect the lives of thousands of men. Then he gazed through the stained window, seeing the midday sun blazing outside. 'We will resume for further talks tomorrow,' he concluded with a clap of his hands.

By his side, Galerius wore a look I can only describe as volcanic. His blocky face was bent into a severe scowl, his skin was a shade of puce and his eyes glowed like smouldering rocks. I did not give him the satisfaction of acknowledgement. Instead, I simply bowed and stepped down from the lectern and made to leave the hall. The corridors outside were thick with chattering courtiers and hurrying slaves. Their babble washed around me and I felt that familiar dark weight settle on my heart again. I would spend the rest of the day alone. Until I donned the mask of Constantine the military hero again the following morning, I would know nothing but despair. Then I sensed another figure walking alongside me.

'You spoke well once again, pupil,' Galerius said through taut lips. 'You have the emperor's court in your palm, it seems. Even the emperor himself speaks of you as if you were... his Caesar.' The last word came with a tremor of ire.

'Then it must be true that you schooled me well in rhetoric as well as military matters,' I answered, donning the mask once more to offer only an earnest smile. This both disarmed and irritated the Herdsman, and if I was so minded, I would have toyed with him more. But his next words negated any such possibility.

'Perhaps, perhaps. And so here is one more thing to ponder – a final part of your training, if you will.' His inky eyes pinned me. 'The persecutions are over, so the Christians can once again see this city as a shelter. So, in your opinion, should the city garrison now be thinned?'

I sensed something coming for me from the depths of his dark glare. 'I... I don't—'

But he cut me off. 'I think it would be wise to keep a healthy garrison, for the streets of this city are still far from safe. A flash of a blade in the darkness is all it takes for a life to end. And the outer wards of the palace are thinly guarded. Remember, you have the safety of your mother and baby boy to think about.' He stepped away from me, a foul grin spreading across his face as he saw that he had broken my mask. 'Until tomorrow, pupil.'

Panicked, I hurried for the chambers in the southern wing in a blur, then halted at the mouth of the corridor. I could not go any closer, you see, for at the end of that passage were the chambers where I had lived in with Mother and Minervina – and that would be too much, even to set eyes on the place. I had not been there in many months. Mother resided there alone, looking after little Crispus. I gazed down the corridor and confirmed that the two sentries I had personally selected were still there, either side of the chamber doorway. All was quiet. All was well. For now. I beckoned one of them, who hurried over to me at once. 'Sir?'

'Summon two more comrades from your century. Place one on the balcony and have another inside the chamber at all times. You and they will be paid handsomely for your efforts.'

'It will be done, sir!' he said, saluting.

Reassured, I swung away and headed to my private quarters in the adjacent wing of the palace: a bare shell of a room – apt for its occupant. What followed had been my routine for nearly a year, beginning shortly after Minervina's death. I heard the door slam behind me as I took up the jug of wine set out there in a daze. I poured a cup to the brim and emptied it in a few gulps. Panting, I waited, longing for the numbness to swamp my mind. Another cup, but still I heard her.

Constantine?

A third cup, and then it came. Dull, sweet nothing. The cup tumbled from my hand, clattering across the floor, and my head lolled. The stupor would fill the rest of my day, and then it would be time to don the mask again.

Many more months passed, and I neither found nor sought escape from my daily routine, altering it only to check upon the four loyal men I had assigned to watch and protect Mother and Crispus' chamber. Equally, I paid little attention to the growing whispers and rumours: fervent talk of new Caesars stepping up into the Tetrarchy.

As I left the marble hall on the first morning of August, I noticed Galerius with his acolytes, whispering, pointing at me. It seemed my fragile state of mind had become common knowledge. This only served to drive me back to my chambers at even greater haste. Once more, I sensed another striding alongside me and my heart sank. This time, the figure grappled me by the arm. I swung to face this one with a scowl.

'I hear you're getting shit-faced and you didn't invite me?' Big Batius grinned. At the same time I felt a wet nose sniffing at my hand. I glanced down to see Ferox, who slurped at my hand in welcome, tail wagging in barely contained excitement.

My anger vanished like a morning mist and I heard a long-forgotten sound. My own laughter. The big man didn't mention the times before when he and Lactantius had tried to dissuade me from retreating to my private quarters like this. He simply beckoned me. We left the palace and entered the sweltering streets. I smelt the sweet scent of freshly hewn wood, heard the tap-tap of hammers and the rasping of saws and noticed the towering and nearly completed new grain silo poking out above the streets ahead. Likewise, many of the other ugly scars from the riots were in the process of being repaired.

Batius threw a leather ball for Ferox as we went, and the hound pelted after it, leaping over low walls and scrabbling under fences to retrieve it. We strolled on into the cool shade of an open-fronted tavern that looked out onto the main way. We sat at a table and Batius nodded to the innkeeper, who brought us a jug of wine, two cups and a plate of bread – plus a bowl of cool water and a marrow-stuffed bone for Ferox. I looked around to see just a few other folk in the tavern. One toothless old man sat near us, alone, roaring with laughter at some imaginary conversation with an equally imaginary comrade. Even he was muttering something about the promised new emperors.

'That's been me.' Batius frowned, jabbing a thumb at the old man. 'Ever since you've been holed up in your chambers I've had to drink alone. I tried talking to Ferox, but he isn't one for conversation,' he said as he scruffed the dozing dog's head and ears. 'Even that old goat and his invisible mate were mocking me at one point.'

The big man's lie was transparent and good-hearted. He had many friends within the ranks of the city garrison and was well liked. Indeed, he was doubtless right now forgoing a rowdy drinking session with them by coming here with me.

I stared at my cup and the full jug of wine, unsure what to say. It had been so many months since I had last spoken with Batius honestly that I felt panic in my breast at the prospect of doing so once again. Then I realised the absurd irony of my situation. 'You saved me from drinking myself into oblivion, to bring me here to... drink myself into oblivion?'

Batius chuckled, then lifted the jug and filled both cups. 'Drink until your heart is content, sir. Just don't do it alone. Don't shut out your family or your friends. Your boy needs you.' He raised his cup. A smile grew across my face, and stinging tears tried to join it as I raised my cup, clacked it to his and then drank. We were soon jabbering, recounting tales of our years on campaign. On the main way at the front of the tavern, people hurried to and fro, babbling, chattering, absorbed in daily life. The shade and the midday heat swirled with the cheap wine and soon I realised that out here it was so much easier to set aside the anguished memories of Minervina. A stab of guilt struck me when I realised this.

'...and then there was the time that Porcus snagged his balls in his scale vest.' Batius rocked back on his seat, his craggy face widening as he roared with laughter and slapped his thigh. When I did not reciprocate, he knew to where my thoughts had strayed.

'Come on,' Batius said, tearing a piece of bread and cramming it in his mouth as he stood, nudging Ferox from his slumber. 'Let's go for a walk,' he said, inadvertently spraying me with crumbs.

The stark midday sun shook the fug of the wine from my mind and we strolled through the market, eyeing the scant collection of stalls and traders. They were facing tough times, as Diocletian's Edict on Maximum Prices remained in force. It seemed to have survived only because so much attention had been placed on the Christian persecutions and their aftermath.

'It lacks all sense,' Batius remarked, seeing one red-faced trader reluctantly handing over a sheet of silk for just a few bronze coins, despite the material having been shipped in from the eastern borders. 'Forced to sell their goods at a flat rate regardless of where the commodity came from and how rare it is.'

I chuckled, equally bemused. 'It's like selling ice to the Caledonians at an inflated price when they are surrounded by the stuff, then shipping it all the way to Syria and selling it there for the same fee, when they would happily pay small fortunes for such a luxury.'

Batius clicked his fingers then. 'Ah, speaking of Syria, have you heard who is coming to this city?'

I cocked my head to one side. When had I last read through the pile of untended messages in my chamber?

'Maxentius' mother, Eutropia, and his young sister, Fausta. They are finally leaving Syria to take up residence in Rome, and they're stopping here on their way,' Batius confirmed.

I smiled, more thinking of my absent friend than of his inbound relations. I knew he was fond of his mother and indeed he missed her. She had spent the last few years in Syria, raising Fausta, while Maximian went about his duties as Emperor of the West, touring the imperial cities there.

'They are due here sometime today. Well, they would have been here earlier, but they insisted on taking the land route through Anatolia – apparently both suffer from seasickness.' Batius' shoulders jostled in mirth as he bounced Ferox's ball on the spot – much to the hound's frustration. 'Though a few months on horseback or bobbing in some carriage might change their minds.'

We strolled past the docks and I inhaled the salt spray from the turquoise gulf. Gulls keened and the waves lapped at the wharf side. The place took me back to that day I arrived here, so full of hope for Minervina and our then unborn child. I turned away then, looking to Batius. 'Thank you, Batius. For today.'

Batius shrugged, curling his bottom lip. 'Eh? You paid for the wine. Thank *you*, sir.' He grinned mischievously.

We headed back towards the centre of the city as dusk approached. Batius bade me farewell, heading off towards the barracks, Ferox by his side, tail wagging frantically. I made my way to the palace, still smiling. Tonight, I affirmed, I would spend with Mother and Crispus. I would eat a hearty meal and sleep without the aid of the wine in my blood. If Minervina came to me in my dreams, I would welcome her – I would stow my self-pity and cherish the moment.

But as I strode along the tall corridor, a sentry hurried to intercept me. He handed me a scroll. It was battered and looked as if it had travelled far to get to me. Indeed, it bore the wax seal of the *Cursus Publicus*.

'A message from Britannia, sir,' the sentry said. 'The imperial courier brought it in this morning.'

I thanked him and walked on towards Mother and Crispus' chambers. I opened the scroll and noticed it had come from an officer on that distant, northern island. I slowed as I read it.

...your father begged me not to concern you, but I fear I must. He is gravely ill, Constantine. If you have any words you wish to share with him then I would urge you to hasten to his side...

My hands fell to my sides. The words were like a sharp jab to my gut and I sensed my spirit sagging. After so many years apart from Father, should I still care for him? The question mattered little, for the fact was I did. I sensed my thoughts spiralling again and I turned on my heel, hurrying back to my own private room. Once more, the door slammed behind me. Once more I took up the wine jug there in a daze. Once more I lifted the cup to my lips.

'Thirsty, are you?' A light voice spoke, halting me.

I swung round, startled. There, in the corner of the room, sat a dark-haired and dusky-skinned woman, cast in the shadows of sunset. My heart crashed against my ribs. I mouthed her name. *Minervina?*

She stood up and stepped towards me, into the fiery red shaft of sunlight that spliced the room. The light revealed a girl, barely ten. She wore a blue silk robe and a shrewd and slightly mischievous grin on her delicate features, and she seemed to be studying me intently. I noticed that she wore a fine, gold crescent moon pendant on her breast: a high-born girl, and a worshipper of Luna, I realised. I exhaled, assuming she was some spirited noble's child who had sneaked into my room. I made to show her the door, but she halted me with her words.

'My brother writes to me often. He told me much about you,' she said.

The familiarity in her words disarmed me. I noticed then that I recognised her, but couldn't place her exactly. *Your brother?* It was then I saw the resemblance. 'Fausta?'

'Very good.' She grinned, wheeling by me to the window, tracing a finger along the sill as she did so and inspecting it for dust. 'Maxentius – when he wasn't too busy lamenting my plans for his imperial accession – told me you were a good friend, and a war hero to boot?'

Shamefully, I donned the mask again, flashing a smile at her by way of confirmation.

Unlike the many others who fawned over me when I did this, she simply frowned and cocked her head to one side. 'That's strange. Your smile; it doesn't seem to reach your eyes. They look… sad.'

I assumed then that this was just the innocent observation of a child, but in the years to come, I would realise that it was her nature, shrewd and astute. I ignored the comment and lifted my wine cup again.

One of Fausta's eyebrows arched. 'Maxentius said many good things about you. But he did not mention that you were a sot.'

Her words stoked my ire. 'I am no such thing!' I roared, the cup a finger-width from my lips. Me, a thirty-three-year-old tribunus of the Roman army, brought to anger by a little girl. But she did not flinch at my booming tone; instead she simply shifted her gaze to the wine cup as I put it back down.

'If you say so,' was all she said with a tune of cynicism.

'Well after a hard day in the imperial court, a man needs to… to wind down, to relax,' I said, annoyed at my stammer.

'I would have thought that both you and my brother would want clear heads over the next year or so,' she countered. She read my puzzled look and sighed. 'You truly must have boiled your brain in that stuff if you do not know of the rumours.'

The damned rumours. 'All that talk of new Caesars? I have heard the chatter, yes, I have heard the panoply of names.' I swiped a dismissive hand through the air.

'Panoply?' she snorted. 'There are but two, and you *know* this.'

I avoided her gaze. She had penned me in like a goat with her words. There were two names being mentioned more than any others. *Constantine and Maxentius.* I scoffed and made to lift the wine cup again. But, like a cat, she bounded over and plucked the cup up before I could grasp it.

'Hold on,' I protested. But she strode back to the window, then unceremoniously upended the cup, tipping the wine out into the gardens below. I heard the spatter of the wine and the angered roar of some courtier below. Fausta sniggered at this, then turned back to me with a scolding look.

'Keep your head clear and your eyes open. I'll tell my brother the same thing when finally we meet,' she said, breezing past me to leave the room.

I noticed her gaze back at me more than once before she slipped outside. I gasped at her impudence, then laughed aloud, seeing that she had made her point and made it well. I grappled the wine jug, walked to the window and exclaimed. 'Thank you, Batius. Thank you, Fausta.' Then I looked to the sunset in the west and thought of distant Rome. 'Thank you, Maxentius.'

I emptied the wine jug into the gardens below with a

voluminous splash. With a more irate shriek than before, the already showered courtier was drenched fully this time.

I swept up my cloak and left the chamber, heading for the quarters of Mother and Crispus. Perhaps, I reasoned, it might be an idea to consider leaving this city. It had once been a beacon of hope, a haven for Mother and Minervina to escape the Christian burnings. But the persecutions had swept over this place like a conflagration. Now it was but a spent ember, a city of dark memories. And still the East as a whole seemed to be a never-ending crucible of trouble.

I wondered then if the western half of the empire – the realm of Maximian and Father – was like this. Or had those two ruled more wisely? The thought of the West as some paragon of hope teased me for a moment; Mother, Crispus and I might find peace in those lands, I mused. Then I heard the distant, playful squealing of little Crispus from the end of the corridor, which scattered my thoughts and hastened my step.

My footsteps echoed along the corridor and I passed several Joviani legionaries posted along the way. These were of the century Diocletian had assigned to be Galerius' personal bodyguard. Most of them wore stony and unflinching glares into the middle distance, but then I caught one pair. They were whispering. I was sure I heard their words. *It's him. Constantine.*

Innocuous words and truthful ones too. But coming from the personal guards of the Herdsman, they were spiced with something else. As I passed this pair they adopted the stiff military stance also, and I was on the cusp of letting my distrust slip away. But I saw something. One of them broke his gaze, shooting a furtive glance at me. A malignant glance that spoke a thousand words.

I thought again of Galerius' recent, barely veiled threats to me, and felt a stony resolution settle in my heart. This city was not just a husk of bleak memories, it was the lair of a venomous asp. But my family lay poised in its jaws, and I knew then that to make a move of any sort would bring its fangs down upon our flesh.

16

MAXENTIUS

ROME, APRIL 305 AD

'You seem to have everything well and truly under control here, Maxentius.' Mother fussed at her slave who was folding one of her favourite gowns in such a way that it would display a strong unwanted crease when unpacked. 'I am sure your assistant will cope with things while you are away.'

I turned in time to catch the look in Anullinus' eyes. The Praetorian Prefect was clearly less than impressed at being described as my 'assistant', especially since his brother had been Proconsular Governor of Africa for the past three years and had been taking every opportunity by missive to rub Anullinus' nose in the gulf between them. Still, in the presence of the wife of the Emperor Maximian – as well as his son – he wisely kept his silence and bent back to his work on the scale model of the city that occupied half the room. Somehow, working alongside the sharp-minded prefect and far from the shadow cast by my father, I had excelled at a level of civic and administrative control, some of the steel that I had always know to lie inside more visible now in my demeanour.

Letting the *stilus* in my hand drop back to the desk, I

looked up from my correspondence. I was already late with my quarterly missive to Theodora, so it could probably wait until I returned. At least now, with Mother and Fausta here, I had two fewer letters to write every few months.

'I wish you would assent to taking ship from Ostia,' I grumbled. 'We could be at Mediolanum in eight days that way. By road it is nearer sixteen; and through lands notorious for banditry.'

'I hardly think we will have to worry about a few thugs with your father's Herculiani escorting us, Maxentius. You will be gone for the large part of a month, perhaps, but no more. You do not have to stay in Mediolanum with us – gods forbid that you and your father actually occupy the same room for more than a day. When the day comes that you are Augustus of the West and young Romulus is your Caesar, remember the distance between you and your father and be sure not to emulate it.'

I subsided into a sullen silence that was far too juvenile really for the master of Rome, and from the flash I caught of Anullinus' expression he had come to the same conclusion. Why was it that no matter how much control I had or how adult I became, even the mention of my father was enough to turn me into a moody adolescent?

Mother and my delightful sister had arrived three days previously, travel-worn and tired after taking a long route to Rome from Nicomedia where they had sojourned briefly with my old friend Constantine. The epic trip had taken them across the Hellespont and along the Via Militaris from Byzantium to Singidunum beyond the mountains, and then turned west, passing into Italia around the curve of the *Mare Adriaticum* and crossing the mountains to Rome, where they had expected to be reunited with my father. Little had they known that Father had uprooted and moved his court to our former home of Mediolanum in the early spring.

And so I, along with the small unit of Herculiani Father had left at my command, would be escorting Mother and Fausta to Mediolanum to rejoin Father. I couldn't help a small spark of jealousy rising in me – not for them reuniting with my father, but for my father who would get to spend time with my mother and the exquisite Fausta, while I would have only the three days in Rome and the difficult days of travel to enjoy their presence. It seemed unfair, since they were a shining light in my life and, as far as I could see, Father hardly noticed whether they were there or not. It had thrilled me to discover that my sister had grown from the precocious girl with whom I had corresponded into a bright, inventive and sharp young woman.

And Romulus would miss them. He loved my mother as much as I did, but with only a year or so between them, he and Fausta had almost instantly become fast friends – more like siblings than aunt and nephew. My boy, as always, had a fondness for active, somewhat dangerous games, but Fausta had taken to looking after him and curbing his most enthusiastic stunts.

Valeria, as always, left her son's care to others, largely ignoring my existence and busying herself somehow. What I did notice was that she at least seemed to be taking an interest in her surroundings these days, and those occasional calculating looks I had caught her throwing me were now also occasionally levelled at Anullinus too, as well as Fausta.

Romulus chuckled at something Fausta said, and I turned with a smile to see the two of them even now playing with the wooden models of the new city walls, giggling mischievously as Prefect Anullinus sought for the next piece to fit to his model of the proposed works only to find that it had vanished by the sleight of hand of two youngsters. With a grumble, the prefect snatched from behind a curtain the tall, a twin towered representation of the newly planned Porta Appia and located the gate on the southern side of the huge model, sliding the hollow block over the current gate to highlight the strength of the proposed changes. At more than twice the original height and with a double set of windows for artillery and archers, twin walls connecting it with a rear gate and turning it into a mini-fortress, it was a perfect example of our plans for the entire circuit. Rome would be strong once more.

'Do you have everything you need for construction to begin?'

Anullinus gave me his usual long-suffering look. 'Yes, Domine. Work will go ahead as planned. By the time you get back, I intend to have two sections of the new gallery walks complete and the southern ditch near the Porta Appia dug and shaped.'

'That fast?' interjected Fausta, and the prefect turned a troubled look upon her, his expression making it clear that he was unsure how to address the young girl, or where she stood in the ranks of the powerful. In the end, he smiled. I always liked Anullinus – perhaps if I had not, things would have been so much different, but the man always said the right thing, no matter the circumstances.

'I have brought in the sailors from the Misenum fleet as well as granting amnesty to a large group of petty criminals in return for their efforts on the project – your brother's idea, that, Domina. With a little creative planning, we have more than trebled our workforce.'

Fausta nodded in the manner of an officer reviewing her men and Anullinus let out a chuckle. 'You approve, Domina?'

My sister straightened and reached out, snapping her fingers. Romulus obediently plopped the section of wall expansion he was holding into her hand.

'Why work on two things at once?' she mused as she turned the block over and over, examining it. 'If you fear for the safety of Rome, concentrate all your efforts on the outer ditch first and then, when that is in place, you can turn to the work on the walls. It will also give you more time to bring your materials in before work begins and supply you with ample earth and turf for an embankment behind the walls if you so desire.'

With a grin, Fausta dropped the wooden expansion over the appropriate wall section and stood back folding her arms. Anullinus laughed. 'I cannot help but wonder, Domina, whether your brother might be better sending me to Mediolanum and putting you in command of the works.'

The room warmed with gentle laughter and finally the prefect stretched. 'If you will excuse me, Domine... Domini... there are a number of influential senators in the council chamber to whom I need to attend. Useful work is oft interrupted by the trivial.'

I gestured my consent and Anullinus bowed and retreated from the room with a click of the latch.

'You leave the Praetorian Prefect to deal with senators?' Mother sounded worried.

'Anullinus knows the senators well – knows who to trust and who to watch.'

'It is not the job of the Praetorian Prefect to mediate between you and the senate, Maxentius.'

'No. But then dealing with them is not my job either, Mother. It is a task that should fall to Father or his court. In his absence, I would rather the prefect worked with those he knows than involve myself in things that are not my business. I am not the emperor, Mother. The day that Father passes into Elysium and power comes down to me – when I am made Caesar – I will take control of such things, but too many ill-fated power-seekers have fallen from such interference in the past and I do not intend to add my own name to that list of the damned.'

Mother shook her head. 'You are making yourself a cross upon which they will crucify you if you are not careful. You claim to have learned from history and yet you put your trust in a *Praetorian Prefect*? I suggest you read your histories again, Maxentius. Why do you think your father and Diocletian founded their new units and relegated the Guard to a civic peacekeeping force? Besides, that *distant* day of your advancement might not be quite as distant as you believe. Surely you noticed Diocletian's decline? Well it seems it continued beyond his days in Rome, and they say that he is quite mad now, that his body follows his mind's descent. And when he succumbs, your father will be the senior Augustus. You could be donning the purple so soon, Maxentius…'

'Enough, Mother! Are you almost packed? If we are to make good time today and reach Sutrium by nightfall we need to set out as soon as possible.'

MEDIOLANUM, LATE APRIL 305 AD

I was weary and not in the best of moods as I stomped through the corridors of the recently refurbished imperial residence in Mediolanum, its walls still fresh with red and gold paint, busts of great men lining the walls, leaded windows admitting the strong sunlight and still failing to alleviate the opulent gloom. I had not seen these buildings since I was young. Then they had seemed so impressive, but then I had not yet seen Rome in those days.

Behind me thumped four men of the Herculiani, chosen for their size and expressions. I was in no mood to deal with my father in anything less than a business-like, speedy manner and then get back on the road south. There was no real reason for my mood, of course, but it had gradually darkened over the past three days as we neared my father's centre of power. The West's Augustus cast a vast shadow, and its darkness chilled me even at a distance.

To compound my mood, the guards at the city gate had been less than welcoming, questioning me in a most unacceptable manner and even peering into the carriage at the women before agreeing to admit us, despite the presence of the Herculiani. Then as we had pushed our way through the busy streets, that same carriage had broken a wheel on a badly repaired gutter, causing Mother to fall within and bruise her head. Finally, as we arrived on foot at the entrance to the palace, the Herculiani there had been unhelpful and even evasive before allowing us to pass and sending for a slave to escort us to my father's *tablinum*.

I huffed as we stamped across mosaics and *opus sectile* in our nailed boots. Ahead of us the house slave slowed and stopped before a door.

'The emperor's office,' he announced.

I looked to either side of the door at the Herculiani guards who stood there, impassive and expressionless. They reminded me all too much of my wife and the realisation did little to calm me.

'Then announce me!' I snapped at the slave.

Recoiling slightly at the sharpness of my voice, the old, bald man bowed his head and then knocked thrice on the wood before entering. I waited irritably, trying not to take offence at the continued indifference of the door guards, until finally the old slave reappeared and held the door open, bowing and gesturing for me to enter. As I neared the door, he cleared his throat and held up a barring hand. 'Not your men, Domine.'

I swear that I almost punched the man then for his insolence, and only held myself back because I knew the orders were not his. I did not relish the idea of facing my father in this mood without the support of the chosen hard soldiers who had accompanied me, but I had little choice. My father was Augustus in the West, and his word was higher than law. Gesturing for my soldiers to wait here, and with a vicious look cast at the slave, I stormed into the office.

The room was bright. Brighter by far than the dim corridors, lit by one huge window facing east and with the dark walls made brighter by the maps hanging over them, depicting my father's domain. By the time my eyes had adjusted and I could make out all the details, the door had clicked closed behind me and I was shut in the room with its occupant.

It was not my father.

I did not immediately recognise the man, but his nature was clear from the fact that he was dressed as a commander of the army and not some affluent courtier. As my eyes picked out the lantern jaw and the broad, muscular frame, the slightly rheumy ice-blue eyes and the weathered, sun-tanned – if ageing – skin, something about him was familiar, despite my ignorance of his name. My anger suddenly boiled over.

'Where is my father?'

The man leaned back from his work at my father's desk, not even bothering to rise in my presence – a fact that irritated me all the more. 'Maxentius. A surprise, I must say,' rasped the man.

I forewent the obvious question as to the man's identity, as my ire was already rolling forth from my tongue.

'I demand to see my father. I have travelled hundreds of miles, abandoning the most important work in Rome, to bring my mother and my sister here. Only a fool would settle his court here and not have adequate watch and scouts, and so I must assume that you had at least an hour's warning of our approach. And yet I get here to find my father absent. Does he not even have the decency to be here to greet us? Would he send one of his soldiers in his stead?'

I noted a shift in the man's expression then, and realised that 'soldier' was clearly belittling his rank. Whoever he was, he was a senior officer of some sort – perhaps even a general. I had a sudden flashback to the court at Augusta Treverorum so many years ago when I had been sent before my father to explain my bruises. This man had been there, arguing with my father. He had been two decades younger then, hungrier but less sure of himself.

Severus. He was called Severus.

'Your father is momentarily absent, Maxentius. He will return presently.'

His slightly breathless, rasping tone brought me right back to that earlier time. I remembered him then: one of the vultures of the court, seeking position and influence. I had not realised that he still stalked the corridors of power – I had not heard tell of him since then. Clearly he still commanded a strong military force. I forced myself to calm down as far as I could – this man was something of an unknown to me, and it would do me no good to become immediately branded as trouble for my temper and my obstinacy. Besides, it was my father with whom I was truly angry, and a misdirected shot rarely ends well.

'My apologies, Severus,' I managed. 'The journey has been trying and...'

'And your father lay at the end of it.' He smiled. 'You are forgiven.'

How generous of you, I thought spitefully in the silence of my heart. Through the clenched teeth in my mask of civility, I managed: 'How go things in my father's court?'

'Troublesome as ever,' snorted Severus. 'That idiot Gaius Annius has made a hash of things in Africa, and your father simply tells me to sort it. I've had to recall him and send the Corrector Volusianus to Africa in his place.'

I nodded. Volusianus was a name known to me. He had been *Corrector Italiae* when I was young and had performed miracles with the Italian economy. The news that Prefect Anullinus' brother was to be recalled was interesting, though. Would he be brought to Mediolanum or sent to Rome? From the few conversations we had managed on the subject, I knew the brothers to be anything but cordial.

'And it seems,' Severus went on, 'that Constantius ails in Britannia and his campaign falters. Your father complains that if the "pale one" dies he will have to travel to that northern shithole to take command himself.'

My heart went out for a moment to Constantine. I hoped that when he received the news himself it came couched in more respectful terms. 'Is that why you are here, Severus? My father's plans for a military campaign?'

'Not precisely...'

Whatever Severus had been intending to say went unheard, since that moment the door slammed open, crashing back against the wall so hard that the hinge almost snapped, the handle chipping the freshly painted plaster. My father's wide frame filled the doorway, and I almost recoiled at the sight of him.

I had witnessed my father angry many times – indeed, it seemed to be his natural state. But I had never seen him quite this furious and with the benefit of hindsight, despite everything that was to follow, I think I never saw him that angry again. I swallowed my own mood, for confronting him now would do me no good at all. His face was a dark purple colour, the veins standing out proud on his temples and his neck. He was actually shaking slightly as he cradled something in his arms as though it were a precious babe.

With surprise, my gaze fell upon a shape in the corridor behind him: Candidianus of all people! I had seen the dull-witted and vicious bully precious few times since the day he had beaten me at Treverorum, but absence and time had done nothing to dull my hatred of him, nor his of me. Galerius' sickening son looked every bit as worn and dusty as I did, and I realised that he had just arrived from a long journey in much the same way.

From where? Had he brought this parcel so carefully cradled by my father? What could hold enough value to be given the son of Galerius as a courier and to draw such reverence from my father? Something vast and worrying was afoot, and I found myself stepping forward towards him, my face a mask now of concern.

'Father? What is it? What has happened?'

Confusion numbed me as my father brushed me aside as though I were irrelevant chaff, taking five long, powerful strides towards his own desk. Clearly Severus had pieced together something I had not, for a wide, sickening grin spread across his face as my father halted and threw the bundle with as much disdainful force as he could muster. The package, wrapped in oiled leather against the elements and tied with a leather strap bearing Diocletian's own seal, smashed onto the table, scattering wax tablets, piles of parchments and styli and coming to rest under Severus' outstretched hand.

I felt the menace of the moment thrill through me like a cold wind, raising my hackles like the waving of barley in the chill breeze.

'Father?'

Maximian, Emperor of the West, looked back only long enough to register my presence and then, his face still dark as an Anatolian storm, marched out of the room, slamming the door behind him.

I turned to see that horrible, sickening smile on Severus' face again. Though I knew not what had just happened, I had the distinct feeling that the whole world had just shifted slightly.

17

CONSTANTINE

NICOMEDIA, 1ST MAY 305 AD

A watery morning sun bathed Nicomedia. For once, this hive of a city was quiet and the streets were all but deserted. The only sign of movement came from the few sentries on the sun-bleached walls and the imperial banners fluttering in the occasional weak breeze atop the gatehouse towers.

Batius, Lactantius and I hurried along the main way, our footsteps echoing in this eerie silence. We climbed aboard the wagon awaiting us by the city's eastern gate and soon it was jostling along the Bithynian highway. Shafts of sunlight and shade flitted across us as we moved through the burnt-gold countryside, dotted with shady ash and poplar groves. Cicadas sang and birds soared in the unspoilt, eggshell-blue sky. My surroundings were faultless. But inside, I had never been more anxious.

I pressed my thumb and forefinger together and tried to focus on pleasant things – like kissing Mother and hugging sweet, little Crispus before I had left my chambers this morning. But every jolt of the wagon wrenched me back to the present. My mouth was dry and my bladder full – despite having tended to both issues only a short while ago. It was akin to the moments before battle, I realised. My back was damp with sweat and the sweltering heat prickled unpleasantly on my skin. My toga – fine white silk edged with gold – seemed uncomfortable and ill-fitting, though Lactantius assured me it was apt attire for what was to come. All morning he had fussed over me like an old hen, even more so than Mother had. Even now, I could tell he was still itching to advise me.

'Sit straight, rest your left hand on your breast and keep it there!' he tutted, gesturing to show how I should change my posture.

And for every line Lactantius offered, Batius seemed determined to counter it with one of his own.

'Leave him be.' Batius chuckled. 'He's never worn a thread of fine silk in his life. Why should he start now?'

Lactantius glanced at the big man. The old goat's face was knitted in exasperation. 'Have you finally pickled your brain in wine?' he said as if talking to a village idiot. 'Have you been so inebriated that you missed the endless preparations, all for this day?'

'Cah! How could I miss it?' Batius swiped a hand through the air and then – as if to goad the old man – produced and then swigged from a hidden wineskin, finishing with an exaggerated sigh of contentment and a watery belch. 'Every bloody street and tavern has been full of chatter about it. Diocletian, Diocletian, Diocletian!' He flapped his fingers against his thumb as if mouthing the words. 'I need a good drink to clear my head of all the talk.'

My heart ached for the big man, for although he was ever fond of wine, his drinking today and in recent times was nothing to do with the affairs of the state. It was a means to distract himself form the absence of his faithful friend, Ferox.

The hound had developed a sudden weakness in its back legs during the winter. Within a month, he was gone. It had broken the big man's heart, but he simply didn't know how to show it. The wine helped numb him to the acute loss, and I understood that well.

As Lactantius and Batius squabbled on, I turned my gaze to the passing countryside. I felt my gut churn, thinking of what lay ahead. The previously empty road was now dotted with men, women, children and soldiers. They were all heading to the same place. To the Jovian Hill, a few miles east of Nicomedia. This was the dusty hummock where Diocletian had been proclaimed emperor some twenty years previously. And it was on this same hill that the man would today relinquish his throne.

The rumours of new Caesars had been the talk of the eastern capital for months, flitting around the streets like a whispering breeze. But that had been overshadowed with the growing reports that Diocletian had been deeply unwell in these last months. Some said he was suffering from some grim illness. Others said he had lost his mind in the years of the persecutions, and was now adrift in endless lament for what he had done – and well he should be, I mused, not for the first time. A brave few suggested he might even have been poisoned.

I dismissed most of these claims as whimsical at first, until I saw the Augustus of the East for myself earlier that year on his return from a tour of the northern frontiers. The shrewd but ailing man who had taken great interest in me in these last years was gone, replaced by a gaunt husk. He had never been a physically imposing figure, but now he was listless, his eyes black-ringed, his back hunched and his gait humble.

I leaned from the side of the jostling carriage to see the hill, up ahead. The many cartwheels, boots and sandals kicked up a dust cloud that stung my eyes and dulled the watery sun, but I could see that thousands upon thousands had gathered around the hill. A hive of citizens swarmed on the flat ground, garrison legionaries ringed the base of the hill, ranks of senators, officers and noblemen lined its slopes, and a detachment of Joviani legionaries guarded the hilltop itself. On the crest of the hill stood a marble temple of Jove and before it, a towering bronze statue of the deity. The statue held one arm skywards, a halo of sunlight dancing on its burnished skin, tall and muscled and so unlike the husk of a man who claimed to be its flesh-and-blood representation.

Just a month ago, when word had spread that the ailing emperor was to address his armies and his people in this prominent spot, the whispered rumours were confirmed. The populace were sure that he was to abdicate. First, there was a wave of shock: this would be the first time in well over a hundred years that an emperor had not died or been slain in office. Then tides of emotion had washed around the city. Laments from his hardy core of supporters, cautious celebration from those who opposed his rule and outright elation from a brave few. Yet the initial groundswell of opinion faded as the populace considered the consequences of Diocletian's retirement. For the tetrarchic system demanded that he be replaced by his immediate subordinate.

Galerius was to be Emperor of the East, senior Augustus in the Tetrarchy and master of the entire Roman world. The Herdsman would be answerable to none but the gods.

A sharp knot formed in my gut and I drew my gaze back inside the carriage. Lactantius and Batius were still bickering, and their debate had followed the same path as my thoughts.

'Today is not a day for celebration,' Batius insisted, despite the cheering from the crowds outside. 'The Herdsman will be the master of the empire by dusk.'

'And that—' Lactantius grinned, wagging a finger as if he had just brought a recalcitrant pupil to heel '—is why Constantine will also be a vital player in the day's events.'

They both looked at me and I felt my nerves jangle. Outside I heard many chanting my name, having spotted me. I adopted a stern, steady look, so incongruous with how I felt inside. 'We know nothing of my role in today's proceedings. Only Diocletian and Galerius know who will fill the void.'

'Nonsense!' Lactantius exclaimed. 'In the West, Maximian will step down and your father will take his place as Augustus.' I felt a touch of warmth at this. My father would today achieve all he had wished for, it seemed. He was to become lord of the western half of the empire, answering only to the Herdsman. I wondered then at his health. I had seen to it that a rider of the Cursus Publicus would bring such news to me: the messages were vague, but it seemed that his illness had faded in recent times.

'And the young wall-builder will be his Caesar,' Lactantius continued, clicking his fingers in search of the name. 'Maxentius!' he finally remembered. 'And here in the East you will be Galerius' Caesar, just as the people have been saying for many months. Diocletian has had you earmarked for this for a year at least,' Lactantius insisted, leaning over, clasping a hand to my shoulder. 'And you can hear the will of the people, so stow your modesty! You are to step up and become Caesar of the East. With you by Galerius' side, he can be tamed.'

The wagon drew to a halt and two Joviani legionaries opened the door. The sea of sweating faces outside was a jumble of inebriation and expectation. Clouds of dust billowed over them and the air was thick with the tang of roasting meat and rich wine. Drums rattled and a cluster of lute-players struck up a shrill melody.

'Constantine the Goth Slayer is here!' one cried.

'The new Caesar has come!' another bellowed. My name swept around the crowds like a breeze.

The Joviani legionaries motioned, ready to escort me to the hill. I readied to step out, when Batius grabbed my arm, halting me. The big man's eyes were narrowed on the hilltop, where Galerius already stood, silhouetted by the mid-morning sun. 'If you finish the day by that dog's side, then I suggest you wear iron, not silk.'

The raucous cheering continued unabated as I came to the hilltop. There, Galerius greeted me with a glacial eye and an odd grin. For once, he was not painted, but he reminded me of a gull that was about to feast. I genuflected as earnestly as I could manage. A few other preferred dignitaries had been allowed up there: some were military men, I guessed, seeing their scarred hands and faces and close-cropped hair; others were grey-haired, soft-skinned senators. And there were the ubiquitous Joviani in full, pale blue ceremonial armour, plumes flitting in the weak breeze. I swept my gaze down around the slopes of the hill, seeing the lesser generals and minor nobles there, Batius and Lactantius too. And then on the flat ground, it seemed as though all Nicomedia – no, all Bithynia! – looked on, mouths agape as they hailed us.

When the cheering lessened, I turned to see that Diocletian had arrived at last. A hush fell on the crowds as they watched him struggling to ascend the slope, even with the help of two Joviani legionaries. The dust clouds cleared and the full glare of the sun fell on the retiring emperor, as if examining his every faltering step. Age had battered the man, it seemed. The stark, white streak of hair that had appeared that day when he burned his wife was now battling to be seen against his almost all-white and unusually unkempt locks. He was muttering to himself, I noticed, shaking his head. *The verse of penitence?* I guessed. A nascent sorrow stirred in my breast at the sight of him, but memories of the many who had died during the persecutions swept it away.

Then I thought of Minervina and wondered again as I so often did: had I been at her side and not tending to the riot that raged on that dreadful day, might she have survived? I plunged even further into that dark well, wondering why I had given my time to Maxentius to help save Romulus from the flames; for by doing so I had unwittingly forsaken the chance to be with Minervina at the end. He still had his boy... I was a widow. I could have saved her. I was sure of it. It was a dark, dark pit of a place.

When Diocletian reached the top of the hill, the smattering of nobles parted, allowing him to step up onto the base of the Statue of Jove. Never had the incongruity between this man and his patron deity been so apparent. Diocletian trembled, head bowed, barely as tall as the statue's ankle. When he looked up, I saw that his eyes were brimming with tears. They jostled there as he beheld the crowd, some darting to wet his cheeks. *Where were your tears on the day you watched your wife burn?* I wondered. *Just one word and you could have spared her!* For once, I felt no anger or loathing for the man, just confusion.

'My people,' he began, his voice weak and high-pitched, raising both arms with great difficulty. The nearby hills did well to amplify his words. 'I have stood at the helm of the empire for so many years. With the strength bestowed on me by Jove, I have guided her through many difficult and choppy waters. Now, I am *tired*. I need to rest. I must step aside.'

This was no surprise to the masses, but they gasped nonetheless. I saw some slave hurrying over to Galerius, swiftly brushing at his skin, applying gold paint. The sight turned my stomach.

'And my gift to the empire, my tribute to Jove, is the tetrarchic succession. When an emperor dies or steps aside, there will no longer be wars of succession, no blood spilled to claim the throne.'

A desert-dry laugh almost spilled from my lungs. Such an absurd contradiction coming from this man. Yet in the years that would follow, I would become that contradiction.

Galerius, daubed in gold, stepped up beside Diocletian. The brute towered over the retiring emperor as never before. His inky eyes swept around the crowd, over the Joviani who were now his. Finally, they swept over me.

Diocletian unclasped his purple cloak, turned to Galerius and handed it to him. 'I am Augustus no more. As I step aside, I now entrust the empire to the man who has been my Caesar for so many years and is now Augustus in my place.'

Again, this was no surprise to the watching crowds. They had long known how the tetrarchic system was to work. But again they cheered. It was an odd sound, riddled with fear rather than adulation. But still, the ground shuddered at the noise and the Herdsman bathed in the attention, sweeping the imperial purple across his shoulders and clasping it into place. He did not even notice Diocletian shuffling down from the base of the statue. Few did.

'My people,' Galerius boomed.

I felt the urge to retch.

'I foresee many glorious years ahead,' he continued.

On he talked, and I wondered if the first of those fortuitous years might be spent listening to his cheap rhetoric on this hill. My mind wandered from his speech, and I tried to ready myself for what was to come. I would have to stand by his side and pretend to be grateful for the right to do so. Batius' warning rang in my thoughts. I would have to tread more carefully than ever around the Herdsman, so the big man was right. One of Lactantius' many maxims echoed up from the vaults of memory too:

The best way to outwit your enemy is to convince him that you are his friend.

As Caesar to Galerius, I could be sure of his motives. More sure at least than if he and I moved in different circles. If I could understand him, then perhaps I could assuage his doubts over me. Perhaps Mother and Crispus might be safe in this city, in the Herdsman's favour?

Galerius' next words snagged my attention: 'On this very day, just as Diocletian, Emperor of the East has stepped down, so too has Maximian, Emperor of the West. Just as I have taken the helm in the East, Constantius has stepped up to take the purple robes in Maximian's place.'

I thought of Father again, at the other edge of the empire in distant Britannia, and prayed he was well.

'And rising to become Caesar of the West by his side is...'

I thought of my friend, Maxentius. The lad would have a hard time adapting to life in such a lofty position, but perhaps, free of his domineering father's influence, he might just blossom in that role.

'...the hero of the northern battlefields, Severus!'

The breath caught in my lungs. I thought of the lantern-jawed dog I had first laid eyes on in Treverorum all those years ago. Then, he was but another man in officer's garb.

In the years since, I had watched him rise through the ranks, following in Galerius' wake like a loyal and vicious mastiff. Severus was no leader of empire. Severus was Galerius' man, utterly. A hardy bodyguard at best. This surely had not been the choice of Diocletian?

'The robes have been sent to Mediolanum and Severus will take up his post at once,' Galerius continued. 'Likewise, I too need a Caesar to sit by my side here in the East.'

Just then, I noticed a slave boy bearing silver paint and a brush, hurrying uphill. This young lad would be the one to paint me silver, I guessed. The new Hercules. I wondered how long I might have to accept such ludicrous ceremony before I could safely shun it. The crowd broke into a keen babble, and I heard my name again. 'Constantine is to be Caesar!' one voice cried. I saw Lactantius and Batius offer me firm nods of encouragement, just as the slave boy reached the top of the hill.

But the lad ran past me. I heard gasps of confusion at this. I was sure to show no reaction. From the corner of my eye, I saw the slave run over to one of the military men, a few years older than me. I recognised him by his wild-eyed glare and feral grin. Daia, he was called. Galerius' nephew. A dark-haired wolf of a soldier who had risen to prominence on the Danubian frontier. I had witnessed him taking part in the persecutions. The man had led many of the tortures and burnings at Galerius' behest. Just like Severus, Daia was Galerius' man. And *Daia* was to be Caesar of the East!

Indeed, the slave boy started dusting Daia's face with silver paint. It was then that I risked a glance up to Galerius. He was already watching me with his gull-stare, eager to see my reaction. His smile was devoid of warmth.

'Gaius Valerius Galerius Maximinus Daia will be my *loyal* Caesar...' Galerius began. I heard little else of what was said.

Batius had insisted this would be a black day. Yet I had never imagined it could be this dark. The Herdsman was master of the Roman world. The Fates of millions dangled at his behest, and he had just cut me loose.

There would be no safety in Nicomedia, I realised. Not for me, nor for Mother or Crispus. But where can a man run, when the world is in his enemy's talons?

PART 3

Si vis pacem, para bellum
(If you seek peace, prepare for war)
– *Vegetius*

18

MAXENTIUS

ROME, AUGUST 305 AD

Romulus looked up at me as we left the forum, our boots clacking on the flagstones and grating on the gravel here and there. The air was filled with that heady mix of sweat, dung and cooking meat that seemed to be the natural aroma of the city in summer, and the searing, stifling heat of the blazing sun in the cloudless sky made every step laborious. Yet still we walked.

'Are we safe, Father?'

It was an excellent question, and not one I felt confident answering with any certainty. I mumbled a vague affirmative while keeping my eyes on the populace around me. No one in the forum could realistically have any idea who I was, of course – not that it mattered since Diocletian's shock decisions in the spring. But with the general mood of the people of Rome, it mattered not who I was, the fact that I wore a toga with a broad purple stripe marked me out as a member of that class currently unpopular with the common folk.

I strained my ears to listen as we passed towards the *Meta Sudans* – the great conical fountain that stood beside the Flavian amphitheatre. The sounds were funnelled along the forum valley by the slopes of the Palatine hill to my right and the imposing temple of Venus and Rome on my left.

Somewhere not far behind, an angry citizen stood on a plinth and harangued the crowds with his denunciations of the empire's masters for what was happening to the city. His voice was hoarse with shouting, but still clearly audible even this far away as he spoke his heart and the crowd hummed their agreement. Soon his voice would die off, when the Praetorian Guard took him down from there – probably on the point of a spear. The fact that he had ranted for so long only went to show just how stretched the Guard was at the moment.

I gestured to Romulus to pause for a moment and we turned toward the Palatine and leaned on the low wall that flanked the entrance to the small bath complex built by the madman Heliogabalus. As we listened to the unhappy mood of the city, I heard a sudden rush of noise back in the forum and then a cry of anger from a dozen mouths... the outspoken orator's voice had disappeared. The Guard had reached him, then.

'Father, why do the people not have enough grain?'

'Because Severus ordered some of the shipments diverted from Rome to Mediolanum in the north, to build up supplies for the army over the winter, and to overfeed the people there, where he now bases himself. And he apparently gave no thought to arranging extra shipments from Aegyptus or Africa to make up the quantities. He thinks only of his current situation, not that of others.'

'But he is Caesar, not Augustus. Will Constantius not be angry with him for leaving Rome hungry?'

Who could say what Constantius *the pale* cared about? I had not met the Augustus of the West in many years, and he had been in Britannia and the north of Gaul for most of his period of power, fighting barbarians. Perhaps he would be angry, or perhaps he would not care at all about a city so far away and unimportant to him. I swear that Romanitas is only to be found in Rome itself, as though honour, respect and deference diminish with every mile from its golden heart.

'You should have been made Caesar, Father, and then the people would not be hungry.'

I snapped my head around and hushed him into silence. He was right, of course... I *should* have been. But what's done is done, and those kinds of words had a tendency to take flight and wing their way to the twitching ears of men like Severus.

'Hold your tongue, lad. Some conversations are not for public places.'

'But something has to be done, Father. Taxes are so high that people are unable to pay them. I have heard that businesses are closing because they cannot afford to both buy stock and pay their tax. And people are starving in summer, when the granaries are supposed to find their job easy. What will it be like in *winter*?'

'I don't know, Romulus, though I *am* sure that Mediolanum will be well fed and comfortable, with Severus in residence. I hear he has officially made it his capital, though I don't know whether Constantius has ratified that decision.' The very idea of Severus the Whisperer embellishing his court in my former home by draining my new home's resources rankled deeply.

'Can Grandfather not do anything?'

I turned with a sigh and gestured for my son to walk with me again, towards the great conical fountain and the amphitheatre beyond.

'Your grandfather can do nothing, Romulus. He has no power or authority at all, now. I think he fumes over being forced to retire just because Diocletian couldn't manage anymore, and he clearly cares more about his own loss of power than the fact that my succession was neatly swept aside in favour of Severus. Besides, your grandfather has left Mediolanum anyway. He sulks down on one of the family estates in Campania, drinking too much wine and abusing slaves to assuage his anger.'

'So we have nothing, Father? And all we can do is watch the city crumble?'

I was about to point out that we were still quite rich and influential, despite the loss of the succession, but in the end I bit down on those words with a slow breath. 'That's about the length and breadth of it, son.'

We walked towards the Meta Sudans and turned to the line of noblemen's carriages before the great staircase of the temple of Venus. My own was the second-most expensive there and the twin steeds that pulled it sleek and white, better fed than most of the citizens. The small private mercenary force who maintained the carriage park and guarded them stood around the edge looking mean and menacing, deterring thieves and beggars from approaching the vehicles.

As we neared them, I watched in surprise as two boys, both a few years younger than Romulus, burst from the crowd and hurled eggs. One smashed harmlessly on the steps of the temple, but the other struck the door of the fanciest carriage – not ours – and the glop slid down the side, marring its perfection. Two of the hired thugs stepped forward with their clubs, ready to deal with the children, while a slave rushed over with a bucket of water and a rag to clean the carriage, but the thugs' interference was not required.

I watched with a heavy heart as the two boys turned to flee into the crowd, sniggering with their victory over the upper classes who watched them starve, only to run straight into a small unit of the Praetorian Guard. The Guard were everywhere in these troubled times, deployed in the streets along with the Urban Cohorts to keep order as best they could, all on the commands of the city's senate, since the emperors seemed not to care.

I tried to turn Romulus away from the scene and towards the carriage, but he kept his neck craned as we left to watch the guards hold the boys down while they removed the offending hands with their swords, using deliberately slow strokes. I turned away before the second boy's maiming, but his screams followed us to the carriage.

I had held out such hopes for this city. My father had all but left me with permission and an open remit to improve, rebuild and expand it, returning it to its former glory, and then, with my removal from the imperial court altogether, that had ended. The Tetrarchy had shifted all funds away from the city and now I had neither the money nor the authority to improve the city in any way. And everything was in decline.

Saddening.

We climbed into the carriage and a moment later it began to trundle off, bouncing and lurching across the cobbles and flagstones as we made for the edge of the city, my day's business done in the Basilica Iulia.

'I heard that Constantius is not well,' Romulus said, breaking the silence after some time. I had hoped that the grisly scene near the amphitheatre had diverted his attention from this subject, but it appeared not.

'So it seems. Though he may already be recovered. News takes a long time to reach Rome from the borders.'

'Or he could already be dead?' Romulus hazarded, and I gave him a hard look. That was the kind of speculation you didn't make out loud, even in the privacy of a carriage.

'We would hear *that* news fast, I am sure.'

'If he does—' another hard look from me that failed to silence him '—then Severus will become Augustus and will have to choose a new Caesar to serve with him. Perhaps he will choose you and all will return to normal.'

'Severus would not choose me, Romulus. Stop speculating on such dangerous subjects. We are private citizens and wealthy ones, but we are nothing more, now. Be content with that.'

'Are you, Father?'

'Enough!'

But *was* I content with that? As a boy I'd watched the powerful all around me and formed an opinion even in callow youth that rulers were people with far more power than sense. Consequently, I had preferred a quiet world of books and privacy. Coming to Rome had changed all that, though. Seeing what had become of the symbolic heart of the empire and knowing how different it could be had changed it. Being given the authority and freedom to take the reins of state and begin to repair the city had changed it. Working with the clever Prefect Anullinus had changed it. I think that the last of the shell of boyhood had fallen away from that steel core in me. Now I still wanted that authority, though I also knew that I had never been further from it. It was an odd, and slightly unwelcome, insight into how my father must have felt upon being told to resign.

With the realisation that I wanted what had been taken from me came another odd revelation. I had recently noticed a change once more in Valeria. Gone was that calculating aspect I had seen rise in her, and the ice queen of our earliest days had returned, and suddenly I knew what it all meant. Here in Rome, in a toga of state and having pushed to gain a small level of authority and control, Valeria had finally apparently seen something in me that had made our marriage potentially worthwhile. Yet now, since it had been taken away once more, her interest had diminished. Did that make her shallow? Probably, though I think even at the time I suspected it went deeper than that.

We bounced and rolled on in difficult silence for some time. I hated being at odds with Romulus. He was the closest human being to my heart. Possibly – it feels cruel to admit that for all that he was my son, little Aurelius's disabilities prevented us from enjoying a similar relationship – Romulus was the only person I ever loved, beside Mother and my sisters. I was about to lean across and mend the broken bridge between us when I realised that he had fallen asleep, so instead I smiled indulgently and stooped over him, wadding up a blanket to wedge behind his head for comfort.

In silence we rattled on and I watched as the city walls passed overhead. Scaffolding covered a half-repaired section, though there was no sign of work, of course, with no money from the Tetrarchy to fund it. No men in evidence, and no tools or supplies. Those belonging to contractors had been taken away, and anything paid for by the state had already been stolen by enterprising locals.

That great crack in the gate tower was still there, untouched, and the sight of it brought back everything that we had lost for Rome with Severus' accession. I had silenced Romulus on the subject – had done so on many occasions – but he had been *right* to ask me if I was content with our lot. I was openly, vocally, happy with my situation. I had offered my congratulations to Severus in a letter and helped the senate lead a celebration in the city dedicated to the new Caesar and his distant master in Britannia. I had given no one any reason to believe anything other than that I was happily retired, just like Diocletian himself.

But inside, I seethed, for my loss had not just been *my* loss. It had been *Rome's* loss. The city had faltered and ground to a standstill as Severus ignored it, throwing funds, glory and food at Mediolanum instead. I had not even been perturbed when the letter arrived for Pescens, the head of my guard, ordering them to transfer to Mediolanum to take up their post with Severus. I had watched as the Herculiani left our villa and marched north, and it had not worried me unduly – though it had infuriated my wife to the point that, in hue, her face resembled a cherry for days. But as the months moved on and the city began to flare with unrest once more, I began to regret the loss of a unit of veteran soldiers to protect us.

I was still brooding on the walls and the lack of attention paid to them when we arrived at the villa and the carriage rumbled in through the gate and to a halt. As I reached across to wake Romulus, the curtains fluttered in a rare gust of air and I spotted three horses tied up at the side of my garden, munching my slightly overgrown lawn. Two of them were ordinary soldier's mounts, but the third – a big black beast called Trojan – I knew well.

Prefect Anullinus was here, then. I had never given my staff instructions to automatically grant access to the man, but they seemed to have taken it as read that the prefect would always be a welcome guest. In fairness, he usually was, but today I was not in the mood. I had spent enough time arguing politics with Romulus already, and at least I could tell him to shut up.

Euna was sitting on one of the marble benches in the garden and, despite propriety and correct form, she remained seated while Romulus and I descended from the carriage. As we crunched across the gravel towards the main house, I saw little Aurelius in her arms, feeding, and I managed a smile. He was wrapped and content and unless one approached and moved the cloth aside, he could have been anyone's perfect, unmarred little boy. I waved at Euna and she inclined her head respectfully at me, concentrating on the baby.

'Where the fuck have you been?'

Anullinus appeared in the doorway at the top of the stairs, arms folded over his moulded bronze cuirass indignantly. I almost laughed. Put him in a pale green stola and a wig and it might as well have been my wife standing there. He even sounded a little like her when he was incensed.

'Greetings, Prefect. What a glorious day. As a private citizen of Rome, I have been dealing with the affairs of my estate and concerns in the Basilica Iulia, and now I am home and intend to make sure my slaves have stoked the bath furnace, for I feel the distinct need to scrape the shit of the forum from my skin.'

Romulus stifled a yawn as he greeted Anullinus and received a curt bow in return.

'You'll have to bathe later. There are half a dozen of the city's most influential senators in your tablinum, ruffled and twitchy and wanting to talk to you.'

I blinked in surprise. 'How did they get in? My staff would not have just invited them into my office without my consent.'

'*I* invited them in, Maxentius. These are some of the most powerful men in the city, and you cannot leave them standing at the gate like street hawkers.'

'Why are they here?'

'They have concerns over the rule of the city, and the only man they can put them to is you.'

I huffed and rolled my eyes. 'Are they aware that I am no more influential than they are these days?'

'You are still the most powerful man in Rome, even without your Herculiani or your father's patronage. You know Constantine. You know his father, do you not? And you know Severus. That's a hefty step above this lot, for all their position.'

With a despairing look, he trotted down the four steps and clasped his hands on my shoulders.

'The city is dying a slow and painful death, Maxentius, and no one here can do anything to stop it. Even the Praetorian Guard is ignored by the Tetrarchy. Severus has not called for its prefect to visit him, so clearly he cares nothing for us. We do what we can to keep the city going, and that is all we can do. Rome is failing. Someone has to do something.'

'I agree,' I said, shimmying out of his grip and walking round him and up the steps. 'But that someone is not me. I am as powerless as you.'

'No you're not. *You* know Severus.'

'We are hardly friends. I have met him twice in my life.'

'But he knows who you are. He has to respect your heritage and your father. You can persuade him to do something.'

'No I cannot. Severus would not kick a pebble aside for me, Anullinus. He certainly will not amend his entire imperial policy for me.'

'Then we are lost.'

Ignoring him, I strode into the house and sat down, removing my boots and massaging life back into my hot, tired feet. All I wanted was to forget about the whole thing for at least an hour and lie back in the bath. As if it wasn't bad enough that my boy was stoking my sense of injured loss over being passed over, now strangers were coming to my house to join in. Anullinus glared at me for a moment, and then without even asking my leave strode into my house, passing me by.

I was about to pull him up on this unacceptable behaviour when I realised that he was bound for my tablinum and the senators who waited there impatiently. Satisfied, I watched him go and then rose, removing my toga and rolling my shoulders in my light linen tunic which was sodden through with perspiration.

The baths.

As soon as Romulus had removed his own boots we were ready – he was too young yet to take the toga virilis, and still wore a tunic of a rather boyish cut. The bath suite lay on the other side of the villa, connected by a covered walkway, and our bare feet slapped on the marble and mosaic as we passed through the villa. We walked through the peristyle and the atrium, where I skirted around the edge in the shade of the columns, half hidden by the statue of a leaping faun at the centre of the pool. As we neared the side door of the atrium and the corridors that would lead us to the baths, I watched the tablinum's open doorway and could see and hear Anullinus in heated debate with a bunch of old men who resembled a flock of vultures in striped togas, their wings flapping as they crawked their displeasure at the prefect.

We hurried on away from the scene.

At the doorway to the bath suite, something made me pause and I turned. The figure of Valeria stood in another doorway across the garden, arms folded, gaze snapping back and forth from the room where the prefect and senators argued, to me. Her eyes had narrowed and that calculating look was back. Without needing confirmation, somehow I knew that it had been she who had let Anullinus and the senators in, perhaps in an attempt to nudge me back towards authority and power. Perhaps she had even been the driving force behind it.

I gave her a weak smile and ushered Romulus on into the baths, leaving them all to it. Looking back on that moment, which was the first time I was called, and the first I refused to answer, I wonder how much of what kept me uninvolved was pragmatism, and how much was simple cowardice.

19

CONSTANTINE

I strode through the dark, echoing palace corridors, marshalled by a pair of Joviani. I wore a thick woollen tunic, but I could feel the icy touch of their spatha points on the small of my back – the steel as cold as the winter storm that raged in the night outside.

The Herdsman had summoned me, you see – as I knew he would. He had heard rumours that my mother and Crispus had not been seen for many days. Now, Crispus was a shy lad and Mother cared little for breezing around the palace like others who lived there; the pair often spent days at a time in our quarters and in the sunshine of our private peristyle in the palace's southern wing. But it seemed that the slaves and the Joviani legionaries had been keeping a keen ear to our walls and heard none of my boy's playful laughter, or Mother's fawning words to him.

And neither would they, the dogs! For both were long gone from this black city and far from the cancerous creature who sat on its throne. I had sent them north, a month ago. Both were dressed in rags and set sail in a trade cog, Lactantius and Batius with them. By now they would have crossed the

Hellespont and be travelling by wagon through western Thracia – far from the menace of Galerius.

The Herdsman well knew this, I reckoned. He did not summon me that evening to find out their whereabouts. He wanted only one thing: my head. His reign had been tyrannical so far: no resident of the palace was allowed to leave without his express permission, you see, and this latest of my misdemeanours seemed like it might be my last.

We stopped at the throne room and one Joviani pushed open the doors. The other grunted and jabbed his blade forward. I took the hint and stepped inside, while they closed the door and remained on watch in the corridor. For a moment, there was only the noise of the winter gale howling outside as I glanced around the dark, cavernous hall: arched, coloured glass windows framed the raised throne at one end, the other walls edged with shadowy colonnade. It was the room where Diocletian had scrutinised me on that dark day of Minervina's death, the white streak of regret freshly emblazoned on his locks.

Today, Galerius was the chief incumbent, seated at his long dining table at the heart of the hall, where two lamps provided bubbles of orange light in the darkness. The two of us were alone, it seemed. The table was laden with food, and the Herdsman was already devouring what looked like his second plateful. His knife chinked and grated on the plate and rasped as he sawed at the hunk of white meat upon it. This was mixed with a riot of gurgling and belching.

'Ah, Constantine!' He looked up like a father welcoming a returning son. 'Sit! Sit!'

His ill-fitting, friendly demeanour was probably the most chilling thing I have ever witnessed. It reminded me only of a hyena readying to feast. I sat, taking not the chair he gestured to next to him, but the one across from him – one that allowed me to keep an eye on the doors. He nudged a platter and the ruined carcass of a chicken towards me.

'So,' he said through a mouthful of meat, spittle flecking the air, 'it seems your family could not make it to eat with us tonight? Such a shame, such a shame,' he purred.

The tall windows creaked as a violent squall picked up outside, and I could see the blizzards that had raged all day thickening, covering the panes in packed snow. The flames in the lamps guttered momentarily. 'They send their apologies. Perhaps they can join us next time?'

The lamplight danced in Galerius' inky, unblinking eyes. 'Next time? Aye... perhaps. Perhaps the gods will even bless us with the presence of old Lactantius too.' He adopted a mock quizzical look. 'Remind me, just where is he again? I haven't seen him since last month either.'

I let his question echo into nothing, waited until his eyes returned to his mess of a meal. Then I poured myself a cup of wine from the jug. 'I hear Daia is taking to his role as Caesar well,' I lied. The truth was I had heard that some legions were on the edge of revolt because of Daia's inflated ego, his constant inebriation and his despotic leadership.

Galerius smiled glacially as he chewed. 'He is many things, Daia. Many things. But one thing that he exudes most of all—' he held up a finger, wagging it like some great tutor '—is *loyalty.*'

Like a hunting dog, mindless of his deeds so long as his master feeds him scraps? I mused.

'Loyalty, Constantine,' he sighed. 'It can lift a man from the gutters to the throne. It can buy a man things he never dreamt of... even...' he paused '...his life.'

Galerius held my gaze for some time as the last word rang in the air.

'Those who are loyal to me reap great rewards. Those who shun me, time and again...' He broke down in a throaty chuckle. 'Well, we will come to that shortly,' he said, returning his gaze to the chicken cadaver to saw more meat from it.

I realised it was time. There was no doubting the Herdsman's intentions now. Nothing but death – only after lengthy torture – awaited me now. Nerves jangling, I slid the small clay vial from my leather wrist cuff. As deftly as I could manage, I crushed it in my grip, and let the viscous contents drip into my wine cup as I moved my hand to take it up. The liquid, Lactantius had told me, would take away pain. *Even the sawing of a torturer's blade would be numbed by this,* the old man had insisted. I knew I had no choice. There was no chance Galerius would let me leave this room alive. It was the only way.

The storm outside keened and my heart thundered as I lifted the cup... pretended to drink from it, then placed it back down, right next to Galerius' cup. I let a tense moment pass, eating a few mouthfuls of meat and a spoonful of warm vegetable stew, before reaching for a drink again. This time, I took up Galerius' cup. It was rimmed with grease and spit, but I sipped at it all the same. The Herdsman seemed not to notice my switch.

I watched the poisoned cup, my thoughts unable to move from it. Galerius sucked the meat from the chicken bones then belched again, before wiping the back of his hand across his mouth. 'You might have hoped to be given one last chance tonight, Constantine.'

I met his gaze, trying desperately not to show any flicker of emotion as he lifted the cup and swirled it.

'And I truly hope you did,' he mused further, his gaze growing distant. Then he placed the cup down, the wine untouched. My heart thudded. 'For there is no finer sight than seeing the hope slipping from a man's eyes... before he dies.' As he said this last word, his demeanour changed. Like a cloud scudding across the sun, the joviality was gone. The Herdsman's eyes shot furtively to the shadowy colonnades surrounding the table. My blood turned to ice. I glanced to the surface of the blunt eating knife in my hand and saw something in the dull reflection. Surging from the gloom behind me. Two dark figures. Wraiths carrying sickles, sweeping them back to strike.

What followed was a visceral blur. I kicked back from my chair and felt my shoulders crash into one attacker's gut. His sickle whooshed through the air, only inches above my head, before he stumbled away and fell. I leapt up, swinging the chair round just in time to catch the sickle swipe of the next assassin. The blade embedded in the chair's timbers, and I saw the moment of fright in the hooded killer's pale face. I hammered my blunt knife down at his chest with all my strength. The blow was dull but true, piercing the flesh between his ribs and bursting his heart. Blood pumped from the wound, the pale face now grey. I spun away as he crumpled to the tiled floor, then faced the first attacker, back on his feet now. He swept his sickle blade down at me and it was a strike that would have taken my head off, had I not reacted so swiftly. I caught his wrist. The curved blade quivered in the air as we each struggled to control it.

I snatched a glance to the table as we fought: Galerius was standing, mouth open, readying to shout for his Joviani legionaries to support his assassins. But he swayed, his head lolling. I saw the cup in his hand. It fell to the floor, empty.

The fool had quaffed the wine while watching me struggle with his assassins! He tried to call out, but it came only as a whimper.

The sickle turned in my favour. Then I wrenched the blade from the attacker's hand and swept it across his throat. Blood sheeted from the wound and the assassin fell, thrashing, clutching at the foaming wound. I turned away, stalking over to the foundering Galerius. The Herdsman slumped to the floor, his eyes closing over as the poison took hold. It would make him sleep and then wake later with a foul head. For a moment I crouched before him.

'You spoke of loyalty. Yet you know nothing of that virtue. Those who follow you do so only out of greed or fear,' I spat, then realised that I had unconsciously lifted the sickle blade to his throat. It would have been so easy to make him sleep forever. But I did not. I reasoned that it would be the wrong thing to do. It would doubtless see Galerius' followers declare some war of vengeance on my father. The fat sack of shit was unconscious, and that was enough.

I stalked to the throne room doors, hearing the murmuring of the two Joviani out there. The door began to creak open. I raised the sickle and readied for them.

I ducked from shadow to shadow, darting across the pools of torchlight on the city streets. But my every footstep was amplified by the crunch-crunch of fresh snow underfoot, and the usual night-time gloom was absent – the slightest glimmer of light reflected on the pillowy white snowfall. Worse, the blizzard had abated, so I had no cover at all.

'Cursed snow!' I hissed, my breath clouding before me in the bitter night air as I dashed into a dark, frozen nook by the dockside forge. My hands were shaking, still wet with the blood of the Joviani pair. After felling them, I had managed to slip from the palace unseen. It seemed that no general alarm had been raised. But one of those Joviani had cut me deeply on my left arm. The pain was fiery and the wound would doubtless hinder my designs. I had spent months planning my escape from the city. *Months!*

I shot a glance back over my shoulder, down the alleyway and into the heart of the city. There, I could see the orange glow of the palace. *How long will the Herdsman sleep?* I wondered. *How long before they find him?* I then risked a glance out from the nook and towards the docks. The streets were empty bar one staggering drunk who seemed to be trudging in circles by the door of a tavern. Beyond, I could see a collection of snow-covered masts. I prayed then that one of them belonged to the ship I had hired. I sent my prayer to Mars – to the entire Pantheon... even to the God of the Christians.

I stole across the street, the chill wind raking my skin, then came to the dockside. I scanned the row of moored imperial triremes there. The watch on the decks and on the wharf side next to them was light. Perfect, I thought. Even better, I sighted the grim trade cog moored at the far end of the dock. It looked like it had been dropped there from a great height – listing badly and in dire need of repair. But it was the cog upon which I had bought a berth, the same one I'd hired for Mother and Crispus to escape on. An anonymous trade vessel. One of many that stopped off at the city every day. I scurried closer to the cog, ducking behind barrels and crates as I went. One garrison sentry strolled past me where I hid, but I could see the boredom in his eyes. He would not spot me, let alone stop me.

I waited until he passed then lurched up, readying to sprint for the cog. But I skidded to a halt after only a few steps. My throat dried in that instant as I saw the grim ornamentation on the trade cog's mast. The grizzled, portly captain hung there, nailed to the timbers with thick bolts through his wrists. His eyes had been put out and the mast was stained red from what would have been a lingering demise.

I shrank back into the shadows, my blood as cold as the whipping breeze now as I saw the dark shapes lining the cog's decks. Not the motley gang of crewmen I had expected, but Joviani legionaries. Twelve of them. Their eyes scoured the night. Somehow, they had not spotted me, and I often wonder if that was due to my far-reaching prayer. But my plan had been thwarted. I would have to fall back on my alternative design.

I peeled away from the docks and headed towards the city's northern gates. Amidst a jumble of slums near the gate was a trade stable. The hand there looked up lazily, his weary features illuminated in the firelight from his brazier. But when he saw the blood on my hands, he was at once alert. He shot to his feet, readying to yell out, when I stepped closer and hissed: 'It's me!'

The alarm faded as he recognised my face – doubtless blue from the chill. He nodded and nervously led me to the horse tethered nearby, inside the stable enclosure. Celeritas, looking strong, well fed and ready to gallop. Damn, he would have to be.

I dropped a handful of coins into his palm, threw on a thick brown woollen riding cloak hanging nearby and led the beast out into the cold. Snow stung me as the blizzard picked up once again. I vaulted onto the saddle, pulled up the hood of my cloak, then turned back to the stable hand. 'And the imperial stables?' I asked.

'It has been taken care of,' he whispered, eyes darting to the red-brick enclosure nearer the northern gates.

Just then, he and I both heard some commotion from the inner city. Shouting and the clanking of armour. Running soldiers. We swung to see the dark shapes emerging from the blackness near the palace area, the puffing of clouded breaths, the flash of blue Joviani armour. The alarm had been raised, it seemed. Galerius had been found.

I turned to ride for the gates. The sentries here had been told to allow a rider through – another purse from my swiftly dwindling monies – and that they did. Moments later I was racing through the Bithynian countryside, the blizzard howling, battering at my face. I could not see the road before me, but I forged on, knowing that a moment of hesitation would bring about my end. I shot a glance over my shoulder with every other heartbeat, certain that each would reveal a pack of Joviani riders, snarling at my heels.

I heard a commotion from the city then; a roar of ire that cut through the snowstorm. A cry that sounded very much like a Joviani *decurion* discovering that his men's horses had been hobbled with irons.

'Ya!' I cried, heeling Celeritas on and into the storm. I squinted into the stinging curtain of white before me and tried to envision the journey ahead. A journey that would take me far from the Herdsman. To far-flung shores and long-unseen faces.

Britannia beckoned.

20

MAXENTIUS

My major-domo bowed as he entered the small chamber where I was busy walking Romulus through the intricacies of the military from the days of the earliest emperors. For all my lack of martial prowess, the academic side of the subject had held my attention as a boy, and Father had been relentless in his education of me in that respect. I could name each unit of note, their highs and lows, their notable commanders and engagements, and even the tactics favoured by some of the best. Romulus was attentive, but I knew that while I talked of archers' ranges and sweeping light horse and the use of *vineae* in sieges, he was simply picturing heroic one-on-one clashes such as Horatius holding the bridge or the cavalryman Claudius Maximus taking the Dacian king's head. He was ever one for such glittering epic, which informed his childish games.

In the corner little Aurelius slept restlessly, shuffling and rustling in the folds of the voluminous materials Euna wadded around him to help ease any discomfort his misshapenness caused him. For a short while – in the absence of my wife, and until the slave's interruption – I had been as happy as I could remember being at any point in my life.

I glanced up at the tired-looking man.

'Yes?'

'You have visitors, Domine. They await your pleasure in the atrium. Shall I show them into your tablinum?'

With a sinking feeling, I pursed my lips. 'That depends entirely upon who they are, Kybios?'

'It is Prefect Anullinus, Domine, accompanied by a number of military officers – Praetorians I would say, Domine.'

I sighed. I had given the staff a talking-to some time ago over their habit of admitting unwanted guests into my office without consulting me first. Kybios had either misunderstood that I would prefer they be kept outside the gate altogether, had deliberately twisted my orders so as to keep the prefect happy or, most likely, Valeria had told him to let them in. I would have to stamp down on this. My wife could play her games but she should not be countermanding my instructions to the slaves.

'Kybios, I do not want these men admitted to the *house* without my express permission, whether it be the tablinum, the atrium, or even the damned latrines! My permission and nobody else's, even the mistress. Do not disappoint me again.' I realised I was grinding my teeth in irritation and straightened. 'Since they are already in the villa and you have no doubt informed them that I am in residence, show them to the office. I shall attend them presently.'

The slave bowed and retreated, his eyes nervous at my tone, which implied an uncomfortable future for him. For just a moment I contemplated striding manfully into the office and dismissing the bunch of them out of hand. It would be satisfying. But I knew myself, and I knew Anullinus well. I would stride in manfully and within three heartbeats I would be nodding along with him. He was ever persuasive, that man. *Too* persuasive, as history will record. In the event, I decided not to sacrifice myself on the altar of the prefect's rhetoric, and instead decided upon petty revenge.

I spent a happy – gleeful, even, given the circumstances – hour in the villa's grounds, playing 'Claudius invades Britannia' with Romulus, using two fairly straight sticks and a bush that might have resembled one of the emperor's war elephants, if only in a bad light and to a deranged viewer. The crisp grass was still frosty wherever the long shadows kept the sun from it, and the air was chilly, our breath clouding as we laughed and leapt, fought and struggled.

When finally the boy tired of the game and decided to go off to the kitchens and demand something sweet to replenish his energy, I strolled through the villa towards the tablinum, steeling myself for the meeting ahead.

This unsought reminder of reality brought with it all the troubles that assailed the city beyond my villa's walls. Rome had wallowed in hunger and dissatisfaction for months now, and I had been reliably informed that no one living could remember a winter with as many starvation-related deaths in the city. The populace was but a short leap from revolt, though I did not fear unduly for my safety. As I saw it, there would be no revolution. There was no one in the city for them to revolt against, after all. The city's nobles and senators were powerless to help, themselves languishing in the pit into which the Tetrarchy had cast them. Perhaps for the first time in history, the nobles of Rome were in the same unappreciated and ignored situation as its poor. The men they would truly need to rebel against were far from Rome, their attention turned to the new metropolises of the empire. Of

course, there *was* still trouble. There always would be, but the
Praetorian Prefect habitually had all his men on the streets
these days, dismounted cavalry included.

I had been blessedly absent on the last two occasions that
Anullinus had come to call, and had spent as much time as
possible withdrawn in my villa or out in the countryside
to the south of the city, avoiding unnecessary trips into the
centre where I might be beset by angry citizens... or worse,
by persuasive prefects.

My heart fell a little further as I approached the tablinum
and my eyes ranged across the heads present. All but one of
them wore armour! I did not recognise three of them, but
the other three were familiar. Anullinus was to be expected,
of course, but the other two were a spirit-crushing sight:
Ruricius Pompeianus, the prefect in command of the Equites
Singulares – the imperial horse guard – and the dreadful,
shifty Sempronius Clemens, currently unemployed, but
former prefect in command of the *frumentarii* – the
imperial spies, agents and assassins. Neither filled me with
confidence.

Again my eyes played across the crowd. Anullinus would be
seeking my backing for something as usual, but he had come
with a full wagon train of support this time. Pompeianus I
knew was outspoken in his denunciations of the Tetrarchy
and their abandonment of Rome. And Clemens... well even in
service to the emperors he had been a devious, untrustworthy
bastard, but since last year and Diocletian's order that his
secretive unit be disbanded, he was truly woe incarnate.

Beside them I could see a tall man with a prefect's uniform,
his nose beak-like and his hair startlingly short – I had
a feeling he was the prefect of the Praetorian cavalry – an
unarmoured man, yet wearing a senior officer's tunic, squat

and unpleasant with black, greasy hair and another prefect in the colours of a legionary officer.

I took a deep breath. This was going to be difficult.

All six heads turned my way as I stepped in through the door wearing my most impassive mask for the gathered military might therein.

'Gentlemen.'

Anullinus took a couple of paces towards me, stepping ahead of the crowd and asserting his position as senior man here. His tight smile showed me little respect.

'Maxentius, it is good to see you again. I was beginning to think you were hiding from me.'

I returned his smile with an even tighter one. Never had someone spoken an unfriendly truth in so offhand a manner. 'I have been busy, Anullinus, being a father. It is time-consuming and energetic work. I would recommend it, however, for it is far more rewarding than public service.' A veiled answer to whatever he was here to lobby me for. The histories had oft taught me that the best military engagements were ones avoided altogether.

'Have you heard the news?' the prefect asked. Straight to the point, no dissembling. This *was* important, then.

'I hear a lot of news. Is this about the new taxes? Or the refusal to reinstate grain shipments? Or the enforced census? Such news seethes around the city like a winter sea. Its mighty waves regularly wash over the walls and flood the villa.'

Anullinus shook his head and I narrowed my eyes. Curious. I had prepared scathing replies for these pieces of news, and had assumed he came to put forth a new case for the city in the face of such tidings.

Rome had always been immune to imperial taxes. It was a statutory right that the city's populace had held since the days of the republic, and was one of the things that defined the privileged status of the city. In some way, not paying that tax was tantamount to saying: 'I am better than the rest of the empire.' Galerius had finally removed that podium, which kept the Roman citizens above their counterparts in the provinces. It was a crippling blow to Rome in terms of both prestige and commerce.

And the grain situation was clearly dire. Starvation was becoming all the more common, and the only sound in the city that drowned out the growling of stomachs was the growling of angry throats.

And the rumoured census? Well it was easy to assume it was simply part of the new tax laws, but it was equally tempting to see it as an appraisal of the city's value prior to stripping it of its worth.

Of course, my answer to all these issues was the same: not my problem.

It rankled somewhere deep inside. I had always held Rome in such esteem, and I knew that whatever glories the Tetrarchy found in, or bestowed upon, Nicomedia, or Mediolanum, or Treverorum or suchlike, Rome was the centre of the world and deserved to be treated as such. It was the womb from which the empire had sprung forth. I would have loved to have seen it receive its due and stand proud at the head of the empire again. But I also knew that I was a private citizen now. I had no influence and no power. Even my father, who had been the second most powerful man in the world, now languished in self-imposed exile in Campania, making a spirited attempt to drink himself to death. I was impotent, and I had to recognise the fact. And in doing so I had to make the Praetorian Prefect recognise it too.

'Anullinus, whatever the latest blow to Rome's pride, it

cannot be mine to deflect. I have no sword or shield. I have no baton of command or unit of Herculiani to do my bidding. All I have are a family, a modest villa and a good toga with a broad stripe, for all that's worth these days.'

'You have no sword or shield?' Anullinus said, archly. 'Then wait a few days and you may take your pick. Swords forged in the best armouries of the empire. Shields emblazoned with the Praetorian scorpion. Mail of the highest quality. Helms with the black crest... all discarded by *imperial order*.'

'Another reduction of the Guard?' I remembered the Praetorians spitting teeth at Diocletian's order that their numbers be cut. A further reduction would not sit well in current circumstances.

'He doesn't understand, Anullinus,' muttered the snake-in-human-form Sempronius Clemens in gravelly tones.

'Clemens has the right of it, Maxentius. When his frumentarii plied the waters of the empire and rode its highways, slipping in among the legions, we knew exactly what was going on in every corner of the empire, almost before it happened. And since their disbanding we are largely blinded. We only hear of momentous events when imperial decrees arrive by courier, like the lowest beggars.'

I cast a brief glance at Clemens. I was less than concerned that the empire had lost Clemens and his reptiles. The frumentarii had become something of a law unto themselves towards the end, and I remembered Anullinus being among the millions who had sighed with relief when the order for their end came. Clearly now he was seeing it somewhat differently. But why?

'What point are you dancing around, Anullinus?'

'News arrived this morning from the East.'

He indicated the short, greasy homunculus in the stained

officer's tunic. He looked little more than a beggar himself, but he stepped forward and gave me a curt bow, one eye looking me up and down while the other false one stayed immobile.

'Domine. My name is Ancharius Pansa,' he replied in shifting, mercurial tones. 'I was formerly one of the frumentarii...'

I might have guessed that!

'...and then transferred to service in the Guard under the prefect here. I have spent the last four months on detached assignment with the First Armeniaca legion in Scythia. I happened to come across a document whilst passing through Nicomedia.'

Again, I snorted internally. '*Happened* to come across' indeed! And why would he be passing through the eastern capital, anyway. My attention was brought back as Anullinus took over once more.

'Galerius intends to disband the Guard entirely, Maxentius!'

I blinked. *Disbanding* the Guard? The Praetorians were an institution almost as old as the office of emperor. Since the days of Tiberius, back before the Jewish Christ had been killed, they had been at the centre of Rome's martial politics. Could Galerius really be thinking of doing away with them?

Of course he could. After all, they had a history of making and breaking emperors, and had rebelled against their masters more than once in the past three centuries. Facing ever worse conditions, Galerius would be worrying that they might try once again to change the balance of power themselves. Moreover, they had been formed as the personal guard for the emperor and it had been some time since an emperor had called this city home. In principle they were already a redundant unit, with a worrying history and presenting troublesome possibilities.

'No Praetorians, Maxentius. No Guard in Rome. Can you picture it?'

It was surprisingly easy to picture, though I did not say so. Anullinus was already riled. 'It will be another blow to Rome,' I tried to say diplomatically, but it seemed to anger the prefect more. He drew himself up and stepped close to me. My eyes narrowed. There was something threatening in his manner now. He had oft been a friend in those early days in the city, and had been a colleague, and lately a pest, but I had never had cause to fear him. Now, I was starting to wonder. He was so close I could smell the sweat seeping out from beneath his arms and the sides of his bronze cuirass. I could feel the heat of his angry face and the whisper of his breath as he spoke again, this time quietly and with force.

'*A blow to Rome?*' He swallowed, pushing his anger down where it seemed to harden into a diamond. 'Think of it, Maxentius. No Praetorians… to guard the palaces and temples from the rebellious plebs. To break up fights in the forum. To arrest wrongdoers and treason-speakers. To prevent riots and reckless destruction. Remember that I have had every man working every shift available these past months and still our glorious temples are profaned. Still noblemen are knifed in alleyways. Still the streets are not safe.'

He gestured to the man in the legionary uniform.

'This is Prefect Quadratus of the Second Parthica. Most of his legion marches in the north with Severus, but half a cohort remains in Albanum as a garrison. He is here to show you just how stretched we are. Albanum is *empty*, Maxentius! Garrisoned only by the sick and wounded. Every able-bodied soldier from that veteran legion walks the streets of Rome, preventing insurrection thanks to his kind offer, intermixed with my Praetorians. Picture the streets if we are disbanded!'

I felt a stone settle in my belly, cold, hard and heavy.

'Then the Urban Cohorts will have to manage, hopefully with Prefect Quadratus' kind assistance.' Even as I uttered the words, I regretted them. I knew the quality of the Urban Cohorts. Little more than street thugs themselves, more than half their training went to the fighting of Rome's interminable fires, and many merchants in the city were more dismayed at the approach of the corrupt and dangerous cohorts than at the disorganised criminals of the poorest quarters. Worse still, since his return from Africa, Anullinus' short-sighted brother Gaius had been made Prefect of the Urban Cohorts by Father – or possibly by Severus – and had soon got to work ruining them just as he had Africa. It made me shudder to think of the state of the city if we had to rely solely on Gaius Annius and his Urban Cohorts for safety and control.

'The *Urban Cohorts*?' Ruricius Pompeianus spat, beating Anullinus to it. 'Even here in your cushioned, well-appointed villa, you wouldn't be safe from them!' the horse-guard prefect snapped angrily. Anullinus gave him a warning glance that silenced him and then turned back to me, a look of long-suffering understanding on his drawn face.

'You have to see, Maxentius! We have been pushed to the edge. How much ledge is there left before we all fall? If the Guard disappear, the city will descend into chaos. No one will be safe. And you, for all your wealth and your personal nobility, are less well defended than some of the merchants with their mercenary guards. We will all suffer. This is not about the pride of my unit, you understand? This is about the very survival of the city...'

I forced myself to straighten and shake my head. Anullinus

was far too persuasive, always, and he'd almost had me hooked.

'No, my friend. I do sympathise, and I understand the dangers. But there is nothing I can do. I have no power and no influence. Severus would as well strike me down as hear me out. Galerius hates me for my father. Constantius is sick and so very far away. And as for this new Daia fellow, I have no idea about him, since we have never met. The only man who might listen to me is Constantine, and from what I hear he may be in a worse, more perilous and less influential position than even I.'

I stepped back. Being close enough to the prefect to be clouded in his breath was beginning to worry me. 'Only one of the emperors can help, now,' I said.

There was a sudden eerie silence, and I felt as though even the gods were listening, pensive, as Anullinus stepped forward, once more almost into my face.

'*Precisely.*'

My blood chilled with that one word.

'Anullinus...'

'We used to have an emperor who valued his Praetorians and this ancient, noble city.' The prefect moved away from me again and swept his arm expressively as if to show me all of Rome beyond these walls. 'Now we have four emperors. *Four!* Two in the East who despise Rome and concentrate on empowering their domain at our expense, one who strips our wealth and might to embellish his new capital at Mediolanum, and a sick old fool busy battering Britons and paying no heed to what goes on at home. We need a *new* emperor. *One* man, not *four*. One man who has the good of Rome at heart...'

He rejoined his companions and I looked at them in disbelief. Could I honestly believe what I had just heard?

All six faces – pale and dark, stretched and squat, handsome and ugly – bore grave expressions and were watching. I felt as though the ground had opened up beneath me and I was hanging by my disbelief alone above a thousand-foot drop into Hades.

'No.'

I hadn't even realised I'd said it until I saw the expressions on the men's faces change. They went from serious consideration to a variety of resignation, scorn, desperation and anger. Not Anullinus, though. *His* expression did not change.

'Do not dismiss this out of hand, Maxentius. You are the son of a former emperor. Though the villains who now sit upon the thrones ripped your birth-right away, we offer it back! You are of the blood of emperors, Maxentius. You were groomed to rule. I saw it when I first met you. I saw it when you put the good of Rome above your personal comforts. When you concentrated on its defences and its buildings. When you took an interest. When you cared! You are the only man to whom the city can turn – can you not see that? You are our only hope!'

I was shaking my head. It was ridiculous. Yes, I had been angered when the succession was taken away from me. Yes, I could see how Rome was sinking and that none of the Tetrarchy would do anything to shore it up. Yes I could appreciate how I was the only name on their list. Gods, but I had even myself come to the conclusion that I wanted it. And my friend the prefect had stated the case succinctly and very well. But in my darkest hours, tossing and turning at night, seething over what had been torn from me, I had worked it all through, calculated it and come up with only impossible solutions. These men had to be made to see the same.

'Anullinus, I understand that. But two things stand against

it long before my wishes are taken into account: firstly practicality.'

I began to pace back and forth in the doorway, accompanying my speech with oratorical gestures.

'Even Severus – the *least* of the four emperors – has numerous veteran legions under his command, and all the money and resources of the empire at his beck and call. If I took the purple at your behest, it would simply make me a target for all four, and we have the Praetorian Guard, the *Urban Cohorts*,' I stressed that just to make the point, 'and three centuries of the Second Parthica.'

I paused in my pacing and thrust my arm at Anullinus. 'You're a strategist. Tell me how long we would last against even Severus like that?'

He opened his mouth to reply, but I was already pacing and waving again. 'And secondly, if you cannot appreciate the fact that sheer arithmetic tells us that we would be dead by summer, consider the history of the Praetorians. Of old, your unit was dangerous to the proper functioning of the empire. Your predecessors slit the throats of emperors as they lounged and raised your own commanders in their place. You *sold the purple*, for the love of Jove! Back after Pertinax, you sold the throne of Rome to the highest bidder! Why do you think the Tetrarchy want to disband you? A good proportion of the reason is your history of making and breaking emperors. And in response to this threat, what is your first thought? To betray the throne and try to raise a usurper in their place? What message does *that* send to the people?'

I stopped pacing.

'No. It is not the way to go. Rome is about honour and respect. You cannot fight corruption by corrupt means. Find another.'

Anullinus rolled his eyes. 'There is no other, Maxentius. You are the only one.'

I stepped towards him, my voice coming out as a low growl. 'Not another *candidate*, Anullinus… another *way*!'

He straightened. 'Maxentius…'

'No.' I knew him well. He'd had time to think while I ranted, and now would be marshalling all his most persuasive arguments. I could not give him the chance to batter me with his rhetoric, lest I succumb. Instead, I rode roughshod over the top of him.

'I have no further word on the subject, Anullinus. It is not a thing I can involve myself in, and it should not be a matter for you and yours either. If you persist in such treasonous notions, I…'

I paused. I had been about to threaten them with denunciation to the rightful Tetrarchy, but I could see clearly how that might work out with six armed men in my office, all with little to lose.

In the end I stepped aside and gestured to my door.

'I cannot help you, gentlemen. I truly hope that this news you came about somehow is not true, and I pray to Jove and Mars and Minerva that something happens to preserve us all and bring things back into order. But it will not involve me.'

Ruricius Pompeianus threw me a glance loaded with disdain and swept from the room. As though he were the first scree pebble of a landslide, the others followed, departing my house in anger and impotence, leaving only Anullinus standing in my doorway, a foot from my face.

'This is your last word, Maxentius?'

I nodded, and he sucked on his teeth like a tradesman weighing up what he can get away with. 'This is not over, my friend. You can argue and bluster all you want, and you make valid points. But deep inside, you know that I am right. This is the only solution.'

I watched as he bowed his head respectfully and strode out, back across the atrium and towards the exit, where my major-domo stood ready to close the door after he had joined his companions outside. I waited for that click and felt an immense sense of relief at the sound. My reprieve would not last long, though, for Anullinus was correct on two counts: this was not over, and I *did* know that he was right.

That I turned to see Valeria in the doorway, wearing a knowing look, did not help at all.

21

CONSTANTINE

BRITANNIA, FEBRUARY 306 AD

My journey west was fraught. I rode alone across the wintry wastes of the Danubius' southern hinterland, every echo of my mount's clopping hooves seeing me glance back over my shoulder in fright. If some phantom tracker was one worry, then the brutal cold was its equal. Ice, snow and freezing fog seemed to have robbed the lands of life and cast them in eternal night. The great plains of Thracia were but white wastes. The sweeping Haemus Mountains too were clad in ice and snow, glowering down at me as if mocking my efforts. The sky remained a filthy grey, its swollen clouds never short of a fresh blizzard to throw down upon me. And I could take no shelter in the many towns I passed, lest Galerius' men waited there or had sent word ahead. Instead, I could only ride past, and cast a jealous eye at the warm orange glow of firelight from within.

Caves and thickets were my home for the next month. I kindled a small fire on each of those nights, shivering, my breath clouding then beading into ice on the thick, scratchy beard that was taking over my jaw. On most nights the fire was barely enough to warm my hands, let alone defrost snow to drink and soften the strips of salt mutton I carried.

One night I could find no dry firewood, and suffered the full wrath of winter: biting wind and snow that whistled around me, searching under my woollen cloak, the chill penetrating my flesh like a wraith's blade. Relentless, ruthless. I looked death in the eye that night and had I not found a hollowed tree trunk to shelter within I might never have seen the light of day again. The very next morning I halted my journey just long enough to track and spear a bear. Its thick brown pelt made a welcome addition to my now grubby and wholly inadequate woollen garb, and I fashioned a coat for Celeritas as well. I tied some of the pelt around my shins and wrists too. When I next caught sight of myself in an ice reflection, I almost cried out; for I looked more like a vagrant Goth than the son of a Roman Augustus. My face was gaunt and black with soot and dirt, my hair long, greasy and matted, my eyes weary.

It was a blessing when I came to the tributaries of the Danubius and left the Eastern Empire behind. For now, Galerius' men had surely lost my scent, and blessedly, winter's wrath seemed to be assuaged by a determined thaw. The land changed into a patchwork of green and patchy white where winter clung on. The babbling of countless meltwater brooks was ubiquitous, and seemed to conjure the first of the spring song from the bravest of birds. So I rode on, turning to the north, finding and following the banks of the Rhenus.

I recognised the fork in the road that led to Treverorum, that path I had taken all those years ago by Father's side. The journey that had ended with me being assigned to Galerius' retinue. But this time, I made no such detour. Whenever I passed ambling, mail-clad imperial equites, chattering as they walked their horses along the main roads, I kept my head down. I refused to take any risks. When I came to roadside taverns and way stations, I bypassed them, preferring the safety of my camps in the woods and in small coves. This was the Western Empire, my father's lands, but I knew it would be folly to assume there was no danger here.

After nearly three months of riding I came to the port town of Caletum, on the northern coast of Belgica. I queued with a motley collection of beggars, seeking a berth on the next ferry to Britannia. I suffered the short voyage by the side of some cross-eyed fellow with rampant flatulence – though he seemed to thoroughly enjoy his own stench, grinning as he basked in every thunderous emission.

At noon, I set eyes upon Britannia at last. There was no stretch of sand and gentle incline leading inland. Instead, stark, white, well-weathered cliffs jutted from the grey sea, with a carpet of lush green grass visible on top. It was as if some giant creature had bitten off the edges of this vast island. We came to Dubris, a harbour town on the island's south-eastern corner where the cliffs at last gave way to a bay. Two towering, octagonal lighthouses stood like sentinels on the cliffs either side of this inlet, keeping watch over the fine harbour complex on the waterline. The sails were drawn in and the oarsmen brought us round the sturdy stone breakwater that shielded a section of water from the rest of the choppy sea like the sheltering arm of a titan, and we docked here.

I disembarked, then trekked under the grand marble arch on the wharf, stopping only long enough to buy myself some fresh bread at a street-side baker's stall. A small risk, I reasoned, but a necessary one, my belly countered. I fished out a bronze nummus to give to the baker, when a voice cut through the air.

'Stop!'

An icy-cold pang of dread grabbed and shook me, for I knew the words were aimed at me. In these last months of flight from Nicomedia, not a soul had spoken to me nor me to them. Instinct screamed at me and my sword hand shot to my weaponless belt as I swung round in the direction of the voice. A huge figure was almost upon me, a blur to my panicked eyes. He shot out an arm at me... then closed over my palm, keeping the nummus there.

'I'll pay for this, sir,' Batius said.

I felt my eyes water and enjoyed the long-forgotten sensation of a smile stretching across my face. 'Batius, how...'

The big man shot an eye this way and that. 'We got here at the start of the month,' he said, paying for the bread then leading me away into the throng. 'I've been watching the docks every day. I was worried for you, sir...'

He led me to a small tavern by a weigh house, and into a little room at the back. There, gawping up at me, taking a few moments to recognise me in my filthy state, were Mother, Crispus and old Lactantius.

I fell to my knees and embraced Mother and my boy. Crispus was three now and I could see Minervina in his fawn skin and dark eyes and myself in his broad, strong face. I would have given anything at that moment to have her there, to hear him calling out as he hugged me: 'Father, Father!'

I ruffled his mop of brown hair and kissed him, sweeping him up in one arm, then held Mother tight with my free arm, kissing the top of her head as she buried her face in my chest. 'I was so afraid that I would never see you again,' I whispered to her, fighting off tears. But she bore a look of serenity on her face as she pulled back from my chest, like an unspoilt pond, that seemed to defy her years. In one hand, she clasped her Chi-Rho necklace. 'I knew you would come to no harm,' was all she said.

Lactantius came over now too, clasping a knotted hand to my shoulder. 'Ah, Constantine...' he started, then his nose wrinkled as he caught wind of my – no doubt pungent – scent of some two months unwashed. 'What have you been doing – did you ride here on a pig?'

I laughed as I clasped his shoulder too. 'You should have smelt the other fellow on the boat.'

I slept like a well-fed dog for that day and the next, neither stirring nor dreaming. When I awoke the following morning, I ate an entire pot of honey and a full loaf of bread, then we left Dubris that afternoon. Mother, Lactantius and Crispus travelled in a covered wagon while Batius and I led the way on ponies. We passed the well-walled city of Londinium, then took the north-west highway for four days. This took us into the first days of March, and soon there was not a trace of snow left. The land was cool with fog in the mornings, then mild, musty and damp throughout the day. We journeyed through oak and ash forests, musty fens, bright meadows and great tracts of farmland, before turning onto a northern road to ride through pleasant green valleys edged with thickets of yew trees.

I had heard much of Britannia: a savage and strange land on the edge of the known world, brimming with fanged, painted warriors who knew nothing of fear or pain. So far, I had seen only the magnificence of the cities, the finely paved roads and the strong garrisons in the forts and watchtowers. Father was doing a fine job of supressing these unseen savages, it seemed.

'We're nearly there,' I said, rolling up the map Lactantius had given me. 'Eboracum.'

'Thanks be to the gods,' Batius replied as he rolled his shoulders and cricked his neck. 'And then we can finally be ourselves again.'

'Aye, no more hiding, no more fear. In my father's city, any of Galerius' spies or whelps who dare to tread there should cower.'

Mid-morning on the seventh day of our ride from Dubris, the grey sky darkened and treated us to some drizzle, and at once the land was alive with the rich scent of earth and damp grass. Shortly after, we came to the banks of a tumbling river and it was then that we saw our destination. Eboracum.

The great northern stronghold straddled the river. On this near side was a civilian settlement, a town with low walls that hugged a jumble of buildings, glistening grey in the rain. On the eastern side of the river, connected to this town by a stone bridge, was a vast, limestone fort – as large as any of the permanent fortifications I had witnessed in the deserts of Aegyptus and Syria. The grey battlements were ancient, with tall, narrow towers of past times. The battlements and gatehouses were topped with gleaming legionaries and fluttering, red standards bearing the markings of the Sixth Victrix.

This was a place of strength, I realised. Then, almost immediately, my mind turned to just how much stronger it could become if rebuilt in the new style – like the great fortifications I had seen and helped design in the East – with thick, rounded and protruding towers and even sturdier walls. I smiled briefly, recalling the conversation I had once had with Maxentius over his fallen city of wooden blocks. This triggered more cutting memories of that long-ago visit to Treverorum: I shot a glance to Mother, and saw her again thumbing her Chi-Rho necklace – her source of strength. I had brought her to safety, but I had also brought her back to her unwanted past... to Father. Guilt buzzed in my thoughts like a persistent gnat. But what else could I do? Where else could I have sought refuge for her and Crispus?

I wiped the rainwater from my eyes and beheld the murky sprawl of the town on the near banks. The gates were open and sodden traders trudged in and out of the settlement. We were met with no challenge at these gates and so on we went through the main way – a straight road that led to the bridge. The air was rich with the tarry aroma of cooking fires and sweat as we passed markets, taverns – plenty of taverns – brothels and workshops. A perfunctory jumble of architecture, in stark contrast to the great fort that loomed up ahead across the river. None of the many faces we passed took much notice of us, most sheltering in the porches of taverns, eyes weary with ale and wine. Then we crossed the stone bridge and onto the northern bank. Now, I heard a dull chatter break out. I sensed many rain-soaked gazes fixed upon our approach to the fort's western gatehouse.

I looked up through the drizzle to the towering, fortified entrance. The legionaries atop the gates looked down at me, rain drumming on their helms. For a moment, I recalled the soldier on the walls on that night of the storm. Oddly, it comforted me.

'Who goes there?' one legionary called down.

'Constantine, son of Constantius.' I smiled.

* * *

Inside the *praetorium* near the heart of the fortress, the lamplight and the crackling fire dried and warmed us. The sound of the heavy rain lashing on the tiled roof and the shutters soothed my weary mind. Slaves hurried in and out of the room, advising that the pools in Father's private *balneae* were nearly ready for us to enjoy hot baths, yet the very basic pleasures of walls, a firm roof and a padded chair were enough to please me after my journey across the empire. As I glanced around I saw all the hallmarks of Father's rise to prominence. Silver chalices and plates, fine silk veils and curtains, gilt-bordered mosaics of the finest quality and even marble busts of himself by the hearth – notably none of these reflected him in anything but perfect health.

One slave entered the room carrying a tray of steaming food. A fat black and white cat came with him, circling his legs and clawing at the hem of his tunic. 'Psst!' the slave hissed, swishing a leg to chase the cat away. 'A constant bane, that creature,' he said as the cat pelted across the room and leapt out of an open shutter. He then placed the platter before me. What a treat for the senses! Steaming pheasant in some delicious-smelling, silky sauce and a cup brimming with dark red wine. I could only chuckle upon remembering my meals of frozen mutton and barely melted snow not so long ago. Mother hesitated likewise, eyeing her food, seemingly without appetite. Batius and Lactantius, however, dispensed with ceremony and tore into their meals. It was only when footsteps approached the room that all stopped and looked up.

The first thing I noticed about him was his smile. It was broad, warm and offered to all in that room. The firelight danced on his features, and in this light, I could see little of the sickly pallor that people had told me of. He wore a thick, purple cloak and a pure-white tunic, a stark contrast to our tattered and mud-spattered garb. I noticed him glancing at Mother. For an instant, that boyish hope I had harboured long ago – that they might reconcile and be together again – played with my heart, until I brushed it away. And Father looked away from Mother too, a furrow of guilt wrinkling his brow. He turned to me and extended his arms, beckoning me. I hesitated, seeing Mother's gaze fall to the floor. But she muttered to me so only I could hear. 'Go to him, Constantine.'

I stood and embraced my father. I felt then the balminess of his skin on mine. Cold, oily sweat. It was at such closeness that I noticed his wan skin and his eyes, black-ringed and sunken, not just a trick of the shadows. And his once thick head of fair hair was cropped to almost nothing, because there was almost none of it left on top or at the sides. 'I have heard you were ill, Father,' I said as we came apart.

'Ha! Messages are too easily twisted in their journey across the breadth of this empire. I could send word that I had bought a new hunting falcon, and by the time the letter reached Nicomedia they would be claiming I had sprouted wings myself!'

'Then I can only wonder what you might have heard of me in these last months?' I replied wryly.

The edges of his lips lifted in an equally wry half-smile. 'Your name has echoed to the edge of every province, Constantine. They say that the Herdsman's rage grows incandescent. They say you—'

'He drank some bad wine,' I cut him off promptly and instinctively, seeing the shadow of a pair of legionaries in the adjoining corridor.

He frowned, then glanced to the corridor and laughed as he turned back to me. 'The Sixth are brothers and I am their father, Constantine. The Herdsman has no influence over the fine legions of Britannia.'

'But you must be wary, Father. He will surely suspect that I have come here. He has spies and agents... like shadows in every corner.'

Father replied with an assured smile. 'I'm sure he does.' His expression darkened, his lips pursing as if recalling some unfinished issues with the Herdsman. 'As have I.' Then he sighed, his shoulders sagging. 'Yet I fear my time to act has passed. I had a chance, Constantine,' he started, his gaze faltering, 'a chance to stand up for your succession. But I did not.'

'It would have been futile, Father. Galerius wanted henchmen by his side, not true Caesars. Nothing would have stopped that jackal, Daia, stepping up before me – nor Severus before Maxentius.'

'Perhaps,' Father said as if trying to convince himself of my words. 'In any case, Galerius has bigger issues on his hands now.'

'Aye?'

'In Rome itself. The Herdsman and Diocletian were always jealous of the spirit of that ancient city and the fire it could kindle in men's hearts.'

'What has he done?' Lactantius said, standing. Batius joined him, both men's faces wrinkling in consternation.

'He has decreed that the Praetorian Guard should be disbanded. Permanently.'

Batius' look of growing alarm faded instantly at this. 'The Praetorians? Ach, they're a bunch of stubborn, cut-throat whoresons anyway.' He blew air through his lips and sat back down. 'Stick a knife in their mother's belly for a purse of coins, they would. Nothing but trouble!'

Father smiled at Batius. 'Ah, Batius – that is why I hired you to stand by my son's side. A blunt, uncomplicated view of the world is often a valuable asset.'

'Thanks,' Batius said, then frowned.

'But Rome is part of the West, your realm?' I said.

'It is,' Father replied with a wry smile, 'but Galerius is the Senior Augustus, and it is his right to dictate to the West as he sees fit.'

I thought then of Rome, of Mediolanum – the new seat of power that had replaced it. 'The citizens of Rome have been stripped of their free bread ration, of their tax exemption... and now the Praetorians are to be disbanded?' I took a gulp of wine as if that would help make sense of it all. 'Does Galerius seek to stoke an uprising?'

Father's face lengthened, his face almost skull-like. 'He has a history of doing just that.'

I tried to envisage what might become of this latest move. His last great initiative, the Christian persecutions, had started that day in Antioch and soon had the whole empire in a turmoil that lasted for years. Then my thoughts settled on something else, *someone* else. Maxentius. I wondered how my old friend, out there in distant Rome, might have reacted: as he did that day in Treverorum, lying down to the bully, or as he did by my side that day when he thwarted Candidianus' ploy to incriminate me, or in the Nicomedia riots, when he fought manfully by my side against the flames?

The flames that kept you from Minervina's side! A voice raged deep within me. I was well used to this now, and so I pinched the top of my nose between thumb and forefinger and blinked hard to chase the anger away. This was no time to wallow in that darkness when there was plenty more of that floating around me. 'Those governing Rome – how have they responded?'

Father did not answer, instead a familiar female voice did. 'My brother tells me that they have yet to comply,' Theodora said as she walked in. Her lithe and relatively youthful frame seemed something of an affront to Mother, but I knew she meant no such offence. 'That is all I know. Maxentius himself has little say in the matter. His word no longer holds the weight it once and briefly did in Rome.'

'So the Praetorian Guard resist Galerius' orders?' I muttered to myself. From the corner of my eye, I noticed Batius drain his wine cup then shrug as if to say *I told you so*.

'It seems they do,' Father said, then clasped his hand to my arm. 'But let distant troubles bother us no longer. Tonight you will bathe, eat and drink until you can enjoy no more, then you shall sleep in clean, warm and comfortable beds.'

I sighed, rubbing at my neck, welcoming his offer. But there was more.

'Because soon,' he said, looking to me and Batius, 'I will need you in armour once again. The Caledonii assaults on the great northern wall grow incessant. The garrison there can only hold them back for so long. I've summoned two cohorts of the Sixth from Londinium. They are good soldiers. And I will need good officers to help me lead them.'

In fact we enjoyed an entire moon of rest and respite. Complications meant the legionary cohorts from the south were delayed. For a time this did not seem like a great problem, for the reports from the wall were that the Caledonii attacks had eased. There was even talk of Father calling off the punitive expedition, sending word south that the Victrix cohorts should remain in Londinium. Then, on the Ides of April, everything changed. A bloody messenger fell from his horse and came shambling into my father's offices. The great northern wall has been breached. The Caledonii had coordinated a strike on one section, overwhelmed it and flooded imperial territory. *They have looted the towns and farms on their way – and left not a soul to bury the slain*, the panting messenger had croaked.

Four days later, the second and third cohorts of the Sixth Victrix Legion arrived and we were on the march. By dawn we had already been on the move for hours. Batius and I rode with Father near the front, each of us dressed in battle armour.

I shot a glance over my shoulder at the marching legionaries. Over nine hundred men wrapped in fine mail shirts and helms, glinting in the first of the sun's rays, their breaths clouding in the early chill and the last of the morning fog swirling around their ankles. Each carried a dark red oval shield, a spatha, a spear and a clutch of lighter *spicula* javelins. These men were grizzled veterans – well used to fighting the rowdy tribes of this island – and not a trace of fear showed on their faces. But something troubled me. Father had avoided my questions on the scale and detail of the Caledonii incursion. I knew from bitter experience that when he was evasive, something grim was usually afoot.

'We cannot call on the first cohort, or the fourth?' I asked, almost thinking aloud.

Father twisted in his saddle, his face wrinkled in annoyance at my questioning. 'The first are needed to man Eboracum's walls. The fourth are far to the south, several days' march away – and they are needed there.'

'And the Fifth?' Batius suggested, daring to side with me.

Father's lips twitched. 'They exist on paper only. Barely eighty men oversee the empty barracks of that cohort.' He sighed bitterly. 'The raids have been incessant, and I have had little time to repopulate lost units.'

Batius and I shared a knowing glance. Over the last decade, Diocletian had begun a process of stripping down the old all-too-powerful legions of over five thousand men, dicing them into smaller legions of just one or two thousand men each. But I had been under the impression that these military reforms had not reached as far as this most northerly province. I rode closer to Father, and lowered my voice so no other would hear.

'I didn't realise you were struggling for manpower. If we are to face a horde in the north, then tell me now. I can help, I have faced long odds on the battlefield before.'

'I've heard of your heroics.' He smiled. It was a warm smile that fought against the cold sweat trickling down his sickly pale face. 'That's why I brought you along.'

'Forget about me – you need another force. I've seen hordes swamp legionary cohorts before. Aye, the legionaries usually fight well and belie their numerical disadvantage, yet they are but the anvil. Something more is needed to finish the fight with minimal losses. We need a hammer to crush the enemy against that anvil. Another brigade is essential. The wars in Persia taught me this and taught me it well—'

'Ah.' Father held up a finger, cutting me off and slowing down. At the same time, the column halted, as if umbilically attached to their leader.

I saw him squinting into the sun. There on a knoll just a quarter mile ahead, a bobbing mass of silhouetted shapes burst over the crest and flooded down across the meadow. Tribesmen, some eight hundred of them, coming straight for us at a charge. They were mostly without helms, long-haired, bearded, wearing baked leather armour or hides, carrying spears and axes. Alemanni, I was sure – ferocious warriors from the wilds of Germania. *Here, in Britannia?* I mouthed.

My heart thumped and I felt the cold certainty of battle. The onrushing warriors howled some foreign cry. I grasped for my sword, readying to swing round and shout the two cohorts into a line. But Father's hand clasped over mine, stopping me.

'Krocus is with us,' he said. 'He and his warriors fought my legions like wolves in Germania – laughed in the face of death. That is why I spared them, then recruited them. Now they are known as the Regii, my most loyal wing of soldiers. I foresee a day in the future when the empire will look to whole regiments of such men – men with no designs or hopes of seizing the purple cloak for themselves – to form an imperial guard.'

I turned back to see the barbarians slow into a gentle run. At last they stopped, their breath clouding in the chill from the exertion of the mock charge, steam curling from their sweating skin. The leader of this pack came to the fore. He was one of the few with a helmet – a finely crafted conical piece, etched with spirals and more than a few sword-scrapes. He wore his auburn hair in a ponytail, and a fiery beard dominated his chin, grown out to a point as if to balance with the shape of his helm. He had craggy features and wild eyes that suggested an edge of madness.

'Domine!' Krocus threw up a gnarled, tattoo-riddled arm in salute.

Batius shuffled uncomfortably beside me. 'Wait a moment... he looks like one of the bastards that nearly took my head off when we were fighting upriver on the Danubius,' he whispered. 'I'm sure of it.'

Krocus' eyes flicked to Batius for just a heartbeat, then back to Father. 'I have mustered all of my men, as you commanded.'

'Excellent, *Rex*,' Father said, then turned to me and grinned. 'It looks like we have ourselves a savage hammer. Now we must make haste. The reports have it that the Caledonii are but a few miles north.' With that, he waved a hand, ushering Krocus and his men into place.

I released the breath I didn't realise I had been holding, relieved that these fierce warriors were with us and heartened that Father's thoughts on what forces were needed matched mine.

As Krocus strolled past, he offered me a solemn half-bow, which I acknowledged with a slight tilt of my head. Then he met Batius' scowl, slowed for an instant and grinned, the madness returning to his eyes. 'I remember you too... how could I forget that ugly head? I nearly took it home that day as a prize!' he said, then threw his head back and erupted in a fit of hoarse laughter, jogging away.

I sensed Batius' hackles shoot skywards.

'The dirty, barbarian bast—'

'Advance!' Father called out, cutting him off. At once, the banners were raised and the legion marched on in search of battle.

The Caledonii were fierce warriors, but sly also. They knew how to strike at the empire's weakest parts, then melt away into the hills, to evade the legions – such as the small army my father had pieced together to tackle them. It took three whole moons – three entire months of arriving at blackened, pillaged towns strewn with dead Romans and not an enemy in sight – to pin down their location. And when we did, we knew we could not simply charge into battle with them, for again they would simply flee and the whole cycle of razing and plundering would continue. That was when I suggested that we had to present to them a weakness, a lure. And what better lure than a small train of soldiers, marching unawares, detached from their main force?

Father, Batius, Krocus and his Regii and I were hidden within a hilltop oak grove. We looked east, over a broad, buttercup-speckled meadow. The mid-morning sun was intense, a pleasant buzzing of bees and chirruping of birds filled the air, and a scent of pollen and honey danced on the hot breeze.

Then, like a shimmering iron insect, one cohort of the Sixth marched into view from the south and through the idyllic lea. I glanced at Father. His eyes were shooting from the Sixth to the northern rise towards which they advanced. Behind us, concealed in the grove, the other cohort of the Sixth and Krocus' Regii waited, primed…

The tense silence ended when Father bristled on his saddle. I swung my gaze to follow his – to the north. There, the rise was deserted still, the air above it rippling in the heat haze. But from beyond, we heard a noise, a terrible caterwauling of one voice. A jagged, foreign call, as if seeking a response from some unseen other. But the reply came not from one, but from countless booming, guttural voices. My skin prickled as the first voice called out again, this time far louder, closer. Again, the thundering chorus of reply shook the land. The cohort in the middle of the meadow halted. The heat haze atop the rise swirled. Then the Caledonii rose into view like a dark tide. Thousands of them.

My eyes widened. The leader wore green trews, a mail vest and a plundered centurion's helmet with a tattered, threadbare plume, and carried a longsword and an axe. His chest swelled and he cried out once more. The swarm of warriors that came with him roared in reply. I counted at least six of them to every one of our legionaries. And they were no ill-equipped rabble. Yes, there were many bare-chested men with wild, flowing locks or limed, spiked hair carrying only crudely fashioned spears. But they also had packs of archers and a core of infantry in good leather, bronze and iron garb.

With a howl of some war horn, they poured down the rise, flooding towards the men of the Sixth, roaring like great beasts. The lone cohort shuffled into a broad line and braced. I watched them, mouthing the drill as the enemy hurtled towards them, feeling the ground quake even from this distance. *Shields together. Feet apart. Spicula... ready!*

As if hearing my anxious thoughts, the line of legionaries rippled, each man lifting a javelin overhead. Swept up in battle fervour and seemingly fearless to the readied missiles, the Caledonii charged onwards. I heard the senior centurion give the order. 'Loose!'

With a flash of steel, the javelins sailed from the legionary ranks, then punched down into the foremost Caledonii. Blood fountained and men were thrown back as the missiles crunched through skin and bone. I saw the leader of the savages duck one such missile, only for it to shatter the forehead of the man behind him, his skull bursting and the contents of his head spurting into the morning haze. Hundreds were felled, but the Caledonii charge only grew more intense for it.

I sensed the cohort with us in the grove shuffle, anxious to join the fray and help their comrades. Krocus' men too were jittery, eager. Then I heard the rustle of boots as a few of them moved to the edge of the treeline, almost breaking cover from the grove. Instinctively, I swung to them. 'Stay where you are! We have the advantage only if they engage with our infantry.'

The scowling warriors halted grudgingly then their grumbles fell silent when Batius and Rex Krocus reaffirmed my command. Father chuckled. 'Aye, you have become all I knew you could.' He fell silent, his eyes glazing over. 'You know, on that journey to Treverorum. Before I married Theodora. I tried to tell you. But I could not. I was ashamed at—' His words were cut short as he broke down in a fit of wheezing and coughing, clasping a hand to his mouth.

'Father?' I gasped, putting a hand to his shoulder. But he shook it off. He tried to hide it from me, but I caught sight of it: the slick of blood on his hand from the coughing. Black blood. His face seemed as white as the few puffs of cloud overhead too. He had been poorly over these months of campaign, but this was much worse. 'You must rest.'

'I am on the cusp of battle,' he snapped weakly. 'Does it seem like a good time for rest?'

Just at that moment, a great crash of iron and clatter of shields sounded as the Caledonii smashed into the legionary line. The war cries were replaced by a crescendo of screams and shrieks. My gaze swung from Father to the clash.

Father kicked his mount from where we waited, drawing his sword and holding it aloft. 'Now, for your empire, for the glory of Mars... *forwaaaard!*' he bellowed hoarsely. As one, Krocus and his Regii burst from the grove with him, bounding forward to keep pace in a tight wedge. Batius and I rode alongside, the second cohort of the Sixth flooding along in our wake.

At once the stillness of the grove was gone, and the wind of our charge whipped over us. The world before me jostled as Celeritas sped forward. My eyes fixed on the swarm of Caledonii warriors, spearing, slashing and hacking at the legionaries. Some of them were even leaping up and over the legionary front line, their comrades using their shields to hurl them into the ranks behind where they seemed to descend into some blood-frenzy, slashing and swiping, heedless of their own mortality. And their fervid efforts were working – holes had appeared deep within the legionary ranks, Roman heads split with axes and limbs hacked from bodies.

Likewise, many Caledonii lay in bloodied heaps before the Roman front, guts torn out by the legionaries' deadly spathas and spears. The stench of torn bowels and coppery blood was rife, and the cohorts were wavering at this vicious onslaught. I felt my mouth dry and my bladder swell, felt my breath come and go in short gasps. I levelled my spear and trained it on the flanks of the Caledonii swarm as we came within strides of them.

I heard an other-worldly wail as Krocus took to blowing a war horn. This gave the Caledonii just an instant to gawp up at us. Some even managed a scream, then we cut through them like a farmer's sickle. My shoulder juddered as I speared down, lancing one lime-haired foe through the shoulder, the point delving deep into his chest. Gouts of blood leapt from the wound, his mouth and his nose at the same time, and he greyed and fell. Then I kicked at another who pulled at my leg, intent on hauling me from the saddle. I brought the shaft of my spear round to whack it on his temple, and he fell back, dazed, before Krocus flew past, slicing his head with an axe. Soon, though, the shock of the charge faded, but only after many hundreds more Caledonii fell to it.

Now the fighting grew primeval, with men snarling, teeth bared. Fists and foreheads were used where blades could not be brought to bear. A longsword tore across my leg and I cried out as my blood spurted and pattered into the mire of red below. Celeritas gnashed at the attacker, biting off his fingers, then reared up, thrashing its forelegs at another, staving in this one's skull. I speared down at a pair who came at me, tearing out the belly of one and pinning the other to the ground through the shoulder. Spearless, I swept out my spatha and hacked at the swell of barbarians around me. I nearly took one foe's head off, but a strip of sinew held it there like an open lid, the eyes rolling wildly and the mouth locked wide open from his abruptly ended war cry. Another spear jabbed up at me, breaking the rings in my mail shirt, gouging deep into the flesh of my breast, inches from smashing through the bone. Hot blood whipped across my face like lashing summer rain as I hacked and parried at this foe. Behind him I saw countless more, waiting to come at me. I wondered then if this was how it would end.

But war is like a storm. One moment it rages around you, the next, it quells, as if it was never there. And so it was here too. First, I noticed the leader of the Caledonii breaking from the fray. He and his best warriors fled back to the rise in the north. That was the moment of change. As soon as the rest saw this, they cried out in panic. The swell of attackers around me relented, flooding away, streaking to the north also. I panted, seeing the tangled carpet of dead they left behind. Broken bodies, jutting limbs and shards of pure white bone. Some three or four hundred legionaries had fallen. Close to three thousand Caledonii lay with them. Clouds of flies were quick to appear, buzzing over the foul mess.

I saw then Batius, caked in gore, his white eyes nightmarish against his haggard, crimson-spattered face. He slid from his mount, nursing a cut to his arm, then plucked up the plundered helmet dropped by the Caledonii leader. 'Seems like the day is wo—' He started, but Krocus cut him off, rushing past and grabbing the helmet from Batius to hold it up himself.

'Victory is ours!' Krocus boomed.

Every man on the field cheered the Alemanni warrior.

The last few patches of unstained skin on Batius' face turned purple with ire.

I turned away from the volley of obscenities he hurled at Krocus, and sought out Father. When I saw him, all else faded from my mind. For he was listing on his saddle, his eyes staring into nothing. I heeled Celeritas into a trot, my heart pounding. 'Father?'

He did not respond. Behind the bloodstains of battle, his skin was grey like an autumn sky, and his lips were dark blue. I looked him over, seeing no wound. His armour had protected him well, it seemed. But, with a rattling breath, he slid from the saddle. I shot out an arm to stop him, catching his weight and cradling him across my own saddle. The pain in my breast wound seared, but I was oblivious to it. I cried out for the *medicus*. The battlefield physician hurried over and helped me lay Father on the ground. But I could see the defeat in the physician's eyes when he saw no wound he could tend to with bandages, acetum or scalpel.

'Domine?' Krocus cried out, hurrying over to us, his eyes wide in shock.

Batius came over alongside Krocus – momentarily forgetting his ire. The big man looked at Father, then me, then shot glances at the fleeing Caledonii. 'What do we do?'

'Forget the raiders – they are broken,' I said. 'We must return to Eboracum. The emperor is dying.'

22

MAXENTIUS

It was the villa's water issues that forced me to return to the city in this hot and dusty season. I rarely set foot inside the walls these days, and I soon remembered why. The crowd over by the rostrum – the podium upon which some of the greatest speakers in Rome's history had stood as they addressed the city – surged and growled out their latest grudges to a desperate-looking toga-clad official atop it, keeping his expensive shoes carefully out of reach of the grasping, dusty hands. The man was doing his best to appease the citizens, attempting to placate them with rhetoric as empty as their bellies. He was losing the battle, and I had a momentary flash of precognition, seeing in my mind's eye the senator being swept from the rostrum and disappearing with a scream among the angry bodies.

I threw off the image, dragging my eyes away from the scene as he tried once again to explain that he couldn't dole out what the city did not have. Beyond the peripheral figures, who hovered uncertainly at the edge like crows waiting to feast on carrion when the predators have left, I could see what now passed for the safety of our city. A detachment of

Praetorians, some dozen men strong and led by a centurion in a dented, badly kept breastplate, stood in the shade of the Arch of Divine Augustus, avoiding the worst of the sun's baking rays, hoping the inevitable eruption of that crowd would not happen and that they could remain in the cool and out of the peril of a small-scale riot.

Experience told them otherwise. Many days ago – was it even months? I was starting to lose track of time now – my slaves and servants brought me news when some uprising occurred in the city and was put down by the troops. Not so now. With small riots being an almost daily occurrence, they were no longer worth reporting. Violence and disorder had become the norm, and only a day that passed in peace was newsworthy.

Over in the shade behind the Temple of Castor and Pollux three thugs were busy beating seven shades of Hades from a poor fellow while an oily-looking criminal observed proceedings as he cleaned his nails with a gleaming knife. When felons could carry out their misdeeds under the very eyes of the public and riots surged beneath the noses of the Guard, it was hard to believe that this was the forum at the heart of the world's most noble city. But the Praetorians, even bolstered with the cheaply equipped and inferior Urban Cohorts and the few available members of the Second Parthica, simply did not have the manpower to deal with every disturbance in the city. Muggings, thefts and murders were carried out by their wicked perpetrators with breathtaking audacity in the knowledge that the Guard would not risk diminishing their numbers in such involvements, when they might be needed at any moment to stop a full-scale riot and prevent the city burning.

I had been forced to dig deep into my coffers to hire a

private guard of gladiators and ex-soldiers, having watched one of my close neighbours being dragged from his villa by thugs who left him for dead after a bloody thrashing while they looted and then burned his property and raped the women. Now I only left the villa when I had to, and only did so with a strong escort of such men, making sure to leave enough to keep the villa secure.

Sidestepping two young boys playing a game of *latrunculi* on a board scratched into the marble step and turning my back on the endless troubles of the city, I forged on out of the hot, dusty air and into the cool and shade of the Basilica Iulia. Behind me, half a dozen men wearing mail shirts, and with knives that could almost be classed as swords, filed between the columns, watching out for any sign of danger, playing rearguard while I entered. Inside, the four men who'd preceded me had fanned out, making sure no one came close.

It was all so different for me. I had never felt unsafe in Rome when we first arrived from the East, and had milled about with the rest of the populace. Now I had a living cage of flesh and iron surrounding me, protecting me from potential danger.

'Looks safe, Domine,' advised Leontius, the head of my household guard, as he stood to one side and swept an arm forth, indicating the clear and peril-free path before me all the way to the small booth of Cleon, the *curator aquarum*, with responsibility for the city's complex fresh water system. Seven of every eight days in the market week, the sweaty, odious little official kept himself in seclusion in his office near Pompey's Theatre, where only official applications and a month-long wait might gain even a senator access to him. But on market day, he sat in public in the forum, briefly approachable by the populace. Two centuries ago, the curator aquarum had been an important role, held by senators, but much had changed since those days and the bureaucracy had flourished like untended weeds, falling into the hands of much lesser men.

Only the fact that the water at the villa had been coming through with a distinctly orange tint had brought me from the safety of home. We had quickly become convinced the water was undrinkable, and running out into the streets to fetch fresh supplies from a public fountain a bucketful at a time was clearly no solution.

Cleon had barely acknowledged my existence until he caught sight of my small force of scarred men. At this, his small, piggy eyes narrowed.

'If you've come for money, I'm an official of the city here to deal with the public. I do not have a strongbox or even half a dozen denarii to rub together in this place, so you are wasting your time. Go threaten someone else. Try Astatius over in the corner.'

I simply rolled my shoulders and breathed through my nose, counting slowly to maintain my temper. The things I had seen on my way here had not put me in the best of moods and the health and comfort of my boys was the paramount reason for my visit, giving me a great deal of focus. I strolled forward, noting with no surprise the lack of any seat for the comfort of a petitioner, and slapped my palms down on the table, making sure to position myself so that the four rings I wore glinted in the beam of light shining down from the high windows, especially the signet ring that marked me as not only wealthy, but also noble and of a powerful family. I have never by nature been a pushy or intimidating man, but my boys were my life, and when their health was an issue I could be fierce as a bear should the situation call for it, and every passing year with their myriad troubles was bringing forth the steel in me.

I was rewarded with a slightly nervous swallow from the man and he put down his stilus and snapped his tablet shut, as if I might be interested in its contents.

'Can I help you... err...?' He left the sentence hanging. In order to afford him the maximum discomfort I dragged out the silence.

'I am Marcus Aurelius Valerius Maxentius, son of the former Augustus, Maximian, and resident of Rome. I require your assistance in a matter of public works.'

The man recoiled as though I had suddenly sprouted poisoned spikes. Clearly the name of my father still carried weight with small bureaucrats, even if it held no authority among the true circles of power. I leaned closer, using the man's nerves to stamp my authority upon his puny person.

'The water supply that feeds my villa on the Via Labicana near the third mile marker is coming through discoloured, and I require that the matter be attended to with some speed.'

Cleon tapped his lips with a well-chewed fingernail. 'That's a low priority area, I am afraid, given that anywhere outside the walls is currently downgraded in favour of keeping the city working.'

I almost faltered then. The city *should* come before the self – it was a principle I had believed in my whole life, and one I thought important. And he almost had me bowing to his words, but I paused, narrowing my own eyes.

'My villa lies a short stone's throw from the Claudian aqueduct and must be fed directly by an offshoot. If there is a discolouration at my villa, then there is every chance that the fault will affect more locations along the *Aqua Claudia*, right into the city itself. You need to look into it and not attempt to weasel out of your responsibilities by playing on my Romanitas!'

I hadn't realised it, but he had made me angry enough then that I had leaned close to his face without meaning to, and my breath must have fogged his eyeballs. He shivered. 'Now that you mention it, I recall sending a small work party to a section of the aqueduct out that way. I will give them orders to expand their remit and check out your own supply.'

'I am most grateful,' I replied, in a tone that indicated quite clearly that I wasn't, and which wafted my breath across his face again. Just to keep him at the utmost level of discomfort I held his twitching gaze in silence for a long moment before straightening.

As I turned to Leontius, I threw over my shoulder without looking: 'Be sure they attend my villa before the day is out.'

Without another word or glance I strode from the booth, back across the echoing marble floor of the basilica. I have to admit that the insistence of my rights over the bureaucratic toad did fill me with something prideful and strong, and I was feeling quite pleased with myself as I prepared for the open spaces of the forum again.

It came as something of a surprise when a swarthy arm, so hairy that it might have belonged to a boar, suddenly slapped across my chest, halting me in my slightly smug stride. I looked across to see the face of Leontius, his bristly chin and scarred, once-torn lip curled as he flicked his eyes between the colonnade and myself.

'What?'

My instant reaction when he had touched me was to launch another tirade, this time aimed at a hired mercenary who thought it proper to manhandle his employer, but when I saw his eyes, the haughtiness caught in my throat and '*What*' was all that came out, quavering with nerves.

The ex-legionary cupped a scarred hand to his ear and flicked his eyes to the colonnade again. 'Trouble, Domine.'

Now I could hear it. The sounds of the crowd out by the rostrum had changed in both pitch and volume. Though I could not see them, the sound had become angry, insistent and shot through with threads of military command. Over the roar and hum of the discontented, I could hear an officer's voice calling for his men to hold. Had a riot begun so swiftly, while I was in the basilica?

As two of my men – a former *thraex* gladiator with a fearsome look and an ex-soldier from some northern land with wild white hair – stepped close to me, their knives readied, Leontius padded over to the colonnade, peering through the gaps at the scenes outside. I waited, tense and impatient, and after a long moment, another of the guards rushed over to the commander at a beckoning finger.

My heart racing, I scurried over to join them, despite the gesturing of the man to stay back. The two fierce killers at my shoulders moved with me, so close one might think they were tethered to me.

I bit my lip as my eyes took in the scene outside. It was startling what could happen in the span of a hundred heartbeats while I intimidated a slimy official over water rights.

The togate man had gone from the podium, though one of his boots remained, which told a worrying tale in itself. The crowd around the block had more than doubled in size in that short time, filling all the open space from this basilica's lower step over to the rostrum, the Basilica Aemilia and the Temple of the Divine Iulius. It had changed from a potential disturbance to a prospective riot in the blink of an eye. I wondered what had turned the tide so suddenly, but my eyes fell upon the answer as they moved up the forum.

Some seven or eight feet from the edge of the crowd, a middle-aged plebeian lay on the ground, his ragged dun-coloured tunic torn by a spear that still stood proud of his chest, pointing accusingly at the sky. A military spear – a spiculum. Had the man on the podium been dealt with in answer to this terrible death, or rather was the spear an answer to the speaker's own fall? Either way, they had been the opening moves that heralded a coming conflict.

The small unit of Praetorians were standing close now, using the ancient *Actium Arch* as a flanking guard, bristling with spears and waiting for the inevitable. I winced. I had witnessed scenes like this before. Curses and imprecations rang out across the forum and angry arms gestured at the Praetorians. Any moment, the crowd might surge forward, as soon as one man's temper reached too high. Or, even worse, one of the soldiers could react despite orders, and throw another spear. The poor prostrate man's death was unfortunate, and might be put down to the will of perfidious gods, but another body added to it would label the whole thing a deliberate attack.

Another of my hired guard appeared with us and Leontius threw a questioning look at him.

'More protesters coming along the roads below the Capitol and the Palatine, sir. Only realistic way out is a quick dash across to the columns, past the *curia* and out into the Subura.'

Leontius pinched the bridge of his nose. The rat-runs of the Subura were hardly safe territory. More nobles had been mugged and knifed in that sprawling maze over the past few months than in the rest of the city together. I looked at the single boot standing forlorn on the rostrum, a mute reminder of the fate of a peaceful nobleman. *Better the Subura than that crowd!*

'Do it,' I hissed at my guard commander, but before we could move any further my vision was blocked by three more togate figures pushing their way into the basilica, panting from running. One of them – the *praetor* Lucretius Ballator, whom I knew and held in reasonable contempt – realised who I was and straightened as he approached me. Leontius stepped in the way, but I waved the former soldier aside. Ballator was an odious weasel, but harmless nonetheless.

'Maxentius! It's chaos out there.'

'We are about to leave via the Subura. Perhaps you would like to accompany us?'

Ballator stared at me. 'The *Subura*? I think not. This situation is out of hand. You should send word to your father. He would...'

'He would do *nothing*,' I snapped, cutting him off. 'He cares for your city no more than the current rulers. And he has no influence.'

'You should speak to Severus. Or Constantius!'

I took a deep, impatient breath. 'Severus has no love for me, and Constantius is barely aware that I exist. Besides, I hear that he has his own troubles in Britannia.' I cast up a breath-long prayer to Mercury for the safety of my friend Constantine, of whom I had heard no word for months since his flight from Galerius' court. I could only imagine that Constantius and Britain were his destination. *May he reach there safely.*

'More soldiers!' someone shouted from the eastern colonnade, and worried citizens in the basilica scurried over to look. I could hear the sound of armoured men approaching from the east. Perhaps with reinforcements, the Praetorians could stop this foolishness before it began. I had a momentary vision of what would have happened if Prefect Anullinus had accepted the tetrarchs' command to disband his unit. The mob out there would be the only law in the city.

'Hold!' called the officer's voice once more, and I could hear the now-larger unit bracing themselves. I closed my eyes. It was about to begin.

Someone out there bellowed a word that we couldn't quite make out and the roar burst out tenfold from every throat in the forum. I kept my eyes closed as I heard the sound of unarmed but desperate and angry citizens hurling themselves at a shield-wall.

'We have to go, Domine,' hissed Leontius, gesturing out towards the area of the forum dotted with honorific columns, beyond which stood the senate house and relative safety.

I stepped through the colonnade, my guards tensed and ready for trouble. Praetor Ballator watched me go, his own nerves claiming him and making him shake like a thin tree on a blustery day.

Leontius barked out a few short commands and the men circled me, their gaze playing across the whole scene. The angry crowd had largely moved off to the right, engaged in fearsome and costly combat with a unit of Praetorians interspersed with members of the Urban Cohorts. However, the troubles were already spreading, and more groups of malcontents were pouring from the other end of the basilica beneath the Capitoline Hill, heading for the fray, with us in the direct line of their charge.

There was a crash and I looked further round to see that one of the twelve statues of the gods had disappeared from above the portico to our left, smashed to the floor.

Moments later I saw the jubilant miscreant pushed from the roof by an angry priest. There was little chance now that the spread of this could be stopped. It might perhaps at least be contained in the forum if the Praetorian commanders were astute enough.

Suddenly I went blind, and panic exploded within me. I felt my legs slip from under me and fell to the flagged ground, wiping away whatever it was that had so blinded me. It was sticky and red, filled with grey mush. As I blinked out the mess and tried to focus I could see the former gladiator who had been just in front of me lying on the floor, shaking. Half his head was gone and the large marble lump that had struck him lay nearby, coated in brain matter.

I heard Leontius shout something, and suddenly all my professional guards were fighting off the angry protesters, doing their level best to keep me safe while staying alive themselves. The public seemed to have found weapons easily enough. Had this been planned somehow?

I had another momentary panic. I knew not what to do. Without Leontius telling me, I didn't know where to run. A woman, perhaps a few years older than myself and wielding a stout length of ash wood, leapt through a temporary gap and ran at me. Before I could react, one of the guards was there and had jabbed a knife into her side, swiftly and professionally, and then grabbed her, drew a line across her throat with it and then cast her aside before returning to his own troubles.

I felt the ire rising inside me. I have never been sure whether the temper I had inherited from my father was really a good thing or a bad one, but on this occasion it served me well. It irritated me that this was happening at all. These were all good people in their hearts. They were bakers and messengers, gardeners and fishmongers. Hunger and desperation had driven them to the edge and they lashed out at whatever authority they could find, despite the fact that these authorities were the only ones actually trying to help them. But for all my understanding and sympathy, given the circumstances, these simple shopkeepers and their wives were now the enemy.

I stooped and felt around in the mess below me, my hand closed on the well-worn ivory hilt of the dead gladiator's curved *sica* sword, and I came up brandishing it. I would not fall here and now.

Four of my guard were dead and two more were struggling, one holding in his own gut-ropes, which were attempting to escape through a jagged rent in his belly. Leontius was still there, and the four other useful men reacted to some command of his, pulling in close together. The bulk of this new crowd were passing behind us now, on the steps of the basilica. What drove them on past us, I could not tell, but Leontius was gesturing ahead, urging us all to head for the curia.

A face appeared in front of me – an ugly face with pockmarked skin and a badly shaved head, his obsidian eyes seeming bottomless tunnels into the darkness of his head. His hand came in for me, swinging a rough wooden mallet of the sort that cartwrights and coopers use. My instincts were good, for all my lack of martial training, and I ducked that ponderous, heavy blow, my razor-edged curved sica lancing out and slicing easily through the man's hamstring while I was crouched. With a cry, he toppled, his leg useless and flopping, the hammer intended to smash out a nobleman's brains skittering off across the forum.

I rose again, feeling at the same time sickened by what

I had done and elated at my victory. Was this how soldiers felt all the time? How did they survive it? It occurred to me that I had often noted the tendency of old soldiers to indulge heavily in drink, and the reason for that was suddenly clear to me. If I reached the villa, I would unseal a jar of *Alban* and drink until I could no longer see that ugly face and hear the sound of honed bronze carving through tendon.

Leontius was suddenly pushing me into the open. I was shaking, felt the overwhelming urge to vomit.

'Fiercely done, Domine,' Leontius said as he and his remaining men moved us further away from the crowd. Why were that mob leaving us alone?

I turned and saw why: a large force of Praetorians, with a banner of the Second Parthica in among their own scorpion emblems, right on the heels of that second mob, marching with determination. I caught sight of Anullinus, the Praetorian Prefect, throwing out orders to his centurions and prefects, dealing with a problem that should have been the province of his brother's Urban Cohorts were they not so ineffectual and slovenly. The prefect caught sight of me and my small group of blood-soaked mercenaries, and he frowned. Leaving a centurion in charge, he hurried over to the open space where we were recovering from our exertions. I was surprised he bothered. Since that last, final, argument at my villa back in late winter, I had refused to see him whenever he called, directing my staff to deny him entrance. The bloody-mindedness I had inherited from Father showing through again, I suppose. Anullinus had stopped coming at all a month ago.

'Maxentius? By the gods you chose a poor day to visit the forum!'

I was still shaking, and most of my concentration was

given to holding in my half-digested noon meal. I would not vomit in front of the man.

'Rome is on the very edge, Maxentius.'

'I can see that,' I managed and shook again.

'You have to do something.'

Not this again! I had seen this play-acted out too many times. Anullinus was persuasive, but his continued badgering was making it ever easier for me to refuse him.

'I have told you time and again, there is nothing I *can* do!'

'You have the lineage, and the noble families will support you. And the Guard are with you, because *I* am with you. Who *else* could do it?'

'Shut up, Anullinus. Isn't it enough that you ignore your order to disband and are now more or less at war with the emperors? You still want to drag me and the city in with you?'

The prefect grabbed me roughly by the shoulders and turned me so that I was watching dozens of citizens being slain by the Guard, who were losing no small number themselves with every passing moment.

'This is only the start, Maxentius. Unless you do something, it will get worse yet. Far worse.'

'For the very last time, Anullinus, *no*! Leave me be.'

I wrenched myself from his hands and stormed off towards the curia, still gripping the sticky, bloodied blade. I heard him start after me and then stop, and I knew Leontius had stepped between us. Then my guard were at my shoulders again as we moved off into the city and away from the sight of so many desperate citizens and soldiers butchering one another because none of them could see another way.

This was not the Rome of which I had dreamed in my youth. This was a poor, damaged, lost place that would soon come undone entirely. And shortly we would have to leave for the sake of my children. But hope, as they say, springs eternal, and I would not leave until I had no other choice.

As we passed into the narrow alleys of the Subura, beyond the grand forum buildings of three centuries of emperors, I took in the hopeless looks in the eyes of the people we passed, and I felt each of those souls tear at my conscience.

I could only hope that my poor, beleaguered friend Constantine was in better straits than I...

23

CONSTANTINE

The principia tent in the heart of the military camp was hot and stuffy, and the scented oil burners gave off an unwelcome, cloying aroma. I knelt by the bed in the centre of the tent, clasping Father's icy hand in mine, growing colder. He had not regained consciousness since the end of the battle against the Caledonii the previous day. His eyes remained closed and his every breath came with a whistle, each a little shallower than the last.

I stifled the latest wave of grief that came to me, stood and moved from the bedside, brushing past his silken cloak of imperial purple hanging on a stand near his armour, coming to the tent flap and drawing it back to look out into the pleasant summer morning. My gaze drifted beyond the marching and parading second and third cohorts in the camp and on to nearby Eboracum's grey walls, less than a quarter of a mile to the south. Again I fretted over Theodora and Mother's whereabouts – Batius had ridden ahead into Eboracum and searched for them frantically, but to no avail. They had travelled to a southern market town that morning with Lactantius and young Crispus, it seemed, and had not yet been informed of Father's condition. And his condition was grave indeed.

After our frantic overnight ride to return to this, the capital of northern Britannia, the medicus had insisted that we stop here, just short of the fortress city. I had tried to protest, but the man's pale expression and curt words ended my objections.

He cannot ride or be carried another step. He is on the very edge of death. Give him his privacy in these last moments... Let him speak with his gods.

So I had barked some command to make camp, the words reverberating numbly in my chest. It was unnecessary to build a fortified camp so close to Eboracum, but my mind was in turmoil. Dutifully, the men of the Sixth Victrix along with Krocus and his Regii had set up this flawless encampment. The soldiers went on to patrol the camp's palisade walls and carry out their usual drills and manoeuvres as I ordered. But now I could see the eyes of every one of those men flicking to the principia tent and to me, like a visceral heartbeat. I swatted away the insinuation and looked across to the northern edge of the camp where the serried ranks of the Sixth Victrix's first cohort were training – having marched from Eboracum to take part in a javelin drill. Perhaps these, the finest of Father's best legion, might offer some form of distraction as they hurled their spicula into wooden posts.

The Sixth were a curious mix, I mused. Most of them worshipped Mars or followed the Mysteries of Mithras. Yet a growing minority were Christian. I could spot these ones now, whether they wore some Christian symbol or not. It was something in the eyes. A sparkle. Strength, comfort, absence of conflict? I had yet to work that out, but they were different. The cult of the Christ was growing – no, burgeoning – despite the trauma of the all-too-recent persecutions. Perhaps it had been different here. For while Christians had been slain in all other corners of the empire, Father had forbade such practice in his lands. A worshipper of Mars, tolerant of those who followed other gods. Loved by his people, and by his army, I realised. For all his failings as a father, he was an admirable leader. I sighed weakly, accepting that my attempt at distraction had failed.

'Give them coins,' a weak voice croaked behind me.

I swung round to the shadowy interior of the tent. He was awake. 'Father?' I whispered, letting the tent flap fall shut and hurrying to crouch by his bedside once more.

'Coins – that will keep the soldiers loyal,' he said again, his glazed and jaundiced eyes glancing to the sliver of daylight where the tent flap hadn't fully closed, 'always does.' He even managed a weak chuckle. 'Harnessing the army, you see – it's like... grappling a wolf... by the ears.' His face split into a trembling smile and he tried to laugh, only to break down in a racking fit of coughing. I took a clean cloth from the pile left by the medicus and wiped up the worst of the dark blood that spilled from his lips.

'They are loyal to you, Father, not to your treasury,' I assured him, raising his head and shoulders just a fraction to aid his breathing. Futile, I realised, seeing the blue tinge spread from his lips and across his cheeks.

But he rallied, his lips quivering. 'Upon my succession, it was only a hearty donative of gold that brought them to... my side,' he rasped, shaking with the effort of drawing a shallow breath. 'Very soon, when I am gone... you will face the same... demands. And there will be many... more choices.' He squeezed my hand and tears danced from his eyes. 'I hope... you will choose... more wisely... than I.'

I could summon no reply, for I saw the colour drain from his face. I saw his chest rise and then fall utterly still with a dull rattle. I held his gaze as his pupils dilated, then put my lips to his to catch his departing soul. When I laid him down, I heard the dull sobbing that seemed to be coming from some unseen other in the tent, yet was my own. I remained there, clasping his hand, kneeling by his side, for so long.

My sorrow came in crashing waves, like claws raking at my heart. It grew and grew until I thought it would strike me down. Then, like an ebb tide, it faded. In moments, the void was filled with anger. All those years we had been apart since the day he chose to shun Mother. All those years I had suffered in the retinue of that dog, Galerius, when I should have been with Father. And it was all Father's doing – spawned from his quest for power and honour. I glanced over his body, then I looked to the purple cloak, wondering if he regretted all he had given up to obtain that fine emperor's garment. Finally, my eyes swung round to the amphora of wine on the nearby table. I had barely touched wine or ale since those dark days after Minervina's death. Now, memories of the numb comfort it offered taunted me, beckoned me. At last I let go of Father's hand, then turned and lifted the amphora and cup. I barely sensed the medicus sweep in behind me. I heard his gasp as he checked for signs of life and felt the swish of the tent flap as he left again.

The wine sloshed around the cup as I filled it to the brim. The harsh, grey world of sobriety, I affirmed, was no place for the grieving. But as I lifted the cup to my lips, something happened. It was as if the summer morning outside had been overcome by a violent tempest. The ground shook, and a guttural, baritone wail filled the air. Thousands of voices. Laments, howls, jagged prayers to Mars the War God and to the Christian God. Next, a *crash-crash-crash* sounded. Spears rhythmically striking shields, a sound unmistakable to a soldier like me. The legionaries knew of their beloved emperor's passing, it seemed, and wanted to honour him. It went on for some time, and my gaze hovered on the surface of the wine, eyeing my sullen reflection. It was then that the iron ranks outside started a new chant. Louder, fiercer, more intense. The ground reverberated and the surface of the wine rippled in time with their cries.

'*Con-stan-tine! Con-stan-tine! Con-stan-tine!*'

My eyes widened and my skin danced in a shiver as I turned slowly to the tent flap. I placed the wine cup down, untouched. I sensed Father's dead eyes gazing upon my back. His last words rang in my head, over and over.

There will be many more choices. I hope you will choose more wisely than I...

And the first choice was upon me, it seemed, with this thunderous *acclamatio* of my father's armies. When I made it, the squall in my mind was calmed. I stood tall, closed my eyes, sucked in a deep, slow breath... then lifted Father's purple imperial cloak. As I swept it around my shoulders, the hem knocked the wine cup to the ground, staining it dark red. Yet I barely noticed nor read this portent.

Instead, I strode from the tent and raised my hands to take their acclaim. Their cheers erupted, like thunder rolling across the skies.

24

MAXENTIUS

ROME, AUGUST 306 AD

I could hear the general tumult and the ebb and flow of noise in the city from the villa, even with the doors shut, though anyone who has suffered a high summer in Rome will know that only a madman keeps his doors and shutters closed through the blistering, stifling heat of an August day.

In the three months that had passed since my blooding at the forum and the riot that had almost risen out of control I had not set foot within the city walls, even for emergencies. I had hired another half dozen men for my personal guard, and had begun to fret over the expense, given that to draw more money from the family funds would involve a trip to the forum. Any time I needed anything, I sent a slave with half a dozen mercenaries for support.

My wife had taken to self-imposed segregation, confining herself to a suite on one side of the villa with its own bathhouse, where she entertained a constant stream of well-to-do hags with more white lead on their faces than brains behind them. What she plotted escaped me, for such women were hardly to be sought for companionship and entertainment, though clearly she planned *something* within the circles of power in the city. On the rare occasions the city was quiet, the peace was spoiled with the cackling, cawing and sniggering of Roman matrons who had nothing better to do than gossip with my beloved.

I occupied as much of my time as possible with the boys, trying to interest Romulus in the plays of our ancestors and the tales of the heroes who made Rome, but the irrepressible lad, now twelve years old, just wanted to practise imaginary fighting manoeuvres in the gardens, and attempting to educate him while he felt the lure of grass and fountains beyond the window was a struggle of Olympian proportions. To help divert myself, I also set about trying to bring little Aurelius out of his shell. He was now over a year old and still seemed little more than a helpless babe. I remembered Romulus at that age crawling everywhere on his elbows, trying to mimic my words and lusting after my solid meals.

Not so, poor, broken Aurelius. He was still surviving on milk and mashed-up food combinations. He barely moved, bar rolling over, and when he did that he yelped with pain. I had taken to keeping our youngest with me or Euna and as far from my wife's sight as possible, for she had threatened to drown him in the Tiber more times than I could count.

And so it was on that pleasant day in August I was sitting alone on a marble bench beneath one of the high cypress trees that bordered much of the villa's perimeter, a copy of Virgil's great *Aeneid* sitting unfurled but unread across my knee, leaning back and enjoying the play of sun on my closed eyelids, while my ears untangled the aural tapestry. The city was unusually noisy today, even beyond what had become the norm, and unless I was much mistaken, the shouting and muttering crowds were spreading beyond the walls and close to the villa, which lay secluded behind its own less impressive walls.

I could make out little of the detail, for in close proximity I heard the wailing of little Aurelius, who even the wondrous Euna seemed unable to calm today, the distant sound of Valeria and her harpies squawking and the shouts, demands and ultimatums of Romulus as he leapt about the garden taking his stick to the statues of emperors, heroes and gods. His life would have been so much more full had he a friend his own age to play his games with, but the city's evil conditions were not conducive to socialising and I had refused to submit him to the children of Valeria's horrendous crowd. In hindsight, I was still treating him as a seven-year-old, and not as the boy who was precious few years from coming of age. Perhaps it would have been better to drag him from his childish games and make him concentrate on his lessons, but the garden of regret is a garden best left to seed, as my childhood tutor had once said.

There was a sudden hammering at the gate. I opened my eyes and turned to look in that direction, but did not make to rise. No sensible homeowner in Rome opened his gate without adequate preparations that summer, and so I simply waited until my major-domo arrived, scurrying down the steps from the villa's main door and across the gravel to the heavy gate while sorting through the numerous keys on the iron ring to find the appropriate one. Leontius and two more of my guard had emerged at his heel and drew their sharp, well-tended blades as they approached the gate.

I frowned as the thumping died away, wondering if it had been opportunistic hoodlums who had given up and moved on at the sound of activity within, but then the hammering began once more, this time more insistent, more urgent. I was on my feet when the slave managed to unlock the door and, as he opened it a crack, the visitors outside heaved the heavy portal wide and knocked him aside. My guards were there instantly, their swords already raised to cause bloody violence, but they stayed their hands upon recognising who had pushed the door.

I felt another wave of dismay pummel me as I saw the shape of Anullinus, the Praetorian Prefect, sweating and dusty but in his full dress regalia for some reason. Behind him came the whole sordid bunch, including Ruricius Pompeianus of the horse guard, Quadratus of the Second Parthica, the squat and peculiar Ancharius Pansa and the master of spies and assassins Sempronius Clemens. I was on my way over to refuse them admittance and have them ejected when I noted with surprise three of the city's more noble and respectable senators – people even I held in regard – close behind. Men whose harpy wives, it suddenly occurred to me, were in my villa already with Valeria.

Before the gate slammed shut again, seemingly of its own accord, I just caught a fleeting glimpse of a unit of the Guard outside keeping the populace away from the wall. What had Anullinus done to raise the ire of the people enough that they would follow him here?

It had been many months since these men had visited me, and the fact that they had come with senators, under Praetorian escort and in full dress uniform, intrigued me enough that my initial urge to throw them out was tempered, and I held back my shout to the villa for more of my guards. Instead, I turned to Anullinus with my most resigned look, preparing to withstand yet another onslaught of his treasonous logic.

Then I saw his face.

'What is it?' I asked, suddenly attentive and serious, casting the scroll to the ground, forgotten and still unfurled.

'You have not heard, then?'

'Another call for the Guard to stand down?' I said. 'A threat from Galerius?'

Anullinus simply shook his head, and I felt a heightening of my nerves. When the man reached out and placed a supportive, consoling hand on my shoulder, I felt positively chilled. Anullinus had been my friend and companion through troublesome times, but it had been many months since we had even spoken civilly, with his continued insistence that I do something and my steadfast refusal to become involved.

'The emperor Constantius has died, Maxentius.'

I closed my eyes. Poor Constantine. I wondered where he was. Whether he had heard? Had he even had the chance to see his father before his passing? I knew their relationship had become troubled over the years once his mother had been brushed aside to make way for my sister, but I knew they remained close at heart, regardless. Closer even after their troubles than I had ever been with my father.

'Did Constantine reach Britannia before...'

My voice trickled away at the look on the prefect's face. He placed his other hand on my other shoulder, his gaze locking mine, only two feet apart.

'Maxentius, your friend Constantine has proclaimed himself Augustus of the West, donning his father's purple cloak.'

I blinked, and Anullinus sniffed loudly.

'They say his father's troops roared their approval loud enough to be heard in Gaul.'

I shuddered. 'Severus will not be pleased.' I don't really know why I said that. It was not what was rushing through my mind, certainly. I simply had to say something banal to give me time and space to think. In my deepest being, I will admit now, all I could think was: *It should be me.* Constantine's father had once been the junior emperor to my own sire's senior. *It should be me!*

'Severus is a whipped dog under Galerius' filthy fist,' snapped Anullinus. 'He should be tied in a bag with rocks and thrown in the river.'

It should have been me...

'Constantine has no regard for this part of the world, Maxentius. He has the Britannia legions, but that is all. If he wishes to come to terms with Galerius and hold on to what he has, he will have to do the pig's bidding and come here to suppress Rome and the Guard.'

'And Severus.'

'*Forget Severus,*' snapped Anullinus. 'He is just a tool of Galerius. He will do as he is told. What we must now fear is your old friend. He might stay out of it for now, but make no mistake: he is outnumbered three-to-one by Galerius, Daia and Severus. If he wishes to hold on to his new power, he will eventually have to seize Rome on behalf of his superiors.'

'Not Constantine. He is not that sort of man. And he hates Galerius more than any other.'

'More than life itself? He has to come to terms with Galerius unless he believes he can conquer the whole empire and wrest it from the others by force. Maxentius, there are fifty-eight legions of varying strength across the empire, and of them, Constantine holds three! A military solution is simply impossible.'

He spoke the absolute truth and I knew it, for all I wished to deny it. Constantine faced the same impossible military odds as I would, one of the prime reasons I had turned Anullinus down so many times. As long as he could not even master the West, with Severus in his path, how could he hope to stand against Galerius?

I pictured Constantine and Severus clasping hands, sealing a deal. How could such a thing be good for anyone? I...

My mind was whirling.

And Constantine had done it so *simply*. No politicking. No pomp or ceremony. He had taken his dead father's cloak and his army and claimed it as his right. His *right*! A right of which I had *more*...

I swear my heart was skipping occasional beats as my head filled with conflict and confusion. Constantine and Severus. Constantine and Galerius. Severus and Galerius. *Anullinus* and Constantine? And where did Rome fit into any of this puzzle? The clear answer through all the chaos in my mind was: *nowhere*. Barring Anullinus and myself, no one with an ounce of power cared a jot for Rome.

A cry of pain cut through my whirl and I swept my gaze to the garden to see Romulus lifting himself from the fountain, blood trickling from a cut above his eye as a sheepish grin spread across his face. Focus came to me instantly for though it was only a small graze, I had needed something personal – something sudden – to snap me out of my chaos.

'Euna: go and help Romulus. Take him inside and have that eye looked at. Make sure he does not go to sleep, too, since it is a head wound. Romulus: go with Euna and I will come and find you shortly.'

Without further pause, I turned to my guests. 'Severus is no Emperor of the West. He never was. He's a lackey of Galerius, who cares nothing for us.' The others were nodding along, and I couldn't help note the gleam in Anullinus' eye. 'Constantine might make a good Augustus... or a good *Caesar*, but the task should have fallen to me.'

The *task* should have fallen to me. Not the glory, the power, the right, the honour. For putting things right in this mess of an empire would be a *task*, and a Herculean one at that. I narrowed my eyes at the prefect.

'You once offered it all to me. You said your Guard would support me, as they have many emperors both good and bad. Are you still of that mind?'

Anullinus smiled as Ruricius Pompeianus stepped around him and cast a wrapped bundle to the gravel. I looked down at it, the sound of my thumping pulse deafening in my ears. The plain cloth wrapping had been knocked aside as it fell, and I could see imperial purple within. The contents of that parcel were unmistakable.

As I looked from it to Anullinus and back, I saw his gaze slip momentarily past me, and I turned to see Valeria standing on the steps of the villa like a statue of Minerva herself, that gaggle of well-connected senatorial women behind her. Her visage was expectant, demanding. Now I knew what the months of calculation had been about, her allowing uninvited officers into my villa, her gatherings of important women. Anullinus could secure the military, but it took a shrewd politician to bind the upper classes of Rome to a cause. Valeria had been preparing the way for me even as I denied the prefect all those months, ignorant of her machinations.

'All you have to do is pick it up,' Anullinus purred. 'The Guard are yours. We are all yours. Rome will stand behind you, senator and pleb, soldier and priest. Pick it up.'

I stared in stunned fascination at the package, remembering that time in Mediolanum when Father had cast just such a bundle at Severus, beginning his journey on the road that had brought us all here.

'*Pick it up*,' urged one of the aged senators, his eyes hungry. The others murmured their support. Constantine in Britannia, Severus in Mediolanum. Two positions... three men. To pick that up was not only to challenge Severus and through him Galerius; it might possibly lead to me challenging my old friend as well. Heart in mouth, I stooped, pulling the wrapping aside. The cloak was new. Freshly produced and well made. I tugged lightly at the fastening.

'Pick it up,' Anullinus repeated above me. I turned my head, still crouched. Valeria said nothing, but her eyes commanded me. She had been sold by her father into marriage with, as she saw me, a weak man with no ambition, yet she had seen the weakness solidify into iron over these past years, and if I lacked ambition, she demonstrated it for me. For the first time in our union Valeria and I were in accord, and I think even valued one another. She would accompany me back into the circles of imperial rule, and I would be at odds with Severus in the West, not with her father in the East. I gave her the slightest of nods and turned back to Anullinus.

'If I do, I do it for Rome. Not for the Guard or for your purses or families. Not for any of us. It will be for Rome. For the good of the city and of its people. You hear me, Anullinus? Sempronius Clemens? Your Guard and your frumentarii will serve me, not the other way around.'

The two men nodded, along with the others. Anullinus simply whispered once more: '*Pick it up*.'

The cloak was lighter than I had expected, though I knew without a doubt that it would become heavy with cares and troubles soon enough. The wrapper gusted away in a whip of wind as I held the cloak up and stared at it. Anullinus reached out and gently took the corners, walked around behind me, draping it over my shoulders, and then came to the front once more, pulling it across and fastening it with a *fibula* of silver, cast in the form of a suckling wolf. *A nice touch, Anullinus.*

'Hail Caesar,' rumbled Clemens quietly, and the words were echoed once each by the soldiers and senators in my garden. Two short words. So small and simple, and yet with the power to change the world.

Quadratus of the Second Parthica stepped into view from the rear, and I realised that he bore a box of highly polished ash some three feet long. I wondered momentarily why he didn't have some lackey carry it for him, but then he flicked open the lid and Anullinus reached inside and withdrew two sceptres of delicately carved ebony, topped with gilded globes of chalcedony and glass – fine symbols of rule, worthy of the great Octavian Augustus himself. I accepted them into my hands reverentially, staring deep into the orbs as though my future might coalesce within.

I turned towards the villa and saw something new in Valeria's expression, and something that in all our time together I had never expected to see: pride. I could say nothing to her, though, for suddenly arms were turning me away. I stumbled as they pulled me towards the gate, and my guard – faithful as ever under Leontius – stepped in the way.

'Domine?' the commander asked.

'I...'

I thought about the unit of the Praetorian Guard outside the gate. They were mine now... or they would be as soon as this claim was ratified in the forum. I stared, wide-eyed, at my private mercenaries. 'All is good, Leontius. Go inside and keep Romulus and Aurelius safe. I will return soon...' I paused. 'Or I will send for them. I'm not sure.'

Clemens had opened my gate now, and as I was urged towards it, I tried to regain my composure as fast as I could. By the time we emerged into the street, I was walking proud, like a patrician of old... like an emperor.

'What now?'

'To the curia in the forum,' Anullinus replied as he gestured to the prefect leading the Praetorian detachment. 'The *radiant crown* of *Sol Invictus* awaits you at the curia. It will be placed upon your brow before the populace, and then the city's senators will pledge their support and ratify your claim with the usual prayers and speeches. The commanders of the Guard, the Urban Cohorts, the Second Parthica and the fleet at Misenum will all take the oath to you. Then there will be the sacrifices, the rites, the donatives and so on. By nightfall you will be emperor according to sacred Roman law in the old manner.'

I shook my head to try and clear the chaos inside and as I stepped into the centre of the street and the Guard formed a protective screen around me, I realised that the increase in the general noise level that I had heard from the villa had come from the population of Rome. Almost *all of them*, in fact, by my reckoning. They lined the street and packed the side alleys and balconies. I could see them massing as far as the city walls that rose above the suburban buildings. As the Guard took their first step forward on the route to my investiture, the crowd began to cheer and throw out a chant:

'*Im – per – a – tor!*'

'*Im – per – a – tor!*'

'*Im – per – a – tor!*'

My eyes taking in the clearly pre-organised scene around me, I glanced across at Anullinus, who walked close by. 'Nice to see that I did all this through my own volition,' I muttered, somewhat dryly.

Anullinus smiled, though there was something in the look that unsettled me.

'One of us was coming out of that gate wearing the cloak. Just be grateful it was you, Domine,' he whispered with a hint of iron in his tone.

PART 4

Inter arma enim silent leges
(In times of war, laws fall silent)
– *Cicero*

25

CONSTANTINE

Celeritas snorted and shuffled, shaking off the light frost that had gathered on his reins, his breath clouding in the chill, clear morning air. I leant forward in the saddle and smoothed the beast's mane, more to steady myself than anything else. Behind me were the regiments I had brought to Gaul from Britannia: a cohort of the Sixth Victrix and Krocus' fiercely loyal Regii. The armoured and crimson-plumed Batius was saddled on his black gelding by my right, and the wolfish Krocus was by my left, saddled on a chestnut mare I had furnished him with. We watched, still and silent as seven iron columns approached from the south and the west. Every day since Father's death had been crucial, but few as much as today. For today, half of the legions of Gaul and Hispania were to gather at my behest, to hear my address, to consider my vision... to *judge* me as their leader. All through my life, I had been told I was born to lead. Today, I would stand or fall by those convictions.

The bitter winter wind cut through me like a Gothic blade, whistling, keening, furrowing the shrubs all across this open heath and the fur on the thick, lined bear pelt I wore over my shoulders. This coaxed a half-grin onto my lips, as I remembered the last time I had donned such garb and the contrast in my fortunes since then. For this time I was no beggar, fleeing through the wilderness from my enemies. Now, I was lord of Britannia. By the end of today, Gaul and Hispania might stand behind me. And tomorrow... ?

I had kept the bear pelt, you see – the one I had crafted in that desperate flight from Galerius' realm in the Eastern Empire. Back then, I had nothing but the clothes I wore and the purse on my belt. Behind me were the Herdsman's hounds. I knew not what I would find in distant Britannia, or even if I would live long enough to see that land. I was alone. But even in the grimmest, darkest moments of that torturous journey, I never gave up hope. Tenacity was a trait of mine that I had always undervalued – taken for granted, even – and now, I would need it more than ever. The pelt would never let me forget.

I watched as the iron columns came to within a quarter mile of us. There, they converged and formed a broad front, arranged swiftly into parade formations by the strained barking of unseen centurions, waving eagle standards and keening buccinas. The ground began to shudder as they marched towards me like this, the clanking and rustling of iron constant. In moments, they would be ready for my address. I smoothed at the fine, purple imperial cloak, enshrouding me under the bear pelt. Father's cloak. Absently, I glanced to the eastern horizon, seeing the hazy pall in the sky that placed Augusta Treverorum just a few miles away. Despite our divergence that day in that very city, Father and I had been reunited in the end. We had made peace with our pasts and with each other. Now I had stepped into the breach left by his passing.

The legions of Britannia had hailed me as their new leader and I had risen to accept their acclaim. It had been a confounding and complex time, with acute grief and a broiling sense of this newfound power crashing together like great oceans in my heart. I had spent the next days trying to understand the sorrow of losing a parent, to explain it to young Crispus and fighting in vain to stem Theodora's tears. Mother shed just a single tear, saying only that she had prayed for Father's soul.

And there were many more affairs to attend to. First of all I had to be sure that the troops of Britannia would remain firmly on my side. So I entrusted Batius with the inevitable task of issuing a donative to the men of the Sixth. *Pay them, and pay them well,* I had instructed him, recalling one of Father's final pieces of advice to me. Meanwhile, Lactantius and I arranged the funeral, a sombre and grey procession that saw lamentations fill the skies over Eboracum. Father's ashes swirled in the roiling sky above the pyre, and I will never forget that sense of finality when he became merely a memory.

Seven days passed after Father's death and my accession, and on that seventh day, things changed. On a pleasant summer's morning that had at last chased away the pall of grey cloud, I was playing with Crispus in the atrium of Eboracum's otherwise deserted principia. Hooves clopping to a standstill on the flagstones outside heralded the Prefect of the Sixth's return from his operations near Londinium. He brought all those swelling thoughts of power and possibility in my heart to the fore with one word amongst his verbose salutation. Just one word.

'Augustus.'

The word had echoed around the atrium's colonnaded

edge. I set Crispus down at once, and locked onto his gaze. 'Say it again,' I replied quietly.

'Augustus,' he said, somewhat unnerved. 'I came straight here. I understand you wanted to gather a council, to make plans to communicate your accession to the wider empire?'

But my head was lost in a strange, crackling mist. *Augustus.* I had heard the appellation on the days since Father's death. Many times. The armies of Britannia had hailed me as my father's successor, and rightly so. It was a moment of fulfilment. A righteous choice and one I did not doubt for an instant. Recompense for the slight of that dog, Daia, being raised into the Tetrarchy before me. My father had been Augustus of the West, so I understood why the legions automatically hailed me as his direct replacement, but what a storm they created by doing so! If they had acclaimed me merely as a Caesar and had I settled for that title, then I would have laid claim to Britannia, and tentatively to Gaul and Hispania... but no more. But by virtue of the legions hailing me as Augustus and by my acceptance of the title, I had effectively claimed the *entire* Western Empire as my own, bypassing that junior post of Caesar. More, I had cast a spear into the dust between the feet of the one I loathed more than any other... I had claimed to be Galerius' equal. Galerius' *rival.* And the dirt upcast by this spear had landed squarely in the eye of Severus the Whisperer. Two grim opponents indeed. *They will rue the injuries and insults of the past,* I drawled inwardly. Galerius, most of all, would bow to me or suffer the consequences.

I realised something then: I had *always* been a rival to the Herdsman. Yet as a mere tribunus I was little more than a minion and my fate and the fate of those I loved had always rested on the blade's edge of his temper. As Caesar of the West I might be able to resist him and his forces, but as Augustus, would he dare to challenge me? As Augustus of the West, could anyone?

Augustus!

At once, I felt taller, broader and stronger. My head flooded with ideas. The armies of the West – how strong were they? The provinces, how contentious or seditious? The borders between East and West, could they be defended if...

My thoughts trailed off to the sound of a tapping cane. I looked up to see that old Lactantius had wandered into the principia too and now stood, rooted to the spot. He was watching me, smiling the wryest of smiles, making the tapping noise slowly and deliberately. He had heard the prefect's salutation, seen its effect on me. The old goat's eyes alone could teach any man a lesson, and so it was that day too. But he affirmed the lesson with one word, just as powerful as that uttered by the Prefect of the Sixth.

'Constantine,' he said. No appellations, no honorifics. Just plain, simple Constantine.

My spiralling ambitions toppled like badly stacked plates. I felt a pinch of anger. 'Tutor,' I snapped, causing him to laugh.

He waved the prefect away like the man was a stray cat. When the prefect was gone, he addressed me with a tone of mild disgust. '*Augustus?* What did I teach you about anger and hubris, Constantine? Both are fool's emotions.' He plonked himself down on a bench, resting both hands on the top of his cane. 'Sit, sit,' he fussed until I complied. 'Your father's ashes have not even turned cold. News of his passing will not yet have reached the four corners of the empire. Yet you have already decided to make war with every one of those places?'

'I said no such thing!' I protested.

'Your eyes said it all. You spent years in my academy at Nicomedia, remember. I have not forgotten the look of glassy boredom that used to coat your eyes when I tried—' he hooted with laughter '—*tried* – to teach you about the many grades of onions one could buy and what recipes they could be used in.'

I must admit that as he spoke, I found my mind wandering.

Click! he snapped his fingers. 'See! And I also recall vividly how you were when I talked of ancient wars, of great campaigns, when I rolled out before you the scrolls of great realms. Sparks seemed to rise from you!'

I laughed wryly. 'If you truly understood me, you would know why.'

His face slackened a little. 'Power, control... they are like nectar to you.'

I sighed and rocked back on the bench. 'You know what I have been through, how many times I have been swung on the end of someone else's rope, discarded, attacked, shamed, plotted against. My loved ones, treated like dirt or used as virtual hostages. No more... no more. It is time to turn everything on its head. Only one man can do that: the Augustus of the Roman Empire.'

'There are two Augusti,' he said plainly.

'And I will be one of them, in my father's place.'

'What of Severus?' he answered. 'He will see it as his right – by the succession law of the Tetrarchy – to take that seat for himself.'

'Then he will be disappointed,' I snapped back.

'And then... there will be war,' Lactantius finished, as if concluding a story. 'How safe will your loved ones be then?'

I let my head droop. From the vaults of memory arose the old noises of battle: thundering hooves, screaming, clashing iron. Blood. Death. Devastation.

'You have worked hard, Constantine, to earn everything

you have. Do not cast it all into the fires of hubris. Remember 'The Tortoise and the Hare'? You have it in you to be either. Choose wisely. Do not give your greatest enemies the excuse to make you the next Emperor Postumus.'

I remembered well the old fable about the tortoise and the hare, and the grim end for the last man to claim more than he should have in these parts.

'Swallow your pride for now,' Lactantius said. 'Spare the world another war.'

It took me some time to respond to him, and when I did, it was with a humble nod.

He patted my knee as he stood. 'Come now. Many things need to be discussed. Batius has brought the maps to the tablinum – along with wine,' he added with a slight roll of the eyes. He waved towards the doorway that led inside to the principia's hall and array of rooms and vaults. 'Shall we proceed?'

And so we had spent that day talking over the panoply of tasks that lay ahead. I made many decisions in the days that followed, issued many edicts and despatched a stable-full of riders on the Cursus Publicus. Probably the wisest choice of all, however, was the one I made in sending an order to the mint in Londinium: ten-thousand gold solidi were to be struck, bearing my image and my title – Constantine, *Caesar* of the West, with Mars as my patron deity and Severus as Augustus and my superior.

I knew that even having heeded Lactantius' advice to an extent, Galerius would doubtless be in a rage at me for accepting the title of Caesar. By striking these coins I would at least have a record of my deference, so he might not twist my announcements. But I swore inwardly that it would not always be like this. When I had answered the many questions over the legions and the defences and the West as a whole, then I could reveal my true stance to the Herdsman.

The cold wind on the Gallic heath howled around me, bringing me back to the present.

'Sir?' Batius spoke under his breath, his lips barely moving.

I glanced up, suddenly aware that the crunch-crunch of marching boots was slowing. The legions were all but assembled before us and many thousands of pairs of eyes were upon me. Silent, staring. Some fifteen thousand men – coming from all over Gaul and Hispania. A sea of iron, shimmering in the winter sun, spear tips sharp and glinting, myriad bright banners rapping in the wind. Famous legions from the empire's earliest days. I spotted the First Minervia, the Thirtieth Ulpia Victrix, the Twenty-Second Primigenia. Great armies of imperial lore. But their fame had faded from those days of past glory. Their cohorts like so many others had been thinned and dispersed as *vexillationes* were plucked from their ranks and sent to the far corners of the empire to become legions in their own right. Perhaps I could restore their lost pride? Another fifteen thousand more legionaries remained in their forts around my realm. Most in the more strategic areas – eastern Gaul where my lands touched on the Herdsman's and the Alpine passes that led to the southern half of the Western Empire – Italia and Africa. And there were some twenty thousand auxiliaries garrisoned around the provinces and along those borders.

And those borders would have to be strong because every corner of the empire had heard of my accession. While samples of my coinage bearing the title *Caesar* might have reached Galerius, I knew that the word of the people certainly would have, carried on the wind of a thousand whispers. *Augustus*. Almost inevitably, my gaze was drawn to the eastern horizon, and the dark clouds there spoiling the otherwise clear sky. What was going on beyond, in the Herdsman's realm, my nightmares could only wonder.

The barking of one prefect before me brought fifteen thousand arms aloft with a cacophony of rustling iron. 'Augustus!' They cried out in unison, as if in brazen disregard of Lactantius' lesson.

Yet while it was a fine salute, it was not matched by the looks on their faces. I saw doubt, fear, furtive scrutiny and, on the faces of the bolder ones, outright disdain. There were doubtless many who were still unsure of me, preferred some general of their own or had some unsettled grievance with my father. Many were surely irked that they had yet to receive their donative. One brute of a man in the Primigenia ranks with an angry, diagonal scar across his face looked particularly disgusted with me. I could have had him flogged or made an example of. Indeed, I had seen some officers do just that to the disobedient in their ranks... and witnessed the rapid deterioration of morale this approach caused. Fear was not to be dismissed, but had to be used carefully. Respect was a different beast. Respect had to be *won*.

I looked to my left to see Krocus eyeing the legions with an assured and slightly manic grin. Batius beheld them with a granite stare. I drew strength from this pair. I was their emperor, I realised, sitting a little taller on my saddle, tilting my head back a fraction more, adopting an austere glower. I heeled Celeritas forward. Some ranks rustled to stand a little taller still. A good sign, I mused. Others remained unmoved, with Scarface and a handful of other soldiers still looking at me askance.

It was then that it hit me: some men needed to be convinced, not commanded. And these men were soldiers. Men who had marched many hundreds of miles to be here. Did they really want some effete show of pomp and grandeur? I relaxed my ascetic grimace, and harked back to the many times I had led men into battle as a tribunus. Harnessing the army, I reasoned, was not a matter of grappling a wolf by the ears, as Father had so pointedly put it – rather, it was to run with the pack, to lead them as one of their own. I sucked in a lungful of crisp air as the whistling wind swirled around me.

'When I was in Persia, I faced a hillman with a serrated blade,' I boomed, imagining that I was speaking to the rear ranks so they and all in front of them would hear me well. I drew my spatha, holding it out before me and eyeing the keen edge as I walked Celeritas along the wide front of the assembled legions. 'The cur was a head taller than me, built like an ox, he was. He laughed like a jackal as he fought me, and seemed ignorant to fatigue. Each swipe of his blade nearly cleaved me or knocked me to the sand. He took care to tell me how he would cut off my balls,' I swished my spatha forcefully through the air as I said this. 'To add to his collection.' I grappled the collar of my cloak. 'He wore them like trinkets around his neck, you see.'

Silence reigned, but I saw one or two of the doubters' faces relax a little, frowns fading and faint smiles replacing them.

'But I ran the whoreson through and took his necklace.' A few eyes widened at this, some scrutinising my collar a little more closely. 'Then I fought a nomad rider in the northlands. He wore the skins of his previous victims as garments, and was likely eyeing mine as a replacement suit. He thought he could toy with me like some cornered game, galloping past me, loosing arrows at will. Only my quick shield saved me. I broke his pony's leg with it and sent him sprawling. The fall killed him and I took his suit of skins.' More dubious looks, this time directed at my garb. 'So when I returned home to find my woman in a foul mood and demanding to know what spoils of war I had brought for her – trinkets, robes and the like – I said: "Why, my dear, I have *just* the things for you…"'

A moment of stunned silence reigned, then Scarface erupted in a fit of belly laughter. Like a heavy rock cast into a still pond, the hilarity spread out across the ranks. Fifteen thousand men were with me for that moment, but I had to seize it before the mood dissipated. I turned to Batius, flashed him a quick half-grin of thanks for appropriating the tale he had once told some years ago, then gave him and Krocus a nod. The pair swung round on their mounts and waved the men of the Sixth forward. They spread out to encircle the seven legions, bringing with them wagons, laden with small, haircloth sacks, handing these purses along the ranks so every man had one. The thick *clunk* of gold solidi – bearing my more modest appellation – brought great cheers from them.

I filled my lungs again. 'I survived the sands of Persia and the wilderness of the northlands not due to my skill as a warrior, but because of the brothers who stood by my side. Their shields and blades were mine and mine theirs. Together, we were invincible. *Invincible!*' I roared this last word, punching my spatha aloft.

The song of many thousands of spathas being torn from scabbards rang out, followed by the almighty din of the hilts and blades being rapped against shield bosses. When the noise fell away, I brought together my hopes and fears and doubtless theirs too, and said: 'You followed my father nobly for many years. I am my father's son, and you are my brothers. And now, brothers, uncertain times lie ahead. Some may seek to challenge our place as keepers of this realm. Indeed, the Augustus of the East will doubtless seek to foist some minion of his upon you in my stead. More, he will surely seek out my head as a prize. But I have no fear except for him – should he dare to face me with you by my side.'

A great cheer erupted once more.

'Fine new forts and watchtowers have been constructed in these last months. Fine billets for legions of your fame and ferocity.' I waved my hand to the east and south, thinking of the passes and roads that linked the two halves of the empire where these legions would now be posted, and the many artisans and workers I had sent to those borders in these last months. 'Camp on this plain tonight. I have seventy wagon-loads of wine and fare being brought for you as we speak. Then, come tomorrow, keep your blades honed and your will iron-strong and remember: any who troubles one of you, answers to all of us.'

They broke out in a chant as the buccinas sounded again, readying them to move to the demarcated marching camp area. '*Con-stan-tine! Con-stan-tine! Con-stan-tine!*' I accepted the gleeful acclaim of many, including Scarface, as they passed. It was a triumphal moment. The armies of Gaul and Hispania had nominally been part of Father's realm before today, but now I knew they were certainly part of mine. When we had the chance to fight alongside one another, then they would truly be *my* legions.

'And now, what of the armies of the south?' Batius said, walking his horse over to stand by my side. 'Italia and Africa. Do you lay claim to them or not? Word has spread there that you are Augustus of the West, yet they see the solidi coming from these lands that mark you as just a Caesar and they exalt another as master of their realm.'

I could have cursed at the big man for toppling my moment of triumph so swiftly. But he was right: I had been avoiding the issue, pushing the news from those lands to one side. 'I need more time to think,' was the best answer I could give. 'Ride with me,' I said, heeling Celeritas into a trot towards Treverorum, waving the Sixth, and Krocus and his Regii with us.

We rode past the train of wagons coming from the direction of the city, piles of amphorae jostling alongside meats, smoked cheeses, bread, fruit and honey for the legionary camp. One such wagon contained nothing but whores, eyes wide in anticipation of a coin-laden evening. I hadn't organised this. I shot a glance to Batius, who shrugged apologetically.

Treverorum's walls came into view as we rode down into the valley of the River Mosa. Here the heath gave way to lush green grass and the gentle babble of the river, with the mighty stone bridge that led across to the city's colossal western gate – a grand arched entrance flanked by two protruding and formidable grey towers. This fine city, once the scene of my divestment, was now my capital. I glanced up at the skeletal outlines of the new basilica I had commissioned within, stretching high above even the walls. This great hall would be a fine way to mark the city as my own, and I had many more projects planned: a fine bathhouse would be started soon, the palace would be extended in the north-eastern quarter and the walls would be bolstered and heightened to make my capital as indomitable as the Sun God himself.

Then I noticed the glinting specks on the battlements. The *Cornuti*, these warriors called themselves, not a legion but a regiment of Frankish warriors raised by my father just like the Regii. They still wore their wing-like tribal feathers on their conical helmets, one above each ear, and their amber shields daubed with red insignia of two serpents glowering upon one another. They would serve as a fine and loyal city guard, disinterested in Roman politics and with no grounds to mount any kind of usurpation.

Alas, this turned my thoughts to the Praetorian Guard and the city of Rome, bringing me back to Batius' question. What to do with the south? Were it simply a matter of bringing the ancient legions there to my side then I would have answered the big man swiftly. But there was Severus – problem enough for any man. More, it had come to my attention just a few months ago that the Praetorians had moved to declare an emperor of their own and saw Italia as theirs with Rome as their capital. That would doubtless have angered Galerius every bit as much as my own raising. It troubled me too, for it demanded that I clarify my ambiguous standing. As a mere Caesar of the West, it would be becoming of me to play no part in quelling the uprising in Rome other than standing to one side and heeding and helping the Herdsman and Severus if and when they marched to quell the rebellion.

Yet if I hoped to command the respect of the armies who lauded me as Augustus of the West, then I would be compelled to intervene for myself – flaunting my status as Galerius' equal... and surely diverting his wrath upon me. Perhaps it would become me to play these delicately weighted dice to my favour, I mused. After all, there was another quarter of the Roman world to be won... or maybe more? And the more of the empire I could call my own the less I would have to dread the rule of others or fear for my loved ones. But in that scroll that brought the news of Rome's uprising, one name had thrown all these first thoughts aside.

Maxentius.

My friend, the diffident youth I had met inside Treverorum's walls so many years ago, was the bold leader of this uprising in Rome. Like so many times before, his path and mine seemed entwined. Son of a wayward father. Disinherited by the Herdsman's meddling, neglected in favour of the loathsome Severus, he had doubtless harboured the many doubts and grievances that had troubled me since Daia had been bestowed with *my* rightful place in the Tetrarchy. Perhaps this shared affront might unite us against whatever punitive actions Galerius might be planning.

Perhaps.

But it seemed that Maxentius was not the boy I knew back in those days or the man I thought he had become. *Princeps Invictus*, he called himself now – the Undefeated Prince. At least that's what messengers told me. Princeps Invictus... a term of modesty like my own, deferential to the Herdsman? Or a fine veil that masked his true ambitions... like my own? Was Maxentius still my friend... or was he a threat?

I had sent Theodora back to Rome in the late summer – before word of Rome's uprising – sending with her gifts for Maxentius and his family. Then, I had assumed he would be pleased to hear of my rise to the purple. Now, I could assume nothing. And if I wanted to retain control of the armies, then I would have to bring him to heel, show that he was subordinate to me, master of the West. I felt a pang of guilt at idly contemplating the future of my childhood friend in this way, but only for a fleeting moment. As we passed under the shadow of Treverorum's western gate, I felt a tremor of ire on my upper lip. *Why* had Maxentius pricked my flesh with such a thorn? This question brought a steeliness to my next thoughts. 'Nobody will stand in my way,' I hissed under my breath.

Batius frowned, only partly hearing me. 'Sir?'

I leaned over, so he alone could hear my answer to his earlier question.

'I will do what has to be done.'

26

MAXENTIUS

'Are you sure it is wise to bend so much effort to civil matters?'

I turned yet another sour look upon Anullinus, who was leafing through sheaves of vellum and parchment covered with delicate, graceful designs submitted by some of the very best architects Rome had to offer. Indeed, there were such wonders of elegance and grandeur across those pages that, had I the room and the funds to bring them to pass, they would have produced a city to raise jealousy in Jove himself. It was then I noticed the oily fingerprints Anullinus was leaving on the papers. The man seemed to spend a great deal of time oiling his blade and armour these days. Reaching out with an irritated cluck, I ripped the designs from his hands and wiped the worst of the oil from them.

'If we are to stand in defiance of the empire's current slew of careless rulers, we must be what they are not. We are Rome. Do you understand? Not just dirty usurpers crawling out from under a rock...'

I caught sight of the slight sneer on the Praetorian Prefect's face, and threw in a barb just for him.

'...or a credulous gibbering fool of the imperial line raised by your Guard in a pool of his predecessor's blood.'

I was pleased to note the change in his expression. I had made it abundantly clear that the Guard would be *my* tool and not the other way around. Anullinus took a deep breath, his hand coming to rest on the pommel of his sword – a habit on the increase even in my presence, I had noted with disapproving eyes.

'I agree that Rome's glory is faded and chipped, and I would love nothing more than to see all that brick sheathed in marble as Octavian Augustus would have had it. I would love to see the statues and pediments freshly painted and bright. I would love to see even the dourest of places embellished and once more worthy of the glory of Rome.' His jaw hardened. 'But we are in perilous straits. Unless we can bring over either a large section of the military or one of the tetrarchs to our side, we are weak and endangered. All I ask is that we concentrate on the walls, and on fortifying some of the posts and cities that surround us. All the beauty in the world is of little value if the enemy are free to rampage among it.'

That sounded rather like a piece of advice Constantine had once given me over a wooden city in Trier. With an irritated breath, I reached across the table and moved another paperweight, jabbing my finger down at another pile of designs, this time of powerful gates and high walls.

'There are your defences. I commissioned the best men to bring me new designs. We will have the latest military advances built into our ramparts, with artillery platforms and archers' galleries. It is all in hand, Anullinus.'

'And yet work has started on your new bathhouse on the Quirinal hill, while the wall alterations are still just plans. Priorities, Maxentius?'

I glared at him for a long moment and finally he sighed and corrected himself.

'My apologies, *Imperator.*'

'The fact is that this city languishes not just in peeling paint, cracked plaster and exposed brick, but in reminders of long-gone regimes. The forum will be the centre of a new project. The temple of Venus and Rome will be restored and improved, a great basilica constructed behind it over the pitiful ruins of the Neronian structures. And beyond that, a new temple to the ancestors of the city. Do you realise that, apart from some restoration work and that self-aggrandising arch of Severus, the forum has seen no construction since the days of the Antonines? Over a century, Anullinus. Rome needs to know that she is valued, that she is cared for. And as for the bathhouse... well the last mark left upon the city by Diocletian was his huge bath complex, and I will not have the city reminded of him if I can help it. I would demolish the damned place if it were not one of the few monuments in this city still clean and in good repair.'

Anullinus sagged. 'I understand, Domine. Really, I do. I just worry for our safety. Perhaps you can push the wall projects forward and have them made a priority? After all, half of the work is still left unfinished from our previous building programme.'

I had to concede the point on our safety. I had bowed to the pressure of my nobles and senators and drawn my family in from that pretty villa out east, taking up residence instead upon the Palatine – that ancient palace of the emperors. I did not like it. Too many tyrants and lunatics had presided over imperial decay from that lofty place. But for now, a residence within the walls seemed sensible.

It suited my wife, of course. After years of feeling as

though she had been foisted off on an underling, she was now an empress in her own right, with the ancestral palace of the emperors of Rome as her home. Though she was still somewhat distant with me, a large part of the clear disdain she had felt was no longer there. I doubted we would ever experience the sort of marriage of which lovers dream, but a meeting of minds with respect and deference was a vast improvement over the gulf thus far.

'I will go over the plans once again this afternoon. But do not look for work to begin until the new year. It is nine days until the Saturnalia festival begins, and that will initiate six more days of feasting, celebrating and chaos. No work will be possible until after the festival. I presume you have prepared your men for some pomp and show during the festivities?'

'I have.' Anullinus smiled. 'And I wondered whether your own son might wish to play the role of King of Saturnalia for the city?'

I smiled, picturing Romulus' face when I told him of this. I could imagine him bursting with excitement. I was expected back at the palace proper for lunch at noon, and would soothe away the winter's cold in the palace baths with Romulus. I could officially consider that to be work, too, since an extension to the Palatine baths was one of the few personal projects I had slipped into the grand scheme.

'I shall ask him presently.'

'Very good, Domine.' With a last glance at the sheaves of designs, Anullinus bowed and retreated, leaving me alone in the auditorium I had selected to serve as my office. I spent perhaps a quarter of an hour finishing off my work, devoting a few precious moments to narrowing down the new tower designs in the military pile to three possibilities. Then, satisfied that the rest could wait until after lunch and a bath, I wandered back through the grand audience hall, the delicate garden with its fascinating octagonal fountain that only seemed to work after there had been a heavy rain, and into the main living area. Some of the paint here had not been replaced since the days of the Flavian emperors, and its faded richness saddened me.

And then I heard something that lifted my heart from that depth into which it was beginning to slide.

Her voice.

My elder sister, Theodora, who had always been a light in the darkest parts of my life, had returned to Rome and to my side following the passing of her husband, Constantius. That she had crossed a quarter of the empire with only a small hired guard said much about her strength of character, which had only grown rather than faded throughout her time with the ailing emperor. She had been with us now for several days, and was undecided as to what she wished to do next. Of course, if Father found out she was here, he would no doubt have his own designs for her, if he could raise his face from his wine cup long enough, that was.

And even *I* was in two minds about her being here. While she brought joy by her mere presence and I would have loved nothing more than to have her permanently by my side, every single day something happened to remind me of the danger we faced in standing against the tetrarchs, and I had to tell myself that there were many places Theodora would be safer than here.

But such worries were not for now. Saturnalia was almost upon us, and it would bring humour and relaxation for all in the city. Moreover, it would guarantee peace for a short while and divert my dark thoughts from the threat of war, for it was against the ancient and unassailable laws of Rome to declare war during Saturnalia.

I managed an easy smile as I pushed open the door to the 'griffin room' to see Romulus and Theodora playing latrunculi upon a teak board with a history almost as long and involved as the building around us. Romulus moved his *dux* decisively as I stood watching from the doorway, jumping a piece of Theodora's, capturing another, and placing him in a good position for closing the game in victory. I had played the game against my sister often enough over the years to know that she was an untouchable mistress of the board, and that she had decided to let her nephew win. She was so good, in fact, that it was difficult to tell that she was losing on purpose.

I waited a few moments until Romulus took the last four of her stones and clapped my hands with a smile. The pair of them turned and looked at me in surprise. Romulus stood, knocking the board askew, and ran into my arms. Theodora smiled pleasantly, though I recognised a look about her eyes that suggested she was holding something back.

'Romulus, I have just been speaking with Anullinus. He would like you to play the King of Saturnalia at the festival. Do you feel up to japes and cavorting and ruining the night for perfectly sensible senators?'

My beloved boy's eyes bulged at the news, and the smile that split his face seemed wider than possible.

'Oh, Father!'

I grinned and ruffled his hair. 'We will have to find you some fitting attire for the Lord of Misrule. I will discuss it with you after lunch when we take to the baths for an hour. For now, hurry along into the *triclinium* and make sure that everything is ready. Your aunt and I will be in presently.'

As Romulus scurried off, already planning the chaos he would unleash during Saturnalia, I turned to Theodora.

'What bothers you?'

Her smile was still heart-warming, even tainted with apparent concern. 'I hear rumour that the grain stores are dangerously low, that the *Horrea Galbae* is empty and that the workers there lounge about idly. There is talk that fruit and meat are scarce, too. Everything you do to promote the status of Rome and its people will be of little use if they starve during the greatest festival of the winter months... a time when people are supposed to be able to relax.'

And there it was: the simple truth rushing in once more and bringing back all my tension and despair, despite Theodora's comforting presence. The grain shipments to Rome had been so dreadfully scarce these past months. Despite my claiming control of the city and the purple cloak, and the sense of jubilant freedom it had ushered in across the city, in practical terms it had done nothing to improve our supply situation. In fact, we were in a worse situation than ever. As Theodora had noted, the Horrea Galbae, which spanned the Aventine and constituted the single greatest warehouse complex in the empire, was indeed empty. And the few smaller, more central grain stores were pitifully low too, Anullinus' men guarding them more jealously than any gold against the criminal elements of the city who would steal it to sell back to the merchants who had originally supplied it.

I had sent messages abroad, trying not to sound desperate. Overtures were made to the Governor of Hispania for garum, grain and olive oil, promising beneficial trade agreements and good prices, all sent with numerous small gifts. Similar gestures were made to the Governor of Africa – the former Corrector Volusianus – and that of Aegyptus, promising a new era of peace and prosperity and my personal patronage if they would send some of the grain earmarked for the Tetrarchy to us in Rome.

Nothing had come of any of it.

The authorities in Sicilia had sent us enough grain to see us through 'til winter, but no more. Hispania, Africa and Aegyptus remained silent. I had more sense than to seek aid from north or east, given that those lands were directly held by my opponents. I had considered sending to Constantine to see if he might come to terms with me, but something had made me hold back.

Saturnalia would be a poor affair, for all its extravagance and languor, but that was as nothing compared to what the new year would bring: starvation and ruin. Once Saturnalia was over and the building underway, I was beginning to think I would have to make a personal appearance in Aegyptus, offering a ridiculous sum for any excess grain they had and hoping that they would not simply label me a traitor and imprison me and my men for transport to Galerius. It was not a possibility I relished.

'Saturn will not see us starve on his festival, Theodora. Even the Christians, whose God seems so impotent and standoffish, believe their Lord will provide when they suffer, and Saturn is *far* greater than he.'

Something about Theodora's agreement suggested that it had been effected merely to comfort me, but I took that comfort and wrapped myself in it anyway.

Time passed with a growing sense of festivity and amusement, though the undercurrent of worry threaded itself throughout everything I experienced. The city prepared for the festival with more gusto than anyone could remember, and that very fact told me that even though there were troubles still looming, one thing I had achieved in this difficult time was to give back to the people of Rome their long-deserted self-respect.

And then, as I leaned on a balcony in the Tiberian wing of the palace, watching the city crisp beneath a hard white shell of frost, the miracle happened.

In the absence of any other hope, I had taken my own words to heart, clinging to the belief that Saturn would not make our people starve during his own festival. Consequently I was here, at the Palatine's most westerly balustrade. Before me lay the huddle of crumbling buildings in the forum and the temple of Saturn that rose at its own western end on the lower slope of the Capitol. My eighth prayer of the day seemed to be going unanswered just like the rest. I felt my heart sink again, but then how could I have known that it already *had* been answered and that I just didn't know about it yet?

The door behind me creaked open and I turned at the interruption, rubbing my hands together against the cold and blowing into them to warm my icy flesh. Anullinus and two of his guardsmen stepped out onto the frosty white of the stone-flagged balcony. The two Praetorians moved to either side of the door and stood at attention as the prefect bowed and approached.

'Anullinus? What brings you out here on such a day?'

'A visitor, Domine. A most *unexpected* visitor.'

I was so taken aback by the unusually deferential tone that I blinked and peered into the dim interior, without acknowledging him further. There were *legionaries* in the corridor! *Soldiers*, in the imperial household! I have to admit that I felt a quiver of fear, then. After all, how many emperors had been brutally removed from office in this palace?

But then the half dozen very polished and well-turned-out legionaries, bearing colours I did not recognise, stepped to either side, lining the balcony between the man they escorted and myself and Anullinus. As my visitor paced out into the cold, I could not help but wonder who he was. He wore a curled beard in the old fashion of the Severans, his face was so tanned as to be almost Arabian, and he wore military dress, though with the broad-striped tunic that still, even in these days of proliferating military fashion, denoted a nobleman. His cloak of rich fur was an expensive item and as he bowed, he swept the hood from his shaggy hair and came up with an easy smile that reminded me at once of both a rabid tax collector and of... *Anullinus*.

'Imperator Maxentius Augustus. I have travelled far in the most dismal conditions to meet you, Domine.'

I tried to think of a reply and came up lacking, so confused was I. In the end, the slightly awkward silence that followed was broken by Anullinus, and I swear that I heard, even in those early days, a tone of disgruntlement and antagonism between the two men. I wondered even then whether there was some history between them of which I was unaware, though neither ever mentioned such.

'Domine, allow me to present Gaius Caeionius Rufius Volusianus, Proconsul and Vicarius, Governor of Africa.'

I blinked. This was *Volusianus*? The man who had repaired Africa after the unstable rule of Anullinus' brother Gaius Annius? Three months previously I had sent him overtures of peace in the desperate hope of an offer of grain and nothing had been forthcoming. All I had hoped for was grain. Instead here was the man himself, standing on my balcony. It occurred to me even then that this man, though he claimed only the proconsular powers bestowed upon him while I claimed the purple, controlled a great deal more land than I, a much more powerful military, a healthier treasury and a booming economy. As the thought struck me I felt more and more like one of the crumbling ancient temples of my city in the presence of the grand baths Diocletian had bestowed upon us.

'Proconsul,' I managed. 'I am honoured by your presence.'

Anullinus gave me a tiny sidelong look to tell me that such deference was not suitable for an emperor, but it was already out and, after all, I needed this man much more than he needed me.

'The honour is mine, Imperator. I must apologise for my appearance, but I have come straight to your side upon my arrival in the city, without the opportunity to change. My ship docked in Ostia mere hours ago.' He straightened in the manner of an orator about to unleash a volley of words. 'It is both my duty and pleasure to bring you the solemn pledges of the *consulares, correctores* and *praesides* of the six African provinces, as well as our neighbours to both east and west. As soon as word reached us that your most noble majesty had been raised to the purple, the legions in Africa and all my subordinates acclaimed you our noble Princeps. I hereby bring you all the lands and the treasury of Africa to supplement your own, as well as the support of the Third Augusta Legion, four supplementary vexillationes, sundry auxiliary and *numera*, and something that I gather is in rather short supply.'

The proconsul, with a victorious grin, swept his left arm out. Past him, almost out of sight – such was the angle – I could just see the wide Tiber at the base of the Aventine, winding off towards Ostia and the sea. I squinted, and it took me long moments to spot the flotilla of barges moving sedately upstream in the cold, gusting wind. My heart lurched.

'You... Is that...?'

Volusianus grinned. 'For the granaries of the Imperator Maxentius Augustus and the relief of the beleaguered people of Rome, I bring you half the grain supply of the provinces of Africa, as well as fruit, oil, wine and... a personal gift. Aboard one of those vessels sits my own personal mosaicist, bearing a supply of stones of the most glorious colours from all over Africa to brighten your palace. On behalf of Africa, greetings, my emperor.'

I swear that in that moment, I thought that my heart might burst.

Food for the starving people! Staunch military support, including one of the most respected veteran legions in the empire. And, perhaps from my point of view the most important thing of all: legitimacy. With the support of Africa, I was no longer alone. No longer an outsider claiming power that had been denied me by my forebears. I was so caught up in the relief of that moment that I missed what I later realised was an important exchange between these two men, carried out wholly with movement of the eyes and shifts of expression.

Thereafter everything changed in the city despite the cold snap that refused to let up and rime-coated the world each morning. Whole areas of the city that never saw the direct sunlight and remained in shadow stayed white and crunchy throughout the day. And yet the people of Rome were overjoyed. The build-up to the festival became more and more cheerful and expectant, and once the first day of celebrations hit and the whole city downed tools, the wine began to flow, every bakery in the city churning out loaf after loaf after loaf of bread, and the atmosphere simply exploded.

Drunken debauchery became the norm and Romulus had a high time on that first night, running amok amid the highest priests in the land and through the most austere temples, throwing buckets of wine over passers-by and ravaging young ones with a fake *spongia*. It felt as though the world had relaxed; had loosened its belt after a large meal. I laughed genuinely and openly for a few days – the first time I had done so for a long time.

And perhaps the last, too, for on the fourth day of Saturnalia as I stood in the great kathisma of the imperial palace, looking over the Circus Maximus, where games and jollity were being pursued, along with no small number of half-naked women, the world came crashing back in, crudely and unpleasantly.

Theodora stood next to me, as did Romulus, still with his impish Saturnalia grin and showing signs behind his ears of the red paint he had worn for his performance. The evening was freezing but it mattered not to the people of Rome, who were determined to enjoy their festivities, no matter how few clothes it entailed.

The door from the palace itself opened and into the light of lamps and braziers, placed there to keep the three of us lit and warm, stepped Anullinus. His face was dark and severe, and I knew then that my personal festivities were at an end.

'What is it?' I hissed and, despite all protocol, Anullinus grabbed my upper arm and ushered me away from my sister and my child. Once we were at the end of the long, deep balcony, my family still intent on the happy chaos below, the prefect took a deep breath.

'Severus is coming.'

'What?' I almost toppled onto my backside at this hammer-blow news.

'Severus. He comes with his legions, making for Rome.'

'But he cannot do that. It is Saturnalia. Even *Severus* cannot declare war now. His men would not allow it. The law is sacred!'

Anullinus folded his arms against the cold. 'I fear the declaration of war was made long before Saturnalia, and if pressed, Severus would suggest that it was you who made it. It would be hard to deny, since we raised you to the purple in clear defiance of him.'

I shuddered. Severus had several legions and a vast army of auxilia, and they were almost uniformly battle-hardened veterans. I had the Urban Cohorts, the Praetorian Guard, a detachment of the Second Parthica, and the men of the Misenum fleet. Sailors, guards and firefighters, and many of those men were ceremonial and had not fought a campaign in years – decades, even. I had appointed an eager young man by the name of Aurelius Zenas as a Praetor with a remit to rebuild the Urban Cohorts into an effective force, a move that had annoyed their prefect Gaius Annius, who now had to answer to someone for his mistakes. His brother's anger and discomfort simply amused Anullinus immensely. Theirs was not a close relationship. Zenas I had noticed bearing that Christian Chi-Rho symbol at his throat, but I had long decided that I could overlook his strange faith as long as he did his job and did it well. And he seemed to be excelling, though it would still be many months before they could be of real value in the field.

The height of our walls was moot. We could not hope to hold Rome against Severus' army.

'Can we call upon any other forces?'

'No. Hispania and Gaul rally around Constantine. Northern Italia and Pannonia are with Severus. The East is under Galerius. You have Africa, but unless Volusianus hid a few thousand legionaries within those sacks of grain, we cannot hope to bring the men of Africa across fast enough to do anything but gather our corpses for burning. We are in dire trouble, Maxentius.'

Again, there: a failure to address me with my title; and yet, given the situation, I hardly cared. This was no time for formalities.

'How long?'

'Who knows? Word comes to us from our former frumentarii friends spying in the enemy's camp. They can warn us of events that are public knowledge there, but they cannot hope to know Severus' mind. If he has everything in position as he would wish it, he could be standing outside the Porta Nomentana and knocking on our door in just half a month. Logic suggests he will take any important cities or strongholds en route, and he will likely move carefully, against the possibility that Constantine makes use of his absence to sack Mediolanum. In my opinion he will not be here until the end of February.'

I felt a blossom of hope in my heart. 'Then that gives us ample time to bring across the Third Augusta and any other African forces.'

'No, Maxentius. It doesn't. Volusianus came here slowly, at the whim of nature. It took him two months to get that grain from Africa to Rome. In winter conditions few sane men sail, remember. It would take at least half a month to get word to Carthago. Then allow a fortnight to reach the legion, who are based at Lambaesis out in the desert and mountains of the south. The legion would have to stand to, drawing in all its vexillationes spread across Africa, and then march to the coast – say another month at least – and then ship across to Rome. Another two. And that's just one legion. The other units we would need are scattered from the borders of Aegyptus to the western sea. It will take months to get those forces across here.'

'But we must *try*,' I pushed. My pulse was pounding. How could everything go from such elation to such despair in so swift a moment?

'I will speak to Volusianus, ask him to start mobilising the African armies. It will not be in time, but they will be ready for the next time. So long as there *is* a next time, and we can survive this.'

'But how do we do that without an adequate army?'

Anullinus paused for a moment, like a man about to deliver more bad news, or pose an unpopular question...

'We should bring your father in.'

'My *father*?' I couldn't believe he would make such a suggestion. His militant and aggressive approach to rule – indeed to *everything* – had always been at odds with my own ways. We had never agreed on anything, and now, since his enforced retirement, he had slid into drink and bitter solitude on his country estate. Could such a man be of any value? The very notion of seeking the help of the man I had spent so much of my life despising chilled me.

'Yes. Your father. I know you and he do not get along, but Maximian carries more weight in purple than you. He is a symbol of the old order, and he is a very able field commander, whatever faults you might have found in him.'

I thought about it for a moment, trying to work through the anger and bile and see it from an objective place. It was true, sadly. I was not the weak youth I had been when Father domineered and sneered, but for all the inner strength I had found, I was no general. What my father had experienced in his campaigns and what he had achieved in war made him a clear choice for the role of commander. I hated the very idea, and wondered even if the old man could remain sober long enough, but he had more military experience in his little finger than any of the officers in Rome, Anullinus included. If anyone could fight Severus off with a pitifully small, out-of-shape force, it was my father.

'Do it. I will write the offer immediately. Have a detachment ride for his villa using the Cursus Publicus. In the meantime, we have to pull all our own forces together. Have the Guard, the Urban Cohorts, the Second Parthica and the Misenum fleet mustered on the plain to the east, past the sixth mile marker on the Via Praenestina. It's time we had our army training and preparing for action.'

Anullinus bowed and retreated from the kathisma, leaving me looking back at my sister and my son. How would I persuade Theodora to leave? Even if Father was coming, she would not abandon me.

And this place was no longer as secure as it had seemed an hour ago.

Severus was coming for me...

...and war was coming to Rome.

27

CONSTANTINE

The earth shuddered around me. The thunder of boots and throaty cries reverberated in the air. Flashes of silver armour surrounded me as my armies swept forward through the swirling, freezing wintry fog, past me and on in pursuit of the fleeing Frankish horde – a sea of dark cloaks, flowing locks, helms and axes flooding back towards the dark forests from which they had poured. Seven thousand of these curs had dared to rise up from the mists east of the Rhine, surge across the fords of the great river and into my lands. They had the audacity to presume that the death of my father had rendered Gaul an undefended prize.

Their feast of rapine had been ferocious: villages and towns had been razed, with women and children left raped and broken for the carrion crows to feast upon; crop fields had been left blackened and fallow, and the grain silos had been drained; villas and imperial tax wagons had been stripped of their precious wares, their drivers and military escorts slain like dogs. At this moment, when the balance of imperial tetrarchic power teetered over four starkly different futures, these bastards had almost riven my plans entirely.

It had taken endless days of riding, marching and scouting around the frozen plains and hills of Gaul to pin them down and then drive them back across the fords. Today, I affirmed through twisted lips and grinding teeth, they would atone for their plunder with a river of blood. It would be a lesson they would never forget.

'Do not let them reach the trees!' I cried, heeling Celeritas onto his hind legs, waving the legions forward. The motion brought a shower of frost from the shuddering plume of my helm. My cry was barely heard over the cacophony of those all around and frustration got the better of me. So I slipped from my saddle and joined the cohort of the Sixth as they swept past. A great cheer rose up as the men saw me do this and I sensed the pace of the pursuit intensify. I hurried through the ranks of the Sixth to the front line, and once there I returned Batius' pithy grin with one of my own. Together, we would lead the centre. The wing-helmed Cornuti, on the right, broke out in a low, baritone growl that grew in ferocity and pitch until it became a chilling, animal howl, trilling as they rushed forward. The *barritus*, they called it.

The javelin-laden, bronze-helmed *Lanciarii*, and two auxiliary cohorts forming our populous left, took to rapping their spear shafts on their shields as they moved. My army was just four thousand strong, but the Franks fled as if it was they who were outnumbered and not us, many of them shooting wide-eyed, panicked glances over their shoulders.

Already, the lesson had begun.

A few hundred strides separated us from the Franks, yet they were just a hundred paces from the myrtle-green mesh of mist-riddled trees and vegetation and the sanctuary this would provide, for they could slip into this wilderness and the advantage of my serried ranks would be lost – indeed, even the bravest legions knew the lore of the Varian disaster and the folly of entering thick woodland. But as the Franks approached the trees, I noticed them slowing. Indeed, they came to a halt by the treeline at the booming, guttural command of their strident kings, Ascaric and Merogaisus – a towering pair on horseback, one with a gemmed helm plumed with dyed-red feathers, the other with a face like a hatchet and a flowing red moustache.

Like a wheat field rippling in the breeze, the Frankish horde turned as one to face us. And no wonder. They had lured my army across the river from Gaul. They outnumbered us, and here, within this shroud of freezing fog with their rear and flanks protected by the forest that they knew my legionaries and auxiliaries could not fight within, they had the upper hand.

And that is just what I want them to believe, I thought, my face twisting into a taut rictus.

The Frankish kings roused their men into a savage war cry, and thousands of axes were raised overhead as we approached. They hurled these deadly weapons at us like a cloud of iron locusts.

'Shields!' I cried.

A deafening thrum of iron splitting wood rang out, the axes smashing through my men's shields. Our advance faltered as many were punched back like kindling, axes splicing faces, smashing ribs and cracking shins. A fine, crimson spray laced the mist. The edge of my shield came away under the blow of one of these missiles, and when I jerked the shield over to that side in fright, another glanced off my neck, just above the collar of my bronze scale vest. The bear pelt there cushioned and repelled the axe where it might otherwise have cleaved my flesh deeply.

I felt the deadly hail lessen, then roared: 'Lanciarii... *loose!*'

As one, the legion of javelin-throwers rippled, hoisting light lances overhead. With the wail of a buccina and the swipe of the Lanciarii standard, the javelins sailed through the fog and thwacked down into the massed Frankish ranks. They fell in droves, blood spurting and bodies crumpling. But still they outnumbered us, and now they had drawn their longswords and braced, grinning, snarling, watching our swift advance and ready for us to close on them. Only a handful of paces separated us.

I caught sight of the two haughty kings, saw the glimmer of victory in their eyes, then turned to Batius. 'It is time,' I growled.

The big man nodded, his expression a grim reflection of mine before he turned away and shouted across the ranks. I heard the buccina sound once more – three short, sharp blasts. At that moment, my lines crashed against the Frankish horde. What followed was a rattle of clashing shields, a cacophony of shrieking men and the rasping of iron tearing through flesh. Our momentum carried us into them. I barged forward as part of the Sixth, shoulder to shoulder with the legionaries around me, just as I had promised them. I pressed on with my comrades, driving into the Frankish mass with our shields. Longswords swept down at me, battered on my helm. Fearless warriors leapt up as if to stab down over our shield wall, only for the ranks behind to run these curs through on their lances. Blood and innards showered us and my spatha flashed out whenever a hint of a gap appeared before me. I felt the jarring of the blade rebounding from Frankish helms or mail, and the dull crunch when it sank into flesh.

Those flanking me thrust out with their spears again and again, rupturing Frankish warriors' chests, ripping out throats and slashing bellies. Likewise, the Franks were reaping a heavy toll of Roman lives. I saw many around me fall in puffs of blood as if pulled from below by some underground predator. One lad's head was cleaved through like ripe fruit by a Frankish blade. Our front began to waver, particularly on the auxiliary left, as our momentum faded and the Franks pushed back on us.

'Hold the line!' I roared, parrying another longsword strike. But I saw pockets of Franks break through our front, swinging their blades around like demons in the packed ranks behind, felling my precious legionaries in swathes. '*Hold!*' I cried again.

Once more I saw the faces of Ascaric and Merogaisus. Their glee was unfettered now, their eyes on me, seeing the Roman shield wall dissolve around me. Then, as if darkened by the shadow of a passing cloud, their faces fell and they shot glances over their shoulders.

I felt it then. The ground thundered like never before. The dark forests behind the Frankish horde shuddered, frost falling from the leaves. Now I wore the Frankish kings' stolen grins. *While you raped my lands, I did more than chase you like a hound. You did not lead my forces here. It was I who drove you to this very spot...*

As if shot from the bowels of the forest by some giant ballista, eight hundred spear-wielding Regii leapt into view and plunged into the rear of the Frankish line.

'*Raaaaa!*' Krocus cried, his face bent in a feral grin as he drove through them like a butcher's cleaver. Warriors were trampled, skewered, thrown to the ground and cut apart by the fury of the Regii. Yes, the legions feared the forests... but the Regii most certainly did not. The Frankish hubris scattered like a flock of doves at that moment, and the horde broke apart. The crumbling shield wall of my legions was suddenly revitalised, and we pressed in and around their flanks like a noose, treading over the wet, red mud and shining white fragments of bone from fallen foe and comrade alike.

'In this last month, every one of these bastards has taken from your families, slit the throats of your loved ones, spat on your lives. Cut them down!' I roared, feeling twice my usual height.

I saw before me only a sea of pale, terrified faces, dropping away one by one as we cut through them. Even as the clatter of discarded swords and spears rang out along with pleas for mercy, I did not stop and neither did my men. At the last, there were but a handful of them surrounding the two kings.

'Cease!' I cried. The din of battle fell away, leaving just the panting of exhausted men, the whimpering of the dying and the cawing of the eager crows.

I beheld the two mounted kings. Ascaric and Merogaisus wore stiff scowls. But something was missing; there was no fear of death. Batius stepped forward ahead of me and held his spatha up to Ascaric's throat while Krocus did likewise with Merogaisus.

'You can never be too sure, sir,' the big man panted. 'And it might be safest to deal with these two the way they dealt with the people of the Gallic provinces.'

At this, Ascaric laughed. An incongruous action for a man with a blade at his throat. But then, this was no ordinary man.

'You had best call off your mongrel, Roman,' he said, addressing me. 'If you want your borders to remain safe, then you should do as your forefathers always have. Make your terms. Give me gold and rights and then I shall be on my way. Then and only then, I might consider holding back the many more Frankish tribes from your lands.'

I felt a visceral, urgent need at that moment to thrust my blade into his gut. But he was right: warriors died, while chieftains and kings negotiated. It had always been this way. I saw the two kings switch their gaze to the forest, no doubt thinking of which grim mud-hole of a village they might retire to tonight after a deal had been struck.

'Put them in shackles,' I spat.

Ascaric swung back round to behold me, his face paling in disbelief. Merogaisus frowned as if he had misheard. I gazed through them and ignored their flurry of jagged curses as they were manhandled by Batius and Krocus, hauled from their horses and thrown to the mire of blood and mud underfoot.

TREVERORUM, FEBRUARY 307 AD

The lands around Treverorum were in winter's deathly grip, the rolling hills encrusted in frost from morning till night and skeletal groves sparkling in the few hours of sunlight. But within my capital, the winter held no sway. Fire roared in my heart and in the hearts of my armies and my people. And never more so than today at the games. After days of parades, processions, feasting and races, this was the climax of the *Adventus* celebration – the official, if belated, heralding of my arrival at the city.

Dressed in my military tunic, trousers and boots – all veiled under the purple imperial cloak and the frost-speckled bear pelt – I climbed the arena stairs to the kathisma and took my seat.

'Augustus!' The pair of Cornuti flanking my chair saluted and a horn sang to announce my arrival. The crowd – tens of thousands of them – turned from the combat on the arena floor to hail me, and I must resist false modesty and admit the sincerity and volume of their cry exhilarated me.

I swept my raised hand around in acknowledgement, then sat to enjoy the gladiatorial bout that was already underway. Someone placed a large cup of watered wine before me, and soon I had almost drained it, the fiery and tart mixture warming me and fuelling my enthusiasm as the combat continued. A *secutor*, bare-chested but with his head and face encased in a smooth, iron helm with just two eye-slits, ducked and jostled, swinging his shield out and twirling his short sword, manfully evading the net cast by a *retiarius*. The two were ancient adversaries – the retiarius' net rendered less effective and unable to snag on the secutor's carefully shaped helm, and the secutor's movement hindered by his narrow field of vision.

The pair were glistening with sweat despite the bitter chill, and their breath clouded in the air. A great clang rang out as the retiarius' trident spear was parried by the secutor's blade. The crowd gasped as the retiarius responded by casting his net. The secutor ducked and leapt clear of the mesh and its talon-like barbed iron weights, then bounded towards his foe. The retiarius fell onto his back and all were off their seats as the secutor leapt, hefting his short sword up to strike. When the secutor landed, the pair froze, the short-sword still hovering overhead and the blow unspent. The crowd fell silent. The retiarius had hoisted his trident spear at the last, and now it rested on the secutor's chest. A thin trickle of blood ran down the central tip where it had split the helmed one's skin. Nervous and panting, the pair looked to the kathisma.

All waited on me. All looked to me. For a moment, it felt as though even the winter sun had halted in its march across the sky and gazed down on me instead, eager for my response. I stood and squinted into its glare, feeling the brilliant force on my skin and imagining myself nimbate, the radiant crown fitting perfectly on my head. I had mused over the nature of gods and power as a boy. I had watched dangerous men wield power and don the guise of gods in the decades since – Galerius and Diocletian had been the men all eyes had turned to in the arenas of Antioch, Nicomedia, Alexandria and more. Their time was over. Today, without question, was my time.

I looked to the almost unnoticed man on the arena floor – the referee. His role was merely to convey my will. When I gave him a slight wave of the hand, the fellow grinned at my decision, then bounded over to gently prize the frozen gladiators apart, before raising the retiarius' hand in victory. The crowd came to life at this, erupting in a cheer that shook the arena.

I sat back down and enjoyed another mouthful of wine. Yes, that foul habit had me in its clutches again. Trying times seemed to have that effect on me.

'Your mother's belief was well placed,' a voice spoke by my side. 'She was sure you would not stain the arena floor today.'

I started, seeing that Lactantius had joined me, sitting on the chair by my side, legs crossed and his bearded chin resting on steepled fingers.

'A wise choice. Men in the past have been raised to power and thought they could buy the loyalty of their people with debauched shows of blood and slaughter, or ensure it by instilling fear within the populace.'

I said nothing. Yet he made a strong point. Like him, many within my realm were Christians. It was uncertain how many of them would have applauded had I ordered a fight to the death between the two hardy gladiators. *But it was my order to give, had I wished to do so,* a stubborn voice challenged in my mind. Yet pandering to the Christian ways had its advantages: it distanced me from Galerius, the great persecutor. *Merely pandering?* I wondered, thinking of the people who I had chosen to surround me: Mother, Lactantius and the speckling of Christian officers in my Gallic armies. I smiled wryly, poured a cup of wine – neat this time – and took a mouthful.

'Gladiators' lives will neither make nor break my ventures. There are more pressing issues on my table at the moment,' I said.

'You mean the manoeuvrings of your friend?' Lactantius replied.

My friend? I had not considered Maxentius as such in these last months. Like each of the tetrarchic claimants, I saw him as a cloud on the horizon, a source of trouble, a threat even. The man had done nothing to challenge me directly, nor had he even made contact with me... but I had heard dark rumours: some months ago I had sent him a scroll announcing my new status as master of the West. With it I sent him a chest of gold, topped with a marble slab engraved with my likeness. I received no acknowledgement let alone gratitude... just tales of how the gift had been smashed on the flagstones of Rome's forum, and my likeness shattered to mocking jeers. I had long ago learned to treat rumours like a pox, but this one fair angered me.

Worse, I had received word of goings-on in the realm he claimed as his own. Now, it seemed, he did not assert authority over just the Italian peninsula, but Africa too – the grain lands of the West. The grain lands of *my* realm.

'Africa was not Volusianus' gift to give, nor Maxentius' to receive,' I said, stabbing my forefinger into the table, causing the wine cup to shudder and a trickle of red to spill. 'Italia too was part of my father's realm – part of *my* realm!' I insisted. My tone was somewhat bitter and I instantly regretted it.

Lactantius took a deep breath, his weary features lengthening. I knew his next words would, as usual, disarm me and render my outburst as petty and hasty.

'You think that Maxentius sees his current situation or the lands foisted upon him as a gift? Do you even remember how he was as a boy?'

I sighed, closing my eyes as the next bout of combat ensued. Images of the boy with the wooden blocks in the halls of this very city surfaced from the blackness behind my eyelids. The boy chained to the imperial bloodline and fated to rise to power. Now, it seemed, Severus marched on Rome with his legions, set on taking the city and Maxentius' head. For the briefest of moments, I must confess my thoughts strayed to what might happen should Severus succeed. One less knot in this mesh of tetrarchic power struggle would mean one less obstacle in my path to claiming the West as my own. I shook off the dark thought with a shiver, then opened my eyes, my bitterness receding, seeing that I had unconsciously pressed thumb and forefinger together.

I hope you have built your walls high, old friend.

I took another mouthful of wine, feeling the heady numbness sweep over me. My momentary weakness vanished. There was no place for sympathy, no place for old, dead feelings. Suddenly, I heard the crowd gasp and saw them rise. Then a series of throaty and inhuman roars erupted. Lactantius leaned forward, his face wrinkled in concern. I looked with him to see that the lions were being led into the arena. Four of the beasts, brought from Iberia, padded and growled, chained and handled by nine men each. The golden-maned creatures snarled and slavered, tugging at their shackles and striking fear into their handlers. The torment these majestic beasts had suffered in their transit had stoked their feral hearts.

'Constantine?' I heard Lactantius say.

But now I visualised the crown of light on my head again. I rose and waved to the men at the arena gate. The iron gateway was raised, and two more figures were ushered out into the centre of the arena floor. In shabby robes and with tousled, matted hair, Ascaric and Merogaisus looked this way and that, eyes wide with fright. Ascaric wore his gemmed war helm – starkly in contrast to his tattered garb and gaunt state – as a symbol of the people who had brought terror upon the Gallic lands in recent months.

'Tear out their hearts!' one voice in the crowd roared louder than any other.

'Gut them!' another screamed.

I saw the ferocity of their twisted faces, teeth bared, spittle flecking the winter air – far fiercer than the lions. Even some of the Christian spectators cursed them. The lion-handlers loosened their grips on the chains, allowing the beasts to maraud towards the Frankish pair, the chains growing tight again only when the beasts' breath lifted strands of Merogaisus' hair. The man's eyes widened in terror.

'Constantine?' Lactantius repeated, his tone desperate. His wise calls for caution went unheard.

I heard only the lions' roaring and Ascaric's trilling pleas for mercy. 'I can bring my people to your side,' he cried up towards the kathisma. 'As a king, you must listen to me!'

I noticed Merogaisus' robes darken around the groin as his bladder gave way.

Then I raised my hand, one finger extended, all eyes on me once more. I fixed my gaze on the two proud kings, and saw the faint hopes of reprieve they might have harboured die at that moment.

I dropped my finger, then closed my eyes and gloried in the winter sun.

I heard the strangled screaming of the Frankish pair and the feral gnashing of the beasts. The screams were short, and soon, the dull cracking and crunching of bone replaced it. But my mind was gone from the arena at that moment, gone and soaring into the months and years that lay ahead. Fate was dangling an empire before me, lifting me so high I was sure I was a god.

28

MAXENTIUS

ROME, MARCH 307 AD

I stood atop one of the tall, powerful towers of the Porta Salaria, feeling distinctly uncomfortable in my military finery as I looked across the destruction to the glittering field of blades and helms that was Severus' army, watching and waiting on their commander's word to advance against Rome's walls. On the next tower I could hear the ballista creaking, at maximum tension with the desperate urge to begin reaping a bloody crop from that field.

The cuirass I wore had been created by the best armourer in Rome gratis, the designs embossed upon its burnished bronze surface displaying gods and heroes and creatures of ancient myth, putting all who saw me in mind of that first great Augustus who had turned Caesar's mania into a legacy of power. I wore a leather garment, called a *subarmalis*, under my armour, designed to protect my flesh from the weight and edges of the metal as well as help dull enemy blows, and which had been dyed white and purple. Compounded with the white breeches of an old-fashioned cut and the purple cloak that whipped behind me in the wind, I must have been an imposing sight to the people around me – to those who did not know me, at least.

The weather had held dry for days, despite a low overcast sky and the constant threat of drizzle, though the winds had cut along the Tiber like an icy knife, ensuring that every fire still blazed even in March. At least, I mused, I wasn't cold in my armour.

The sword hung at my side with the weight of twenty generations of lives lost in the defence of this city. How many times since the days of the man I was dressed to emulate had Roman drawn sword against Roman? *Too often*, of course, was the somewhat sad answer to that question.

Beside me, emitting a cloying aura of superiority and smugness, stood my father, in more functional military garb though displaying just as much purple in his attire. I felt sickened at the need to rely upon a man I saw as symptomatic of the decline of the world into vainglory and militant might. And yet I needed him.

Our uncomfortable pairing was accompanied by Anullinus of course, as well as his brother, who seethed gently in the shadow of young Zenas, Volusianus – the Governor of Africa – and any man in the strange cobbled-together army of Rome above the rank of prefect; quite a few of *them*, too. In fact, the tower top was rather crowded, and I noticed with irritation how my father had acquired a space around himself through sheer presence, while officers crowded closer to me than was proper for my rank.

Rank! Now there was yet another bone of contention jutting from the ragged wounded body of our family. Though I could sense my father's hunger to resume power in the empire – something that in itself almost persuaded me to refuse him – there had been aggravating and intense negotiations, and

Father had only come to Rome to aid me on the promise of an equal share in the power and the title of 'Augustus'. Of course, I had been hailed as 'Caesar' in the hope of avoiding aggravating Galerius into direct war but that did not deter the megalomaniac old man, who simply doused himself liberally in my best wine and announced that he would only be willing to settle for 'Augustus'.

I had almost exploded then and began a tirade against him, freely expressing a number of opinions that cooler heads might have kept hidden – that pig-headedness which had passed down from Father to myself led to dreadful disagreements between us at times. But Anullinus had stepped in and persuaded me – that man could talk a donkey off its legs – to accede to my father's requests until at least the current crisis had passed. And so my father – the *Senior* Augustus of Rome – had stepped in to take command of the military while I retained civil control.

Valeria had exploded at the news, of course. She had expended so much time and effort in making me, her husband, the legitimate emperor of Rome, and within months I had been forced to defer to another. She had hissed and spat invective as she railed against the decision. I had stood and taken the tirade stoically, noting with mild interest that if my wife and I had only one thing in common it was a mutual loathing of my father.

When her fire had finally burned itself out and she subsided into huffs and hisses, I had asked her what alternative *she* would have sought. She had blustered and argued for a while before admitting weakly that there was none. Maximian was a soldier emperor like those of old, and if any man could galvanise our meagre forces into something that could stop a full-scale invasion, sadly it was the bloated old bastard.

Despite the uneasy divide in power, with Father believing himself my superior and my refusal to acknowledge as much, I had retained a military garb for the time being, and it was to me that the senate, the people, and most of the officers – especially the Praetorians – looked to for rule.

And I would rule as I could. But what lay before me, outside the walls of Rome, was daunting to a degree I had not previously considered possible.

The Porta Salaria was one of the north-eastern gates in Rome's newly refurbished walls and one of the most impressive, and I was glad that it was here that this scene had unfolded, and not at one of the half-finished and much lower gates in the south of the city. From this lofty eyrie a man with keen eyesight could see every foot of the suburbs all the way to the bridge that crossed the narrow Anio River, two miles away and just half a mile from its confluence with the Tiber. A man with a light heart might in better days have stood here and looked with a smile upon the cheap, fire-trap wooden houses that filled that intervening space with the lowest strata of life. Dirty children playing in the streets with balls and sticks. Poor women washing their drab clothes in the Anio and hanging them on lines between the houses to dry. Men drinking their wine in the shade of the timber lean-tos. Lighter hearts, in better times, seeing simpler things.

Now, I looked with stony heart upon the shattered remains of what had once been a thriving, if poor, community who had been steadfastly loyal to me and to Rome. Of course many of the residents had fled inside the city's walls when danger loomed and some had brought everything they owned with them, preferring the uncertainty of living on the streets to the certainty of what was going to happen to their neighbourhood. Others had refused to leave, disbelieving that their noble betters would do to them what we all knew they would.

The area had been cleared with an iron fist and no sympathy for the humanity therein. Severus' forces had simply butchered anyone they came across and driven the young and the old alike into the Tiber to swim or to drown as the Fates decided before levelling their property.

And we had stood here and watched.

They had set up camp on the other side of the Anio, out of reach of any of the heavy artillery on my walls, and waited, leaving us staring at them across a wasteland of death and destruction. Word had come to us that much the same thing had happened to any city, town, village or even farmstead on this savage emperor's path to my door, particularly if a garrison or settled veterans there declared for me.

And after three days of the most unpleasant, tense waiting, this morning Severus himself and his officers and bodyguards had approached the walls. I had been tempted to have a ballista loosed at him as he approached. It would have solved a lot of problems. But he came bare-shouldered in the old manner to signify peace and a wish to parley, and I would not sully the traditions of Rome for personal gain, even if it might save many lives. Besides, my father had almost convinced me this would be bloodless.

Almost.

I turned to Father. 'How sure are you about this?'

Maximian, *Augustus* of the West and renowned general of numerous legions, scratched himself somewhere below the waist and smiled a drunken smile that did not instil any more confidence in me. 'Leave it to me, boy. Trust me. You promised to defer to me, after all.'

I could hear my teeth grinding even over his words. I had made that very promise, curse the Fates for the necessity.

'Just remember, Father, that my promise holds in military matters alone. In civil affairs, my decisions are my own.'

My father gave me a sidelong sneer that left me under no illusions as to just how much he cared about my plans for building, religion and commerce, and I only felt my irritation grow with the confirmation.

Severus halted his steed far enough from the walls that he did not have to crane his neck unduly to see us, the breathless rasp of his voice hard to make out atop the gatehouse in even a mild breeze.

'What did he say?' I was forced to ask of Anullinus, who I knew had keener hearing than I.

'I'll give you a bloody guess, Imperator,' he replied sourly and with tone and attitude totally unfitting an address to his master. I bridled, but if I'd argued and admonished I'd have missed the next rounds of speech too, so I glared at him as I strained to hear the old vulture below croaking at me.

'...will accept your peaceful abdication and the handing over of Rome's command to me in exchange for my promise of leniency.'

'Leniency?' my father scoffed from the tower top.

'The false, usurping emperor will be allowed to retire somewhere remote in exile on the condition that he never again attempt a political role within the empire. Refusal will result in war, and my force is unmatched in this peninsula.'

Maximian nodded with pursed lips as though he were considering the offer. I had to force myself to believe that he *wasn't* considering it, though I had an awful moment's fear that it might be true. And then Father cleared his throat.

'And what of myself: Maximian, once your own master

and de facto ruler of the West? Might you grant me the same tolerance?'

There was a moment's pause and I wondered what was going through my enemy's head until Severus straightened in the saddle as though speaking to a superior – another thing that annoyed me intensely. 'I had heard the former Augustus had put in an appearance with his mewling boy. I will give you this advice, Maximian: go back to your villa and your amphorae. Politics is a young man's game, and you are past your best.'

I frowned at the idea that Severus thought himself a young man, but already my father was chuckling that unpleasant gurgling laugh that made men who valued their skin move away from him. I watched, fascinated. Father had taken the whole matter of Severus upon himself to settle in the half a month since he had reached my side. I had been rather grateful really, since it kept him away from me and limited his interference in other matters, but now I was regretting our separation, since I had no idea what he had planned. My eyes scanned the walls for some surprise. Perhaps fire-throwers?

Instead, my father stepped up onto the battlements themselves – a thing I would never have done in a thousand lifetimes for the fear of falling. The drop was certain death. There he stood, magnificent, like some furrow-browed, rosy-nosed Hercules astride the gates of Rome with his own purple robe whipping in a wind that threatened to send him to his death. It was an awe-inspiring sight, even for those of us who knew his baser side. To those below, he must have been god-like.

'And you will cultivate a new generation of rulers, will you, Severus the Whisperer? You will plough furrows in my flesh with your blade and seed a future without my dynasty? And whose army will you command against me?'

'Do not play feeble word games, old man,' Severus rasped. 'You can plainly see the army I bring. It dwarfs your pitiful forces. Accept my conditions and be on your way, unless you seek oblivion?'

And all of a sudden I knew what was happening. I knew what my father had done. *Whose army will you command*, indeed?

The officers around Severus began to polarise as I watched, though the man himself remained blissfully unaware of it without the benefit of my high viewpoint.

'I will offer my terms one last time...'

And his hoarse voice faltered as he suddenly realised that he was almost alone. Most of his officers had moved away from him in two groups, leaving only a handful of senior commanders surrounded by bodyguards, all looking equally perplexed at this turn of events.

'Think again, Severus horse-buggerer.' My father laughed. 'Look around you. You are blind to true power, for you cannot see beyond your own radiant halo. If you could see past your *ego*, you would have realised before now that almost every commander and almost every soldier in your army once swore an oath to me, and I marched through Gaul and Germania and across the most brutal, unforgiving lands in the empire alongside them; *fought* with them; *ate* with them; *bled* with them.'

Severus had realised his folly quickly and was looking around himself with increasing desperation.

'And you, Severus, arse-wiper of that fat blob of dead worms Galerius, have done nothing to win their loyalty. Nothing, except attempt to lead them against their true commander. Are you sweating, Severus? Because I would be if I'd done what you have done.'

Marvelling at my father's simple, astounding solution, I watched the now-panicked Severus rattle out some desperate instruction to the commander of his bodyguard, a man with a Praetorian crest astride a big roan. The man simply backed away, and my father laughed loud.

'You forget how you and your fleshy shit-pile of a master have treated the Praetorians, Severus. Do not think to curry favour with them now, nor with the frumentarii you know of in your army, for each and every one of them entered your ranks after leaving the Castra Peregrina in Rome at my behest. Do not forget that under my former colleague's edicts, their ranks are no longer officially in service.'

Severus was wheeling his horse now, along with perhaps half a dozen panicked officers who were no part of the conspiracy against him.

'I see you have a few units with you that did not previously serve with me. Do you think them strong enough to seize Rome?'

The old soldier down on the ruined ground outside the walls had no answer for my father, for there was now only one thing on his mind: flight. He heeled his horse urgently and began to race for the river Anio, his desperate allies close behind. Those officers who had declared for my father with their meaningful silence remained motionless, gazing up at the tower top. Father chuckled darkly. 'What are you waiting for, boys? Gut the bastard.'

I watched as the assembled commanders of legions and cohorts urged their horses round and raced off after the fox-flight of Severus. Father waited until they were already away towards the Anio before dropping back down from the parapet.

'What now?' I asked quietly, feeling an admiration for my father that was almost entirely alien to me.

'Leave him to me. Even without the bulk of the army, he has a few faithful cohorts beyond the Anio, and he will attempt to flee with them. The forces loyal to me should be able to halt him in his tracks, but if he crosses the *Septem Balnea* valley he'll escape.'

Septem Balnea. The Anio was perhaps two miles from this gate, within easy reach for the fleeing emperor. Beyond, he and his few loyal men would have to move quickly to cross the causeway that traversed the wide marshy valley of the Septem Balnea some three miles beyond. If he passed that causeway he was free, but if he was caught this side of it...

Father started to hurry down the steps from the tower top, though his age-increased bulk forced him to take them slower than he would like. I watched him go, feeling rather impotent and glum, until I felt a presence at my shoulder and turned my head to see Governor Volusianus wearing a strange expression.

'The people love a strong emperor... a *martial* emperor. Do you want your *father* to be the people's hero, Domine?'

I stood for a moment, turning over what the man had said, weighing up potential dangers, the strange panicked thrill of defying my father's wishes even now as a grown man, and the agreement we had made to separate our spheres of power. But I had made my decision immediately and was now simply attempting to justify it. My eyes caught those of Anullinus, who was shaking his head fractionally, trying to urge me against the decision, then the Praetorian Prefect's fiery gaze turned on Volusianus as though he could burn him to ash with a look. With a last glance at them both, I leapt into the stairwell.

I felt strange and exultant as I took the three staircases to ground level two or three steps at a time, leaping from the bottom of each and racing to the next. In the lowest chamber I passed my father, who stood rubbing his knee and cast me an enraged look as I raced out into the chilly morning and grasped the reins of my horse, taking them from the *equisio* who had kept all the officers' horses for them during the parley.

Father had gathered a small force inside the Porta Salaria, with the bulk of our army on the walls, and I had wondered why until now. As I looked around the wide thoroughfare I realised that the gathered force here were all mounted men – no infantry. The *exploratores* from the Castra Peregrina, the small cavalry detachment from the Second Parthica at Albanum and the Praetorian cavalry. Father had known he would need the horse for a chase. With a grin, I hauled myself up into the saddle and turned to the assembled horsemen.

'The false emperor Severus flees north, his army deserting him. A bag of gold *aurei* to the man who stops him before he reaches Septem Balnea.'

I gave the gesture to open the gates of the Porta Salaria, and the guards did so as speedily as they could, for discipline in the street had been obliterated by my perhaps o'er hasty offer. As the wide oak gates creaked open, riders were bursting through it, ripping swords from their sheaths even as they crossed the boundary.

I heeled my horse and slipped in alongside them, the men respectfully leaving me plenty of room. No one knew whether I would be a good horseman, after all.

I pelted through the gate with the rest, wishing I was

attired in the shushing mail shirts that most wore and not this glorious, unforgiving bronze lump that held me rigid in the saddle, bruising me and causing me almost endless discomfort. I felt a pulse-racing panic as I tore my expensive, decorative spatha from its scabbard and kicked my horse to ever more speed. I had been in precisely two fights in my life. Once as a boy, when I had narrowly avoided being kicked to death amid my toys – saved by Constantine, who now claimed the same throne as I – and then almost a year ago, during the riots in the forum. But I had never fought a real fight. I had never drawn a sword in anger. I had never ridden into battle, and the bone-chilling excitement was almost too much.

My heart thumped in my throat and my bowels threatened to loosen more with every passing moment as I hurtled out across the ruined, cleared neighbourhood outside the walls in the wake of my cavalry, eating up the two miles to the Anio with a breakneck pace. Perhaps it was the excitement, or perhaps the quality of my horse which was, after all, the very best, but I was soon passing many of the other horsemen and moving into the lead formation, driven by the exploratores, whose horses were by their very nature good quality.

As we thundered across the heavy ancient bridge that spanned the Anio I marvelled at the army Severus had brought south to crush me. I had never imagined so many soldiers in one place. How could a general hope to command such a force? The logistics alone seemed insurmountable. But the watchword for Severus' army on that day was 'confusion'. The revolt of the officers loyal to my father had taken the actual legions and cohorts mainly by surprise and to discover that they were suddenly sharing a camp with their enemy had caused a certain amount of chaos. Here and there fights had broken out between units with opposed loyalties and many of the forces milled about in confusion as their newly returned commanders tried to rein in the chaos.

The passage of Severus and his men was clear, though. Like the bent stalks of a wild meadow that deer have crossed, the army had been neatly bisected by the fleeing emperor. Clearly he had managed to gather some of his loyal forces as he passed through, and some sort of clash was going on at the far edge of the enemy camp, though with the din of small melees breaking out all across the plain it was hard to tell what exactly was going on.

In truth I would have floundered there and then, unable to identify my enemy and with no clue as to how to proceed, but it appeared that my cavalry had a much better grasp of the situation than I – especially when driven by the promise of gold – and without pause or thought, they raced on through the army's camp. Glad of their lead, I followed.

As we passed the last vestiges of Severus' camp and entered open countryside again, I reckoned we were but a mile from the Septem Balnea crossing. I could see a cavalry force ahead. Presumably Severus had abandoned his loyal footmen to find their own way and took to the gallop with his cavalry – a sensible decision. Severus was bearing down on the causeway and my heart sank as I realised that we had little chance of catching him before he escaped across it. My irritation only increased as I recognised my father's voice not far behind distributing orders to the men rather breathlessly as he rode.

I *would not* be outdone by him this time. I kicked my horse to a pace that would eventually break him and raced out among the lead riders in the force. My head came up, my hand already feeling heavy with the long blade in it, the muscles in my arm straining. Ahead, the bulk of the enemy had moved onto the causeway, while a small group of riders had formed up at the southern end to discourage pursuit.

I do not know whether it was a vain pursuit of glory, or the desire to prove my mettle to the soldiers around me, or possibly pure irritation at the combination of my foe's now-clear escape and my father's arrival, but I threw caution to the wind that morning, charging the causeway guards head-on along with a dozen or so of the more gold-hungry exploratores in my pay. We hit them hard and fast, with fury, and no quarter was given. I slashed with my blade as though scything wheat. Warm crimson spray filled the air, along with screams of man and horse, and the ring of metal on metal. I revelled in the simplicity of butchery.

For a short while, I almost lost myself.

Of course, while it felt as though I was the personification of Mars himself, slaying my enemies in a welter of blood, I am under no illusion as to my martial abilities. I was probably slow, weak and not very effective. Almost certainly the men around me had to save my life numerous times. I know that I came out of that engagement with a savage cut to my upper arm that needed the urgent attention of a medicus and required nine stitches, though I remember being more put out that the blow had snicked off four of the purple leather *pteruges* hanging from my shoulder.

When it was all over and I sat astride my whinnying horse amid wounded and disconsolate men – they had each lost a potential bag of gold coins, remember – I watched the flight of Severus, already two miles away and gaining. Blood ran freely down my arm and joined that of others on my blade. I turned a gore-spattered countenance to my father, who was looking at me with a sort of grim curiosity, as though a cat had just recited Ovid. Not pride so much as interest, but even that was new and welcome.

'What will he do?' I asked, my voice shaky.

'He will flee to a safe location. Not Mediolanum without his army, for that is too close to Constantine. My guess is Ravenna, where the fleet is still loyal to him.'

My father may have been infuriating and cold but he knew his business, and I always did well to rely on him in military matters. 'What to do now, then?'

'I will take the army, hunt down the dog and nail him to the gates of Ravenna,' Father growled with low menace.

'Respectfully, Domine, that would be a mistake.'

I turned to see that Anullinus had joined us, his hands clean and sword still sheathed. I opened my mouth to argue but the Praetorian Prefect did not wait for contradiction. 'The false emperor has no army left now. He cannot hope to attack us with the Ravenna fleet and, while the few cohorts that are still loyal to him might manage to reach Ravenna and join him, he is no threat now. Constantine and Galerius, however, still pose the greatest threat. You cannot take the army east and leave Rome unprotected.'

Sense had been spoken. A war at Ravenna would just put Rome at risk, and after all we had done to save her, I would not countenance that now. My father opened his mouth to argue, but I hurried out my words to make an imperial decision before he had the chance.

'We move the army back to the city. Our forces have grown and we must reorganise and take stock now. It is time to fill the ranks of the Second Parthica and return it to the status of a full legion. Anullinus? Have a deputation ride for Ravenna in the morning. I will give them a letter for Severus.'

'Your solution is to send him post?' my father grunted, a twitch making his top lip jump.

'My solution is to end this without a costly war, Father. I will send word to Severus offering him leniency in return for his support. If he will agree to abdicate his position and declare for me, I will see him unharmed and treated with the respect due to a Roman citizen of note.'

My father opened his mouth to object but Anullinus was already saluting and turning to leave, and I suspect that at that moment Father realised something. I was no longer a mere boy, and he had considerably less power over me than he had assumed. Moreover, for all his confirmed position as my co-ruler, Anullinus was *my* man, which meant the Guard were mine. And the people of Rome knew me as their champion, and knew my father only as a name from the past. I had the edge over him, and I could see in the narrowing of his eyes that he was already trying to work out how to change that. But for now, he watched the Praetorian Prefect go with my orders.

'This is a mistake,' he muttered.

'No. This is what it is to rule Rome. Not everything is about blood and steel, Father.'

Of course, I was wrong. In the end, it always comes down to blood and steel, doesn't it?

Almost half a month went by in a strange lull. The dreadful war we had been anticipating for so long had somehow missed us and as a result our army had strengthened immeasurably. We had received no news from Severus or from our deputation and I had become convinced that the defeated emperor had fled to his master Galerius for aid. But I had little time to brood on whether my father had been right about hunting him down, for the city still required my attention. The great works I had planned were moving apace, and the walls of the city were strengthening by the day. After all, we may have beaten Severus and stolen his army, but there were greater, darker threats out there than he.

One of whom preyed on my mind a great deal.

Constantine.

My former friend was growing into the role of emperor now every bit as much as I. His martial skills were undiminished as his defeat of the tribes across the Rhenus told us, and his strength of character was surely growing, for the armies of the western provinces were flocking to his banner according to all accounts. But something had changed in my old friend. A blood-chilling tale had reached us that he had ordered two barbarian kings torn apart by beasts in the arena. That did not sound like the Constantine I remembered. The hero of the Sassanid Wars, and the voice of sanity and reason amid the persecutions of Nicomedia. A man I knew to have sympathy for the Christians in his court through his family's faith.

I began to feel cold and alone. I had never truly believed that my old friend Constantine would stand against me. I'd always assumed that something would happen and everything would work out with us sharing the responsibility for the West in opposition to the stark evil of Galerius and his cronies. The idea that my friend had become the sort of man to torture someone to death – even the leaders of the enemy tribes? It seemed alien and worrisome. Such a man might not baulk at a war with an old friend.

And so we strengthened and reordered the army – the latter keeping my father busy and largely out of my hair. And then one morning, as I sat musing over the numerous problems facing us, the spell of the last half month was broken.

There was a knock at my tablinum door and when I called for whoever it was to enter, it turned out to be a procession of my peers: Anullinus, Volusianus and my father.

'Good news, Domine.' The Praetorian Prefect smiled, and I felt my tension begin to ease. 'I have a message from Severus. It seems he accepted your offer some time ago, though the messengers never reached us with his answer. Perhaps they fell foul of bandits in the mountains? Whatever the case, Severus is now at Tres Tabernae, not fifteen miles from this very room, with only his personal household and a few guards. He wishes to publicly declare his support for you as emperor in return for his life and his freedom.'

I narrowed my eyes. I had never offered him 'freedom' but his life I would grant him. The tension continued to ebb as one of my most dangerous opponents finally disappeared from the great board.

Volusianus leaned past the prefect and cleared his throat. 'Domine, I know it is not my place to offer advice, but I feel compelled to do so. You have Severus now, close by and poorly guarded. Do not let him live, for he will always be a danger. Kill him now, while you can.'

I blinked. 'I'll not renege on a promise I gave, Volusianus. What kind of emperor would that make me? No. He must be spared and his voice must be heard in support of my claim. But his freedom was never on offer.'

To my surprise, my father nodded. 'Agreed. Severus is Galerius' pet. And if Galerius should decide to move against us we will have Severus as a bargaining tool, or at the least to threaten.'

I cared not about my father's reasons. The fact was that

he supported me in the decision, and the two other men muttered their acceptance of the order. Severus would be brought to Rome, would acknowledge me, and would pose no further threat as he lived in luxurious captivity in my capital. Galerius would ever be a threat, but now I faced only one direct opponent in the West.

'Constantine,' I muttered, without realising I had said it out loud. Father gave me a look that I recognised and gestured at the other two men. 'Anullinus? Volusianus? Could you step outside for a moment?' I asked.

The two men shot me concerned looks but I returned them with an easy smile and they left, closing the door behind them. Father waited until he was sure we were alone.

'I have been giving thought to the issue of Constantine,' Father mused. 'He claims to be Augustus just as you and me...'

A flash of annoyance hit me at that tacit equality between us. That and a question: '*Augustus*? Did he not release coins as a *Caesar*?'

'And if I sit in a sewer, does that make me a turd? No, he sees himself as Augustus, regardless of his displays. But he might be willing to accept the role of Caesar – or at least some compromise in the same manner as you and I have managed – if we can tie him to us closely. After all, his old wife is now long dead...'

'A marriage to Theodora? She was his father's wife. It might be a little strange for him to marry her, but she would be good for him, I think, and closer to his age than his father's, after all. And there's been enough time since Constantius' passing that it could be seen as proper.' I felt a thrill. Theodora and Constantine would be a good match, and Father was right. She would tie him to us. We might be able to pull this together and form a united West against Galerius. A strong and stable future was almost within our grasp.

'Not Theodora,' Father replied. 'Fausta.'

I pictured my little sister in that moment, with her sharp mind and mischievous humour. She had just turned thirteen, I realised with surprise. Easily old enough for a good marriage. She was still small and carefree, and somehow that always reduced her age in my mind, in much the same way as I never seemed to see Romulus growing, even though he was now a similar age. I pictured Fausta and Constantine together. Interestingly they seemed to fit like perfect puzzle pieces, and the thought brought a smile to my face.

'I agree. She will suit him well, and perhaps turn him a little lighter once more.'

'She will make a well-positioned piece in the game,' Father corrected with a calculating expression. Personally I had trouble picturing wonderful Fausta manoeuvring Constantine on Father's behalf, but I kept my peace for, though his reasons were cruel, his decision was a fine one for all concerned.

29

CONSTANTINE

TREVERORUM, APRIL 307 AD

J ust last year when I returned to this city as its master, the
fabrica had been deserted: the great workhouse was a
cavern of echoes and still shadows, its furnaces lying cold
and its hammers silent. A void of torpor. But today, like
the many months since my return, it was a riot of activity.
In the permanent twilight of this vast hall, chains clanked
and carried swaying crucibles of molten iron to and fro, the
smelted, bright orange ore peeking from the edges of each
like demonic eyes. These conical vessels were tipped into
channels and moulds, spilling out and taking the shape of
sword blades, spear tips, and arrow heads.

When the red-hot liquid had solidified and significantly
cooled, each piece was lifted and taken to the furnaces. The
back wall was lined with such kilns, where smiths worked
the bellows like great lungs, sending black smoke spiralling
up the chimneys and out into the air over Treverorum like
a demon's breath. They would draw an iron piece from
the flames only when it was the colour of a morning sun
before chiselling and hammering it into the weapon it would
become. Men scurried back and forth, faces soot-stained

and glistening with sweat as they carried tools and hand carts. Hammers chattered rhythmically like iron birdsong as the new blades were forged, worked then finished over a line of anvils.

It was early spring and the days were still crisp and fresh, yet inside this great brick workhouse my skin was slick with sweat and my tunic and purple cloak damp through as though I was once again trudging through Persian sands. A savage *hisssss* sounded right behind me and I started, swinging round to the noise. A young and rather sheepish smith's striker had just plunged a newly forged blade into a slack-bucket of briny water, and tried to hide his embarrassment behind the grey-white cloud of steam that rose from the cooling metal.

'Domine.' The nearby smith genuflected hastily, then bundled the striker back with a muted volley of curses.

'Hmm,' Batius mused, lifting the discarded and nearly cooled blade from the tub with a rag, shaking the water from it. 'Give me one of these on the battlefield, still glowing hot.' His smile, uplit in orange from a passing crucible was, quite frankly, terrifying. He jabbed the blade up as if into some imaginary foe. 'Right up the ar—'

The deafening clang of a sledgehammer muted the remainder of his strategy, but Lactantius, walking with us, wore a scowl that suggested he had heard well enough. In any case the old man had worn a disapproving look for most of the day – one that only grew as he saw the war machine I was establishing. I saw his face souring further when we passed a vast stock of spathas – enough to arm the new legion I had raised – stored upright in timber racks like an iron crop field.

'The armour works are over here,' I said, seeing scornful words form on his lips.

'When is it time, Constantine; time to say... enough?' he said, refusing to be distracted.

'When the armies of my realm have means to defend themselves and to strike out at those who might challenge us,' I snapped.

'Yet you have arms and armour here bounteous enough to equip every man, woman and child within Treverorum's walls.'

'Thus, you understand the scale of my concerns. Thousands of men march in my armies and must be equipped. Ancient legions fight with a mixture of tattered garb and weapons just as archaic as their reputations, or recent but poorly crafted kit. New regiments have been raised: thousands of men who need sword, shield, spear and helm of any sort. Aye, my armies are growing, but still they are dwarfed by those of Galerius and rivalled by those of...' I saw Lactantius hang on my words, confident that I had wandered into his trap. I feigned a coughing fit and left the rest of my sentence unsaid.

'Of your old friend?' he finished for me.

I pretended to be distracted and briskly ushered them on to the far end of the fabrica, opened to the morning light by five huge doors, each wide enough to drive two wagons through abreast. Here, the workers fashioned mail shirts, scale jackets and helms. Outside, the courtyard was lined with circular tanner's pits and the air was laden with a vile stench of dung, urine and offal as skins were soaked and worked in the foul soup of waste by barefooted wretches coated in the stuff. Lactantius covered his nose and mouth with a rag. I couldn't help but enjoy the relief and silence this brought. The stink even caused Batius – a man who had spent much of his life in the malodorous environs of legionary *contubernia* tents – to gag.

'I know we've talked this over already, but do we really need leather armour?' the big man croaked. 'Seriously, I spent two years with a tent-mate who lived off cabbage stew. The cheaper he could buy cabbage, the better. If it was a little black around the leaves – no problem.' He shuddered at some olfactory memory. 'But this place tops anything he subjected me to.'

I chuckled, heedless of the smell. Then my humour faded. I regarded the pair with a look I knew they would not misread. 'Were we to fight the Goths, then I would have our legions clad in iron. Were we to face the Persians, then I might opt to train swift cavalry with no armour at all. But we do not have the luxury of knowing our enemy, which direction they might come from, upon what terrain we might meet them.' I pointed to the wagons laden with the new mail shirts and those with the fresh leather cuirasses and saddles, then to the bundles of newly fletched arrows and *lancea* javelins. 'Stealth, strength, range... we will not be caught out,' I finished, pushing a fist into my palm. 'The Herdsman has been making a great din about ending my reign and crushing those who support me. You have both witnessed what that dog is capable of.' I sighed, wishing my troubles ended there. But they did not.

Batius curled his lower lip as if about to submit to my reasoning.

Lactantius, however, was not to be assuaged. 'And?'

I feigned a blank look as if clueless to his allusions.

'Italia and Africa?' he added. 'You were busy telling us of your enemies at every side: Galerius and all the armies of the East. Yet you forgot to mention the lands of Italia and Africa.'

I gave him a sideways look with narrowed eyes. 'But you did not, old goat.'

The rising in Rome had been a curdled mix of blessing

and bane for me. Maxentius' claims to the Italian peninsula and the rich lands of Africa had stung my pride and stoked that fiery ruthless streak in me. But his seizure of those lands had also drawn the attentions of Galerius and his armies from me and onto him. Severus, Galerius' dog, had marched upon Rome and it seemed that the city would be his. I had waited anxiously on my messengers to bring me word – for as soon as Maxentius' realm was seized by Severus, then surely Galerius would then turn all of his attentions back on me. Yet it had not come to pass. Maxentius had won his first great victory. The boy with the wooden blocks was now a hero of the ancient city, it seemed. Rome remained his and Severus the Whisperer had been swept from the great board. The delicate balance had remained: Galerius, me, Maxentius. A balance that groaned with tension. Then it had all changed just under a month ago.

Lactantius studied me as if hearing my every thought. 'You spend your days commissioning new armies and stockpiling arms. Yet Maxentius brings to you not sharpened steel, but an olive branch.'

I blinked and my lips moved to speak but no sound came out. Suddenly my thoughts of steel and sundered realms crumbled away. Long-forgotten memories rose to the surface in their place: things lost to me since Minervina had left this world.

'When does she arrive in Arelate?' Lactantius pressed me. *She.*

With that single, simple word the old man had turned my thoughts from martial to personal matters almost irrevocably. Almost.

'Fausta will travel to Arelate in the new moon,' I said at last.

The whole thing had come about so suddenly and so unexpectedly. It began when a messenger from Italia had arrived at my planning room on the Ides of the month. The bright young girl I had met in Nicomedia in those dark days after Minervina's death had been offered to me as a symbol of union between our families. At first the offer left me stunned, then I had laughed aloud, looking to my retinue and to the messenger in turn, sure they too would crumble and laugh with me. But the messenger's awkward silence told me it was no jest.

I had spent the rest of that day on the balcony of Treverorum's palace, oblivious to the icy winds that swept around me, my eyes combing the letter again and again. More than once I spoke into the ether, asked Minervina to guide me, but heard only the wind keening in reply. This was to be my choice and mine alone. Was it truly an offer of familial union? Was it perhaps a tacit acceptance of guilt – for Minervina died because I was not there, because I was busy running through flames to save Maxentius' boy. *He owes me,* I thought, my mood falling into that dark pit again.

I came in off the balcony when night fell, my mind made up. I would accept the offer and Fausta would be my wife. We were to be wed in the port city of Arelate in Southern Gaul in just over a month's time. Maxentius' family and mine were to be united and, ostensibly at least, we would be allies once again. But the haste and timing of the offer spoke of motivations not recorded on the message scrolls. The rumours of Galerius' impending punitive expedition into Italia had surely fuelled this sudden yearning for an alliance.

'An olive branch?' I muttered, my eyes locking upon a

smith's hammer, falling upon a glowing blade and sending sparks flying in all directions with every strike. 'We shall see. We shall see...'

ARELATE, MAY 307 AD

I t was a clear and almost clement day when I travelled to the southern coast of Gaul, where the city of Arelate sat perched on the shore, overlooking the tranquil, silky-blue Mediterranean, fed by a grand mill on a grassy hillside north of the city and watered by a fine aqueduct.

Mother and Crispus travelled with me in the imperial wagon. I chattered and played with Crispus, and enjoyed hearing the spirited lilt in Mother's voice as she joked with him too. I glanced from the wagon and back down the road to see the cohort of the Sixth and the Regii who marched in our wake. In my stead, Batius rode at the head of the soldiers, enjoying the chance to berate those who strayed even a step out of line and particularly relishing the chance to order Krocus around. We passed through Arelate's northern gates at noon to a crescendo of cornua from the gatehouse.

Up on the overlooking balconies I saw senators, dignitaries and magnates. Marinus, the bishop of this city, was there too – there were rumours he was keen to give a Christian blessing to my joining with Fausta: such a stark contrast to the persecuting leaders in the East and their bloody and fractious relationship with the Christians there.

The streets were lined with people. They hove petals from spring blooms before and over my carriage, and I saw in their faces pure, unbridled joy. They hailed me as some sort of hero, yet I wondered – as I often did in those days – just what darkness I might have brought upon them with my claim to the purple. Did Maxentius think these same thoughts? And Galerius... no, the Herdsman's conscience had surely died long ago.

We were soon in the palace on the small hill at the heart of the city, and by dusk I found myself alone in my chambers. I gazed out over the balustrade and across the compact and populous streets. Tomorrow, I would be wed to a mere girl. A marriage of convenience. My thoughts were swift to turn to Minervina.

If you were with me now, my dear, I mouthed, envisioning her as always in the gardens of Antioch.

A delicate knock sounded on the door. Oddly it seemed to be in response to my question.

'Enter,' I called over my shoulder.

The door creaked open and a hunched, bald man entered. Another fussing official who would oversee the wedding, I guessed. A troop of them had buzzed around me all that afternoon. I sighed hotly and waved him away. 'The preparations are all in hand, man. There is enough pomp, silk and silver in this palace to smother a king.' When the man did not move or respond, I shot him a sour look, but he gestured to the door and stepped to one side before I could berate him further.

'Domine.' Fausta bowed.

I beheld her in the golden sunset, and saw how she had grown in the years since last we met. Still but a girl, I realised, yet tall as a woman and with broad hips and a growing bosom. Her dark, spiralling locks hung to her waist and her shrewd, dark eyes were set aflame by the ochre she wore on the lower lids. I felt a sense of shame for momentarily enjoying her beauty, then a sense of absurdity: she was to be my wife, yet it would be a few years before we could lie together.

The bald man backed out of the room and we were alone.

'The preparations are in hand, I presume?' I said in a staid tone.

Fausta's eyes narrowed. 'If I am questioned one more time on what colour of blooms will decorate the bridal route to your hearth room then I might just need to borrow that sword of yours.' She nodded to the spatha lying with my ceremonial armour in the corner of the room.

I chuckled, relaxing a little. She moved to stand beside me by the balustrade and look over Arelate's southern districts. 'Another city, more armies... men riddled with tension.' She sighed, toying with the Luna amulet on her neck chain. Her devotion to the old gods was one thing that set her in stark contrast to Minervina. I was sure there were many others that I would discover in time. 'What has changed since last we met in Nicomedia?' she said, then added with a ludic smile: 'You are sober at least.'

I acknowledged the comment with a flicked half-smile, thinking guiltily of the bad habits I had fallen back into in these last months. Although I was clear-headed today, wine and I had become close friends once again. I saw her trying to appraise my lack of reply, then swiftly changed the subject. 'Rome is faring well?' I asked. I would put these questions and more to her father later in the evening – we were due to dine with Maximian soon and I was to talk with him alone after dark – but I sensed that Fausta might be a more earnest conversationalist.

'Rome is Rome,' she said with a shrug. 'A jewel, a prize, a seething bed of murderous intent.' Then she looked at me like a mother might behold a shy child. 'Maxentius is well. He asks after you.'

Then why does he send his father here and not attend himself? I mused bitterly. Had my old friend harnessed his once-domineering father so much as to despatch him across the empire as a lackey much as Galerius had done with Severus? Or was Maximian the one who held true power?

'Valeria, Romulus and young Aurelius – they are well too?' I added, sensing Fausta's gaze reading my furrowed brow and taut lips.

'You ask after his wife as if her good health might be a virtue?' she replied with a mischievous smirk.

Again, she had me. 'Aye, perhaps next time I will ask instead if she has fallen down a well.' I chuckled dryly.

'His sons are well: Romulus is as brave and reckless as ever with his games, while Aurelius...' She paused, her eyes betraying a pang of sadness. I knew only that the lad had been born with misshapen limbs. I bowed my head, annoyed to have stoked her sadness. 'Aurelius is well looked after in the halls of the Palatine,' she said at last.

We shared a silence, watching the sun slip below the horizon until we were both bathed in deep red light. 'Tomorrow, our families will be united,' I said at last. 'It is something your brother and I would have heralded with bright hearts had it happened some years ago.' My tone grew sober. 'Now, I wonder at what has brought us togeth—'

'Galerius readies to march upon Rome,' she said cutting me off. 'We are to marry in order to stand against the Herdsman as one family, one dynasty. Is that not virtuous enough for you?'

Her strident tone impressed me. The truth of her words troubled me, for the rumours that had circled since Maxentius' defeat of Severus had proved well-founded: the Herdsman was indeed on his way to Rome in an attempt to do what the loathsome Severus could not. Reports had come in over the past month of Galerius' legions mobilising, gathering in Pannonia and readying to pour into Italia to seize Rome and avenge Severus' ignominious defeat. Yes, Galerius was Maxentius' problem right now, but if the Herdsman defeated my old friend, then he would be swift to turn his wrath on me next. I tried as best I could to rid my mind of this tangled future, focusing instead on the steps already taken to face it: the marriage would provide Maxentius and me with a better chance of withstanding Galerius' armies, and in any case, a series of meetings had been arranged for the days after the wedding, where we would discuss our strategy thoroughly.

We turned from the sunset to face each other. She continued, now in a gentle voice: 'Such political weddings often see women forced into matrimony with brutes, slavering old men or those who would rather spend their time with boys.' She shot a shy, coltish look at me, her confidence wavering. 'I am not disappointed as those countless women might have been. I will, of course… serve you and bear your children.'

I wanted then to tell her to put such things from her mind. There would be a time when she was ready for such matters. Until then, she would be a companion and a young mother for little Crispus. This brought another smile to my lips: a mother for Crispus – yet just eight years separated them! How wicked fate is, for in years to come this reality would leave me bereft… but that is a story for another day.

'And I want you to know also that I will be loyal to you.' The shyness was gone as she said this. 'To you, Constantine. Not to my brother, nor my father.'

I searched her eyes for some confirmation of these bold

words. Were they hers, or those of Maximian and Maxentius, planted on her tongue to position her securely by my side to their advantage?

'Tell me, then; what truly goes on in Rome? The tales I hear of Maxentius do not sit well with the memories I have of him: sweeping Italia and Africa into his palm? Leading a cavalry charge and slaying Severus' companion cavalry? They say he was drenched in blood as his Praetorians hailed him.'

Fausta balked at this. 'And do you know what he asked me, just before he saw me off from Rome's gates? He asked me to find out what had happened to you. He longs to hear that tales of your blood-games and beasts feeding on men in your arena are untrue. Can I tell him so?'

I swung away and gazed back to the last vestiges of light.

'I thought not,' she said. 'But I am just as sure that things are not entirely as they seem? The mighty Constantine does not condemn men to death at the jaws of lions for frivolity, but because of the great threats that hover so close to his dominion?'

I said nothing. Guilt silently scourged me.

'Maxentius has made the best of a grim lot. Had he not taken up the mantle and donned the purple cloak, he would have been murdered on the end of the Praetorian blades. Snakes surround him, Constantine, *snakes!*'

'He should have talked to me before claiming Africa as his own!' I hissed.

'Had he hesitated, then his body would by now have been swept down the Tiber and be lying washed up on the coast, the bones picked clear of flesh. Volusianus and Anullinus sit on his shoulders like quarrelsome crows.'

'And your father? What part does Maximian play in this

game?' I asked, convinced by the passion in her voice that I was at last hearing how things truly stood.

'Maxentius understands our father more than ever before. But Father has grown shrewder, bolder in his autumn years.'

I tried to judge that statement, to ascertain Fausta's true loyalties. I could not.

The gentle knock on the door sounded once more. The bald man entered.

'Domine, Domina... the dining hall is ready.'

A waft of roasting meat swept around the room, and I heard also the booming laughter of Maximian. The man knew how to put on a show, and I wondered then if I was part of his latest fete. Lutes twanged and timpani throbbed as we walked together towards the hall. The trilling voice of some orator rang out along the corridor as we approached, lauding Maximian as if he were father of all the gods himself.

'Maximian, greatly missed Augustus of the West, bravest of generals, first to cross the River Rhenus in the face of the barbarian hordes, conqueror of Africa, you have bettered your Olympian best and returned from the obscurity of retirement. By bravely forging your way back to the forefront of imperial...' The man's words trailed off as we entered the feasting hall. Many hundreds of faces, painted in lead or ruddy with wine turned to us. I glowered at the fat orator, incensed by his brazen exaggerations and outright lies.

His face paled and he continued, in a more humble tone: '...by being graciously *brought* back to the imperial court by the magnanimous twin rulers of the West, Constantine and Maxentius.'

His hastily sweetened words only served to needle me further. Maximian and I had yet to discuss the exact terms on which Maxentius' rule of Italia and Africa would sit under my control of the Western Empire as a whole. *Under my control – that is how it will be,* I vowed once more. I met Maximian's eyes then, hooded as ever, his bloated, rubicund form dominating the head of the huge main table. He stood with great fuss, knocking over a wine cup that was caught by some scrawny acolyte at his side, then he gestured to the two seats at the other end of the table. 'Sit, my son,' he said then swung a finger overhead as if about to proclaim some great discovery. 'Ah, *son!* To think that tomorrow I can call you that in earnest!'

A rumble of applause and cheering greeted his words. When it faded, I heard only the crackling of torches and shallow breaths of the many watching me. I glanced at the chair, at Fausta – already seated – and at Maximian again.

All those years ago, Father had traded much – too much – to wed into Maximian's bloodline and assure his place in the Tetrarchy. Tomorrow, by marrying the daughter of the old Augustus of the West, I was seeking that same legitimacy and allegiances against Galerius and his eastern forces. But who did this bargain truly favour?

The look in Maximian's eyes gave me a cold and unwanted answer.

The hall was empty bar me and my soon-to-be father-in-law. The feasting tables had been cleared and the fire crackled and spat, slowly dying. Maximian had consumed a wagon-load of wine, yet still he seemed no less in control of his faculties. Indeed, he eyed me like his next cup, and it troubled me greatly to wonder what his agenda was.

He is no longer a man to fear and defer to, a voice spat in my head. *You are master of the West! You!*

I swigged my watered wine as these belligerent thoughts irritated me for a moment, then I realised they were correct. Maximian was a guest in my dominion. More, he was nothing but a dignitary, representing Maxentius – himself merely a hopeful subject in my Western Empire. *My Western Empire,* the voice hissed again.

'My blood runs in Maxentius' veins,' Maximian said, breaking the silence. 'Augustan blood.'

So there it was. The challenge. I resisted the temptation to snap back at the corpulent old bastard and let his words blister in the air between us instead.

'When he could call upon just the patchwork army of southern and central Italia, he was weak. But when he harnessed Africa and its veteran legions too, he became a force to be reckoned with,' Maximian said, his eyes on the surface of his wine as he swirled it. 'But you know what truly gave him power?'

I thought of that ethereal commodity, the nature of which had puzzled me since that childhood storm in Naissus. 'Enlighten me.'

He looked up, his eyes glinting in the firelight. 'When I took my old legions from Severus and brought them to his side. *I* granted him the power he now commands.'

'Only because it suited you,' I replied. 'You are a man who has rested uneasily in retirement. Bringing Severus' legions to Maxentius has levered you back into the imperial court. Right to the top.' I leant forward a little, being sure to offer no hint of friendliness. 'Look at you now – you sit in the court of the Western *Augustus...*'

Maximian's top lip twitched at the manner in which I drew this last word out, but that was the only sign that I had found a fissure in his armour. He sighed and tapped the edge of his cup. 'Augusti should be careful when dining alone with ambitious men. I hear the wine can bring on a fearsome headache.' He said this with a burgeoning grin.

His allusion cast me back to that hall in Nicomedia where I ate with Galerius on that dark wintry night: the snow piling in the corners of the windows, the wine, the poison... the assassins in the dark. For a moment, I imagined the icy presence of Maximian's men somewhere behind me, but let the fear pass, supping my wine confidently. Maximian boomed with laughter, clearly seeing through my veil.

'So you aim to bargain for your son's position, I presume?' I spat, my patience cracking at last. 'You seek to install him as Augustus of the West, just as you once were? Most absurd of all, you think I will meekly stand aside and forgo my father's legacy?'

Maximian shook his head. 'I *know* you won't. That is the flaw of the Tetrarchy: your father was Augustus of the West, and so when he passed, you took on that mantle as any noble son would. Yet in the Tetrarchy there are many fathers, and even more sons.'

I bristled, waiting for some barbed follow-up.

'As I said, I understand power,' Maximian purred, 'in a way that few men do.'

Intrigued, my mind again flashed with images of the storm and the lone legionary on Naissus' walls.

'I understand when it is advantageous to support your kin... and when it is not. Tomorrow, you will marry my daughter. That day and every day after, you will continue to rule the West as Augustus.'

His words waylaid me. It was like the moments after battle when the buckled armour is shorn and the weight gone from your shoulders. 'You will support my rightful claim?'

Maximian nodded. 'And when I hasten back to Rome at the end of the celebrations, I will see to it that my son does too.'

I stared at him and through him, struggling to stay focused and stave off the instinctive sense of elation that this shrewd old leader had bowed to my demands. After so long, first as a concubine's son, then as a commander in the legions but merely a puppet of the emperors, then in this last year as an emperor plagued with cries of illegitimacy from his opponents... finally, I would be recognised, accepted.

'Maxentius and I will serve you as your father once served me, Augustus,' he said, bowing.

My elation faded as I searched his eyes, knowing that the serpentine mind behind them had revealed to me only a fraction of his intent...

30

MAXENTIUS

I have rarely in my life been as angry as I was that afternoon when my cursed, hag-ridden, wine-sot of a father strode into my tablinum as though it were his office and I merely a supplicant awaiting his pleasure. You see, I'd had a couple of days to marshal my thoughts since the rather credible rumour reached me that the old snake had offered the position of senior Augustus to Constantine. It made a mockery of the whole system of the Tetrarchy, of course, there now being three emperors in the West – Constantine, Father and myself – with a somewhat nebulous order of priority, barring the fact that the other two clearly considered me to be the lowest in the hierarchy.

While I owed Constantine a great debt for saving my son that day in Nicomedia, I could not repay a personal debt with Rome as collateral, for the matter of imperial power was not a personal one for me, but a matter of doing what was best for Rome, and making Rome bow to a power ruling from Germania was not an acceptable solution. No. Constantine could be my equal, for sure, but he should bow to Rome, not the other way around.

Two days; and instead of calming down and reaching a sensible level of clarity I had instead slept fitfully, disregarded my duties, shut myself away from the children and raged, festering in my ire. The only consolation I had found was that Valeria was as furious as I and had urged me to have my father arrested as a traitor. Gods, but I had considered it, too. How far apart can a father and son drift when one considers condemning the other to vile execution?

In the end, we had both reasoned that to deal with Father in such a way may turn a large part of our newly healthy military against us, and now was not the time for that. A more subtle solution would have to present itself.

I thanked Minerva to her wise core for the fact that I was dressed togate and unarmed as Father clomped in across my delicate marble floor, for it would have crippled my reputation among the higher echelons of society in Rome had I hacked my father to death in my office, and that is undoubtedly what I would have done had I a sword within reach. As it was, I found myself gripping a stilus and wondering if it would penetrate his thick skull.

'Prepare yourself,' Father said in a calm tone.

'Oh I am very well prepared,' I hissed in return, causing him to lean back in confusion. 'You think that news like this follows in the wake of its instigators?' I threw in with a steely tone. 'That rumour does not spread like a forest fire even in the wilder quarters of the empire?'

Father made towards my desk and – petty, I know – I stamped across to it and sank into the room's only seat before he could do so, forcing him to stand opposite me on the other side of the wide oak surface.

'Then what do you plan to do about it?' he asked quietly.

It was my turn to frown. In all my mental images of how

this meeting would play out I had never imagined this sort of question. 'Do? What *is* there to do? The matter has been settled without my consent!'

Father's brow creased further until it looked as though his face was about to collapse like a badly mortared bridge.

'Well, have you deployed the army in my absence?'

I was now baffled. 'I am incensed by the matter. I loathe and detest the whole issue, but I cannot see how deploying troops would improve matters. After all, we are family and he is my co-ruler, whether I like it or not!'

I was shaking now, not so much through the rage I had felt the past few days, but from the strange combination of anger and confusion.

'What are you blabbering about, boy?' Father snapped finally, straightening with thinned lips.

'I refer to Constantine, you old snake. You think to put him above me? And what of you, since you also claim such a position? Are you now both to be Augustus of the West with me as your junior to clean up both your messes?'

I faltered. Instead of the anger or smarmy superiority I had expected, all I could see in Father's face was confusion, with a touch of something else... Could it be fear?

'That?' he said, in tones that suggested I had interrupted important matters with trivialities. 'I sweetened the deal in order to seal it. Constantine is proud and would hardly accept subservience to you, after all. The important thing was to bring him into the fold, into the family; to have him acknowledge you in Italia and thereby legitimise your position. Don't forget, boy, that there are three of us, but the Tetrarchy has room for four!'

'Only if we dispatch Galerius or his pet monster Daia,' I snapped.

'Anyway,' Father said a little too loudly, sweeping a hand across in the air above the desk as if to push aside the matter in its entirety, 'the title I offered your friend is not the issue to which I am referring. You have not heard the news of your eastern counterpart then?'

My heart skipped a beat at that. *Galerius?*

'No.'

'That sack of dog vomit has moved earlier than anticipated. He is in Pannonia as we speak, gathering his crack legions to cross the border and do to us what Severus could not.'

My blood chilled. Galerius was coming for me *so soon?* Severus had been bad enough, and Galerius was a far greater worry, but I'd assumed I had many months – a year even...

'How soon will Constantine's support reach us?'

'What support?'

I stared at my father in disbelief. 'Surely you secured his military support as well?'

'Constantine is busy building his forces to secure his position. He is hardly going to throw them away against the empire's most powerful leader to save you and me, boy. Use your brain.'

I was stunned. 'So you gave Constantine seniority in the West, even over me, and my sister as his wife, and all you asked for in return was that he pat me on the head and tell people that I work for him? I should have sent Anullinus to him and kept you here!'

The anger had returned, which was useful as it covered my growing fear that Galerius was coming for me.

'Don't be a fool, boy. Constantine will acknowledge you in time, and likely help you when he himself feels secure, but he will no more send men to stop Galerius marching through Italia than you would send your Praetorians to the Alpes to stop Galerius marching on Treverorum. Can we now put aside squabbles and petty recrimination? There *are* more pressing matters!'

I seethed, wide-eyed, but whatever I would have liked to say, Father was right.

'How long do we have until Galerius is on Italian soil?' I asked, calming myself with some difficulty.

'Half a month would be my guess.'

'So the end of July? And he could be outside the gates of the city by perhaps mid-August if unopposed.'

'Just so. We cannot be sure what size army we face, but be assured that it will be a large force of loyal veterans. He will not make the mistake of fielding only a small force like that with which Severus lost. Also we cannot be certain where he will enter your territory, though I can make a solid estimate.'

I tapped my lip, my eyes closed as I tried to picture the terrain. 'By land, I presume? Around the north? Tergeste and Aquileia then down across the mountains.'

'Precisely. We cannot entirely rule out a naval landing at, for instance, Ravenna, or Ariminium, or even Fanum. But if he decides to do so we can add a month or more as he organises transport and his army makes the slow, laborious crossing. No, I believe he will come on foot, around the north of the sea and across the mountains.'

I pursed my lips. 'We have solid garrisons at all three ports you mentioned, as well as half a legion at Tergeste. We should have held on to Pola. It belongs to the West, after all.'

'Pola is more difficult to defend and too distant. Tergeste was the prime choice. I would have chosen Aquileia in truth, had I been expecting something like this.' Our quarrel forgotten, he swept my work to one side of the table and retrieved the map of Italia – something that had rarely been out of reach this year – from the cabinet, stretching it across the surface and pinning down the corners.

'Our garrisons at the main ports can stay where they are. I do not believe they will be engaged at all, and if they are, the ports are defensive and can hold until we divert reinforcements. No. We must concentrate on a land invasion. After they subdue the garrison of Tergeste, they will march across the plains and marshes of Venetia, to Ravenna and then along the Via Flaminia to the walls of Rome. We need to set redoubts along their line of march to harry them.'

I felt my stomach flip. Were we really discussing war with Galerius? I resisted the urge to suggest any attempt at reconciliation. That thought was the work of fear alone and a fevered dream at best. And we were at least better prepared this time than last, for our army now included the bulk of that which Severus had led against us. 'And if the Herdsman chooses a different route?'

'He will not. He is a predictable man. Hard and fierce, but not sly. If I were in his position, I would think to bring my force that route. So will he.'

I may have disliked my father, but he was a proven military tactician and he knew Galerius better than I. 'Eight points of defence leap at me from the map,' I noted.

'Seven. Tergeste then Aquileia at our eastern border. Nothing else in Venetia due to the marshes and flats. Then coastal Ravenna, which serves the dual purpose of sturdy redoubt and supply port for any army who secures it, then Ariminium with the same benefits. Then across the mountains by the Via Flaminia, where we have the solid defences of Helvillum, Hispellum and finally Narnia. You also consider Falerii Novi, I presume, but that city is too close to Rome. If

Galerius makes it past Narnia, then we should fall back to your new, very high, walls.'

It made sense. 'We have forces already spread out as far as Hispellum, though mostly concentrated near Rome.'

'I will take care of the army,' Father said. 'The more distant units can be moved forward to Aquileia and Tergeste. The ones near Rome can move into position from Ravenna south. I will issue the standing command to abandon any position that becomes untenable and fall back to the next. That way survivors of any engagement will be available to bolster the next line of defence. The Ravenna fleet is fiercely loyal to you, just as the Misenum one, so I shall move them south to Fanum to keep them from falling into the enemy's hands when they take the ports. Then, once Galerius is coming across the mountains, the fleet can fall upon his supply chain behind him, in his absence. With Fortuna and Neptune on our side, we can make him pay so heavily for every mile of the Via Flaminia and thin his supplies so close to starvation point that his invasion falters. If it comes to sheer numbers and strength, he will win, so we must be cunning.'

I fretted at my beard, which was longer than I found comfortable after my two days of sleepless raging. 'Anullinus may have to defer to Volusianus in active command of the Guard. He knows Rome's defences well, but Volusianus has proven himself in the field under the emperor Probus against Roman usurpers. He not only has experience of campaign command, but clearly has no qualms about facing other Romans.'

'Put whoever you wish in command, but the Guard will stay in Rome along with the Urban Cohorts and that vexillatio of the Third Augusta that arrived from Africa last month. We must keep the city secure, despite manning redoubts against Galerius.'

I agreed. Anullinus then could retain command. Along with the now better trained and equipped Urban Cohorts under Zenas, the Praetorians would be an effective defence force. I had acceded to the suggestions of Anullinus at least and removed his brother Gaius from command of the Urban Cohorts, assigning him to a minor role in the administration of the city's mausolea. I presumed even he could not make too much of a hash of the long-dead. Anullinus and Zenas would be more than adequate.

'Very well,' he finished, rubbing his hands together in a business-like manner. 'I will attend to these matters immediately.' He made to sweep from the room as abruptly as he had entered, then paused, tapping his forehead in thought.

'Have Severus readied. If Galerius makes it to Narnia, we can peel the Whisperer's flesh from his bones and parade him before the invaders. If they are already tired, sore and hard-pressed, the fear may break them.'

I opened my mouth to object, but he was gone in a flap of cloak and a crash of door, leaving me alone in my office, my thoughts and emotions in turmoil.

I was at war again for the second time in a year. I had been lucky with Severus in having a trick to play in the form of my father. I doubted it would work again. But one thing was certain: I was the emperor of Rome and on my word, he would not be harmed.

That evening in the halls of the Palatine brought one of the more difficult conversations of my life. I entered the imperial apartment slowly and carefully, treading on eggshells. I found

Valeria standing at a window, her expression as cold and bleak as it had been in our earliest days.

'Word has reached you then?'

She turned and locked me with a piercing gaze. 'I am in an impossible position. I am loyal to my family. My father is a true emperor of Rome, no usurper or underling, and he is the most senior of all. His word by rights should set the law in the empire. And he comes for you, to remove you from power. I cannot stand against him. He is both my father, and right in his decision.' She sighed. 'Yet I have staked everything I have on putting you where you are. I have sold my reputation, my lineage and all to the families of Rome and the empire to make my husband its ruler. How can I abandon that? I cannot cheer you on against my father, and I cannot support him against my own world. I am in Hades.'

She turned back to the window, shivering. I felt for her, more than I ever had. What must it be like to hold one's father in such esteem? In her position I would have sold out my father in a heartbeat. I wandered over and stood beside her. 'I am ruler in Rome, Valeria. I am an emperor in more than name, and ten times the emperor my father can be. In time, Father will fall once more, and I can brush him aside. But I cannot delay so with your father. Galerius comes to remove me, and I shall resist with everything that I have and everything that I am. But just as I have vowed that since Severus proclaimed for me I will not have him killed, I promise you that, despite my father, I will do all that I can to end this without the death of your father. What I cannot avoid, I cannot avoid, but I shall try nonetheless.'

* * *

VILLA OF HERODES ATTICUS, SEPTEMBER 307 AD

The past two months had been fraught, though mostly for those around me. I had spent much of my time with Romulus, who I had discovered was still regularly playing his childish – if often death-defying – games. I had begun to have him taught skills with a blade, and I watched and commented when I felt capable, taking my turn in trying to educate him in the noble past of Rome's greatest warriors and generals. Soon he would be a man and would take his place beside me as my pride and joy, and I wanted him prepared. Besides, these days even the son of an emperor was wise to know one end of a sword from the other.

I endured the increasingly common bickering between Anullinus and Volusianus and mediated between them as best I could without alienating either – for one commanded my Guard and the other had brought me Africa. And I continued my building works, albeit with the focus squarely set on the defences for now.

I ruled.

Around me my father moved like a crow in a field of corpses, dipping his beak into a thousand aspects of rule and command, always with a ready excuse as to how it impacted on the invasion that was his priority. And in his wake generals and officers, spies and politicians all carried out the business of war, making sure that none of it landed on my plate, despite my father regularly picking from it.

Not that I wished to argue, for I was happy to administer Rome in the meantime and glorify the brick skeleton of that city with new marble coats and fresh paint. And I had no *cause* to argue, either, for Galerius had done everything Father had said he would. And despite the size and experience of his

433

army, every engagement on his path to Rome had cost him dearly. This was not the easy campaign he had expected and word was that the Herdsman raged at his generals for their incompetence, since he had expected to be in Rome picking over my own corpse long before now. Instead, after a month and a half of slogging his way across Italia, paying a blood price he could barely meet, he was finally closing on Narnia and still far from certain of victory.

Indeed, Father was smug, convinced in himself that he had beaten Galerius. He assured me time and again that Galerius would come no closer than Narnia and, while Anullinus fretted about increasing the defences of the city, Volusianus – who had fought in such campaigns before – agreed with my father that the end was near and would result in our victory.

And I would be at Narnia to watch it.

Father and I would ride out with an honour guard of Praetorians to join the army at Narnia and watch Galerius' sea of men crash harmlessly against its walls. But there was one thing that needed attending to first. Consequently, I had quit Rome while the court prepared to move to Narnia, and travelled a mile and a half south along the Via Appia to this place.

Here, standing off to the left of the road on a low rise, stood a grand villa that had once belonged to Herodes Atticus, the great friend of Hadrian. Here, for the past five months, the former Emperor of the West, Severus, had lived in relative luxury – albeit also seclusion – guarded by four centuries of Praetorians and two of legionaries. He had not set foot outside the villa's grounds in almost half a year, such was the value of his imprisonment and the danger of freeing him.

I left Anullinus and the rest of my small retinue at the villa's gate and entered, the Praetorians guarding the place snapping neatly to attention as I passed. It was a stunning villa in a wonderful location, far grander than the one in which I had lived prior to my investiture. I found myself envying Severus this place over the past few months. It was not majestic enough for an imperial residence, of course, but the rural setting and greenery suited my tastes far more than that brick and marble eyrie in which I nested upon the Palatine. When the wars were over and we could live in peace, I thought I would like to find somewhere like this. Or to build it, even.

Through beautifully painted atria and corridors I passed, escorted by a Praetorian centurion, every space decorated with cleverly painted scenes that confronted me with fake spring landscapes and wide seas. Through peristyle gardens that most senators and governors would envy, and to a marble balustrade with a half-moon bench beneath an arbour covered with vines. As I beheld the lone figure on the marble seat, I turned to the centurion.

'Leave us.'

A look of dreadful concern lit the officer's face. 'Domine?'

'The villa is surrounded with your men. Severus is ageing and unarmed. Leave me. If I require you, I will call.'

The centurion, still disapproving, retreated to the house, though I saw him stop in the shade of the doorway, where he could still keep an eye on me. I had not the heart to argue. Today I had no heart. I could not afford to. I had buried it beneath a stone of necessity.

'Severus.'

The figure on the bench turned and inclined his head in respect. He did not stand or genuflect, but I was surprised in truth that he afforded me even the respect of a bow.

'Maxentius. How goes the business of rule?' His hoarse

voice perfectly fitted what was now a very drawn, pale face. I smiled, my smile as empty as his false lightness.

'You have heard news of your master?'

'Galerius marches on Rome. He will not succeed. He is stronger than I, but I was a better general than he. I underestimated you. Galerius will do so too. Congratulations.' His bitterness was undisguised.

'Would that I could set you free...'

'To raise opposition to you?' Severus rasped. 'No. You, I believe, might actually *do* such a reckless thing, but that is because you are a romantic fool. Your father keeps me as collateral, because he knows my value as a tool in your regime. He is cruel and treacherous, but he is no fool.'

It disturbed me a little to realise how perceptive this man was, here at the end.

I fell silent and stood for a while as we both gazed out across the valley below the villa, to the tombs and mausolea that lined the Via Appia, the aqueducts in the distance and beyond them the purple-blue peaks of the spine of Italia. It really was the most stunning prison in which to be incarcerated.

Finally I cleared my throat. 'My father will send for you this afternoon. We move to Narnia to witness the failure of Galerius' invasion, of which my commanders are now certain. You are to accompany us as his prize captive.'

'There to be beheaded before the armies of Galerius, no doubt,' he replied. 'A deterrent. A morale-killer. As I said: cruel, but not stupid. I can see the value of his decision.'

I felt a fresh loathing of my father fill my soul then, for I knew the truth.

'Not quite. I have seen the group that are to accompany you. In addition to the Praetorians, there are three former members of the frumentarii, including one who worked...

well let us just say that his career kept him in the cellars beneath the Palatine and he made few friends.'

Severus gave an involuntary shudder, which told me that he understood well enough. Nonnius had been packing his pincers, knives and brands when I saw him. He was an expert at his job, and his job was to make a man wish he was already dead.

'He is no fool, curse the man.'

I felt cold. Despite everything he had done, I had now a small knot of sympathy in my belly for him. No man deserved what was planned for Severus – an agonising death despite my given word that he would live. My father was breaking my oath for me.

I removed the hand I had kept beneath my toga and held it before Severus, palm up and open, the knife lying across it.

The former emperor stared at the weapon. It was a beautiful article, said to have belonged to his namesake, that powerful emperor Septimius Severus, the African. Decorative and rich, it remained nonetheless razor sharp and lethal, just like its original owner.

'This is the only offer I can make,' I said.

I became aware of a shout from behind and glanced over my shoulder. That damned centurion had sharp eyes. He'd seen this from the doorway and was already running, blowing his whistle to summon his men.

'And this is the only chance you have to take it.'

Severus blinked at the knife and reached a shaky hand up to it. As his fingers closed on the hilt I stepped back out of reach, my nerves overcoming my common sense. But I had no need. Severus was no threat to me now, even armed. With a simple nod, he unsheathed the blade and looked at his reflection in the cold Noric steel.

'I look ancient,' he rasped, smiling weakly. 'I hope that when your time comes, young emperor, someone is generous enough to make you such an offer.'

Men were running across the gardens now in a clank and clatter of armour, vaulting low box hedges and converging on the bench. The centurion was shouting warnings at me, but I was unheeding, unhearing.

Instead, my eyes remained locked on the former emperor as he reached up and jammed the tip of the blade into his neck below his left ear, sinking it in a good inch with a hiss of pain. With a brief rasp of agony, he somehow dragged the blade around to his other ear, cutting through skin, flesh and cartilage, the blood fountaining from the wound and soaking the area, missing me only because I had stepped back.

I watched his eyes glaze and the blade fall from his nerveless fingers and clatter across the stones. Blood flowed from him in a cascade. I was astounded by the quantity, and by how fast his face greyed. Then, while I watched as if in a dream, the centurion was there, pulling me away from the scene, his men trying to see if Severus could be saved.

He couldn't.

He was already dead, even though the crimson torrents still poured from him.

Insofar as I could, I had kept my oath.

Would I be able to do as much for Valeria's father?

Narnia was impressive. I had never been here, but I could immediately see why Father had selected it as the last fortress before Rome. Nestled on a sharp spur of land at the end of a wide valley, it was also separated from the hills by a narrow ravine that held a river. The only easy access was from the south, along the spur on which we stood, and that was not wide enough to house a large army with siege engines. I had seen drawings once in a book of that great Jewish fortress *Masada*, and this looked like its smaller, greener sibling.

Several cohorts of Galerius' men had occupied that southerly approach, sealing off the city while the bulk of his army spread across the plain below. It was a monstrous force. Enormous. How could we hope to stop it?

While my father oozed confidence, he would not look me in the eye, nor speak to me. He had not done so since my compassion had denied him the pleasure of killing Severus.

We travelled with the bulk of the Second Parthica and a sizeable detachment of Praetorians, and were more than a match for the cohorts on the hill, if not for the mass below.

'How do we hope to enter the city?' I asked of Anullinus, who rode alongside with Volusianus at my other shoulder like twin *lemures* – spirits of the malevolent dead.

The Praetorian Prefect gave me a knowing smile. 'I am not privy to your father's plans, Domine, but I have seen numerous former frumentarii visit his chambers recently, and half a month ago the old Herculiani standards were retrieved from storage.'

Another of Father's little tricks. But while I could be disparaging, their efficacy was never in doubt. He knew what he was doing.

'There are so many,' I murmured.

To my other side Volusianus cleared his throat. 'Look again, Domine. Their army is widespread. They cover the plain, but they are not dense ranks. There are far fewer men in that valley than there appear to be. According to the estimates I've read that force must number but half of the army he led against Tergeste when he crossed the eastern border. And I note a distinct lack of supply dumps in their midst. They are ill-equipped and hungry and trying to look more impressive than they are. This is the gambit of a man who knows he is almost lost and is making a last attempt to grasp a victory.'

I couldn't see it myself, but all my advisors seemed happy with matters.

As we reached the open ground and faced the first of Galerius' forces between us and the gates of Narnia, my father gave a quiet order to his musician, who raised his horn and blew out a series of rising notes into the tense, warm afternoon air.

As the musician fell silent, his refrain echoing back around the valley, we sat quietly watching. I was nervous beyond belief.

And then it happened. One of the enemy cohorts before the walls answered the call. The standard – an Illyrian legion flag atop it – disappeared from view and a moment later it rose once more with the black-on-red eagle standard of the Herculiani – my father's old guard unit.

I stared as the action repeated and spread. As the moments passed, more and more banners went up proclaiming allegiance to Maximian, and thereby to his son... me.

I watched in astonishment as all but one cohort on the hillside declared for us. There was a brief, violent struggle between the two sides, but the single remaining enemy cohort was seen off with relative ease, and fled down the slope back to Galerius' army below.

I stared, my mouth still open in surprise, as the army before us parted to grant us entrance to Narnia. I glanced past them down to the plain below. Even down there among Galerius' main force, I could see red and black banners here and there, defying their commander. They were in trouble, for they were greatly outnumbered by those loyal to my enemy, and many were quickly put down, but others ran for the slope to join us. The balance had tipped on one tuba call!

A ragged cheer went up from the high walls of Narnia on its precipitous hill.

Again, we had done it.

This time, I'd not even seen the armies until the very end, but the fact remained that within a year we had seen off two invasions by emperors of the Roman world, each force superior to our own. It was barely credible, but it was true nonetheless. Galerius was finished in Italia.

'He's leaving,' I noted, my eyes having scanned the plain and fallen upon the Joviani standards of our enemy. Sure enough, the command section was already on the move as Galerius made to flee the field. Like a vast ebb tide his army, responding to echoing calls, turned and began to swarm back towards the north-east. Not only had we achieved the impossible victory, but it seemed that I had also kept my promise to Valeria. Her father's invasion had been crushed, but he would live on as emperor.

'He was already beaten. I just wanted to draw matters to a close,' Father said. 'More cohorts would have joined us had I shown them Severus' body. But that was not to be.'

'When will our forces pursue him?' I asked, aware that Galerius may not yet be safe.

'Never.'

I turned a surprised expression on my father, trying to hide my relief. It suited me well, but it seemed so unlike my violent father. 'What? Why?'

'Because there is no need. He is beaten and makes to flee.'

'But you could capture him now.' I had given my word to Valeria, but if Galerius could be captured alive, then perhaps he could take Severus's place in that villa, living a life of quiet retirement. Then very idea that I could offer Constantine the East as my co-emperor while I ruled the West was incredibly tempting. 'The Eastern Empire is in the palm of our hands, with its master riding ahead of his army down there.'

'You are thinking like an excited boy,' Father grunted, 'not a leader of men. We would lose many thousands of men trying to harry him. We cannot afford in our position to diminish our forces chasing down one man. Better to diminish those of someone else.'

My frown deepened, and Father chuckled darkly.

'Many days ago now, I sent a rider on the Cursus Publicus with a purse of sweetening gold and documents ceding a couple of unimportant northern border positions to Constantine in return for his support. He would never have committed his men to protecting you from Galerius, but now we have beaten the man, there is no reason for Constantine to baulk at catching the fleeing shit-sack on his way back east and doing away with him.'

My eyes bulged. 'You treated with him without even telling me? You gave him our cities without my knowledge? You go too far!'

But for all my indignity over giving away my towns, I found myself realising that Galerius was going to die at my old friend's hands. What a neat solution. I had kept my vow to Valeria, and yet still Galerius would be removed.

'Better to risk others than ourselves,' Father said, 'and you know me well enough to realise that anything I give him is trivial.'

Like my sister? I felt the seething in my blood rise again, but held my tongue. We were surrounded by the great and noble, and open conflict between us would do irreparable harm.

Father went on as though I hadn't spoken. 'Do not think that the East will open up to us so simply, even if Constantine catches him, though. Daia reigns there in Galerius' absence and if his master died, he would simply assume the mantle. I doubt he would be any easier than his master. No. The East is still closed to us. Savour the victory and the fact that we have preserved much of our army. Now we must consolidate our position before the next threat raises its armoured head.'

I watched the enemy swarm from the valley and clenched my teeth. Though he had said *we must consolidate our position*, it was not those words I heard. To my practised ear, I heard *I must consolidate my position*.

Almost as if to confirm my suspicions, as I turned to him I saw Father giving me an appraising look that he quickly hid behind a feral smile.

The gulf between us had widened again. How long before our alliance was no longer viable? I caught both Anullinus and Volusianus throwing pointed looks between my father and I, calculating, and I cast up the latest in a long line of prayers to Minerva.

31

CONSTANTINE

The lower Alpes were shrouded in winter's grip, ice and snow clinging doggedly to the rugged contours of the granite massif and the higher peaks stretching off into the angry grey sky. I was crouched in ankle-deep snow behind the lip of a ledge; the deep, windswept gorge I looked down into was streaked with white and beset with a driving blizzard. My face was numb and the bitter chill searched inside my bear pelt, armour and woollen robes. This was no place for man nor beast. But today, great swathes of the empire's armies were close by. I looked to my left: all along this lengthy ledge were my legions, the Sixth Victrix and the Primigenia, and my guard regiment, the Cornuti – all stretched off for miles along this lofty track. Behind them, the Minervia, the Thirtieth Ulpia Victrix and the Lanciarii. Serried steel braving the fierce cold, not one of them offering a hint of complaint. To a man, they were crouched like me, hidden behind the lip of the ledge and from the eyes of any down in the defile below. Occasionally, their heads rose, eyes darting down into the gorge floor. I too risked a glance, training my eyes on the col to the south – the pass that led from Italia to Pannonia. Empty and silent bar the moaning winter gale... but not for long.

A bracing wind like never before swept over us and seemed to penetrate right to my marrow. Even Batius, by my right, lost grip of his resolve.

'Ahhh,' he said, badly disguising chattering teeth, 'nothing like a nice, crisp day, eh?'

I looked to him and noticed his nose was nearly sapphire-blue and his eyebrows were white with frost and snow. He wore a scowl like a bear wakened from hibernation with the prod of a sharp stick. I would have laughed had we not been on the precipice of such a vital moment.

'What's it to be then, sir?' Batius asked me.

I dipped my head down and pretended to examine the hidden ranks by my left. *Damn him,* I thought, *can he do nothing but find the most pertinent questions?* But the big soldier was only right to do so. I prised the scroll from inside my cloak. My fingers were numb and the paper nearly weightless, yet it felt like an iron burden in my hand. The rider had brought it to me at Treverorum and I had ended court immediately upon receiving it. Sitting alone in the throne room – the very room near which, so many years ago, the young Maxentius and I had first met – I opened it.

Bring your armies to the mountains. Crush Galerius. End his reign.

The request was an enticing one. But the offer was stained... for it had come not from Maxentius but from *Maximian.* Just what was the old man's agenda? I snorted at this. *Power! I* mouthed. *All men seek power in various guises!*

Despite my misgivings, the situation was stark. The Herdsman's army had been put to flight at Narnia and would be retreating through Noricum. I had but days to act, and act I did, bringing my forces to this pass. Still, though, the decision lay in my hands. At that moment, I looked at the scroll and thought of the Chi-Rho and the spear in the hands of that lone legionary on the night of the storm. One man, power, choice...

'Sir!' Batius hissed.

My eyes snapped to the col, following his gaze. The wintry waste there was empty, then I saw what he had: banners coming over the horizon. The pale blue cloth and the eagle emblem. *The Joviani!*

The pass at once filled with the rest of the Herdsman's legions.

'So the rumours were true?' I cooed, seeing the thinness of his ranks. Legions marched as little more than cohorts. Their step was erratic, hurried... panicked even. More and more regiments came into the pass until I counted some twelve thousand men. Yes, the Herdsman had lost much of his army, but this was still a sizeable force. And the numerous legions that he had left in place in Pannonia, Asia Minor, Syria and Aegyptus meant the events below Narnia's walls amounted to little more than a dent in his pride and prestige.

Unless I was to crush him, strike the life from his sorry heart right here in this pass.

My forces – fifteen thousand strong – outnumbered his, and we held the element of surprise. More, we had the flanks, the high ground. We had it all. My hand rose, readying to give the order. I sensed the eyes of my regiments waiting on it to be so. Thousands of breaths held, muscles tensed, javelins, slings and bows readied.

Power...

But I realised I had halted, my hand not quite raised. What had brought me here? Was it my will to see the Herdsman wiped from history? Was it the traces of my once-filial loyalty to Maxentius? Or was it not my will at all – but an answer to Maximian's call, like a dog to his master? The man had asked me to throw my armies against the Herdsman's. Thousands of lives would be lost should I give the order to do so. Yes, the Herdsman might be crushed, but my armies would be seriously weakened too as a result. And for what prize – to have Daia, Galerius' mongrel, pursue my head in vengeance... or for Maximian to then dispense with his veil of allegiance and march upon my lands and against my weakened legions? More, the Bructeri – a fearsome tribe that numbered many thousands – were pressing on the Rhenus forts in the lands to my rear. Would it not be prudent to preserve my forces to tackle them?

The voices gnashed in my mind.

'Sir?' Batius asked, urgency in his voice. 'They are about to pass us, below!'

I glanced over the ledge and saw the Joviani, Galerius in their midst, the rest in his wake. Now was the moment to act. *Now!*

My heart pounded, my breath quickened. Such moments and such choices defined men. My eyes narrowed. 'Stay where you are. Watch for my signal,' was all I said. With that, I pushed back from the ledge and hurried back through the mountain path to where Krocus and his Regii waited in their leather and furs along with a turma of silver-armoured equites on fine mounts. Here, in the lee of the mountains, the driving blizzard abated. All was silent and snow fell gently around me.

'You want us to go down and spill across the pass?' Krocus whispered, eyes narrowing on the winding downhill path that met with the gorge floor.

'No, but bring me Celeritas, then ride with me.' I gestured to him and the thirty equites.

We mounted then walked the beasts down the icy, winding path then spilled out across the gorge and into the full wrath of the blizzard. Snow flicked up from our mounts' hooves as we faced Galerius' army, just twelve of us. It was as if we were Titans, for the unexpected sight of us brought great terror to the Herdsman's legions. They cried out, horses whinnied, eyes shot around, and they came to a halt.

I ignored the soldiers. My gaze was fixed on the Joviani and the man at their heart. Likewise, it seemed, Galerius sought out only me. His Joviani parted and the Herdsman walked his stallion to the fore.

'Constantine?' he said in that jagged, thick tone I had not heard in so long, his blocky and age-lined face quivering with ire. '*Constantine!*' he repeated, this time as a roar that matched the blizzard.

This was the first time we had locked eyes since that night in Nicomedia when he had tried to slay me and I had drugged his wine. The fire blazed in my heart and in his eyes.

'You bastard whoreson,' Galerius snarled, his lips curling back to reveal a yellow-toothed, animal rictus. 'You vile, vermin-fucking beggar. You dare to face me? I will dine on your heart... *Seize him!*' he barked, waving his men towards me.

The Joviani looked to one another, then a century of them surged forward. They made it only a few steps when they froze like the ice clinging to the gorge-sides, for my hand shot up and with it, my army rose to standing on the ledge. Thousands of spears, javelins and arrows were trained on the Herdsman's legions. Bows creaked, slings whirred... Galerius stared, agog.

I clicked my tongue and Celeritas walked forward. Galerius' stunned expression turned from my forces on the ledge to me. 'You insolent dog,' he growled, but his voice was cracking as he spoke. As I neared him I saw just what the Herdsman had become in the years since I had fled his court. His belly and thighs were swollen and misshapen under his armour, and his skin was ashen, reminding me of Father in his final year.

As I walked Celeritas towards him, the Joviani parted like water. As I slowed before the Herdsman, he half-drew his gem-hilted spatha. I clasped a hand over his, forcing the blade back into its sheath.

'Draw that blade and your bloated body will be torn apart.' I shot a glance to the ledge. 'They await my word. Just one word.'

Galerius shook uncontrollably. It was a mix of fear and anger, I was certain.

I hesitated before speaking again. The decision was still unmade. What I said next would define the fate of many of the soldiers there on that day. It would define me as a person. More, it would surely alter the future of the empire.

I pinned him with the steeliest of glares. 'Take your armies home, Herdsman, and never return. I hold sway in all these lands. Britannia, Gaul, Hispania, Italia and Africa are *mine*. For I am Constantine, Augustus of the West.'

Galerius' breath clouded as he took this in. His eyes searched over my face, doubtless contemplating what his one-time charge had become. Then, like a recalcitrant but scolded child, he gave the curtest of nods. Just once, but it was all it took. He parted from me and his armies marched on, heads bowed in fear and deference to my forces watching over them. As I watched the last of his column leave the pass and return to Pannonia, I realised that something had ended at that moment. The dark threat Galerius had always posed had been broken at last. The myth of the Herdsman had been dispelled before the eyes of my army. Now, unquestionably, I was master of the West.

32

ROME, APRIL 308 AD

The spring of that next year – a year that defined all our lives in new ways – taught me one of the most important lessons in life: trust no one. It was a lesson I should have learned earlier and certainly should have adhered to in latter times, also. I had felt the deepest sense of betrayal that a man I had considered my friend above all else, and who had taken my sister to wife, had failed to come to our support in the harrying of our mutual enemy, Galerius. Consequently the most dangerous man in the empire had now returned, free to cause havoc, back east. Indeed, the man's army had looted and raped any settlement in their path of retreat. Constantine had taken his army back north without a word of explanation or apology to me. I felt let down to an extent I had previously not thought possible.

I had lived with a debt to the man hanging over my head all my adult life. He had defined our relationship when he saved me from Candidianus and had cemented it when he rescued Romulus, but in one bitter move, he had swept all that benevolence away in favour of his own goals. What value friendship now? Why concern myself with such debts any longer? It was, I think, the moment that the fraying bonds between my brother-in-law and myself began to snap. We clung on for some time, but it is clear that this was when everything began to change.

Yet the betrayal of Constantine, while the most shocking event for me, was not the most dangerous. That terrible honour fell upon a date that should have been the most glorious and celebrated of the year.

For in late April in the city of Rome is observed the rustic festival of the Parilia, and along with it the commemoration of that greatest of days, the dies natalis Romae – the founding of the city of Rome. As you might expect this particular festival was closest to my heart. I ever saw Rome as the centre of the world, and the date of its birth could only be the most auspicious of occasions... or inauspicious, of course.

The city's populace was feeling jubilant, not because of the festival, though the people were bursting with anticipation for that, too. No, the cause of the high spirits was the belief that Rome was now safe. A sovereign state with an emperor of the greatest pedigree, supported by a father with an equally recognised history and a record of military successes. We had vanquished the opposed 'emperor' Severus, against all odds. We had tied ourselves by bonds of marriage to the rising star of the West – Constantine – and for all the good that appeared to be doing us, the people still saw it as a step forward. We had even withstood and humiliated the most powerful claimant to the purple: the legitimate Emperor of the East, Galerius. We seemed unassailable.

There was even rumour that the legions of Aegyptus might come over to our banner, following the example of their neighbouring forces in Africa, and if that happened, we would secure the greatest sources of grain and gold in the empire.

It was almost enough to make me forget Constantine's failure to support me.

Almost.

I threw myself into the revival of Rome as the favoured jewel of the world. No longer under direct military threat, the army was garrisoned appropriately and then put to work repairing aqueducts, bridges, roads and city walls where required. The Second Parthica was now back up to full legion strength at Castra Albana to the south of the city. The Urban Cohorts were becoming a true force of soldiers again. Grain flowed and the people prospered.

Rome bloomed.

I attended in purple and helped lay the foundation stone for my new grand basilica at the eastern end of the forum, while my workers toiled to raise the nearby great temple of Venus and Roma from the ashes of its fire-damaged skeleton. I watched with satisfaction the city walls reach completion. I reconstructed the long-ruined temple of the *Penates* in the forum – my son's favourite building, for which he had repeatedly nagged a restoration. I tested the completed bath complex I'd added to the great Palatine sprawl despite the fact that I had no intention of remaining in that place. Lastly, in the monumental heart of Rome, my *curator aedium sacrorum* – the official in charge of maintaining sacred buildings – had a fine bronze equestrian statue of me raised on a large marble plinth. The first testimonial raised in the city to the glory of my principate, I dedicated the statue with a plaque – worded by the curator – dedicating the statue to Mars and the founders of Rome, in thanks for the city's repeated deliverance, and referring to me as 'Lord Imperator Maxentius Pius Felix, Unconquered Augustus.'

Unconquered Augustus!

I have to admit to a little pride there. And *Pius* I felt an apt description. As for *Felix* – lucky – well that was a different matter entirely...

Beyond the walls of the city I began my other great project. In my august position, I had clearly outgrown the old family villa on the Via Labicana, and the more time I spent on the Palatine, the more I became conscious of the villains that had inhabited the place while bleeding Rome dry. It was unsuitable for an emperor of Rome for other reasons, and I would leave it as a place of administration and business, and not a residence.

I had looked at the great imperial villas along the Via Appia to the south of Rome, but quickly dismissed the old villa on the Ox-Head hill as too cramped and messy, and could not countenance the Quintili villa for its association with the despicable Commodus and his megalomania.

But closer to Rome lay that sumptuous villa that had played the role of Severus' last home. I had decided to rest my laurels there, and set the best architects in the empire to creating a new design for the most modern palatial structure, which would retain the best features of the original. I would move out there from the hubbub of the city once it was complete, taking the children where they could breathe the fresh air of Latium and not the fetid stink of a Roman summer. The villa had an added, underhand purpose if I am quite honest.

My wife had stated in no uncertain terms her unwillingness to leave the city, and any move I made with my family out to the Via Appia would be without Valeria, who would remain and stalk the echoing halls of the Palatine. In her opinion, my sharing of power with my father was a mistake, and she warned me that should I move from the heart of Rome, it would not be long before my father was ruling and I little more than a hanger-on. Whether she truly cared about my future or merely saw in it the potential rise and fall of her own I cannot say, but I was in truth already beginning to think on ways of ousting my unwanted co-emperor from his position.

April came around fast, bringing with it Rome's traditional rain showers interspersed with blue skies that retained a certain chill. And as the festivals of Venus and Ceres and Tellus passed, the citizens began to celebrate more, feeling that the world was returning to peace and prosperity as the summer loomed on the horizon.

Furius Octavianus, my curator aedium sacrorum, arranged for the newly repaired temple of Venus and Rome to play host to an imperial spectacle that would form the climax of the festival of Rome's founding. My father would reprise his old role as Hercules – though these days without the gleaming painted face – while I would fashion my appearance after Octavian Augustus, the first emperor of Rome. I refused to adopt a more divine character when there were so many great Romans who had been born as men.

My staid belief in the value of such imagery did not hold for my children, of course. Romulus, now growing into a tall and studious young man, I had fashioned as his mythical namesake, displaying my poor twisted Aurelius as his brother, Remus. We would hold a great sacrifice of a fine white bull reared in the sacred fields at Paestum. I would bless the people and the city of Rome in my role as *Pontifex Maximus* and would bestow various titles, including *Saviour of Rome* upon my father for his defeat of two invading forces, *Loyal and Faithful* upon the provinces and military forces of Africa, and the induction of a new *Dux Militum per Italia* – master of the army in Italia – for Volusianus, granting him seniority of all the military barring the Praetorians, who still fell under Anullinus' command.

A flock of pure white birds would be released into the sky – birds that had been trained by the priests to fly en masse to the Capitol and to settle upon the roofs of the great temples there. Then there would be massive donatives, with chests of money being cast out into the crowds by my soldiers, linking in the minds of the public the military might of their emperor with beneficence and civil prosperity.

It was to be a master stroke of imperial publicity.

The day came, and I rode through the streets on a well-appointed chestnut mare, surrounded by senators and courtiers, my father, my wife and children, my advisors and senior military officers, all togate rather than arrayed in military kit. As we arrived at the huge platform of the temple that overlooked the great Flavian amphitheatre and the colossal statue of Sol Invictus, we dismounted, the Praetorians around us forcing a wide path through the cheering crowd.

Even the interminable showers seemed to have granted us respite for the day, and all looked good. Then, as we climbed the newly refurbished marble stairs to the temple itself, the first omen struck. My foot came down upon a step which contained a freakish fault, and which snapped under my tread, forcing me to correct myself in order not to fall. The crowd around us sucked in a nervous breath and many made warding signs against this clear omen, but for me, I considered it good, for I had not fallen.

And then, beggaring belief, as I reached the top, the *same damned thing* happened beneath my father's foot on an entirely different step, and he fell, damaging his knee with an audible crack. The crowd almost collapsed in on itself with all the warding signs they made. I held my breath. What could it mean? The answer was to come swiftly after.

The bull stomped and lowed in the background, and the people began to settle, unsure as to what the signs meant. Eventually, the priest officiating at the temple stepped forth and made some introductory speech. I paid little attention, for something had caught my eye as I lifted a fold of my toga and draped it over my head in the old style, marking my role today as Rome's chief priest. Along with the gathered crowd and numerous luminaries, my Praetorians were visible, keeping the open space below the temple in order. But my eyes were picking out other uniforms among them. Prefects of other units who had, as far as I was aware, no role today and no right to attend in any other manner than as members of the public.

I was watching them curiously as I heard the priest's cue and knew the time had come for my carefully prepared speech on the value of the Roman ideal and the unassailability of our noble city. I opened my mouth to speak the words, still unable to tear my eyes from the soldiers, when my father's voice unexpectedly rose over the top.

I blinked in surprise as Father appeared beside me. It took a moment of confusion to clear before I started hearing what he was saying.

'...so do you really need a stripling boy with no military prowess to defend our lands? Do you truly wish to place your future in the hands of an untried academic who makes enemies of the great men of the empire? We have a strong army now, but Constantine raises more north of the Alpes, and Galerius will not let us rest now he has been humiliated. You, my people, know that it was *my* hand that stopped Severus, *my* hand that halted Galerius. *My* hand that built your new army and saved Rome. I have been Augustus with the noble Diocletian and helped pull the empire back from the brink of chaos. I am Hercules reborn, the master of Rome and the rightful and *only* Emperor of the West!'

I was so stunned by this sudden turn of events that my voice failed me, my protestations dying as croaks in my throat while my father drove the knife into my back.

'You, the people, know my pedigree and my ability, and I call upon you to renounce my son, to proclaim me your only emperor.'

I floundered in astonishment as my father ripped off my purple-edged toga, leaving me standing in a simple tunic and boots. Valeria had been right, but Father had not even waited for me to quit the city to betray me!

'I call upon the armies to follow me,' he boomed, 'as I rebuild Rome to become the military power-centre of the world!'

I heard a loud crack, and didn't immediately see from whence the blow came, but my stunned gaze soon picked out my son with a face like thunder, rubbing his stinging knuckles as Father staggered back and dropped the purple-edged toga. Emitting a roar, Father lunged for Romulus with an answering blow, but I stepped in the way just in time, his punch knocking me from the podium to crash painfully on the steps before falling into the mass of soldiers below. I was dazed, I realised. I had struck my head at least once in the fall and could feel blood trickling in my hair. I tried to stand, but failed dismally.

It could all have been over then, so quickly.

But hands reached for me, lifting, supporting, consoling. I was borne aloft by the proud Guardsmen of Rome and brought to rest once more atop the stairs as my battered brain swam in my skull. My lurching sight caught moments to which I later applied significance:

Volusianus at Romulus' side, sword out protectively. My father's carefully selected officers among the crowd shouting slogans, attempting to rally the Praetorians to his cause. The Praetorians failing to a man to respond to the calls, and brutally putting down the rebel officers. The crowd chanting my name.

My father had made a dreadful miscalculation. He believed his erstwhile power and his twin victories enough to win over the Guard and the people of Rome. But he had ever been harsh and aloof, playing at being a god with little care for the common folk. And I? *I* had given Rome back its pride. I had seen the people fed and healed. I had glorified their city and rebuilt the houses of the gods. I had cradled in my hand the heart of Rome and watched it, after a century of atrophying, start to beat anew.

The people knew that and were not fooled by an orator's militant haranguing. And the Praetorians knew that Maximian the Augustus had been part of the regime that had limited and effectively disbanded their force, while I had *empowered* them.

Critical failings, and the omen of the broken steps became clear.

As the crowd roared their support for me, and my wits began to steady, I saw Anullinus and his men fall upon Father, grasping him by the shoulders and pushing him to his knees in the pose of a man awaiting execution.

'Yours is the order, Imperator,' murmured my Praetorian Prefect as his biggest man pulled my father's head back by the hair and positioned the point of a blade in the 'V' of his throat.

I stared.

I was now undisputed emperor of Rome. I had power of life or death over anyone, even my father. I ruled with ultimate power, as had the great emperors of old: *Trajan, Augustus, Marcus Aurelius...*

I closed my eyes.

...Nero, Commodus, Gaius Caligula...

'Release him.'

Anullinus stared at me. It was foolish, perhaps, to prevent the act. Freeing a potential enemy is oft the move of a foolish and short-sighted man. But to order my father's death at that moment would be to define my time as emperor of Rome in exactly the fashion I could not stomach. I would be a Trajan, or a Marcus Aurelius, or an Augustus.

I would *not* be a Nero.

'I said, release him.'

As the Praetorians let go of my father and he staggered painfully to his feet, rubbing his shoulders, Anullinus and Volusianus – two men who had been likened to rival stags in mating season and had not once in all their time together agreed on a single matter – both appealed to me.

'Domine, you *must* finish him!'

'My emperor, he *has* to die for this!'

But my decision had been made as I had realised that my entire principate might be defined by this moment. I turned to my father and ripped the toga from his shoulders, watching it fall to the temple podium leaving an overweight, ageing mess in a rich tunic.

'I will not desecrate this sacred place with patricide,' I snarled. 'This is a day for celebration and rebirth. I am reborn Augustus, emperor of Rome. You are reborn a private citizen and no more. Get you hence from Rome. You will take nothing with you – no weapon or coin or personal treasure. You will be gone from this city before the gates close tonight and if you ever return, your head will be forfeit. No citizen of Rome or Italia will give you shelter or succour. You are hereby exiled beyond my domain to wherever you can find shelter. Go!'

I pointed my finger towards the Oppian hill, which loomed beyond the temple and the great colossus. I didn't really care which way he went, so long as he went. My father turned, casting a black look at the soldiers who had held him, and then turned a murderous gaze upon me, but wisely held his tongue. The crowd, who had fallen silent during those moments that had defined Father's fate, began to chant again: *Imp-er-a-tor, Imp-er-a-tor, Imp-er-a-tor!*

Rome had given my father his answer and as he made his way down the temple steps, his malevolent gaze falling upon all who opposed him, even the lowest of those in the crowd began to spit at him. I wondered if, despite everything, my Praetorians might take offence at that and discipline the crowd, for my father had been a great man. But no. Instead, the Guardsmen joined in, hawking and spitting on the failed usurper.

I watched until Father was almost out of earshot and then leaned close to Anullinus.

'Take a squad of men. Make sure he leaves the city unmolested but unaided. Once he is beyond the walls, abandon him to the Fates.'

For a moment, I thought my prefect might argue, but then he turned and was gone, leaving me on that podium, the trickle of blood from my head wound skirting my eye and dripping from my chin.

I watched that retreating figure as one of my attendants

mopped the blood from my face and another collected my fallen toga and carefully draped it back into place, covering my head once more.

'He was to be *Saviour of Rome*,' I murmured. 'He was *consul*!'

Volusianus, suddenly at my elbow, cleared his throat. 'He could not even save himself, Imperator. He did not deserve the consulate, let alone such honours.'

As I stood in confusion, I heard him announce my name to the public as the new consul of Rome, with Romulus as my suffect consul, the priest confirming his words, which were then echoed by the gathered senators. I turned to see Romulus smiling at me, pride suffusing his features as he flexed his bruised knuckles.

The betrayal of my father had come so swiftly on the heel of that of Constantine, and yet for all the evil of that treachery, it had brought something good. Finally, after so long, I was free of the shadow of my father, and undisputed master of Rome. I smiled. Nothing could go wrong now.

33

CONSTANTINE

'Loose!' the Lanciarii *Campidoctores* bellowed. The bronze-scale ranks rippled and a thousand javelins sailed across the target range, thwacking into timber butts and sending splinters into the air. I saw how most of these lethal missiles had stayed true and wondered how many Roman lives such a volley would have claimed? Yes, *Roman* lives. For the empire teetered on the brink of civil war.

I turned away from the javelin-throwers and waved my Cornuti escort with me across the Field of Mars below Treverorum's eastern walls. These four offered no conversation and this suited me. As I walked through the training field, I observed my legions in the throes of formation drills, manoeuvres and swordplay – *thrust, cut, stab, feint!* – but my mind was absent, wandering like a drunk through the turmoil of recent events. It seemed that my brazen denouncement of Galerius at the Alpine passes had stoked an almighty conflagration of pride. The Herdsman had returned to the East, shamed and angered like never before, bent on revenge. More cuttingly, my one-time friend, Maxentius, had taken it as some kind of affront that I had chosen to exact my authority so on those wintry defiles. So much so that he had now taken to calling himself the Unconquered Augustus, as if to spit on my claim to that title.

The quiet, unassuming youth I had met all those years ago was gone, it seemed, devoured by the black maw of power on Rome's Palatine Hill and reborn as a strident leader, fortifying his cities and swelling his armies, even exiling his father. And so the whispers had begun. Which of my enemies would act first? What would come across the horizon to my lands – steely legions or venomous embassies? I was prepared for both, but I relished neither.

Many days I had spent like this. Numb days. Watching, waiting, the Gallic air growing cold and the woods around the Mosella valley turning golden brown. But on this day, at last, the horizon stirred. Not with the legions of Galerius from the east or Maxentius from the south, but with a simple riding party. An embassy, I thought, seeing that they carried no banner marking them as my men or those of the other factions.

My legions slowed in their training, many thousands of heads turning and a babble of curiosity breaking out. The Cornuti with me closed together like a set of fangs as the riding party approached, only relaxing when I waved my hand. For I did not fear this group of horsemen. They numbered just five. Four simple, mail-shirted equites, black cloaks stained with dust and both they and their mounts emaciated and dirty. But the one they screened, he was different. I shaded my eyes from the noon sun, seeing how he rode haughtily, back straight. This was no ordinary horseman. He was as thin and bedraggled as those who guarded him, yes, but he held himself with the poise of a nobleman. As he approached, a creeping sense of realisation stole across my skin. The unkempt beard, the hooded eyes, the ruddy complexion.

Maximian!

What had become of the fat sack of wine I had once known and loathed? This form that approached me was withered, gaunt and bruised. His fingernails were cracked and caked in dirt, his hair and beard were unkempt and filthy, and his robes were soiled and torn. Had the one-time Hercules been living like a wandering bandit in the months since Maxentius expelled him from Rome? It shames me to this day that I took great pleasure in seeing him like that.

He came to a halt before me, his lips pursed as if withholding sour words. When he did speak, it was with the contrived tone of a man who knew he had run out of all other options. 'Augustus,' he said with a slight bow of his head.

Had my mind not been in such disorder, I might have erupted in wry laughter. This was the man who had deigned to bequeath me with the title on my wedding's eve, like a charitable father. Today, he came to me like a grovelling son.

'Maxentius knows of your journey to these lands?' I asked.

He shook his head then said with an expression of a man who had just swallowed a spoonful of salt and was trying not to react: 'My son would not know or care had I stumbled into a ravine.'

Then that makes two of us, I thought, my eyes narrowing just for a moment.

'I come to you for sanctuary,' he added humbly.

What obligation was I under to provide such for this man? A raft of black ideas sped across my thoughts. It was only the hurried footsteps behind me from Treverorum's eastern gate, and the trilling voice that accompanied it, that broke my thoughts.

'Father!' Fausta cried. She hurried to the side of his mount, took his hand and kissed it, then helped him from the saddle. 'I heard terrible things. They said you were dead!'

'I am very much alive,' he replied. 'And here, under the shelter of the true Augustus of the West, I will remain that way,' he said, hugging her and looking up to me for confirmation.

Now it was my turn to take a spoonful of salt. Fausta turned to me, her eyes full of hope.

No! my heart screamed. To harbour this man would stoke fire in the heart of his son. To offer Maximian shelter would be like inviting a wolf to dine with my lambs. But Father's words from years before guided me. *The enemy by your side is an asset, the foe unseen whets his blade.*

'It is so,' I said flatly.

I spent the next few days locked in discussion with the bitter and broken Maximian. He spoke through clenched teeth of the armies Maxentius was gathering in Italia. No longer could his son rely only on a patchwork of vexillationes and those damned Praetorians, it seemed; every legion within Italia and Africa were now firmly Maxentius' to command. Despite this I remained stoutly confident in my veteran legions, should it come to that... Then Maximian told me of the possibility that Aegyptus might declare support for his estranged son. I left him then, to gorge on food alone and replenish his lost gut, while I sought some solace outwith his company.

I climbed the staircase and onto the rooftop balcony of the palace, glad to be away from venomous talk. A bracing autumnal wind caught me and swept the clouds from my mind. For they were all there: Mother, Fausta, Crispus, playing together. Batius stood, one arm resting on the balcony, a soldier's grin on his anvil jaw as he watched the horseplay. Lactantius was sitting, enduring the cold to enjoy the moment, cajoling Crispus into sprinting from Mother's arms to Fausta's and back again.

'Come here, lad,' I said with a hearty chuckle, crouching and extending my arms. Young Crispus spun to me and his face brightened like a ray of dawn sunshine. Then he ran to me, giggling, leapt and wrapped his arms around me, his laughter muffled as his face burrowed into my bear pelt. I smoothed his hair and stood, lifting him and swinging him from side to side, making the noises of an angry bear. This only stoked his laughter further. When I set him down he staggered back and swiped up Lactantius' cane. 'Back, monster!' he yelped between eruptions of hilarity. I pretended to stalk from side to side, unsure. Crispus kept a keen eye on me, stepping back as I edged a little closer to him. I saw Fausta creep up behind him in silence, her face split with a smile, one finger raised to her lips to keep me quiet. Then she seized my boy, lifting him by the armpits, before nuzzling into his neck and trying as best she could to imitate my baritone bear cries.

Crispus kicked out and shrieked, then the pair fell to the marble balcony floor, overcome with laughter. I wiped a tear from my eye as I watched them. That moment I remembered something long-forgotten: that the simplest of pleasures were often the sweetest. Despite this game of power that was in play across the empire, Fausta had been united with her father and she had been joyous that rumours of his death had proved unfounded. Likewise, I had all of my loved ones here, safe, well and shielded behind the great screen of power I had seized as my own.

Then I saw something, approaching the city just as had

happened so recently, but this time from the eastern road that led here from Mogontiacum. A dust cloud. Another travelling party, and not an ordinary one, for they bore Joviani banners – the Herdsman's colours. My laughter ebbed.

Fausta stood, leading Crispus over by the hand. 'We should get this young man washed and changed before his evening meal,' she said, her voice still high-pitched from the jocularity but her eyes narrowing as if she had noticed my change of mood.

I smiled, though it was less exuberant this time. I ruffled my son's hair as he went, complaining that he was not finished bear-hunting. 'And the bear has not finished hunting you, scamp!' I retorted, then my eyes swiftly returned to the approaching party.

Mother stood to follow Fausta and Crispus. I saw her glance to the east and the incoming riders. She had noticed the change in my demeanour too. She knew what it meant. She knew me like no other, as she always had. She rested a hand on my shoulder as she passed. 'Choose wisely, Constantine. If he brings wrathful words, do not reply in kind.' I noticed she was thumbing her Chi-Rho as she said this. 'Sometimes power comes in the form of submission.'

Never, I thought, though did not dare affront her with such a response.

I placed a hand over hers, felt it slip away and watched her go. I realised then that she had watched my journey all these years. From the eager youth in Naissus to Augustus of the West. I had once assumed she felt pride at my choices in life. But in these last few years, I was not so sure. The ever-rising tensions since Father's death had driven me to black places, usually nestled behind a wine cup whilst watching men being savaged by lions in the arena or observing fresh legions coming together month after month, ready to fight for me... ready to die for me.

As she left with Fausta and Crispus, I walked over to the balcony edge. Lactantius and Batius flanked me. The three of us gazed east, the wind bathing us.

'Aye, they're the Herdsman's lot,' Batius remarked glibly as the riders came to the great eastern gatehouse, slipped from view for a few moments, then reappeared inside when the tall gates opened. Twelve iron riders in pale blue cloaks, with some kind of ambassador in their midst. 'I can smell their pig-shit breath.'

Lactantius studied the party's path as they made straight for the palace. I could see that the old man was anxious. He stroked and tugged at his beard and was constantly licking his lips as if eager to speak but wary of the response he might receive.

'Rest easy, old friend,' I said. 'My mood is light today. They come to talk and conversation is all I will subject them to.'

'Why don't we wait until we hear what this cur has to say?' Batius countered, sourly eyeing the ambassador in the centre of the party.

I watched as the unarmoured rider amidst the Joviani dismounted inside the palace gates and was then ushered inside, marshalled by a pair of my feather-helmed Cornuti.

'He can say what he likes. The only certainty he can guarantee is that come sunset, I will remain undisputed Augustus of the West.' I cast Lactantius an apologetic sidelong look. 'I did not say it would be a pleasant conversation...'

My words trailed off as I heard pattering footsteps coming up to the balcony. The three of us swung to see the sweating rider dressed in a brown tunic, green trousers and a grey woollen cloak. At once I felt guilty for having eyed him as the enemy. This man was a messenger and no more. I held out a hand and took the scroll he offered. I barely noticed Maximian appearing on the rooftop too, eyes narrowed in interest, that hooded gaze locked on the scroll as a raven might eye a mouse.

'Jove Incarnate prays this reaches you well,' the rider said, genuflecting before me.

I noticed two things. *Jove Incarnate?* Was Galerius taking this title now? And the man had not addressed me. Neither name nor rank. My hackles stirred as I unfurled the scroll. As I read it, I felt the wind whipping around me, sure its contents would conjure my anger to the fore. But the wind stilled and I looked up. I turned to Lactantius and smiled.

'Everything will be fine,' I said. The old man's face reflected mine.

'Domine?' Batius said with a quizzical look.

'The Herdsman has been put in his place, it seems,' I said, tapping the scroll. 'Diocletian has returned to the imperial court from his retirement palace. He has watched the events of recent years in dismay. He seeks to end the turmoil.'

'How, exactly?' Batius scoffed. 'Does he think he can reprise his role as master of the empire? Does he plan to take his sword to the Herdsman, to us... and to Maxentius?'

I fixed Batius with a confident smile. 'No, his return is temporary – to arbitrate and rectify matters. He has called for a conference.' I gazed out to the eastern horizon, and for the first time in so long, I did so with hope.

'We have been summoned east... to Carnuntum.'

I was about to roll up the scroll when my eyes drifted across the list of attendees and snagged there. *What was this?*

'Interesting,' Maximian purred, reading it over my shoulder.

34

MAXENTIUS

I had demanded of the architects and workers how long the villa on the Via Appia would take to achieve a basic level of habitability. I had ideas of residing in one extant wing while all the work was carried out to put my modern stamp on the rest of the beautiful palace. Though the weather in Rome had once more become acceptable after the dusty heat of August and the stifling September, the icy coldness of my wife drove me to look for alternatives anyway. Sadly, there was no feasible way I would be able to move into the new villa until the next summer at the very least, and so I resigned myself to remaining in that sprawling chaos of bad taste – the Palatine – and avoiding any contact with Valeria – at least that was easy in such a vast complex.

There was nothing political to occupy my mind for the first time in so many months. No one was massing troops on my territory's border and planning an invasion. Rome was peaceful and well fed. Africa was loyal and steady. Rumours continued to reach me that Aegyptus was considering coming over to my banner, though the only physical sign of that was a number of lesser military units who had left their unfavourable postings and crossed into Africa to take up arms for me.

In fact, my army was growing at a surprising rate. A few units from Southern Hispania who considered Rome their spiritual capital rather than Germanic Treverorum had crossed the sea and reposted in Sicilia. Various units – including more than one legionary cohort – had crossed the border from the Herdsman's territory following his ignominious retreat, and had reformed under my banner. And in addition to all of this, while Anullinus had concentrated on rearming and training his Praetorian Guard, Urban Cohorts and various elite cavalry units, Volusianus – my new Dux Militum – spent a great deal of time and of coin from my treasury raising and equipping new legions across Italia and Africa. My commanders were determined that the next time a man in purple crossed our border they would find an army the likes of which had never trod Italian soil.

I tried not to dwell on such matters. For any time I thought on invaders and armies, my mind inevitably settled upon Constantine, who had come to my aid in the past, but had not supported me on the one occasion when Rome truly needed his help. I had spent days wandering the Palatine, hammering my fist on walls in anger just as the Augustus of old had done when let down by his general in Germania. How could Constantine have let Galerius go? How could he not see that he had saved our most vitriolic enemy and allowed him to regroup? Not only had he betrayed me by letting my erstwhile invader flee unharmed, but he had also let live a man who hated him beyond all others and who almost certainly coveted his title for one of his own lackeys. It was madness. I could only assume that Constantine had been fevered and temporarily struck senseless.

See how even now the subject sends me on a rant from which I find it difficult to calm myself? No. Despite our ties, Constantine was no longer my ally. There were even rumours that my father had run to his court after he had been ejected from the city. I could see the logic of such a move, of course: Fausta was the link between he and my former friend. But I simply could not see Constantine granting sanctuary to the old sot. He was so clearly untrustworthy, and Constantine was no fool, for all his blindness over Galerius. If the rumour turned out to be true, then I would know Constantine's betrayal to be complete. To harbour a father who had tried to depose me would be the last nail in the crucifix upon which our tattered alliance hung.

But musing and speculation were all that was open to me. As I said, we were under no threat and the world was bountiful and peaceful. I turned my thoughts back to the various building projects I had begun, but even those were either complete or well underway and needed little attention from me. I tried to hold court in the traditional Roman manner, with occasional banquets for my closer friends and advisors, but found the conversation of senators and their wives to be no more diverting than a stroll across the Palatine, and any time spent in the presence of both Anullinus and Volusianus guaranteed me a day-long headache. The pair bickered like an old married couple, and I could see the time coming when there would be blows between them. I was constantly tempted in wicked amusement to make the pair joint Praetorian Prefects in the old way and watch how long it took before one of them disappeared mysteriously. See how little occupied my days that such plans were given consideration?

Valeria had come back into her own. She had congratulated

me guardedly on my handling of Father's usurpation. I had been wise, she said, to be seen by my people as benevolent and merciful, though she did add that if it had been her she would have then had him knifed and left in a gutter out of sight of the people. Appearance was one thing, and wisdom another. She was right, really, though even across a chasm of dislike it takes a lot for a son to order his father's death.

Still, Valeria was content. Once more sole empress of Rome, she set about ordering everything changed on the Palatine, securing the continued support of the city's old families and even wrote a missive to her father, urging him to acknowledge me as legitimate Augustus of the West over Constantine, a move with which I could hardly argue, given my old friend's betrayal.

In the end, I spent a lot of time with Romulus and little Aurelius. I had somewhat neglected the boys in recent months in Rome, the dreadful danger we were all in taking precedence in my mind. But now, with peace, came time for family.

Aurelius, now approaching his fourth year and still unable to walk more than a few painful steps, had passed from the care of Euna and into the ministrations of a medicus who had trained early as a priest in the temple of Aesculapius and who had prayers, potions and balms to ease my poor son's constant aches and pains. Aurelius had learned to read and also to talk, though his mouth was deformed and his speech difficult, and so he rarely did so for fear of provoking a sour reaction. He had never had such from me, of course, but my darling wife was less concerned with his feelings.

While I spent patient hours with him working through ancient tales of Trojan heroes and trying to help him with pronunciation, I had actually once witnessed his mother kick him out of the way when she came across him in a corridor.

He may have been ill, but he was the son of an emperor; *my* son. He deserved whatever we could give him, and I had a distressing feeling that beneath the impenetrable façade of deformity that had been in turn encased in a shell of self-loathing, there lurked a truly clever and good boy.

The tears over him came at night when I was alone, and they oft drove me to visit his brother's room, to watch my older boy sleeping the sleep of the content.

Romulus seemed to have grown again in the past few months. I had assumed he had stopped growing, since he was now aged fourteen summers and rapidly closing on the taking of the toga virilis and becoming a man, but he seemed to have shot up again. Another summer like this and I would be looking up at him. I was surprised when I saw him that October morning, which became ingrained in my memory for more than one reason. How did the time pass so quickly? Seemingly an hour ago he had been a little boy playing with a stick and ball.

Now here he was in the great Palatine complex, tall and rangy and with a voice that alternately warbled like a lark or grizzled like a centurion, cracking from the one to the other continuously. I smiled as I emerged from the main palace and saw him sitting on the balcony, leaning back against a delicate column, silhouetted by the garden's autumnal light. No matter what else happened in my life – bloody wars of succession, familial betrayals, a cold and calculating wife, aides who could not speak civilly to one another – despite it all, there was one golden glow in my heart and one constant in my life: Romulus.

'I've been waiting for you, Father,' he warbled, the last word cracking into a growl.

'I was signing documents for Anullinus.' My eyes narrowed.

His new grey and silver tunic was already torn near the hem and dirty. I had bought him it only two days earlier and this morning had been its first wearing. How could he take on the man's toga when he was still throwing himself around in the dirt like a child?

I had to stop thinking of him as a little boy!

'Your tunic?'

He rose on the low wall upon which he sat and my heart lurched as I realised he was teetering on the edge of a thirty-foot drop to the peristyle garden below. He seemed unconcerned, examining the tear in the fabric at his hip.

'Sorry, Father. I had a bit of an accident.'

'How?'

'Ruricius Pompeianus was teaching me a few sword moves this morning, but the grass is slippery and wet. You'll be pleased to know that I caught him on the leg as I fell. He'll have a bruise to remember the practice by.'

I pinched the bridge of my nose, not so much in despair at such activity, but more with the difficulty in concentrating on his words when his voice jumped up and down like a cat on hot tiles.

'Perhaps you should dress more appropriately for sword lessons?'

'It was just an unexpected practice, Father.' He slid from the wall and approached me. Gods, he was getting tall. 'I have a question for you,' he said.

'Yes?'

'When my voice settles, will I take the toga?'

Lose my little boy? I felt a shiver. My son becoming a grown man. No one can stop the march of time, of course, but the very idea that someday soon Romulus would be a man seeking a wife and moving away from me broke my

heart at the very core. If I didn't have my beloved Romulus
to run to...

I hardened myself and forced an encouraging smile on my
face.

'Of course.'

'Then, will you allow me to take a commission as a prefect
in the army?'

Where had this come from?

My voice failed me.

'It is a good start on the *Cursus Honorum*, Father, and I
would rather earn my place in society than have it handed to
me because you wear a purple robe.'

Pride. Fear, for sure. But pride also. This was my boy and
how could his father deny such a noble and honourable
request from him? Besides, junior prefects were never in any
danger. They carried messages, watched the action and drank
good wine while they waited for their service to end so they
could become *quaestors* back in Rome. Of course, Romulus
was already my suffect consul, despite not yet being entered
into the rolls of citizenship as a man. The son of an emperor
has never been tied to the traditional ladder of advancement.

A prefect!

The idea of my son in uniform was strangely thrilling and
terrifying in equal parts.

I suppressed my need to keep him close; my fear that
when he left my side, my life would become empty. 'I will
think on the matter, Romulus. You should certainly take
on a military role, though I am thinking it might be in the
Guard. After all, you are already consul along with me, and
you will be consul again next year. A consul should remain
close to the heart of Rome.'

It was a feeble excuse really, intended to keep him as close as possible. I had already twisted the traditions to allow him his first consulship while still a boy in the eyes of Rome. He would need to take the toga virilis soon, so that his second year as consul was a true one. Fifteen summers, and already looking at being a prefect in the Guard and a second term as consul.

I smiled.

Romulus, a look of gratitude and satisfaction suffusing him, stepped back and leapt up onto the low balcony above the garden once more.

My heart lurched again as I saw his foot slip, the sole of his shoe still muddy from his sword practice. As seems to always be the case in such moments, the world slowed to a leaden pace, my heart thumping out a stately, ponderous beat, despite the fact that in myself I knew it to be racing with panic in truth.

I saw him going over the edge.

I leapt into action, but even as I loped the three steps to the balcony edge, I knew I would be too late. I screamed something... I cannot remember what.

And then the world recovered.

Somehow, Romulus managed to wrap an arm around that slender column and his feet repositioned, his weight moving back to a balanced poise.

I felt as though something inside me had burst as I watched him right himself and then flash me a wicked grin.

'You worry too much, Father. My balance is impeccable. You know that.'

The words came out in growls and trills, but all I could do was shake uncontrollably.

'Get down from there. It's too far down and your shoes are muddy. You nearly broke my heart... and your skull!'

With a light chuckle, Romulus dropped back to the flagged floor and scraped the rest of the mud from his shoes. I was busy clutching my chest, sure I had had some sort of heart failure, when my boy looked over my shoulder.

'Hello. What's this, Father?'

My eyes still wide and slightly teary, I turned. Volusianus was crossing from the main palace doorway towards us, Anullinus close at his heel. Both wore dark expressions and for the first time in many months they were not arguing, and that realisation made the hair stand proud on the back of my neck. *That* fact boded no good whatsoever.

'What is it?'

The two military commanders, who between them defended my realm, shared a look, an unspoken conversation passing through their eyes.

'We have confirmation that your once-noble father is indeed at the court of the false emperor Constantine, Domine.'

It might have been more of a blow had I not been already reeling from the near fall of my dear son. Instead I felt only a slight pull as one of the last few ties that connected me and my former friend stretched and snapped.

'Unfortunate, but not a surprise.'

'The time is coming when you may have to declare an open state of war with the man, Domine.'

I blinked, but as the words sank into my head I realised that he was right. If we were no longer allies, then any further deterioration in our relationship would see us enemies. And if the man acknowledged my father's title, then the pair of them could be Caesar and Augustus of the West with no use for a rival emperor in Rome. Only if my father was removed from the equation could there be a hope of reconciliation between us.

'I will not do so until there is no other choice.'

Volusianus pursed his lips. 'Then we must await the result first, Domine.'

'Result of what?'

My Dux Militum took a deep breath and looked me straight in the eye.

'Diocletian has returned from retirement to settle the current succession crisis. He has called a meeting of all the "legitimate claimants" to the purple – his words, Domine, not mine. The meeting is to be held next month at the great fortress of Carnuntum on the Danubius.'

Good. Diocletian may be old and frail now, but despite his dangerous and extreme persecutions, under his hand the empire had at least been steady and not at risk of civil war, and the people would still respect his decision. Clearly he intended to prevent such a disaster occurring. I wondered whether this was the result of Valeria's letter to her father. Had Galerius decided to make me Augustus at last?

'Carnuntum is almost half a month's journey,' I mused, 'even if the sea is calm, which is unlikely in October. The old Augustus has not given us much notice. We shall have to pack and depart tomorrow to be sure we are in time. Romulus can come with us, and Valeria will want to see her father, but my little one will have to stay here. It would be dangerous provocation to turn up with an entire Praetorian cohort, but some sort of honour guard is important...'

I stopped, concerned at the strange look that passed between my two military advisors as I rattled out my plans.

'Respectfully, Domine, we are only aware of the conference through our frumentarii hidden among Constantine's court. No invitation has been dispatched to Rome. In fact, as we understand it, the attendees named in the missive are Galerius, Daia, Constantine... and your father.'

Both men lowered their gazes as I tried to take in the meaning of this. Diocletian intended to confirm four men as the Tetrarchy, *but none of them were me!* He had invited to the conference all those he considered 'legitimate' claimants. *And none of them were me.* Even my purulent, betraying, ignorant wine-sack of a father had been invited. *But not me.*

I took a step back in shock.

Valeria's plea had fallen upon deaf ears. Either that or Galerius had decided in favour of me but the old emperor had denied him. I knew that Galerius considered me a usurper, and therefore likely so did Daia. But Constantine had been in almost the same position as I. In fact, I had always had a closer claim to the purple than he. Yet *he* had been invited.

Not me.

Had the old former emperor finally slipped into insanity? Shaking my head in disbelief, I stared at my two advisors.

'What does this mean?'

Anullinus cleared his throat. 'This means, Domine, that very likely the next few months will see our array of enemies double and our support in other provinces wither.'

'This means,' Volusianus growled, 'that we should redouble our military recruitment.'

I stood speechless. For some reason it irked me that we were in the heart of that great Palatine sprawl and I could not look out over the city and the walls to the distant horizon. Perhaps it was good that I could not, for now no horizon would satisfy. If this news meant what it appeared to mean, I could say farewell to the potential support of Aegyptus, and to any military units fleeing from the territory of others to my banner. West and north lay Hispania and Gaul – steel-clad lands of Constantine. East lay the empire of Galerius, who now would have no compunction about bringing the sword to my domain. South lay Africa. Loyal, worthy Africa. But I could see it in the eyes of Volusianus, who had initially brought me that land: with no outside support to my imperial claim, how long could I rely on Africa?

We were an island of tradition in a sea of tetrarchic ambition.

And, like an island, we stood alone.

35

CONSTANTINE

I rested my elbows on the side of the bireme and surveyed the grey, bitter-cold morning. The roar of the Danubius was as ferocious as I remembered, and the sprawling, frost-veiled pine forests on the northern bank were as dense and dark as ever – harbouring an army of shadows. Just how many mad-eyed tribesmen watched my flotilla approach the dock of Carnuntum? Just how many of them knew what was to take place this day?

I stood tall and turned away from the northern banks, instead sweeping my gaze over the twelve warships that sailed downriver with me. Each was well-manned with crew and a contingent of the Sixth Victrix – the agreed maximum of three centuries' worth of men that each party coming to Carnuntum could bring. These stony-faced legionaries knew what was happening today. Batius, standing with one foot up on the prow while munching into an apple – he knew what was to happen today. And me? I had thought of little else for many days.

Glancing downriver, I saw Carnuntum's tall, red-brick walls rising into view on the river's southern banks. This city had a proud history: Marcus Aurelius had scribed part of

483

his famed *Meditations* here and Septimius Severus had been raised within those walls. Now it was esteemed mainly for its healthy amber trade. Carnuntum was nominally part of the Western Empire, but in truth it was a border settlement, with my legions stationed just a half-day's march to the west and Galerius' a similar distance to the east. I saw how the city's towers and gates had been draped with purple insignias and banners and noticed a group of bronze-clad buccinators atop the towers.

Today, Carnuntum would serve as a neutral ground – a no-man's land of sorts. I could not help but liken what was to come with the moments before battle when opposing generals discuss resolution by peaceable means. *Resolution,* I mouthed. Indeed, in the many days of riding to the river's upper stretches, then the voyage downriver that followed, I had thought of little else. For today, I was to be officially recognised as true Augustus of the West, as Father had been before me. The buccinators on Carnuntum's towers erupted in a heralding chorus, the imperious tune bolstering my thoughts.

A shiver of excitement leapt across my skin, despite my thick winter garb and the ever-present bear pelt. By nightfall, Galerius would no longer be a threat: the Herdsman would have to attest his acceptance of me as his western counterpart. Diocletian would then return to his retirement palace. The succession troubles would be over. I even let my thoughts turn to what my next steps might be – a conciliatory hand across the Alpes to Maxentius, perhaps? My one-time friend certainly did not lack intelligence, and surely he would see sense in complying with the decisions made today. This kindled a few fond memories of better times we had shared, and it almost brought a smile to my lips... until my gaze snagged on something.

A waddling figure, ambling towards the prow, hands clasped behind his back. Maximian had emerged from whatever corner of this vessel he had been hiding in. The old man had piled on weight since arriving at Treverorum, and had now regained the look of a portly sot. He had been quiet during his time in my city, and that was all I could ask. More, Fausta had seemed buoyed by his presence. She was no fool, as I am sure you realise by now – as clever as her brother, at least – and she knew her father's flaws only too well, but she fawned over him nonetheless.

I wondered if Maxentius had heard of my sheltering of his father and wondered more how the temporary Keeper of Rome felt about this. Angered? Almost certainly. But I hoped that, when the anger faded, he would realise that I had done us both a favour: under a tight bridle within my palace, Maximian could be watched. More, Maxentius would not have to worry about him wandering around Italia with his tattered band, stoking trouble and sowing dissent.

That was my thinking anyway – until the Carnuntum scroll had been delivered. A momentary hope, followed by a swirl of confusion when I saw who was to attend: myself, Diocletian, Galerius... and Maximian. At first I had read that last name swiftly and assumed that Maxentius had been invited. Perhaps there were grounds for him to be installed as my Caesar? We could work together as we had so often in the past. The possibilities had blossomed in my mind. But no, not Maxentius. *Maximian.* The retired Augustus of the West had been summoned instead. There was no place at this event for the Keeper of Rome. And what troubled me more was how Maximian had just this morning opted not for his grey woollen robes, but for an opulent purple gown. His hooded eyes had always given the impression that he knew more than he was letting on. This time, they seemed more hooded than ever.

The buccinas blared again. This time it was a shiver of doubt that crossed my skin.

When we came to the dock, a line of Joviani legionaries in ceremonial armour emerged from the dock gates and onto the wharf then greeted us with a fanfare of salutes. Batius, Maximian and I disembarked then waited on the three centuries of the Sixth to form up with us. I noticed how the air almost crackled with tension as my scarlet-shielded legionaries shared stony glances with the Joviani in their pale blue regalia. *It couldn't happen, could it?* The thought had crossed my mind like a persistent hornet with every day of travel towards this place. *What if Diocletian plans to end the strife in the most time-honoured of fashions? What if he or the Herdsman has brought not a few hundred men but a thousand?* My three centuries would not save me if this was the case. I imagined then a full cohort of Joviani waiting inside the gates, ready to fall upon us, slit our throats then dump our bodies in the Danubius. The chill in the air seemed to have intensified.

The gates opened and we were led inside. No ambush. Just a babble of voices from the populace within, who hushed and parted, the sea of faces gazing at us intently. As we passed under the gatehouse, Batius leaned a little closer to me so only I could hear. 'I don't like this. Something's not right...'

If I had felt a tense chill at the docks, then the air in the meeting hall the following day seemed to be as dense and cold as ice. The heat from the torches that crackled in sconces on the walls barely registered as I stood there in the doorway, flanked by

Batius and a pair of my legionaries. My eyes searched through the crowd of fine-robed officials and nobility: senators, ambassadors and high-born men. A few Joviani legionaries were stationed around the sides of the room.

Then I saw the focal point of the affair, my eyes locking onto the pair I had not seen together for over three years: Diocletian and Galerius. They sat there on their twin thrones upon the dais like so many times before. They were not painted in silver and gold as they once had been, though perhaps this would have been desirable, for it might have masked the ravages of time. Diocletian was withered, painfully shrunken, his wispy hair now all-white. His twitching cheek and trembling hands were all too apparent and he was erupting in little fits of absent laughter to himself no matter how serious the faces of those around him. And his eyes? They were more lost than ever. The great Jove was approaching his final days, surely. I wondered if it was a combination of this and perhaps one last bout of penance too, for his misdemeanours of years past, which had brought him to attempt a peaceable resolution to the troubles.

Galerius, by his side, did not look much healthier – now even more pallid, drawn and misshapen than when I had faced him at the frozen pass. The pair did not notice me at first, continuing some fraught debate over the issue of religious persecution; it seemed that the Herdsman had taken to burning and torturing Christians once again, and his subjects had railed against this.

'Let them burn, let them riot... Their God will die with them!' Galerius said through gritted, yellowing teeth, one fist clenched. I noticed blood on his gums.

Some of the senatorial types around him piped up in agreement, only for a brave few to squabble against the notion. I gestured to Batius and the two legionaries, who read my signal and waited by the door while I stepped forward into the hall.

Diocletian waved a trembling hand through the air as if in dispute with the Herdsman. 'But their God only grows stronger,' he said weakly, then moved his lips to continue.

'Then strong men are needed to oppose them and their God!' Galerius snapped. Diocletian visibly shrank at the bitter retort. I wondered then just how much of a willing participant the frail old emperor was in this gathering. The thought chilled me more than my earlier fears that he might have brought legions to slay me. 'They claim that death is not the end, well, when there are none of them left—'

He stopped mid-sentence, his gaze switching round to me. Diocletian followed suit. The Herdsman's eyes held no hint of welcome. It was only to be expected though, I assured myself. This meeting was never going to be a reunion of old friends.

A hush descended as all eyes in the room momentarily fell upon me. It was only now I noticed the wolfish Daia amongst them, standing with a pair of personal guards. Galerius' dark-haired underling now bore white flashes at his temples – time had marched for him too, it seemed. He was speaking with a fat-faced, short-haired man in his fifties – a fellow who wore a look of unbridled superiority. Licinius, one of Galerius' many acolytes, I realised, recalling his face from previous engagements. As the hubbub of discussion picked up again around me, I turned my attentions back to Diocletian and Galerius.

'Domini,' I said, genuflecting towards the pair. Maximian echoed my greeting.

'Ah, Constantine,' Diocletian said in a feeble tone, beckoning me. I stepped forward to the foot of the dais with

Maximian by my side. The crowd parted before us. 'It has been some time. Much has happened in the years since last we spoke.'

'Indeed, Domine. Some of it regrettable, though much of it—' I flicked my gaze to Galerius '—necessary.'

Galerius laughed dryly, then clutched at his lower belly as if racked with pain. 'You should learn to mask your contempt in front of your betters, especially when you do not have your legions to shield you.'

The Herdsman and I remained locked in a fiery gaze as Diocletian welcomed Maximian. 'Shall we proceed?' Galerius said at last, clicking his fingers.

At this, Diocletian stood, a guard helping him rise, then waved Daia over to the foot of the dais. 'We are gathered here to discuss a peaceable end to the troubles of late.'

Daia stood by my other side, shooting me a disdainful sidelong look, his nose wrinkling.

'The Tetrarchy was designed to bring stability to the empire,' Diocletian continued. 'Yet of late it has been used as a ladder for the ambitious.'

I felt a sting in his words, but convinced myself they were aimed more at the absent Maxentius.

'And today, we must end the uncertainty. Today, each of us here will bear witness to the true tetrarchs, and uphold and support each man in his rightful position.'

I nodded guardedly. Diocletian's words could not be faulted.

'The East will remain under the stewardship of Galerius as Augustus, with Daia as his Caesar.'

'Domine,' the pair said.

'The West has been guided by many hands in these last years.'

My heart thumped under my robes as Diocletian gazed down upon me.

'Constantius ruled well until his death. Severus' reign was short and brutally ended. The one responsible for his death is not here, and nor shall he be recognised by any part of the empire as a legitimate ruler. This *Princeps Invictus,* as he calls himself, is naught but a maggot, festering in the flesh of the decaying capital, reaping the grain of Africa and poisoning the minds of the legions in his lands. Shamefully, having overseen the slaying of Severus, he then masterminded the unjust attack upon Galerius – the *senior* Augustus, no less – and the legions that marched for Rome in an effort to free the city from his tyranny.'

Galerius nodded knowingly, almost righteously, as Diocletian spoke.

'He has attacked the tetrarchic system, its true leaders and its people. Thus, he is to be known from this day forth... as an *enemy of the empire. An enemy of Rome!* Just as he cast his father into exile, *he* is now the outcast.'

Cheers erupted from the onlookers.

At that moment, I closed my eyes and saw my old friend in the darkness, imagined the great blade of Damocles dangling over his head. *But when I am confirmed as master of the West, I can remedy this,* I mused. And I was sure it could be done. Though a part of me, a tiny morsel of my being, hidden in a dark, forgotten corner wondered: *Why should I care about Maxentius? He has become an arrogant man and I owe him nothing. Nothing!*

'And so, the maggot will be cleansed from the imperial flesh. But to do so, the West needs strong rulers.'

I stood tall. By my side, Maximian also straightened. And it was Maximian that Diocletian addressed first.

'Old comrade, once we ruled as brothers,' Diocletian said, his eyes glassy as if recalling those distant days before the black years of the persecutions.

'Aye, that we did, Domine,' Maximian agreed, his chest swelling as if preparing to accept a purple robe on his shoulders. *What was this?* I thought, my anger kindling.

'But our day is past,' Diocletian added.

Maximian's shoulders and face fell.

'After today's gathering I shall return to retirement. I shall tend my fine vegetable garden at the palace near Salona and enjoy every day the gods bless me with. This, too, must be your path.'

Diocletian said no more. I saw from the corner of my eye Maximian's pale, aged features sag further, and I thought for that moment that his spirit was broken. Then he bowed and said: 'So it shall be, Domine.'

I might have believed him – indeed, my anger faded – were it not for the faint rising of his lips. Perhaps it was only me who noticed it. Perhaps it was my imagination. But it was the embers of a smirk that said he was most certainly not finished with his business in imperial circles. My musings were scattered when Diocletian turned his rheumy gaze upon me.

'Constantine, I call upon you before all in this chamber, before all in the empire…'

This was the moment. The pretenders were absent or had been denounced. All I had sought lay right before me. Legitimacy. The means to ensure that no man could take from me, no man could harm those I loved. Power. Undisputed power.

'… to relinquish your claim as Augustus of the West.'

I blinked. A babble of intrigue rang out all around me.

But I was numb to it. The blood running through my heart turned icy cold. A nausea squeezed my gut. I noticed Galerius watching me, a sickly grin etched on his wan features. I saw how Diocletian looked to the Herdsman, as if for approval, which was given in the form of a contented nod. Diocletian's lips flapped as he continued, but I heard only snippets of it. Licinius, the fat-faced man whom Daia had been talking to before, strode up the steps of the dais, beckoned by Diocletian. I saw from the corner of my eye Daia bristle at this.

But Diocletian handed the fat-faced one a fresh purple cloak. 'Gaius Valerius Licinianus Licinius, from this day forward, you are to be Augustus of the West. Constantine will be your loyal Caesar.'

A roar of dispute broke out amongst the crowd.

I heard Daia's protests now as he flicked up a hand towards Licinius in ire. 'This man is not even a tetrarch, yet he leaps ahead of me to become an Augustus?'

My lips moved as if to add my protest, but no sound emerged.

The crowd swamped round the foot of the dais. Daia's two guards hurried to flank him. Swords were half-drawn and Joviani legionaries rushed into the crowd too in an effort to calm the sudden strife. I backed away, noticing how Galerius' sickly grin remained, his bloodshot eyes pinning me through the chaos. I felt that ethereal sword swing from Maxentius' head to mine and back again, like a dead man on a noose. I was to be demoted to Caesar of the West? Was this Galerius' idea of a wry gift for sparing him in the icy passes of Noricum? Or was he simply positioning me for his assassins? Dread gripped me as I backed towards the door. The only thing I could be sure of was that if I agreed to this, then I would be the pawn once more, my fate in their hands. Galerius and yet another of his dogs, Licinius, would be my masters, not my equals. And the look on Galerius' face told me all I needed to know about what he had in mind for me. The chaotic shouting and dispute around the dais had grown so loud that the room shook.

I had almost backed off to the door, when a fury overcame me.

'I *refuse!*' I roared.

The words cut through the squabbling. All heads turned to me, eyes wide. Licinius, red-faced from arguing his case. Daia, his features wrinkled in deep, dark ruts of anger. Maximian, watching with those hooded, unreadable eyes. Diocletian, his expression pale and bewildered. Galerius, leaning forward on his throne, the grin now bestial.

Was this why I had truly been called here – to provoke this reaction from me? Not to confirm my role as Augustus but to rob me of it and rile me into defying the ruling of the conference?

Diocletian gazed through me.

'You... *refuse?*' Galerius hissed.

'The West is in my stewardship and there it shall remain,' I replied, a flash of ire in my voice.

Galerius roared with laughter at this. 'The West is in turmoil, you fool. You have meddled in affairs there for years now and still it remains a mess.'

I ignored the Herdsman and met every other eye in the room. 'The West is mine, and you know this.' I swept a finger across all of them. '*All* of you.'

With that, I turned my back on them and strode from the chamber, Batius and my two men rushing to screen me. I barely noticed Maximian coming with me too.

'Sir?' Batius said, unease tightening his voice, his eyes darting back to the meeting hall, now shrinking as we strode through the corridor that would take us from the palace. I looked back too, seeing those around the dais eye me as a venue of vultures might ogle a lame goat. A pack of Joviani legionaries seemed poised, ready to come after us. 'We have to get to our centuries.'

'They would not dare harm us. *They would not dare!*' I growled. In truth, my insides were melting with white-hot terror, sure the Herdsman's legions might do just as I had feared – slit our throats and toss us in the Danubius. But they did not come after us, and as we left the palace, swept through the streets and gates then were reunited with our centuries on the wharf, I tried to put shape to what had just happened.

'And I thought you were a shrewd man,' a voice said as we boarded the bireme.

I turned with a scowl to see Maximian, munching on a leg of goose he had taken from the hall, beholding me as a cat might eye a bowl of cream. 'What?' I snapped.

'You walked right into their trap,' he said, shaking his head as the flotilla departed Carnuntum's docks under power of oar. 'I knew nothing of what they had planned,' he added quickly, palms up as if to pacify me, 'but I quickly saw what they had in store for you.'

'Speak cogently or shut your mouth!' I hissed.

'Think about it,' he said, tapping his fleshy temple. 'They... *he*, backed you into a corner, knowing how you would react.'

I closed my eyes. Had my temper beaten me again?

'What are your options now?' Maximian pressed.

I strode away from him and over to the prow then gazed upriver in an effort to disguise my anger. I saw in my mind's eye a map of the Western Empire – Africa and Italia in the grasp of the pretender who was once my friend. I saw Maxentius' face, stern and unforgiving, gazing upon me like those dogs back in the meeting hall. His hold over Italia and Africa was a stain on the western lands and it validated the claim that I was unfit to serve as Augustus of that realm. Then I saw Galerius' sickly grin and imagined his glee at the *casus belli* I had cast down in that meeting hall by my refusal to stand down. I imagined the cur's sermons to his numerous legions as he readied to march upon my lands. *To slay the false Augustus!*

Maximian was right, I realised. I now had a choice of poisons: to stand down and throw myself at the mercy of Galerius and this Licinius; to continue to defy them from my lands in Gaul, Britannia and Hispania and face the wrath of their combined forces for such defiance; or to prove them wrong... by crushing Maxentius and seizing control of the West absolutely.

'What now, sir?' Batius said, coming alongside me.

'Now, the talking ends, Batius. Now, I will no longer wait for scheming men to bequeath my rightful titles upon me nor will I cower on my borders in fear that they might come to take my lands. Now, we sharpen our blades and march from our forts.'

'Sir?' Batius persisted.

'Didn't you hear what happened in there?' I growled, stabbing a finger back towards the shrinking outline of Carnuntum. 'They knew I would not stand down. They knew I would refuse. They want a war, Batius.' I grabbed the big man by the collar of his tunic.

'A *war!*'

Epilogue

ROME, 18TH NOVEMBER 308 AD

I stood in the shadowed marble glory of the private Palatine basilica, sombre and silent, in the company of only those who held power within the city and my increasingly isolated domain. Outside, the world continued as it had done before, as though nothing had changed. The huge three-day Plebeian Market festival had begun that morning and already the clamour and din of the city was inescapable even in this serene, darkened hall. I had attended the opening ceremony a few hours previously and received the adoration of the people, despite the undercurrent of rumour that Rome had again been disenfranchised by the Tetrarchy and that we stood alone.

If I stood alone, I did it alongside a million other souls.

I looked around at the gathered faces. In such a short time since donning the purple, they had become an integral part of my world, as much as any hearth or wall. Some had been with me since the start, others had risen to the fore in more recent days, yet all were the foundation stones of my rule.

Publius Anullinus, in his Guard commander's uniform, gleaming and martial, his auburn hair and beard close-cropped.

My Praetorian Prefect, my first ally and supporter in this city and in this great endeavour. A man who had stood by me time and again and even now remained strong, showing no sign of nerves.

Caeionius Rufius Volusianus, former Governor of Africa and now my Dux Militum, dressed in a toga, his hair shaggy and with that wild look that was clearly the product of half an hour with body slave and styling tongs, his beard curled tightly. With his dark skin tone, he could be another Septimius Severus and, like that ancient great soldier-emperor, he gave off an aura of extraordinary military strength.

He was my sword as Anullinus was my shield.

Ruricius Pompeianus, the commander of the imperial horse guard, in uniform and wearing his usual severe expression beneath dark eyebrows that sat at odds with his short, golden hair. Since our early days of coolness to one another, Pompeianus had become something of a fixture in the palace as he had taken it upon himself to teach Romulus the art of the sword.

Romulus.

My son stood at my side. He wore his tunic and gold *bulla* locket, signifying his status as a child, though that would change in the coming months. For all his attire, he was clearly already a man. Had I missed so much of his growing up that he'd seemed to switch almost magically from the one to the other? My son. The centre of my world and my reason for all. He seemed pensive; and well he might, given the situation.

Aurelius Zenas, the praetor and de-facto commander of my Urban Cohorts and a man who had re-created what had been a defunct and corrupt organisation as an efficient, loyal and proud force. His Roman nose and hairstyle did nothing to hide his clear Greek origins, and when he spoke it was with a thick accent, but his tongue was as still today as everyone else's.

Sempronius Clemens, the head of my frumentarii, disbanded by the Tetrarchy but thriving in my city and responsible for much of my intelligence regarding my opponents. A man who simply by his choice of career should not be trusted, and yet in whom I had placed my faith, forced thus by necessity. Without Clemens I would know little of what was happening outside our borders.

Seven of us standing silent and dour in that shadowy, echoing hall. Myself, my son and five warriors who constituted my advisors and personal council. Telling, perhaps, that all those upon whom I relied were soldiers.

It had been seven days since the conference at Carnuntum, and still no news. Clemens had assured me that his men who had been there among the military guard of Daia – do not ask me how he had managed such a thing – should have been back in Rome with the news two days ago. He had secured the Cursus Publicus so that his man could make for Rome on horse relay, and had been firm that, even allowing for unexpected problems, the man should not take more than five days to reach our gates from Carnuntum.

It had been seven, and Clemens was at least as twitchy as I.

Our attention was drawn back to the centre of the basilica, where the haruspex had finally finished his intonations, accompanied by the muted sad sounds of the ritual pipe-playing from the room's corner. A white sheep lay on the temporary altar slab, its legs bound, eyes rolling, but now still after much struggling had rendered it exhausted. Zenas closed his eyes for a moment and I saw his lips moving in prayer. He could be as Christian as he liked in my domain, but no amount of disapproval for such divination would excuse him from attending at such a moment.

The blade came down and I realised that I was holding my breath.

The sheep bucked and thrashed as its lifeblood poured out onto the stone in a flood. With expert cuts, the haruspex ensured that no arterial spray touched the attending masters of Rome.

We watched in tense silence as the man intoned further ritual words and then took his knife and his fingers and got to work opening up the sheep from below. The haruspex was careful to work from such an angle that those of us attending the divination could all see what he saw, so as to be in no doubt as to the truth of his findings.

Which is why I know that what we saw was no trick, and no fakery.

The innards slithered out from the opened carcass as the sheep finally expired and shuddered to stillness. The haruspex had his arms inside to the elbows now, carefully sliding his hands around internal organs, and already the bulk were out and slipping around in the gore on the slab.

And among the grey-pink innards, tiny fragments of metal caught the light from the lamps and braziers around the room, glittering and reflecting the glow. Dozens of tiny steel fragments. Zenas was busy making his *cross* signs and had paled visibly. The others were equally shocked, their expressions reflecting the clear dreadfulness of such an omen.

The haruspex removed his hands, the knife shaking, his eyes wide as he looked down at the tiny fragments of metal. How they had got inside a sacred sheep that had been reared in seclusion for this very purpose was unfathomable. His lips quivered as his sacred intonations died on his tongue.

'What does it mean?' I whispered in the echoing chamber.

The man's lips flapped silently for a moment as he stared in horror at the animal's metal-studded entrails, and finally his voice reappeared, hollow and quiet.

'Steel is approaching. Much steel will be revealed in the coming days. Steel in the gut. *Killing* steel. Steel that will bring death and destruction. These fragments are the serried ranks of your enemy, Domine, and the sheep is Rome.'

I nodded bleakly. I had assumed as much. Thank all the gods we had decided to make this divination a private matter and not held it in the forum or on the Capitol. There would have been panic on an unprecedented scale. I pulled myself together as best I could.

'No hint of this leaves the palace.'

Volusianus exhaled quietly and I saw his fingers play on the pommel of the sword at his side. I knew that he would do what was necessary to stop knowledge of this leaking out. I felt for the haruspex and the musician, who would be silenced for the good of the city, but I would not stop it. My eyes took in the dreadful omen on the slab and the pool of blood that surrounded it, and followed the rivulet that had already poured from the raised stone and down to the floor of the basilica. It came as no surprise to see that the slow-flowing stream of crimson was snaking its way towards my feet. I needed no haruspex to translate *that* for me.

Pinching the bridge of my nose, I turned from the grisly sight and walked to the door that led into the *Aula Regia* – my audience chamber and throne room on the Palatine. I could hear the boots of my companions following me, each man lost in his own shocked silence. Not all of them, though, for I heard the brief cry as the haruspex met his quick, efficient end on the tip of a Praetorian blade, closely followed by the young musician.

No one would tell what had happened here.

At my command, the doors were opened by the Guardsmen outside, and I was surprised to see a man standing in the centre of that great audience chamber, which had seen the best and the worst of Rome's rulers issue commands.

I had not set eyes on the warped homunculus Ancharius Pansa in over a year. The frumentarius who had worked among my enemies' commands for so many months was exhausted and travel-worn, filthy and stinking.

I cared not, because the expression on his ugly face was less pleasant than any other aspect could ever be.

'Carnuntum?'

The others were with me now, Volusianus hurrying to catch up, wiping his sword on a torn piece of the haruspex's robe, sheathing it and dropping the bloody cloth in the shadowed hall before stepping out into the light with us, the guards closing the doors on the scene of butchery.

Pansa nodded, his face bleak, one eye regarding me darkly, the other as ever immobile.

'Tell me.'

'Domine,' the squat spy began with his strange silvery tone, 'the Tetrarchy has been confirmed by order of the great Diocletian and ratified by his peers.' The man twitched. *I* was supposedly one of those peers, after all. I simply waited for him to continue. 'Galerius and Daia retain their positions in the East. Your father has been forced to relinquish all claims. One Gaius Valerius Licinianus Licinius, a former aide of Galerius' has been acclaimed as Augustus of the West, with Constantine as his Caesar, though *he* refused to accept the decision.'

I blinked. I had somehow expected my father to weasel in as the Caesar to Constantine's Augustus but I had not considered even for a moment that the old emperors might try to drop Constantine to a lesser role. I could imagine my old friend's reaction – that fiery temper that lay dormant much of the time beneath a calm shell exploding at such treatment by men he despised. Not that it would likely improve my own position.

My thoughts churned as I realised that my situation was becoming ever more isolated. Galerius and two of his cronies now officially ran the empire. Constantine would either be forced to accept the decision, or would prepare himself for war. Could an accommodation be reached? Were we now in a position where standing united against three of the tetrarchs was possible?

I shook my head at the thought. Constantine had not accepted a role as the junior Caesar even from the hand of Diocletian himself, whose decision no military commander or senator would deny. The only hope I could have that he might join me against the others would be to renounce my own claim to Augustus and become his junior. And even if I considered that an option – which I did not, given my stronger claim to the purple – I had little doubt that the support of my military advisors would melt away should I defer to him, possibly even turn on me. And Africa would probably shift its support.

No. As long as I lived and ruled in Rome, I had to be Augustus. And as long as I claimed that role, Constantine would not throw his support behind me. I had learned that lesson hard as my old friend had failed to come to my aid and stop Galerius those months previously.

Whatever the man truly thought of me now, he was no

more my friend or my ally than Galerius, who hated me, or Daia, who apparently considered me an upstart, or this Licinius, to whom I was an impediment, or Diocletian, who clearly thought me nothing at all since I was not even required at their summit. Constantine and I may not have been at war, but nor were we confederates.

And if he finally accepted the decision, which it seemed he must, then Constantine would become their attack dog, in an attempt to achieve what Severus and Galerius could not.

No friends, just different grades of enemy.

'There is more,' Pansa coughed in a troubled voice. I waited, my face carefully blank.

'Because your investiture to the purple has not been ratified or accepted by any of the new Tetrarchy, Domine, you have...' he looked down for a moment, steadying himself before raising his eyes to mine '...been declared an enemy of Rome, "to be hunted and removed by all loyal sons of the empire." Their words, Domine, not mine.'

I closed my eyes. Not just a nothing, then. Not a usurper to be faced across a field of steel and flesh. A criminal. Less than nothing. An enemy of *Rome*!

How could I be the enemy of Rome? While the tetrarchs had cared nothing for the city and had let it crumble as they glorified their distant cities, I had re-created Rome in glory. I was the *saviour* of Rome. The *protector* of Rome. I was the *emperor* of Rome!

Aurelius Zenas cleared his throat. 'There is another solution, Domine, however distasteful. Renounce the purple and seek the support of Constantine. You might be permitted to retire with your heir.'

Anullinus and Volusianus turned baleful glares on their colleague, confirming my suspicions as to what might happen if I deferred to Constantine, but Zenas' face said it all. He didn't want me to do that, but he felt it his duty to clarify my only chance of escaping what was to come, for my family's sake if not for my own. Christians always seemed to have a knack of bringing it down to family in the end.

'No.'

I turned in surprise at the single, flat word, to see Romulus regarding me with a stubborn expression and a set jaw. That stubbornness so deeply bred into our line seemed finally to be exhibiting itself in my son. He brandished one of the chalcedony sceptres that were my symbol of office as though beating down our enemies with it, and the fire of resistance blazed in his eyes.

Slowly, I straightened and squared my shoulders.

'Then an enemy I shall be; but not an enemy of Rome, for those who would remove me are the *true* enemies of Rome. News of this will soon reach every corner of the empire. We must look to our defences and to our subjects' loyalties. Volusianus, have your successor in Africa confirm his allegiance and that of his province and his forces. Anullinus, look to the control of the city and the readiness of the Guard. Clemens, have your frumentarii move among the enemy as much as possible. I want to know a great deal more of this Licinius, and of Constantine's intentions.'

As the men nodded their acceptance of the tasks I had assigned, I took a deep breath.

'The world has set itself against us, gentlemen. War is coming, but Rome will prevail.'

Rome *would* prevail. And so would I.

* Here ends book one *

Historical Note

Part 1 – the world of the late 3rd/early 4th century

Constantine and Maxentius were born into an empire that had suffered over half a century of turmoil. The third-century crisis, as it is known, saw new emperors raised from the armies to the throne almost yearly, their short reigns ended more often than not on the end of the blades of the bodyguards who replaced them. This instability bled the imperial coffers dry and resulted in horrifically debased coinage. Outbreaks of plague played their part in rocking the empire to its core and then enemy invasions from Persia and Gothia were compounded by a revolt and the formation of a splinter empire in Gaul and Britannia.

Diocletian may have had the best intentions when he established the Tetrarchy in order to predetermine succession and end the successionist wars. On paper, it seems like a good approach. However, any system is only as strong as the people who use it, and the people involved in the first decades of the Tetrarchy brought some of the most dangerous of human qualities: greed, ambition, jealousy and bitter agendas. Galerius is offered little sympathy from contemporary chroniclers and modern historians (the biggest compliment he is paid is that he was a good military leader – though there are recorded examples of his failings on the battlefield), and there is much suggestion that he used his influence over

Diocletian to firstly clamber aboard the tetrarchic system and then to instigate the Edict of Christian Persecution.

In the time of our story, Christianity had been on the rise for centuries, spreading mainly through the urban centres of the empire, particularly the great port-cities. Viewed as a humane religion, it did not permit the aborting of unborn babies or the killing of female children (something common within the old Roman religion). Quite possibly the third-century crisis helped drive people towards this new faith. But the big problem with Christianity was that, unlike the old gods, it demanded of its worshippers no loyalty to the emperor. This was seen as a clear threat by the tetrarchic incumbents of Diocletian's time, and resulted in the brutal wave of torture and slaughter depicted within our tale. It should be noted, however, that some accounts of the persecutions are written in retrospect by the jaundiced eye of devout Christians (Lactantius being a prominent example).

As always, we have employed a little author's licence here and there, and it is our duty to advise and discuss such matters here. The meeting of our two protagonists in Treverorum in 286 AD is speculative, though entirely plausible, as Constantine's father was probably present in Treverorum at this time to witness Maximian's raising as Diocletian's co-Augustus. The later meeting at Maxentius' wedding in Sirmium is also speculative but credible. The portrayal of Diocletian burning his wife is strongly believed to be apocryphal, but it served as a succinct metaphor for the empire's self-destructive tendencies in those brutal times. The death of the Deacon of Caesarea Maritima did not occur until 17th November 303 AD, a year or so after we have described his demise. Our detail of Constantine's flight from Galerius' court in Nicomedia to seek shelter with his father in

Britannia is unashamedly panegyric in its nature, telling of his sole survival through blizzards and uninhabited wilderness. It is more likely that he fled with the company of a strong escort of soldiers and enjoyed a warm bed most nights.

These aspects aside, the timeline and the events of the rest of the story are as true as we could align them to a history that required little tweaking to add drama or tension. Constantine and Maxentius were indeed drawn into the chaotic world of the Tetrarchy and soon found themselves at its apex, staring across the Alps at one another, faced with war.

Part 2 – Maxentius

Evidence for Maxentius in terms of both actions and personality are extremely rare. Even secondary texts for him are few and far between. Physical evidence for his reign is little better. Most of his buildings were later claimed by Constantine and are remembered for him (barring the villa on the Via Appia and the basilica in the forum.) Most of his statues were re-chiselled into the likeness of Constantine (it is now believed that the fragments of the 'colossus of Constantine' kept on the Capitoline, were originally parts of a statue of Maxentius that was altered after 312.)

And what little evidence we have in primary sources for the life of Maxentius is at best suspect, if not downright lies. Maxentius was a pagan emperor in the manner of his forebears, while the history of this troubled time was written by Christian writers after the fact, who naturally demonise and vilify Constantine's opposition.

To some extent this makes piecing together what happens on Maxentius' side of this great shake-up of the Roman world much more difficult. Huge leaps in logic and judgement are required even to settle on basic matters (did he have a beard or not? The few statues seem to vary.) Creating a timeline for Maxentius is troublesome. And, of course, while Constantine gallivants around the world raising armies and fleeing traps, Maxentius essentially sits at Rome becoming steadily more troubled and isolated. Not an easy situation in which to build a gripping tale.

But, every hill has a downside and an upside. The upside of Maxentius' sparse details is that the writer is given a great deal of licence in his portrayal of the character and events. Consequently, we have built an image of Maxentius based on logic and assumption, trying to throw out anything that seems to be clearly based on later Christian propaganda. When the chaff is cleared from his reputation, what seems to remain is a very traditional, pacific, family figure who finds himself in the midst of a maelstrom of troubles. And thus was the Maxentius of this tale born. Take a look at the few remaining busts of the man (we know of only around half a dozen surviving) and we suspect you will see our Maxentius gazing out from the marble.

A mention must be made about Anullinus. The name causes some confusion in the time of Constantine and Maxentius' troubles. There are suggestions that the Anullinus who is recorded as a Praetorian Prefect is the same Anullinus who had been Governor of Africa and Urban Prefect (Gaius Annius Anullinus). Chastignol and Barnes both suggest, though, that the two men were brothers and not the same person. It is this approach we have chosen, naming our protagonist Publius Anullinus to distinguish him from Gaius Annius. We have by necessity minimised Gaius Annius Anullinus' role in the entire affair for clarity of plot and ease of reading.

Part 3 – Constantine

The sources portray Constantine as an enigmatic character and this presents a tricky but welcome challenge for a writer. What little personal detail we have of him is contradictory: devoted to his loved ones – particularly his mother and his first wife, Minervina – but also capable of showing ruthless ambition and aggression when required. In this respect, we have chosen to represent him as a man driven to protect his precious few by any means necessary. Indeed, in the short spell with his mother and Minervina in Antioch he does find tranquillity for a period... only for the persecutions to ruin everything. Quite possibly it was this and his wife's death (it is likely that Minervina died of eclampsia during childbirth) that escalated his propensity for boldness and rashness in later years.

Constantine's father, Constantius, is described as a man of noble lineage, but this was most likely grafted retrospectively onto historical records by Constantine himself in an effort to portray an aristocratic heritage where there was none. This indicates a sensitivity about his origins, and our depiction of Constantine's bitter shame at his mother's estrangement (an effective statement of her and his illegitimacy) is designed to support this theory.

Constantius 'Chlorus', or 'The Pale One', is thought to have suffered from some long-term ailment, and modern historians believe this was a cancer. Whether he was aware of the terminal nature of his illness or not, he lived and ruled Britannia and Gaul until that day in Eboracum in July 306 AD, when he finally succumbed. This was the moment when Constantine's destiny was defined. The troops hailed and raised him, and he truly seized the moment. By accepting the purple, he probably saw at last a means of protecting his loved ones and ridding himself of the threats that had hovered around him for so many years. Also, it presented him with the chance to write his own history and crush the rumours of his perceived illegitimacy.

In this book we have only brushed upon Constantine's stance on Christianity with allusions (in the prologue) to his 'vision' on the eve of the Milvian Bridge and Maxentius' observations of the odd, seemingly Christian emblems on Constantine's shields the next day during the battle. The meaning behind these things and the progress of Constantine's 'journey' will come into sharper focus in the remainder of the tale.

Constantine and Maxentius' story is not yet complete. Book two 'Masters of Rome' will be coming soon, and we hope you will join us and immerse yourself in the pivotal years of history that are to come. In the meantime, we'd be delighted to hear your ideas, thoughts or questions, and you can contact us at our websites, below.

Best Wishes,
Gordon Doherty (Constantine) & S. J. A. Turney (Maxentius)
www.gordondoherty.co.uk   www.sjaturney.co.uk

Glossary of Latin Terms

Acclamatio – The formal recognition of a new emperor.

Adventus – Ceremony held to celebrate the arrival of an emperor into a city.

Alban – One of ancient Italia's three great wine regions, immediately south of Rome.

Aureus (Aurei) – Gold coin, the highest denomination currency of Rome.

Balneae – Private baths or bathing complexes in houses, villas and palaces.

Barritus – War cry, specific to the Germanic peoples.

Bireme – Roman galley, both military and civilian, with two rows of oars.

Buccina – Curved horn used by the military for signalling and issuing of commands.

Bulla – Amulet worn by Roman boys until their coming of age.

Campidoctores – Legionary officers tasked with training the ranks.

Capitolium – A temple dedicated to the main Roman deities.

Castellum – Detached fort or defensive site, often used as a signal station or bridge-head.

Casus Belli – 'Cause of War'. The justification for attacking an enemy.

Cataphractii – Persian heavy cavalry completely covered in armour, both horse and man.

Consul – One of the two highest administrative positions in Rome, below the emperor.

Consulares – Provincial governor, originally the role of an ex-consul.

Contubernium (plural contubernia) – The smallest unit formation of the army, eight men sharing a tent.

Cornu (plural cornua) – 'G' shaped horn used in imperial games and ceremony.

Correctores – Senatorial officers with specific command to reform provincial administration.

Cosmeta – the slave or servant of a lady who applied make-up, tended coiffure and dealt with accessories.

Cubicularius – An imperial chamberlain.

Curator Aedium Sacrorum – Official responsible for the upkeep of Rome's religious monuments.

Curator Aquarum – Official responsible for the maintenance of Rome's water system.

Curia – The senate-house of Rome, located at the west end of the forum, beneath the Capitol.

Cursus Honorum – The ladder of positions a Roman nobleman was expected to climb.

Cursus Publicus – The empire's state-run system of couriers and transportation.

Decurion – Roman cavalry officer in command of a *turma* of 30 riders.

Dies Natalis Urbis Romae – festival honouring the founding of the city of Rome.

Dimachaerus – A gladiator bearing two swords.

Dominus/Domine – 'Master'.

Derafsh Kaviani – Legendary royal standard of the Sassanian Persian kings.

Equisio – Individual assigned to the care, supply and grooming of horses.

Equites – Cavalrymen of the empire. Originally a term for Rome's noble 'knight' class.

Exploratores – Scouts and reconnaissance riders of the Roman military.

Fabrica – Military workshops of the empire, often manned by the soldiers themselves.

Fibula – Brooch.

Frumentarii – 'Grain men.' Imperial agents who moved from unit to unit on clandestine business.

Haruspex – Individual trained in divination by reading the entrails of a sacrificial animal.

Horreum (plural horrea) – Granaries built on raised platforms to allow air circulation and prevent rot.

Imperator – Emperor.

Insula – Roman apartment block, often of many storeys, with shops in the ground floor.

Kathisma – Greek term for the imperial box at an entertainment venue. Cf. *pulvinar*.

Lanciarii – Term applied to various unit types, all armed with the *lancea* – a thrusting spear.

Lanista – Gladiator trainer or owner.

Latrunculi – 'Bandits.' A board game similar to *Draughts* or *Go*, played with stones on a grid.

Lemures – Restless malevolent spirits of the dead in the Roman world.

Loricate – 'Armoured'. Term used to describe a man wearing, or statue depicted in, armour.

Ludus Magnus – The great gladiator school in Rome.

Medicus – Term applied to doctors in both the military and civilian spheres.

Murmillo – a class of gladiator with a high-crested helmet, usually covering the face with a mesh, a gladius and a shield.

Numerus (plural numera) – A small, irregular military unit, outside the army's standard organisation.

Obstetrix/Obstetrices – Midwives, often highly skilled and able also to deal with illnesses.

Optio – Second in command in a Roman century. Hand-chosen by the centurion.

Opus Sectile – an art technique where marble, mother of pearl, and glass were cut and inlaid into walls and floors to make a picture or pattern.

Penates – Protective deities, both in the household, and on a grander scale in the city.

Pontifex Maximus – The chief priest of Rome, a title traditionally bestowed upon the emperor.

Praepositus – A title given to officers of various ranks given temporary command of a unit.

Praesides – Aide to a provincial governor, acting as a vice-governor in his absence.

Praetor – An administrative role held by a Roman noble, part of the *Cursus Honorum.*

Praetorium – The headquarters building at the centre of a Roman camp or fortress.

Prefect – Commander of a legion. In the later empire, this post could be aspired to by 'career soldiers' who impressed in the ranks.

Primus Pilus – The chief centurion of a legion. So called, because his own century would line up in the first file (*primus*) of the first cohort (*pilus* – a term harking back to the manipular legions).

Protectores Augusti Nostri – 'Protector of our Augustus'. A coveted position awarded to Roman officers who came to the attention of the emperor for their deeds of valour.

Pteruges – leather strops attached to a garment worn under armour, protecting the upper arms and thighs.

Pulvinar – Latin term for the imperial box at an entertainment venue. Cf. *kathisma*.

Pushtigban – The elite bodyguard of the Persian king, well trained and one thousand strong.

Quaestor – Title applied to men in various administrative posts in Roman government dealing with finance.

Radiant Crown – (also *radiate crown*) a diadem of stylised sun-rays, associated with *Sol Invictus*.

Retiarius – Nimble gladiator type who uses a net to ensnare his enemy and a trident to wound.

Rex Sacrorum – The Priest/King of Sacrifice.

Romanitas – Romanism, the Roman way or manner.

Secutor – Gladiator designed to fight the *retiarius*, with a smooth helmet to negate the net's value.

Shamshir – Single-handed straight infantry blade of the Persian armies.

Sica – Curved short sword from the Balkan regions, often borne by the *Thraex*-type gladiator.

Singulares – Personal cavalry guard of the Emperor.

Sol Invictus – 'Unconquered Sun.' Later Roman Sun God adopted from the eastern regions.

Spatha – Double-edged sword, longer than an old-fashioned gladius, originally a cavalry weapon.

Spiculum (plural spicula) – Throwing javelin of the Roman infantry, replacing the earlier *pilum*.

Spongia – Sponge on a stick used for cleaning the posterior after latrine use.

Stilus – Tapering, often metal, writing utensil for making indentations in wax tablets.

Subarmalis – Leather garment worn under armour.

Tabernae – Roman shops of many varieties, often located in the frontages of apartment blocks called *insulae*.

Tablinum – Room set aside in a Roman residence as the master's office, where all work is carried out.

Thermae – Public bathing complexes, often of great size and intricacy.

Thermopolia – Low-class commercial premises for the sale of food and drink. Early bars and restaurants.

Thraex – Well-armoured gladiator type, named for the Thracian region where the equipment originated.

Toga Virilis – Plain white toga adopted by male Roman citizens when they come of age in their teenage years.

Togate – 'In a toga.' Term used to describe a man wearing, or statue depicted in, a toga.

Tribunus – By this period in history, the term 'prefect' was used to denote a legionary commander, but 'tribunus' was still used at times to denote high-ranking officers.

Triclinium – The dining room of a Roman household.

Triumphus – A ceremonial procession to honour a military victory.

Turma – Roman cavalry unit of 30 men, the subunit of an ala of 120 riders.

Vexillatio (plural vexillationes) – A detachment of legionaries from the main body of their legion.

Vicennalia – A festival held to celebrate 20 years of an emperor's reign.
Vigiles – City watchmen, who acted in the roles of both police and firefighters.
Vineae – Mobile hide-covered sheds used in sieges to protect attacking soldiers from missiles.

About the authors

SIMON TURNEY is from Yorkshire
and, having spent much of his childhood visiting
historic sites, he fell in love with the Roman heritage
of the region. His fascination with the ancient world
snowballed from there with great interest in Rome,
Egypt, Greece and Byzantium. His works include
the Marius' Mules and Praetorian series, as
well as the Tales of the Empire series and
The Damned Emperor series.

www.simonturney.com   @SJATurney

GORDON DOHERTY is a Scottish author,
addicted to reading and writing historical fiction.
Inspired by visits to the misty Roman ruins of Britain
and the sun-baked antiquities of Turkey and Greece,
Gordon has written tales of the later Roman Empire,
Byzantium, Classical Greece and the Bronze Age.
His works include the Legionary, Strategos
and Empires of Bronze series, and the
Assassin's Creed tie-in novel *Odyssey*.

www.gordondoherty.co.uk   @GordonDoherty

Their rivalry will change the world
forever...

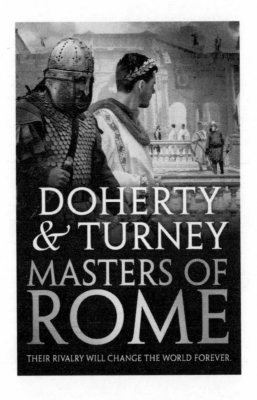

Read *Masters of Rome,* book two in the
Rise of Emperors trilogy.

Y034300